JO'

"In
I've
colorful small-town people doing small-town things
and bringing 5 STAR and GOLD STAR rankings to
the readers. This series should be selling off the
bookshelves within hours! Never have I given a series an overall review, but I feel this one, thus far,
deserves it! Continue the excellent choices in au-
thors and editors! It's working for this reviewer!"
—*Heartland Critiques*

We at Jove Books are thrilled by the enthusiastic critical
acclaim that the Homespun Romances are receiving. We
would like to thank you, the readers and fans of this wonderful series, for making it the success that it is. It is our
pleasure to bring you the highest quality of romance writing in these breathtaking tales of love and family in the
heartland of America.

And now, sit back and enjoy this delightful new Homespun Romance . . .

MAGGIE'S PRIDE
by Deborah Wood

MAGGIE'S PRIDE

DEBORAH WOOD

J
JOVE BOOKS, NEW YORK

MAGGIE'S PRIDE

A Jove Book / published by arrangement with
the author

PRINTING HISTORY
Jove edition / March 1996

The Putnam Berkley World Wide Web site address is
http://www.berkley.com

ISBN: 0-515-11830-3

A JOVE BOOK®
Jove Books are published by The Berkley Publishing Group,
200 Madison Avenue, New York, New York 10016.
JOVE and the "J" design are trademarks
belonging to Jove Publications, Inc.

PRINTED IN THE UNITED STATES OF AMERICA

10 9 8 7 6 5 4 3 2 1

This book is dedicated to Gail Fortune,
my editor, who inspires me to strive to
do my very best and helps me accomplish this
goal. You are indeed a very special lady.

Chapter 1

October 1861

Two crows, perched atop an old wagon wheel, watched as men hauled bales of hay, barrels of flour, and sacks of grain down the gangplank of the *Maggie* to a nearby warehouse. Maggie Foster, captain of the small stern-wheeler on the Willamette River, stood on the main deck with her dog, Cap, at her side, overseeing the unloading of goods. It was the third week in October, and with sunset creeping into the afternoons earlier each day, she was anxious to have the freight ashore before dark.

Down the street a dog barked, but Cap sat quietly at Maggie's side. "Take care with those sacks or you'll pay for them," Maggie called down to one of the men. A gentleman with a little boy in his wake started up the gangplank. At the same moment, one of the men headed down with a barrel balanced on his shoulder, and she shouted, "Hey mister, watch out!"

Her warning startled the roustabout, and several things happened almost at once. The barrel slipped from the roustabout's shoulder and fell into the river; as he teetered on the edge and fought to keep his balance, the gent steadied him, while another man jumped into the water and hauled the barrel ashore.

"Thanks, Bert," Maggie called to the man in the water. "I owe you a beer after you dry off."

"Best offer I've had all week!"

Maggie chuckled. Then she noticed the gentleman from

1

the gangplank standing in front of her and sobered. "How can I help you, mister?" *Goodness, he's better looking than Asahel Bush*, she thought, comparing him to one of the handsomest men in the valley. At any rate he should pay for Bert's beer, but she couldn't afford to anger a possible customer.

"Ma'am, I'm Samuel Adams. I'd like to see Mr. Zeke Foster." Sam gazed at the woman staring up at him. A soft-brimmed man's felt hat shielded her face; the large jacket and a skirt, which didn't quite cover the bottom of the trousers hidden beneath it, concealed her shape.

She felt slightly taken aback at the mention of her late husband. "He . . . isn't here." She pushed her hat back and pulled off her right leather glove. He was a tall man, kind of lanky, but his piercingly deep-blue eyes and thick, dark brown hair were almost worth getting a crick in her neck. She held out her hand. "I'm Maggie Foster, captain of this boat. May I help you?" Her stern-wheeler had two decks, only one smokestack, and no fretwork or gilt finials, but it was all hers, free and clear.

"I've come a long way to speak with Mr. Foster." He respectfully clasped her hand. Her authoritative grasp was surprising, as were the rough callouses on her hand.

She met his gaze. "Zeke was my husband. He passed away a little over a year ago."

"I'm sorry," Sam said with heartfelt sincerely. "Please accept my sympathy." He glanced at Jeremiah but saw no sign that the boy recognized her and began to realize how little he knew about him.

"Thank you." She felt the warmth of Mr. Adams's hand and really looked into his eyes. There was a boy named Sam from her youth, but that name wasn't uncommon. At twelve, the sixteen-year-old was nearly a man, and she had loved him with all her heart. She tilted her head. "If you don't mind my asking, where're you from, Mr. Adams?"

Her jaw was firm, some might say defiant, and her dark brown eyes seemed to bore into him. "Of late, San Francisco." The breeze lifted several strands of her light brown hair. Her stare was unwavering, as if she expected something more, so he added, "Before that, Ohio . . . Meyers Ferry." A smile softened her mouth, and her eyes seemed to grow larger, as if in recognition.

At the mention of her hometown, she scrutinized his features, and her heart pounded with excitement. He'd been a rangy boy, and her mama had said, more than once, that it wasn't fair for a boy to have such beautiful thick hair, the envy of most girls and women. He was now a lean but solidly built man, though the boy's reserved gaze had been the same. Suddenly she realized Sam didn't recognize her.

She looked at the little boy crouched down by Cap. He didn't look much like Sam, but not all boys took after their papas. "I'm sorry, Sam. You've come a long way."

You've come a long way, echoed in his mind. She couldn't have been more correct. He'd brought the boy all the way up to Oregon City, Oregon, from San Francisco—just to find out his uncle was dead. Sam didn't want to believe it. But at least the boy would have his aunt, he thought.

He didn't take her announcement well, and she wondered if she'd been wrong. Maybe he wasn't "her" Sam after all, but she needed to be certain. "I should be crushed you don't recognize me, but I don't look twelve any more." She paused. "I'm Maggie Carter . . . Foster." She crisscrossed her arms at her waist, and twisted two fingers for luck, hoping it *was* him.

After a long minute, Sam narrowed his gaze. Maggie . . . There had been a girl, four or five years younger than he was. She had tagged along with the boys and preferred wearing her brother's pants to skirts. Could she be the one who used to chase after him and climbed trees as well as any of the boys? He'd dismissed her as a real little hoyden for a time—until she had talked him into going fishing with her one afternoon and he'd discovered how much fun she was to be with.

"Maggie?" He pictured the girl and smiled at the woman. He'd noticed the calluses on her hand, proof she worked as hard as the men, which seemed to conform to his memory of her, and he'd spotted those men's trousers under her skirt. "Is it really you? After all these years . . . what a wonderful surprise."

She laughed softly, still feeling as if she'd conjured him up, though in truth, she hadn't thought about him in many years. More years than she wanted to claim. "You gave me a fright. I'd almost decided I was mistaken."

"I'm surprised you remembered me."

You're one of my fondest memories, she thought.

"How long have you been here? I had no idea." She had sure grown up, he thought. Although a hint of mischief, so like the girl's, still danced in her deep brown eyes.

"We'll talk later. I have a few questions to ask you, too." He hadn't forgotten her, and that knowledge made her feel like singing.

"Hey, Maggie," Bert shouted. "I'm ready fer that beer ya promised."

She reached into her jacket pocket and withdrew a five-cent piece. "Catch," she called out to Bert and flipped the coin down to him. "Thanks for rescuing that barrel." When she looked up at Sam, he was actually grinning.

"You didn't forget."

She gave him a puzzled look. "Forget what?"

"How to flip coins." Sam knew the moment she remembered that he had been the one who had showed her how to flip a coin straight. She really hadn't changed all that much, he decided. Her thoughts were mirrored in her eyes and the curve of her lips.

"You were a good teacher," she said, laughing softly. The child at his side was dressed in a little suit with short pants that exposed his spindly legs; his dusty brown hair had been slicked back, and his shoes had a shine under a fine layer of dust. "Does your boy have your talent?"

"My . . . this isn't—he's not—" Sam put his hand on the little boy's shoulder. "This is Joshua Foster's boy, Jeremiah, your nephew." The boy trembled, and Sam went down on one knee. "Jeremiah, this is your Aunt Maggie."

Oh Lord, Maggie thought as she shook hands with her young nephew. "I'm very happy to meet you, Jeremiah." His hand felt so small in hers, and his eyes, the shade of weak tea, looked so big. There was only one reason she could think of for the boy being there, and it wasn't a good one.

Jeremiah wanted to be back home with his mama, but he couldn't help staring at this other lady. His mama told him about Aunt Maggie a long time ago, but he didn't remember what she had said. His aunt smiled, but she didn't look too happy, and she didn't dress like his mama. He wasn't sure if that was good or bad. He licked his lips and patted the dog's head. "Is he yours?"

"He sure is. His name is Captain, but we call him Cap." She grinned. "He's not a pup any longer. Golly, he's almost eight years old."

Jeremiah glanced at his aunt. "I'm six." Cap pushed his nose against Jeremiah's hand. He looked into the dog's brown eyes and rubbed his neck. Cap's ears were floppy and soft, and his dark fur was as long as Jeremiah's fingers.

"He's only a little older than you are." It was dusk, and the evening air was chilly and damp. Maggie met Sam's gaze. "We can talk in my cabin. It's getting cool out here." She turned to lead them up the main stairway and nearly walked right into Ely, her friend and engineer, the one who kept the *Maggie* steaming up and down the Willamette.

"Slow yer engines, girl," Ely said, stepping back. "Thought ye'd want ta know, Thad'll have to clean out the boilers in the mornin'. Must be a ton a mud in there." His glance passed over Sam and the boy, then focused on Maggie. "I gotta go check that cam. Thought ya oughta know."

"Thanks, Ely." She motioned to Sam. "I'd like you to meet an old friend of mine, Sam Adams. Sam, Ely Cole." She rarely saw Ely without his cap on. It did hide his graying black hair that had grown a bit thin, though not the leathery, lined face that she had come to love.

Sam started to raise his hand, but Ely gave him a curt nod without quite meeting his gaze.

Maggie held her hand out toward her nephew. "And this is Zeke's nephew, Jeremiah, Joshua's boy."

Ely studied the boy and cleared his throat. "Jeremiah, now that's a fine name."

Even in the dim light, Maggie couldn't miss seeing the emotion that sprang to Ely's eyes. He and Zeke had been close friends for years, long before she married Zeke. She guessed how Ely must feel meeting Jeremiah. He did bear some resemblance to his uncle. It might be the way he looked at Cap and rubbed him behind the ear, the same way Zeke had, and the dog had taken to Jeremiah as if he understood the situation.

"Take your time in the morning, Ely. We're not scheduled to head back up river until noon." She had the feeling she was in for a long night and was glad she wouldn't have to be up at sunrise. "I'll have the stew warmed up in a little while."

Ely shook his head. "Don't ya worry 'bout us. Thad n' me'll eat at Miz Hanson's."

Maggie nodded. "Her cooking's better than mine." She understood Ely's change of plans. He usually kept to himself. "Thad's the fireman," she explained to Sam. "I'm sure you'll see him later." Anticipating her direction, Cap darted ahead of her up the stairway and trotted back to her cabin beyond the passenger saloon. Her quarters contained a main room she referred to as her parlor, her bedroom, and a small kitchen, which she stubbornly refused to call a galley. She pushed the door of her cabin open, and the dog darted inside.

She lighted a lamp, stirred the fire in the wood stove, and added wood. "Please, sit down. It'll warm up soon." She hung her coat and hat on the pegs near the door and then put Sam's next to hers. Jeremiah shivered, and she thought he might want to keep his jacket on for a while.

Jeremiah dropped down on his knees by Cap. The boy had been so distant following the death of his parents, Sam was relieved to see him showing an interest in the dog. When Maggie stepped into the next room, Sam sat down on the quilt covered armchair and relaxed for the first time in weeks.

The room was small and neat with little bric-a-brac other than her framed marriage certificate, Zeke's pilot's license, and a tintype of her parents, the Carters. Sam remembered them smiling a lot; he was a shoemaker and none of the children in town had ever gone without.

The furniture was just as down-to-earth as Maggie seemed to be: aside from the chair he had chosen, there was a little armless rocker, a small sofa, a corner writing desk, a chest and two small tables. He had the feeling Maggie didn't have many callers. The boat wasn't as grand as some of the steamboats he had seen on the Mississippi, but Sam had noted the pride in her voice when she had introduced herself as its captain. He sensed a sadness in the sparse furnishings, but he assumed Maggie had her treasures on display in her home.

After dashing into the kitchen, Maggie stirred the fire in the cookstove and put the stew on to heat. Finding Sam on the deck of her stern-wheeler after all these years had been a shock. He'd filled out real nice, she mused. She washed her hands and stared at the rough dry skin. She'd changed, too. She quickly dried her hands, hurried into her bedroom to slip off the trousers she was wearing under her skirt, then returned to what passed for her parlor. "You still stay for supper, won't you, Sam?"

He nodded. "I hope we didn't put Mr. Cole out." He noticed the difference in her immediately. Her hair had been dark blonde as he remembered, not light brown as it was now, but she was now round in all the right places, and her smile seemed to come from within.

"He'll be fine. He doesn't take to strangers easily." She sat down on the armless rocking chair. "The last time I saw you, you were leaving for university." *And I thought I would die of a broken heart,* she recalled, but she couldn't admit that to him.

"You came down to the landing and watched me board the *Marietta*." He shook his head. "As I remember, you used to watch most of the boats arrive and depart."

"Both of us did." She glanced at his hands—clean, smooth nails, no scars and lightly tanned—the hands of a man who probably didn't do hard labor. "Are you an attorney? That's what you said you wanted to be."

"I am. I worked in a law office for a few years, then I

heard stories about California and decided to see it for myself." Sam felt the boat drift slightly with the current. He watched as Maggie glanced at Jeremiah and realized she must have questions she'd rather not ask in front of the boy. "Looks like you're doing what you used to talk about doing, too."

She stared at him, amazed he had recalled her fascination with riverboats. "I didn't know it when I married, but my husband had been a steamboat captain." She shook her head. "Strange how things turn out, isn't it?"

"Mm. Are you happy, Maggie?"

"I have what I always wanted. Why wouldn't I be?" She rocked the chair forward and stood up. "I'd better check on the stew."

Maggie watched Jeremiah. He had fallen asleep on the floor beside Cap, while Sam told her about San Francisco. "Let's take a walk around the deck."

Sam nodded. "Good idea." He helped her into her coat, slipped his jacket on, and followed her out onto the deck. "The falls are loud at night, aren't they?"

"There aren't as many wagons or people around to compete with the noise. I like the sound of the water spilling over the ledge, and in the autumn, watching the salmon jump over the falls on their way upriver." The Willamette Falls was horseshoe shaped, with Oregon City on the east side and Linn City on the west. Sometimes on a sunny day she liked to stand down by the basin and watch for a rainbow in the spray.

"You really like it here, don't you?"

"Yes. Don't you?" She glanced at him.

"It . . . 's a good place." It reminded him of home, that small town on the Ohio River. As he grew to manhood, he'd been so certain his fortune and happiness would be found in the city, a big city—Boston or New York City, and then he tried San Francisco, a much younger city. Fifteen years later he wasn't so sure. "Does it remind you of Meyers Ferry when we were growing up?"

She gazed along the riverbank at the sprawling town. "Yes, I guess it does. Have you been back there?"

"Not since the family moved to Council Bluffs, Iowa. Three years ago they moved across the river. They have a farm just south of Omaha, in the Nebraska Territory."

Once in a while, late at night, she had wondered about people from back home. "Do they like it there?"

"For now." Sam chuckled. "My father used to say *I* had the wanderer's eye." He shook his head. He'd forgotten that until that moment. "If I do, I came by it naturally."

As they strolled past the boilers, she glanced at him. "What happened to Joshua and Clarissa? Were you his attorney? I don't understand . . . I wrote and told him about Zeke's death a year ago. It—"

"I didn't know." Sam reached over and lightly pressed his finger over her lips, stilling her flow of questions. "You would've made a good lawyer yourself." He linked arms with her and continued on toward the bow. "I waited until now to explain what happened to them. Jeremiah's been through enough and didn't need to hear this. Earlier I mentioned my hotel in San Francisco. I sold it to Joshua Foster."

She glanced at him. "Your practice must be doing fine. I'm happy for you."

"It didn't cost that much. The owner lost most of the price of it to me in a poker game. I ran it for awhile and discovered I'm not suited to standing behind a desk or worrying about clean slop jars." He shrugged. "I hired Joshua to manage the hotel, and I left town for awhile. By the time I returned, I had decided to sell, and he wanted to buy it. He signed the papers and gave me partial payment. Five days later, the first of this month, a fire spread through the area, and the hotel burned to the ground. Joshua, Clarissa and one of the boarders were trapped inside. An old miner was able to get Jeremiah out." He took a deep breath and let it out slowly.

"Thank the Lord." She shuddered. She couldn't imagine a worse death, and their poor little boy . . . A horrible thought occurred to her. "Please, tell me Jeremiah didn't see them."

"I was told he hadn't." *But he surely must have heard their screams for help,* Sam thought.

"He must have been terrified." She shuddered. "What about Joshua and Clarissa? They were—"

"Yes." He gave her arm a reassuring hug. "They were buried, and it took me a few days to settle my affairs and prepare for our trip up here."

The boy wasn't much more than a baby, and he would have nothing to remind him of his parents. "No wonder he seems so lost. He probably cries himself to sleep every night."

"He's over that now." He stiffened his jaw. "I've never felt so helpless. I would never have sold that building if I'd thought—"

Turning to him, she placed her hand on his arm. "It wasn't your fault. Don't take the blame for their deaths. I've heard that fire is common in San Francisco."

"It is."

She took a deep breath. "I—" She shook her head. Two paces later she paused and faced Sam. "How did you know about Zeke? Where to bring Jeremiah?"

Sam heard the confusion in her voice and noted the tension in her posture. "When Joshua and I were negotiating the price of the hotel, he talked about his brother. He sure was proud of him. He planned on talking him into moving down there." Sam gazed at her and covered her hand with his. "I didn't remember everything he told me—just Zeke's name and that he had a stern-wheeler on the Willamette River." He glanced at a reflection of a light shimmering on the river. "When we arrived in Corvallis, I asked around."

"Zeke told me once that Joshua always seemed to look up to him." She had, too. With an almost twenty-year difference in their ages, Zeke had been more like a father or close friend.

"Maggie, there was *nothing* left after the fire. If Joshua hadn't told me about his brother, Reverend Roth would have had to find Jeremiah a home." They continued walking, and Sam wished he had handled the telling better. "I had to bring him here, Maggie. The boy needs his family. Zeke was his only relative, but now at least he has you."

"Wasn't there a Bible? A diary? Or any letters? Jeremiah must have kin somewhere. You're an attorney. Don't you know how to find people?" This couldn't be happening, she thought. She had never even met Joshua or Clarissa. After nine childless years of marriage, she had accepted the fact that she wasn't meant to be a mother.

He shook his head. "Do you know Clarissa's family name? Where is she from?"

"We exchanged letters once a year, but I never met Joshua or Clarissa." She shook her head. "He must not have received my letter about Zeke's death."

Her chin was set just the way he remembered, and he knew she was digging in her heels, but he could be equally firm. "You have to take him."

She slipped her arm from his and stepped back. "I can't raise the boy. I won't. I'm a steamboat pilot, not a mother. He should go to school." She paced to the rail and back.

"There must be schools here. Why can't he go to one near your home?"

"*That's* the problem. I live on this boat. We . . . I have a little cabin upriver—it's north of Champoeg, at the bend in the river—but I haven't seen the inside of it in over a year. And I can't live there *and* pilot the steamboat." She glanced at him. "Have you thought about boarding schools? There're several in the valley, one that's suppose to be good, Trinity School, in Lake Oswego."

Sam stood with his legs apart and his hands clasped behind his back. "That is out of the question. He needs a family." He almost felt as if he were in a courtroom. "Couldn't you hire a pilot?"

"Maybe," she said, shrugging, "but I couldn't pay a living wage." She waved her arms in frustration. "Grannie's biscuits," she mumbled. "Sam, I hardly earn enough to keep the old boat running. I've had to keep my fees dirt cheap to compete with Oregon Steam Navigation's boats on the river."

"I didn't realize." He frowned. "Can't you join the company?"

She shook her head. "Zeke wouldn't have any part of them, and I won't sell my boat. It's all I have, and they wouldn't hire me to pilot her."

He reached out and clasped her arm, forcing her to halt. "But Jeremiah has no one else. At least think about it."

"Zeke and Joshua had an older brother, Jedediah, but he passed away over three years ago." As she stared at him, an idea came to her. "What about you, Sam?"

She smiled, unmindful he felt sure, of the effect that simple act had on him. "What about me?" Her eyes sparkled, and her face almost glowed. Her excitement was contagious, and he felt himself caught up by her enthusiasm, though he wasn't sure why.

She slipped her arm through his and encouraged him to walk along the deck moist with dew. "I've watched you with Jeremiah, and he trusts you." She gazed into his eyes. "Are you married, Sam?"

Chapter

2

Sam dropped her arm and stared at her as if she were a snake. "Oh, no you don't, Maggie. I'm only the courier . . . Jeremiah's chaperon." He should have remembered, he realized. Years ago, she had entangled him in more than one of her wild-haired schemes.

"Won't you even ask your wife? Jeremiah's such a sweet little boy." *Please, Lord,* she pleaded, *Sam must be a good man, and he'd make such a good papa.*

He stared at her, marveling at the easy way she attempted to hand the responsibility of the child over to him. "I'm not married."

"Well, neither am I."

"But you are his aunt, the only relative of his I know of."

She gazed heavenward, then at Sam. "What would I do with him? I told you I live on this stern-wheeler. I steam up and down the upper part of the river every week."

"As I recall, you earned good marks in school. Why can't you tutor him?"

"I could teach him to read, write, do his sums, and a spattering of history. That wouldn't be enough for him the way I see it."

"No, but it would be a good start. He'd have to go to university. Think about it." He glanced at the water and back to her. "We're staying at the Main Street House. I'll be here a few days. It will be easier if you get to know him."

"I'm going back upriver." She raised one brow, giving him a that's-what-I-mean look. "The *Maggie* leaves tomorrow."

He ran his fingers through his hair. He'd thought this trip, from start to finish, would take ten days at most and he would be able to return to his latest venture, a sheep ranch, well before the first of November. Now it looked as if it could take much longer. "We'll sail with you, if you have room for us. I can help out. I haven't forgotten what I learned on the Ohio."

"We'll see." She smirked. "Someone would have to keep an eye on Jeremiah."

The tension eased, and he chuckled. "You said you'd be a captain of a riverboat. And you are. Who would've guessed?"

"Not me," she said, surprising herself by the note of sadness in her voice. "When we came cross-country, Zeke said he wanted to have a farm. He'd heard the Willamette Valley was so fertile anything would grow, and I guess he wanted to try farming." She shrugged. "He tried it for a year, then the *Hoosier* was hauled around the falls and made a trip south. Next the *Canemah* began carrying the mail on the upper river. He felt the lure of the current." She paused and stared into the dark night. "He told me he'd worked on riverboats, not that he had been a pilot on the Mississippi and lower Ohio rivers." She hadn't told him how fascinated she was with riverboats, either, back then. But neither of them had talked about their dreams. Surviving the hardships of the Oregon Trail and settling in the Territory had kept her too busy to think about childhood fantasies.

Her voice had grown soft, but she didn't sound melancholy, so he asked, "When was that?"

She gazed at him and suddenly she felt younger than her twenty-seven years and completely at ease with him. "In fifty-one. I was seventeen and delighted to discover one of my dreams might come true." She tilted her head. "Now, tell me about you." She leaned back against a spar. "I used to think about you at university and wonder if it was as grand as you had described."

If he hadn't known better, he could easily have believed she had been interested in him, but he did know better than that. She had been too young for anything more than friendship. "Grand? Compared to Meyers Ferry, it was. Thank goodness Mama had taught me proper manners. It took me months to adjust to dressing in my Sunday best every day, not to mention the city noises and smells, and the social life, so different from home."

"Mm." She smiled, recalling her own innocence. "We had such dreams."

"That we did." When she smiled at him wistfully and linked arms with him, he felt drawn to her, and not merely as an old friend. "You haven't given up dreaming, have you?"

As she gazed into his eyes, her smile widened, and she shook her head—though if the truth were told, she had little time for dreaming. He held her arm snug against his side, and her heart beat a little faster. She had had no idea he would become a romantic. "There's a small cabin on board you and Jeremiah can use." *At least we'll have a few days to renew our friendship,* she thought.

Maggie stirred beneath the covers. All too soon she felt Cap's cold nose on the palm of her hand. Oregon City was still considered rough by many. She had learned that lesson firsthand. A month after her husband's death, Ely had caught a man sneaking up to her cabin late one night. She'd brought Cap into her room after that, for company and protection. "I know. You need to go for a walk." She dragged herself from the cozy bed and let the dog out for his constitutional along the riverbank.

Though she wasn't steaming upriver this morning, she did have work to do. She wasn't used to staying up and visiting late into the night. She hurried through her ablutions, put on a dress, wrapped her hair in a loose coil, and left Cap's dented old pan with his food on the deck outside her door.

Clean linens and extra blankets had to be put in the small cabin. She found an old cot in the storeroom and set it up for Jeremiah. When she was finished, she inspected her handiwork. Most of her passengers made day trips and traveled in the main cabin, but she kept the two little cabins ready in case someone became ill or wanted privacy.

After straightening up in the saloon, she returned to the main deck. Cap was watching Thad clean out the boilers. She continued on to the engine room, where Ely was up past his elbows in oil. She peered over his shoulder. "Will that cam rod last a while longer?"

"Still has a few trips left in it." Ely didn't look up. "How's Thad comin' 'long?"

"Almost finished."

Ely nodded. "He can fire her boxes by noon." He stood up and turned to face her with the oil can in one hand. "You're not dressed for a trip. Ya know ya shouldn't come in here in that finery. Aren't we settin' off upriver t'day?"

She brushed her skirt, feeling a bit self-conscious. "I'm not changing our schedule." Upriver was south. It had taken her a while to get used to the Willamette River flowing south to north, instead of the reverse. Now, she gave little thought to it. She held Ely's gaze until he nodded. "Jeremiah and Mr. Adams will be with us for a few days."

"Ain't none of my concern, Maggie," Ely said gruffly. "Ya know that."

"Sam and I grew up together. We were friends back in Ohio." She put her hand on Ely's shoulder. "He wants me to keep the boy, Ely, and raise him. He doesn't understand why I cannot. I think he needs to be shown."

"Not many city folks unnerstand our way a life." He shrugged. "Unless he's slow minded, he'll soon see the right of it, girl."

"He's not city folk." *Although he acts and dresses like one,* she thought. "His uncle was an engineer on the Ohio River, and Sam worked with him." She shrugged. "He even piloted a few boats. He should know well enough why the boy can't live here." In the next few days, she realized, she would have to think of a good family, one who would not only take the boy but love him, too.

"Mebbe." Ely rubbed his forehead with his shirt sleeve. "If'n that's all he's up to," he mumbled.

Maggie stared at the spray from the falls as she thought

aloud. "Jeremiah seems like a good boy. He deserves better than this." *Or than me for a mother.* She could pilot her steamboat along a shallow channel past snags, shoals, and over rough water, but she knew nothing about raising a child.

Ely looked sideways at her and picked up a bucket. "He could do worse."

"And a good sight better." She stepped back out of his way. "I'm going into town. I'll check on Peterson's shipment."

It was clouding over and the air smelled like rain. *'Bout time,* she thought. It wasn't unusual for the Willamette to fill her banks in the winter, but the high water was welcome whenever it came: it made piloting the stern-wheeler much easier. After she watched a small limb from a maple tree slip over the falls, she called Cap to go with her and left the boat.

Her first stop was at the Oregon Steam Navigation Company office, where they tolerated her checking on potential passengers arriving from up north. There was regular service from Portland to below the falls at Oregon City, where there was a portage around the falls to the upper landing where travelers could continue their trip south.

Next, she went to Mr. Peterson's general store. She placed her order with him and assured him that she would deliver his shipment before nightfall at Fairfield Landing. His cargo and her supplies would be delivered to her boat by the time she returned.

Mr. Peterson craned his neck, looking at the door. "Is that mongrel outside?"

Maggie chuckled. "Of course. He's my protector."

"A Mr. Adams was in a while ago. Said he and the boy are steaming south with you."

"They are. Jeremiah is Zeke's brother's boy."

"I thought he might be an admirer of yours."

"Not likely." *Not even fifteen years ago,* she thought as she turned to leave.

"Hold up a minute," Mr. Peterson said, and went to the back room. When he returned, he handed her a hastily wrapped package. "For Cap."

"This is his favorite stop. Thank you."

Lastly, she wanted to pay a short visit with her friend, Caroline Dobbs.

Both Maggie and Caroline were something of an oddity in the valley—neither had accepted any of many recent proposals of marriage. Caroline had told her that she wouldn't remarry unless she found a better man than Mr. Dobbs. As for Maggie herself, she was enjoying her newfound freedom, took great pride in her work, and she couldn't imagine turning her little old steamboat over to anyone else. Besides, she was quite sure she made a better riverboat captain than wife. When they reached Caroline's house, Maggie gave Cap his prized bone from Mr. Peterson and pointed to the stoop.

Caroline's dressmaker sign was hanging out front, so Maggie went in without knocking. The small brass bell over the door rang softly, and she called out, "It's me—Maggie."

"About time you paid a call," Caroline said as she came into the parlor wiping her hands on a towel. "I haven't seen you all month." Caroline paused, eyeing Maggie. "Who's getting married?"

Maggie glanced down at her faded brown-and-yellow calico dress. "What're you talking about? I just came by to pay my respects." She frowned. "Are you feeling all right?" Caroline wore her thick, reddish-brown hair in a loose coil at the back of her head, and it was always as neat as if she'd just done it up. In fact, she possessed all the domestic talents any man would expect to find in a woman, abilities Maggie had never truly grasped or had ever wanted to master.

"Right as rain. How about you?" Caroline stared at the hem of Maggie's skirt. "You're not wearing trousers."

When Caroline raised one finely arched brow and her hazel eyes sparkled with mischief, Maggie grinned and shook her head. "They're warm, and I don't *always* wear them." She glanced around the room expecting to see Caroline's cat. "Where's Tucker? He usually greets everyone." Caroline had named him after her uncle, who she said was also a character.

"He was curled up in his basket a while ago." Caroline

motioned for Maggie to take a seat and joined her. "I can't recall the last time I saw you so fancied up. Do you have time for a cup of dandelion tea?"

Maggie perched at the end of the sofa. "I really don't. We're leaving at noon but the strangest thing happened, and I . . ." As she looked at Caroline, Maggie thought about how her friend had sometimes talked about wanting a large family.

"Whatever is it?" Caroline leaned forward. "You're acting rather peculiar, even for you, Maggie Foster."

Maggie smiled. She had a bad habit of letting her mind drift off in different directions at the oddest times. "Zeke's nephew is here. Jeremiah. He arrived last evening, all the way from San Francisco. He's six, and the cutest little tadpole you ever laid eyes on."

"I'm sure he is," Caroline said absently, still clearly confused.

"I'll bring him over when we get back."

"That will be fine. Did Mr. Foster's brother come to pay his respects?"

"No. Sam Adams thought he was bringing Jeremiah to live with his uncle." Maggie shook her head. "There was a fire. The boy's parents were trapped and perished in it."

"The poor little tyke. At least he has you."

"That's the problem. I can't keep him." Maggie heard the edge in her voice and took a deep breath. "But I'll have a couple days to talk it over with Sam."

"Sam?"

"Mm-hm. We grew up together."

"Imagine, meeting a childhood friend here after all this time." Caroline paused, watching Maggie. "Were you . . . close friends?"

Maggie brushed her fingers over the sofa. She felt a trifle ill at ease, even though it seemed silly. "When I was all of twelve years old, I was completely taken with him. I heckled, pestered and dogged him unmercifully."

"Goodness, Maggie, you're flushed." Caroline grinned. "Are you still smitten with him?"

"Of course not."

"Is his wife with him?"

"There is no Mrs. Adams, except for his mama. And wipe that smirk right off your face. I didn't come here to talk about Sam. I need to find a good home for Jeremiah." A slow smile spread across Maggie's face. "How is Mr. Bennett? I haven't seen him since summer."

"He's the same."

Maggie nodded with a slight smile. "Are you still keeping company with him?"

"I see him occasionally. You know him. His favorite topic of conversation is still politics. What has that got to do with anything?"

"You know I'm plain speaking, so I'll just say it out." Maggie knew Caroline had wanted children, had lost two babies and had had no more. "This is a chance for you to have a cute little boy. Would you consider adopting Jeremiah?"

Caroline's wide-eyed stare slid from Maggie to the floor. "Mr. Bennett and I aren't . . . We haven't even discussed . . ." She shook her head. "I couldn't possibly consider that." She clenched her hands into fists and took a deep breath. "If you don't keep him, he should go to a real family."

Maggie reached over and covered Caroline's tightly clasped hands. "I didn't want to bring up the past, but I thought this might be a wonderful opportunity for both of you."

"I know, Maggie. Two years ago, before Mr. Dobbs passed on, I would have felt blessed." She sniffed and added, "But not now."

"I understand." Maggie withdrew her hand and glanced at the clock on a small side table. "I'd better get back." She stood up.

"When are you going to let me make a new dress for you?"

Maggie shrugged and started for the door. "After this one wears out?"

Caroline followed her, laughing. "I'll start cutting out one for you," she said, eyeing her. "Something to wear when you see Mr. Adams."

Maggie held up her hands. "He'll be leaving in a few days, and I don't need anything special for him." She impulsively gave Caroline a hug. "I'll see you soon."

As Maggie left, Caroline called out, "I'm looking forward to meeting Mr. Adams. You will bring him with you when you get back?"

"I'll try." Maggie waved, signaled Cap to join her, and hurried down along the street, hoping she hadn't opened a tin of worms by mentioning Sam to Caroline.

As she approached her gangplank, she saw Jeremiah and Sam. The man was even more handsome than she thought the night before. Today he was wearing boots, a heavy jacket, and practical trousers, as if he weren't planning on staying in the saloon the whole time. "Hello," she called out.

Startled, Sam glanced over. Maggie's cheerful expression reassured him. "Good morning. You're bright 'n' sunny for such a gloomy day." Her smile seemed to bubble from inside her. The next few days should be interesting. "I hope we're not late."

Unaccustomed to compliments, she pulled her shawl a little tighter. "No. We leave at noon." She teasingly eyed his luggage. "Looks like you're ready for a *long* trip."

"You haven't changed your mind, have you, Maggie?"

A terrible thought occurred to her. Surely he wouldn't take off and just up 'n' leave the boy. "No, Sam. I haven't changed my mind about *anything*." Her gaze drifted to Jeremiah. He was clutching a good-size package to his chest. She grinned at him. "I heard you'd been to the store earlier. Did you get a peppermint stick?"

Jeremiah peered at her. "No," he glanced at Mr. Sam and added, "ma'am."

"Well, we'll have to get some after we stow your gear."

Cap walked up to Jeremiah and looked at him as if to say, See my new bone. Jeremiah patted the dog's head and followed him onto the boat.

Maggie quietly said to Sam, "The peppermint will settle his stomach if he doesn't take to the boat."

"Good thinking." After motioning Maggie to go up the gangplank ahead of him, Sam watched her skirt sway gently with each nimble step she took. He wondered if she would now be any more sympathetic to taking the boy.

She led them to the cabin she had readied and she opened the door. "Jeremiah, I made up the cot for you." Cap started into the room. She snapped her fingers, and he changed his mind.

Jeremiah looked at his bed and set his bundle on it.

"There isn't a wardrobe, but there're pegs on the wall." She stepped back from the doorway so Sam could enter. "While you get settled, Jeremiah and I'll see about those peppermint sticks." I'll make it plain from the start, she thought. We're not on a fancy Mississippi riverboat, and I won't be his steward.

"Lucky boy." Sam set his bags on the bed. "I'll see if Ely needs a hand." His hopes soared. From what she had said the night before, he hadn't thought she would be anxious for Jeremiah's company. If everything continued to go smoothly, he could depart for his ranch from Salem or Corvallis.

Chapter

3

Maggie reached out and took the last passenger's hand. "Mrs. Tillman, paying a visit to your sister?" Mrs. Tillman's hair was more white than black; her back was straight as a spar, and she was always cheery. She carefully tended her garden and raised a wonderful variety of fruits and vegetables to barter for her expenses.

"That I am. I haven't given up on Lavinia. I'll get her to move in with me one day. But don't you worry. Even when she does, I'll still bring you jam and fruit, dear." Mrs. Tillman handed Maggie her basket. "I hope this is enough. The whortleberries were especially good this year."

After accepting the basket, Maggie gave her a hug. "You know you can ride any time you want." She lifted the cloth and peered at two jars of jam, a crock of butter, a loaf of bread, eight eggs and two large onions. "Thank you. You know my favorites." While secretly very grateful for the food, she had given up complaining about Mrs. Tillman's overpayment long ago. They were both equally stubborn.

"Maggie," Sam called, as he approached her and smiled at the elderly woman standing with her. "Ely said to tell you her fireboxes're filled and the cam rod's turnin'."

"Mrs. Tillman, I'd like you to meet Mr. Adams, a friend of mine from back home. Sam, this is Mrs. Tillman, my favorite passenger."

Sam met Mrs. Tillman's appraising gaze. Her light blue eyes were lively, and she was dressed in varying shades of gray except for the snow white lace at her neck. "It's a pleasure, ma'am."

23

"Glad to meet you, Mr. Adams." Mrs. Tillman eyed him from his dark hair to the tips of his dusty boots and met his amused gaze. "You don't look like John Q."

Sam stared at her, wondering if she was serious. "I'm not surprised. There aren't any presidents in my family," he said, glancing at Maggie, who was unabashedly amused, "but I have a cousin who's a postmaster."

Maggie managed to keep her laughter to a chuckle, glad he hadn't lost his sense of humor. "Do you know where Cap's gone off to? He usually greets everyone with me."

"I left him with Jeremiah in our cabin. I should have told you."

"It's all right." Maggie linked arms with Mrs. Tillman. "We'll walk with you. Thad's built up a head of steam, and I'd better get this boat moving before the boilers blow."

After they left Mrs. Tillman at the door to the saloon, Maggie led the way up the ladder to the pilothouse. It was one of her favorite places. All four walls had glass windows, affording a clear view in all directions. It wasn't a large room, but it felt even smaller with Sam standing right behind her. As he looked around, she watched him from the corner of her eye. "What do you think?"

"I always did like the view from the pilothouse." He motioned to the other side of the river. "Is that part of Oregon City?"

"No. That's Linn City." She looked at the many warehouses and wharves that lined the narrow shelf of the river on the west side of the horseshoe shaped falls and beyond. "Most of the stern-wheelers dock over there, but I'm partial to this side of the falls."

As he gazed past her to the lower deck, he rested his hand on her shoulder. The engine was idling and the deck vibrated. Her hair brushed his cheek and a feeling of sheer joy rushed through him. Then he became aware of his fingers holding her shoulder and stepped back. "Since you're short of deckhands, what can I do to help?"

When he lowered his hand, she shivered. His touch had been comforting and warm, and she couldn't remember the last time she had been so aware of a man. He smelled of store-bought soap and clove-scented hair tonic, and his low-pitched voice had the same stirring effect on her as the sound of the falls. *This is ridiculous,* she thought. "Where's Jeremiah? If he gets in Ely or Thad's way, he might get hurt."

He nodded. "I'll watch out for him." For a few minutes she had softened, then as though he had turned a page in a book, she was all business, which was logical, when he thought about it. She had a boat to pilot and she was responsible for everyone aboard and the cargo. "But don't forget, I piloted Captain Thornton's side-wheeler on the Ohio. I'd be happy to spell you—any time."

"Thanks, Sam, but I wouldn't know what to do with myself if I weren't at the wheel."

"The offer stands," he said on his way out.

She listened to his light step descending the rungs of the ladder, and called down the pipe, her only way to pass orders to the engineer from the pilothouse, for Ely to reverse the engine. She rubbed her cheek on her shoulder and smiled. Not now, she thought, she had to get to work. She took the wheel, piped Ely to change to the forward gear and maneuvered the *Maggie* along the east bank. Then she crossed the strong downstream current to the slack water on the west, where it was easier going upstream. The *wsh-wsh-wsh* of the paddles slapping the water beat the familiar rhythmic patter.

As the stern-wheeler made its way upstream, she glanced at the yellow leaves of the ash and cottonwood trees as they fluttered in the breeze. The trees grew so thick in some stretches of the riverbank that they blocked out the prairie beyond. Suddenly the wind gusted, scattering dried-out leaves across the river, the sky grew darker, and, after she passed the Tualatin River, it began raining.

Maggie kept a sharp eye trained for snags in the shallower water. She had been piloting her boat up and down the river nearly every day for more than five years. Experience had taught her not to take the course for granted, but she couldn't help thinking about Sam, wondering where he was and what he and Jeremiah were doing. *Blame my buttons,* she thought, *that man has the oddest effect on me, almost like when I was twelve.*

Cap sat near the bow of the steamboat as if he were a sentinel. Sam gazed at the swift current of the river off the port side and took pride in Maggie's skill as a pilot. He glanced at Jeremiah. "How's that peppermint stick?"

Jeremiah pulled it out of his mouth. "It's good." He pushed his free hand in his pants pocket and asked, "You want one?"

"Thank you, not now." Sam watched the first drops of rain splatter on the river. He took Jeremiah's hand and led him back into the cargo area under the boiler deck. "Have you ever been on a riverboat like this?"

"Unh-uh." Jeremiah looked up at Mr. Sam. "I been on a ferry."

"What do you think about riding on the river?"

Jeremiah stared at the high pile of sacks and barrels at his side, then down at his shoes. "How come the floor growls like my innards when I'm hungry?"

Sam chuckled. "On a boat, the floor is called the deck. It rumbles because of the engines that turn the big paddle wheel at the stern—the back of the boat."

While Jeremiah mulled that over, Sam thought back to when he himself had been six years old. His family lived above his papa's store in town. He spent his time either there, where his ma had taught him to cipher and read, or at Uncle Henry's farm at the edge of town, where he learned about the land, the seasons, and the importance of having hope. Of course, at the time, he hadn't been aware of life's lessons—*any more than Jeremiah is,* he thought.

Although Sam knew the boy's father had managed a hotel in Des Moines, Iowa, while his mother had run their boardinghouse, he hadn't learned any more from the frightened little boy during their journey from San Francisco. Sam reached down and raised Jeremiah's collar. The child seemed so vulnerable, and he himself felt at such a loss. Surely Maggie wouldn't disappoint either of them. If his memory was correct, she had been the first to defend the underdogs and faced the bullies for the weaker children. She had given Freddy Burns a shiner for teasing Georgie Tubbs about his crossed eye. "I bet there're a lot of big fish in the river. Do you fish?"

Jeremiah shook his head. "I saw mama fry fish in the big pan." He stared out at the rain and watched the water run along the floor. No, Mr. Sam said it was a deck.

"Maybe we can go fishing, Jeremiah, if you want to." There was a light of interest in the little boy's eyes, and Sam continued. "Your Aunt Maggie used to fish."

Jeremiah did meet Mr. Sam's gaze then. "She did?"

"Mm-hm." Sam suddenly recalled Maggie wading out into the stream near her house, her skirts bunched up, as she pursued the catfish she'd snagged. He smiled. "We'll have to ask her if she still does."

As her stern-wheeler came round the first sharp bend in the Willamette River, where it turned due west, Maggie hung close to the bank. Just beyond the stand of alder trees lay the cabin her husband had built for them on their donation-land claim. They had sold most of the original six hundred and forty acres to pay off the stern-wheeler. However, her attention did not waver from the swift current. She had returned to the cabin just once shortly after Zeke died. Just knowing it was there was enough for her.

A few minutes later, the sound of someone climbing the ladder to the pilothouse surprised her. No one ever came up there unless there was a problem. Then she remembered that Sam was aboard. The door opened. She cast a fleeting glance over her shoulder at Jeremiah and Sam.

Jeremiah stepped into the little room and stuck his wet hands into his coat pockets. He watched his aunt, but she didn't look back at him again. Mr. Sam seemed real glad to see her. She smiled a lot, and she had gotten him the candy. One stick was in his pants pocket. It tasted good, but he was saving it.

"Sam, why'd you bring him up here in the rain?" Maggie spoke without taking her attention from the river again.

Sam picked up Jeremiah and settled him on his arm. "You'll be up here all day, right?"

"Except when we stop."

"Well, I thought Jeremiah should see what you do, and see the view." Sam pointed out the jackstaff, the tall narrow pole at the bow used to judge distance, the tall smokestack, and the paddle wheel. "It looks different from up here, doesn't it?"

Jeremiah stared at the big wheel and down at the river. It was so far away. He put his arm around Mr. Sam's neck and held onto him.

The small arm around Sam's neck was soaking wet, as was the rest of the boy, he slowly realized. "Guess this wasn't the best idea I've had. He's drenched. I'd better get him warmed up."

Maggie reached over and felt Jeremiah's leg. It was so thin and cold, and the trouser leg was dripping wet. "Use my cabin. There's plenty of wood. I can't leave the wheel until we stop at Fairfield. With this current, that'll be two hours or so from now."

Sam gave the boy a reassuring nod. "We'll be fine, won't we, Jeremiah?"

"Uh-huh."

"Sam, strip and rub him dry, real good, from his hair to his toes." She frowned in concentration as she eased the wheel around to avoid a fallen tree sticking out from the bank. "There should be a couple towels on the washstand. And drink something hot, both of you."

Sam felt reassured by her concern, but he said, "Don't worry yourself." Her directives sounded like a mother's—or a boat captain's, he amended as he reached for the door handle.

Maggie had to trust that Sam could manage below. The rain continued pelting the windows and made it difficult to see. Fortunately, she could trace the course of the river in her sleep, so her attention was focused on hazards that came and went by the hour or day. In the fall and winter, the storms usually came in from the south, which meant the rain not only helped raise the level of the Willamette but also the streams feeding into it from the south.

Almost three hours after Sam's visit to the pilothouse, she made it past Thompkins Bar and neared her first stop. Her arms, back and shoulders were aching and stiff, but she had reached Fairfield an hour before sundown, though they wouldn't see it that evening. She pulled the cord, blowing the whistle to signal their arrival. Her little steamboat pulled up to the landing. After she went down to the main deck and made sure the cargo was being unloaded, she hurried to her cabin.

She rushed inside and quickly closed the door. Gracious, she was soaked. She hung up her jacket and glanced around. Sam was sitting in the quilt-covered chair, an open book in his hand; Jeremiah was on the rag rug leaning back against Sam's leg; and Cap was stretched out beside them on the floor. She shivered. "Oh, it's toasty in here. I'd better change, too, before I steam up the room. Won't take me a minute."

Glancing down at Jeremiah, Sam set the book aside. The boy was tuckered out. He ran his palm over the top of the child's head and sighed. No fever. True to her word, Maggie returned in less time than he would've thought possible. "Feel better?" He eyed her coarse trousers, minus a skirt.

"Much. Wet pants are bad enough without a drippy skirt on top." She shrugged. "But I'm up and down the ladder to the pilothouse. These are serviceable." She sat down across from him. "Is he feeling all right?"

"He's fine." Sam leveled his gaze on her. "I assume we won't be spending the night here?"

"No. Mrs. Tillman's going to Wheatland. We'll spend the night there." She arched her back and rolled her shoulders, glad Mrs. Tillman was the last passenger. Steaming against the current was exhausting work.

"In California they say it rains here year round. No wonder everything's so green." He watched the spark come back to her eyes as she settled back on the chair. Her light brown hair was coiled on the top of her head, though several strands had worked loose. He couldn't help wondering how a woman who dressed like a man could look so pretty.

"We're just coming into the rainiest season, but I don't

think we get more rain here than back home. Maybe that's why I like the storms. The air smells so fresh, and I don't know of one farmer who couldn't grow any crop he planted." She cocked her head, listening to the voices below. "I have to get back to work. We should arrive in Wheatland within the hour." She stood up. "I'll see you then."

"Depend on it."

She murmured, "I will," as she shrugged into her large coat. Climbing the ladder to the pilothouse, she wondered at her words. Oddly enough, she was looking forward to spending another evening with Sam.

"Hello, Mrs. Phipps." Maggie put Mrs. Tillman's valise under the bench seat and gave her a hand up to her sister's buggy. "You two have a good visit."

"Thank you, Maggie." Mrs. Tillman patted Maggie's gloved hand. "I'll see you Friday."

"About two o'clock." Maggie hurried back to the boat. She stopped for the night a little further up stream near a stand of trees, then went down to the boilers to see Thad. "How are we doing on wood?"

Thad dragged his shirtsleeve across his sweaty forehead. "We'll need more, ma'am. Fightin' the current took most of our supply. You picked a good place to spend the night."

She nodded. "Are you up to gathering wood?"

"Yes, ma'am." Thad glanced at the woodpile. "Better now than mornin'."

"Good. It can dry out a bit before we'll need it."

Thad nodded. "That's what I figured."

"I'll see if Sam will help you. You and Ely had a rough afternoon." She started for the stairs and paused. "Will you eat supper with us? Or would you rather eat down here?"

Ely joined them just then, and Thad glanced at him before answering. "Down here'll do fine."

Maggie nodded and went up to see Sam and Jeremiah. She hung her coat on the peg by the door and set her gloves on the woodstove hearth. Holding her cold hands out to warm them, she smiled over her shoulder at Jeremiah. "How do you like steaming along the river?"

Jeremiah's gaze darted between Mr. Sam and his aunt, and he licked his lips. He didn't know if he liked it or not. If he didn't like it, would she get mad? "It's like a house on the water . . . only there's no yard or chickens." He wished his mama was there, holding him. His eyes were wet, and he wiped them.

He's missing his mama, Maggie thought, and of course that was to be expected. "No, but if you look real hard, Jeremiah, you might see fish in the river—there are a lot of big salmon—or maybe a critter in the bushes or trees."

She turned to warm her backside and met Sam's gaze. It should seem strange having him waiting for her, and in her cabin, but it didn't. A tremor slithered down her back. *You're being plumb silly,* she chided herself. "I don't like asking, Sam, but would you help Thad gather some wood? Ely's tuckered out and I should get supper started, unless you'd rather cook?"

Her white hands, strong and calloused, were tinged now with red, and so were her cheeks. "I've been in here all afternoon. The fresh air will do me good." He leaned forward and rested his arms on his knees. "Why don't you sit down? You're tired."

The idea sounded inviting, but she still had chores to do. And Sam looked for all the world as if he were at home in her parlor. What a notion; Sam as cozy as a flea on a hound in her parlor. "I will . . . after we eat. We haven't had a chance to visit."

"We will, later—if you don't fall asleep first." Sam stood up and stepped around Jeremiah.

"I do this every day, though the current hasn't been this strong since last spring."

Jeremiah rubbed Cap's neck. "Can I go with you?"

"It's still raining. Maybe next time. Okay?" Sam grabbed his coat and opened the door.

Cap stretched his back legs as he got to his feet and went to the door. Maggie grinned. "Do you mind if he goes with you? He usually takes a walk when we stop."

Sam held out his hand. "Lead the way, Cap." He followed the dog, but his mind was still on Jeremiah. The boy had grown used to him and seemed to trust him. If Jeremiah spent a little time with Maggie, Sam felt sure he'd trust her, too. "Cap, I hope you're ready for a good outing."

Once the door closed, Jeremiah looked more woebegone than ever. *The poor little tadpole,* Maggie thought. "I'm going to get out of these wet pants." She quickly exchanged the wet trousers for a flannel petticoat and skirt. She stepped back into the parlor and held out her hand to him. "Want to help me fix supper?"

Jeremiah put his hand on hers. It was warm and hard, and he let out the breath he'd been holding. At least she hadn't grabbed his hand and hauled him along with her. He'd seen mamas dragging young'uns like dogs. But he looked over his shoulder at the door, wishing Cap and Sam would come back.

She glanced down at him. He was gnashing his lips, and she wondered what had given the boy such a fright. If his pa had been anything like his uncle, it wasn't likely he'd been beaten. "After we eat, would you like to give Cap his supper?"

"Mm-hm."

"Good. He's taken a real shine to you."

Jeremiah glanced around the kitchen. Aunt Maggie sounded nice, but he didn't think she liked him all that much. He didn't know why; it was just a feeling.

She got a pan from the shelf. Her kitchen was snug and tidy. When meals were served to more than three people, the table was downright crowded. She poured several dippers of water into the pan from the bucket. "You can wash the potatoes off while I get the fire going." If she had any extra money, she'd hire a cook. Growing up, she'd paid more mind to what her papa was doing than her mama's instructions in the kitchen. She settled Jeremiah on one chair, the pan of water on another, and the potatoes on the table.

She built up the fire in the cookstove, put the corned venison in a kettle of water, and set it over the fire. Turnips were put in another pot with water. She watched Jeremiah clean the last potato. "You did a real fine job." When he finished she handed him a towel to dry his hands, and she set the potatoes on the little dry sink. "We're done in here for a while."

She picked up the pan of water Jeremiah had used to clean the potatoes. "I'm just going to dump this." She walked outside, went back toward the paddle wheel, and tossed the content of the pot overboard.

Holding the pot out to rinse it in the rain, she listened to the soothing sound of the drops falling on the river. It wasn't coming down as hard as before, but it was steady. When she stepped back into the cabin, Jeremiah was staring up at the oil lamp on the wall. After she set the pot on the dry sink, she returned to the parlor and lighted the lamp. Maybe he was afraid of the dark.

"Is that better?" she asked, wondering what was on his mind.

"I never seen one like that." He watched the lamp hoping to see it move. "Mama put ours on the table."

Maggie grinned, pleased with his curiosity. "All of mine are on the bulkhead—that's a wall on a boat—so it can't fall over if the river gets rough. It swings," she said, lightly tapping it. "See?"

"Oh."

He began fidgeting, and she realized how little there was for him to do. She glanced around trying to see the room through his eyes. There were no pretty pictures, no knick-knacks, not even any dried flowers to look at, not that he'd be interested in any of those. She should—

"Ma'am?"

She smiled. "Do call me Aunt Maggie or just Maggie." She dropped down to his level. "Do you feel okay, honey?" She placed her hand on his forehead.

He stood on one foot, then the other. "I gotta go. *Real* bad . . . an' I don't know where it is?"

Chapter

4

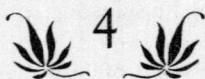

Sam shook the raindrops from his coat and waited for Cap to do the same. Then he hurried into Maggie's cabin, right behind the dog. He hung his coat on a peg and realized he was standing in a puddle of water.

Maggie met him with towels. She handed Sam two. "Don't worry about the water. Go stand by the stove." She knelt down and began rubbing Cap with the other. "You didn't happen to stop by your cabin for a dry pair of trousers, did you?"

Sam went over to the stove and stood on the small stone hearth. "I'm not used to keeping a dry change of clothes with me." He towel dried his hair. "These'll dry out before long in front of this fire."

She grinned. "And parboil you, too." She eyed him, gauging his size. He had slender hips, narrower than her own, she realized a bit self-consciously. "I kept some of Zeke's trousers," she said, heading for her bedroom.

Cap came over to him and sat down at his feet. Jeremiah glanced at him, but he didn't say a word. "Something sure smells good. You must be hungry, Jeremiah."

"Aunt Maggie said I can feed Cap after supper." Jeremiah dried Cap's face with his shirtsleeve.

Sam smiled. That's another good sign, he thought, as if keeping score.

Maggie returned with a pair of pants and handed them to Sam. "Your belt will hold them up but there's nothing I can do about the length. He wasn't as tall as you."

He accepted her offer and motioned to her room. "Mind if I change there?"

"Not at all." When he started to leave the room, his shoes squished, and she added, "If you leave your boots by the stove, they might dry out a bit, too."

He nodded. Then he went into the bedroom and closed the door. There was a lamp over the chest of drawers, and a modest-size mirror reflected the light in the small room. The chest was sturdy and unadorned, but the wood held a rich gleam; there was a sea chest in one corner by the wardrobe. However, it was the bed that dominated the room.

The oversized quilt was made of pieces of varying shades of yellow fabric with occasional red and yellow roses. There were several pillows with intricately stitched cases at the head of the bed. Maggie had clearly made this one small corner of the boat hers and hers alone.

Sam quickly stepped out of his shoes and put his soaked pants in the bowl on the washstand. The dry trousers certainly did feel better. He peeled off his stockings, wrung them out over the basin, and carried the wet clothes to the parlor.

A drying rack had been placed by the stove. He laid everything out and glanced into the kitchen. The table was set, but he didn't see Maggie. Just then, Jeremiah came out with Cap following behind, licking his lips. Sam hid his grin. "Supper 'bout ready?"

Jeremiah nodded. "Aunt Maggie said we can eat."

"Without her?"

Jeremiah pursed his lips and shrugged. "Guess so."

Sam went over to the kitchen door for a closer look. "Where did she go?"

"Said she had to take Ely and Thad's plates down to them."

Maggie rushed in and quickly shed her coat. She gazed at Sam and smiled. "Warmer?" His thin white ankles and feet stood out against the dark shabby trousers and floorboards.

"Much. Why didn't you ask me to take their food down before I changed clothes? There was no need for you to get wet, too."

"I didn't." She glanced at his bare feet and grinned. "It's not bad when the wind lets up." She started for the kitchen. "Let's eat." She paused at the head of the table. "Sam, you can sit there," she said, indicating the seat to her left. "And Jeremiah, you can sit across from him."

Sam reached over to pull out her chair, but she stepped over to the dry sink. He motioned for Jeremiah to sit down.

She filled one glass with milk and two with water. She set Jeremiah's milk down near his plate. When she returned to the table with their water, Sam stood with one hand on the back of her chair. She set their glasses down and met his gaze. "We don't stand on ceremony around here, Sam, but thank you." Being treated as if she were a lady felt odd, though pleasant. Men treated her with respect, but she made sure she did her share. After all, lace and crinoline wouldn't pilot a steamboat.

"You are most welcome, Miss Maggie." She was as outspoken now as when she was twelve, when she had tried to be one of the boys. And yet over the years, when he thought of her, he had pictured her as the mother of several rambunctious boys of her own.

She served Jeremiah, passed the plate to Sam, then cut her nephew's venison into small bites. She glanced at Sam. They had not only grown up, they had grown in different directions. She took a sip of water and accepted the platter from Sam.

Jeremiah looked over at Cap seated in the doorway. *Poor boy,* he thought, *you're hungry.* The dog drooled, and Jeremiah stared at his plate. He shoveled a bite of meat into his mouth and wondered if his aunt would make him eat everything on his plate the way his mama had. His eyes got watery, and he swiped at them with the back of his hand.

"This venison's much tastier than those tea cakes you made for one of our fishing trips." Sam hid his grin and reached for a piece of bread.

She chuckled. "As I remember, those cakes sank like stones when we tried to skip them across the stream." She grinned at Jeremiah. "I was better at fishing than cooking."

"Girls don't fish."

"Some do." Watching him cram his mouth with meat and potatoes, she frowned. "Slow down, Jeremiah. You'll get a bellyache."

Jeremiah struggled to chew his food. His mouth was so full he had to swallow several times. He nodded and took a drink of milk. His throat still felt funny, and he hadn't even cleaned his plate.

Sam watched Jeremiah and looked at Maggie. "I've never seen him eat that much food in one sitting." The boy's appetite had improved in the last few days, but he had still only worked himself up to eating four or five bites of meat and a few small pieces of a potato or vegetable. "Would you mind if he shared his meal with Cap?"

"Not at all." Maggie glanced at Cap, then Jeremiah. "Eat what you want. You can give the rest to Cap after we finish. He's used to eating last."

Jeremiah poked his fork into a piece of turnip. He wasn't full yet, and his ma said he'd grow to be a big man like his pa if he cleaned his plate. He chewed the bite and swallowed.

Sam glanced at Maggie. "How long do you plan on piloting this boat with only Ely and Thad to help?"

"As long as she holds together. Why?"

He shook his head. "If you keep this pace, you'll join your husband long before you thought you would."

She grinned. "Haven't you heard? Work is good for body and soul." She glanced at Jeremiah and added, "I've been thinking about working one of the feeder streams. The Clackamas might be a possibility or the Tualatin."

Sam swallowed the last bite and wiped his mouth. "Would either of those rivers make your work any easier? Or Ely's?"

"A little." She shrugged. "If I made the move next spring, and the business is good, I could hire a young man to help out." She sat back and eyed him. "What are you getting at?"

"I'm concerned about you. At least allow me to help while I'm here." Jeremiah pushed a piece of meat around his plate, and Sam took pity on him. "If you're full, Jeremiah, lay your fork down on the plate."

Jeremiah set his fork down and looked at his aunt. "Are you full, too?"

Grinning, she glanced from Sam to Jeremiah. "Yes, I believe we are." She stood up and filled Cap's pan with scraps and the leftovers. She handed the pan to Jeremiah. "If you hold up his food, he'll sit up for you."

"Can he eat in here?"

"No." She motioned to the dog. "He's going to the door because he gets fed outside on the deck."

Jeremiah opened the door. Cap trotted out ahead and sat down. Jeremiah looked back at his aunt and held up the pan. "Up, Cap." When the dog sat back on his haunches and raised his front paws, Jeremiah grinned. "Good, boy." He set the pan down on the deck. He had asked his pa for a dog, but he had been told the city was no place for a dog. As he watched Cap, Jeremiah wished he could stay with Aunt Maggie. She wasn't mean. Maybe she would learn to like him, the way he had just learned to eat turnips.

Maggie opened the door to Sam's cabin, dropped her jacket on his bed and lighted the lamp while he laid Jeremiah down on the cot. The boy had fallen asleep after she had finished cleaning up the kitchen. "We'd better loosen his belt and take off his shoes. He'll sleep better."

Sam unbuckled the boy's belt and unbuttoned the top buttons of his shirt, while she took off Jeremiah's shoes.

She pulled the covers up and tucked them around Jeremiah's neck. He looked so small and so young. She leaned over, kissed his brow, and softly said, "Happy dreams, Jeremiah."

Sam glanced at her and added another piece of wood to the stove, then closed the door. He stood up as Maggie leaned forward. Her hand slid down the back of his jacket, and his arm brushed against her firm breast as she bent to set Jeremiah's shoes by the stove. The deck gently swayed, and he met her wide-eyed gaze.

Her heart seemed to skip a beat as she stared into his eyes and said the first thing that came to mind. "He's fast asleep." Her thoughts were a jumble with the rush of excitement his touch roused. She felt a little confused by it, until she tried to remember how long it had been since she had experienced such intimacy.

"Good." He motioned to the door. "Want to stroll around the deck?"

She smiled and picked up her jacket with a shaky hand; he slipped on a pair of shoes; and they left the cabin. The rain sounded like a spring shower. It was coal-dark, but she didn't need to see to find her way past the boiler. Just short of leaving the protection of the boiler deck, she stopped and slipped into her jacket. "If it weren't raining, we could walk along the bank. It's beautiful."

"I'm beginning see why you like it here." The deck shifted. He raised his hand to her waist, intending to steady her, but she moved with the boat as naturally as if she were born to it. "Did you ever stowaway on any of the riverboats without telling me?"

She chuckled. "I used to dream about what it would be like, and I planned to many times." She shook her head, absently watching her breath form a cloud. "I wasn't brave enough to try it alone. You would've skinned me alive if you'd caught me." She tucked her hands in her pockets.

"I think you could do just about anything you put your mind to. You must know lady pilots are rare." He moved behind her and leaned against the bulkhead at her side.

"Only because most men would rather women remain at home. Women plow fields, drive teams of oxen, walk alongside wagons for hundreds of miles, and still tend to daily chores." She turned around and gazed up at him. "Have you ever known a riverboat pilot that had to hurry home to wash the laundry, feed the family and clean house?"

"You left out motherhood." He grinned. "Men have it easier there, too." So she was a women's rights advocate, he thought. He recalled jokes and cartoons about a women's rights convention in the late forties but that took place somewhere in New York, and he was sure she hadn't attended that.

She laughed. "I'm surprised you're not married. You

must have the girls buzzing around like bees in springtime."

It was his turn to chuckle. "If you think I'm a rogue, why did you come out here in the dark with me? Aren't you afraid I'll ravish you?"

Oh, Sam, if you only knew, she thought. "I'll take my chances." The water lapped against the hull, and the little stern-wheeler gently rocked. "Tell me about some of the places you've been. We came west on the trail with a wagon train. There weren't any towns to speak of. I haven't even been down to Jacksonville. Why don't you start there?"

"We arrived there at dusk, spent the night in a hotel and continued on early the next morning. From what I saw, it was a busy town."

"You used to tell such stories about New York City. Did it live up to your dreams?" Cap returned from his outing and pressed his cold wet nose against her hand. She rubbed his neck, and he padded over to the rail.

"One night it did. I spent most of my savings on a ticket to see Jenny Lind at Castle Garden. She was marvelous. I wasn't close enough to see her face clearly, but I couldn't miss her russet hair. No one in the audience made a sound when her glorious voice rang out."

As she listened to him, the soft patter of rain fell on the river, and Sam spun a web of other sights and sounds. Though she couldn't imagine Miss Lind's voice, Maggie pictured the ladies' satin and silk gowns, and the gentlemen's elegant cutaways and top hats. "What a wonderful memory to have."

"The first ticket sold for two hundred and twenty-five dollars."

"For *one seat?*" In all her days she'd never heard of such a thing.

Her shock was enough for him to keep the price of his ticket to himself. "That's almost paltry compared to the one thousand seats that sold for more than ten thousand dollars each." Her mouth dropped open. He raised one brow and nodded.

In her opinion that was beyond extravagance. It was plumb crazy. He sounded so highfalutin. She hadn't realized how very much he had changed. "That's more money than I've ever seen." She glanced around at the *Maggie*. If she had the price for one of those outrageous tickets, she could outfit her boat in style and never have to worry about bills or taxes. And she could raise Jeremiah and pay for his schooling. Sam was watching, his amusement obvious in the curve of his lips. "What we have is gatherings. Not as grand as Miss Lind's, but there's usually a fiddle player or someone with a mouth organ or banjo." She gazed into the darkness. "The music sounds best here on the river. Tell me more, Sam."

"Mm, let's see." He struck what he hoped resembled a meditative pose. "Riding for the Pony Express sounded exciting. But I'm too old."

His deadpan expression was a give-away that he was teasing her, and she grinned. She had missed his straight-faced humor.

"Besides, I was running the hotel when they started up last summer. Instead I decided to explore some of California. That's when I hired Joshua to run the hotel, and I visited a few mining towns in the Sierras."

"Did you pan for gold?" His sense of adventure roused hers, and she was curious to learn more.

"I tried my hand at it a couple times but by then the streams were about played out." He leaned closer to her. "How about you? Did you and your husband try your luck down on the Rogue River?"

"He said the merchants were the ones getting rich."

Sam nodded. "Saloon keepers got a good portion, too."

"I heard that some used to search through the sweepings for gold dust." She shivered. "It's getting cold. And time for me to say good night." As she moved toward the steps leading to the upper deck, he put his hand on her elbow. His touch was warm and tender, and she wished the stairs weren't so close. She paused at the first step and smiled at him. "See you in the morning."

He stared at her a long moment. He didn't want the evening to end, but she had worked all day. "Sleep well, Maggie."

"You too."

She patted her leg, and Cap trotted up the steps ahead of her.

After a quick breakfast of potato fritters and stirabout, Maggie guided the stern-wheeler upriver. The sky was clearing, and it promised to be a beautiful day. She stopped twice to pick up passengers going as far as Salem and Lincoln. She blew the whistle and went down to the main deck. Sam and Jeremiah were standing near the bow hatch.

Sam helped her set the gangplank. "You're making good time."

"There's only a light breeze." Jeremiah came over, and she dropped down to one knee. "Did Sam take you back to watch the paddle wheel?"

Jeremiah shook his head.

"Maybe he will later." She thought he looked a little tired, and she wondered if he felt okay. "Does your tummy feel okay?"

"Mm-hm."

"Ho, Maggie."

She stood up and waved to Mr. Timms. He was waiting at the foot of the gangplank with several hogs.

"Can you take us to Salem?" Mr. Timms called out, waving his arm at the hogs.

"Come on aboard." She looked at Jeremiah and spoke to Sam. "Maybe you should take him up on the boiler deck until we reach Salem."

The hogs started up the gangplank. Sam picked up Jeremiah. "Let's go see the paddle wheel."

As soon as the hogs were on board, Maggie returned to the pilothouse. The stern-wheeler backed away from the riverbank, then continued south. The deck vibrated in response to the increased speed of the paddle wheel. The river was clear up to Darrow Chute. Five miles further up river, they arrived at Salem. It was midday, and she was on schedule.

Cap was the first down the gangplank. Maggie let the passengers off. She motioned to Mr. Timms. "Are you still getting a better price here at your brother-in-law's slaughter house?"

He nodded. "If not, I'll take'm to Independence."

"Good luck." Mr. Timms waved and herded the hogs away. Maggie looked for Sam and Jeremiah on the boiler deck, but they weren't in sight. Passengers boarded, and cargo bound for Portland was stored. She went up to the pilothouse and found Sam holding Jeremiah up and pointing to some building in town.

"I wondered where you'd gone." She stepped over to blow the whistle, then eyed Jeremiah. "Do you want to blow the whistle?"

"Can I?"

"Just pull this rope. Two times." Sam stepped over, and Jeremiah took hold of the rope. Maggie covered his small hand and helped him. The whistle blew, and Jeremiah's eyes grew round. She let him pull the rope a second time.

"That's loud."

"It has to be heard far away."

Sam stepped back out of Maggie's way. "What's our destination?"

"Back to Oregon City. Heading downriver with the current, we'll make it by nightfall." Maggie waited for Thad's signal over the pipe, then pulled out into the current.

"Aren't you going to have dinner? Jeremiah and I are starving, aren't we?" The boy nodded, and Sam gave her an encouraging look.

She flashed a quick glance at them and then concentrated on the river. At times Sam acted as if she were playing at being a steamboat pilot. She wasn't. Her survival depended on her wits and her ability to earn a living with the boat. "Sometimes Thad fixes something during a long stop. You'll have to make your meal. There's plenty of food. Jeremiah can help. He watched me last night."

Sam stared at her a moment, but her concentration was solely on the river. "All right."

He and Jeremiah went down to Maggie's cabin. When Sam opened the door, Jeremiah hung back. "Aren't you coming in?"

"I wanna see Cap. I'll come right back."

Sam heaved a sigh. The boy had spent nearly every minute of the last three weeks with him and probably needed time to himself. "Do not go on the outside deck. And don't stay too long." As soon as he spoke, Sam knew he might sound like his own father one day, but he didn't think he would sound like his mother.

"Yes, sir." Jeremiah hurried down the stairs to the main deck. Cap was lying by the woodpile. Jeremiah went over and squatted down by him.

As Thad shoved a log into the fire, he saw the boy and walked over to him. "Does Miss Maggie know you're here?"

Startled, Jeremiah stepped back. "Mr. Sam does."

Thad nodded. "Just didn't want them worrying."

Jeremiah buried his fingers in the dog's thick fur. He knew Ely was down in the engine room. "I'll be right back." Jeremiah made his way down more steps and saw him. The engine was so loud, the noise filled his head.

Ely reached for the oil can and saw Jeremiah. "What're ya doin' down here?" he shouted, going over to the boy. "Get tired of the cabin?"

"Yeah," Jeremiah shouted, looking past Ely.

"That's the engine. Big, ain't it?"

"Mm-hm. How come Cap stays by the stairs?"

Ely shrugged. "He likes to know what's goin' on. What about you? Does Maggie know where ya are?"

Jeremiah shook his head. "Mr. Sam said it was okay. Can I stay?"

"Nah, lad. It's not safe." Ely checked one of the valves and went back over to Jeremiah. "Ya ever been on a steamboat b'fore?"

"I was on a ferry."

Looking away from the boy, Ely cleared his throat. "Ya haven't got sick. Ya must have some of yer uncle's feel fer the river."

Jeremiah frowned. "What-d'ya-mean? You can't feel the river."

Ely smiled knowingly. "Ya kin feel the water. That's a

fact. If ya stay here long 'nough, mebbe ya'll learn to read the river."

"Can you teach me?" Jeremiah licked his lips. "Mama was teachin' me to write my name. She said I was . . . real bright." He had never heard of anyone reading a river, and he wanted to learn how.

"I bet yer ma was right. Let's see." Ely rubbed his chin. "You have a lot to learn if you're goin' to be helpin' out."

Jeremiah nodded. He looked around the room. "What can I do?"

Ely thought a moment. "Do ya think ya kin haul some wood for Thad?"

"Sure I can, but can't I help you?"

Ely shook his head. "Not down here. Yer aunt wouldn't like that. You go along now. If ya wanta be a mate, ya gotta take orders."

"Oh, all right."

"But don't ya go tryin' to put any in the firebox." Ely eyed the boy. "Ya hear?"

"Oh, I won't." Jeremiah dashed up the stairs. He patted Cap's head and said, "Come on," as he hurried to the woodpile. He carried a chunk of wood over to Thad.

Thad took the piece of wood and threw it into the firebox. "You don't have to do this."

"Ely said I could help you."

Thad grinned. "Good."

Jeremiah had only carried a few pieces over to Thad when Mr. Sam came down.

Sam waited for Jeremiah to make two more trips to the woodpile before he spoke up. "Dinner's ready. I think you'd better wash up now."

"Can Cap come with us?"

"If he wants to." Sam held out his hand. When Jeremiah joined him, Sam whispered, "Don't forget to say good-bye to Thad."

Jeremiah went over to him. "Thanks. Can I help you some more another time?"

Thad nodded to Sam. "As long as your aunt or Mr. Adams says you can."

Jeremiah petted Cap and looked up at Mr. Sam. "Can I have some water?"

"This way."

Jeremiah patted his leg the way his aunt had and called, "Come on, Cap."

Chapter

5

Steaming downriver with the current and the sun at her back felt easier as Maggie steered the stern-wheeler into the deeper channel around one of several brush covered islands in the river. She stretched her back. She continually scanned the river, but her thoughts drifted to Sam. And eventually, to his reason for being there.

They had laughed, talked and shared memories, but each of them had avoided dealing with Jeremiah's future. She had no remedy, knew of no family who would be eager to take in the boy, and her circumstances should be clear to Sam by now. Anyway, she hoped so.

When she came to Doak's Ferry crossing, she waved and gave one blast of the whistle. Three farmers boarded at Matheny's Landing. And so she continued north, picking up passengers, letting others off. This was her routine, her life, and it was as comfortable as her old pair of gloves. She couldn't imagine what else could bring her as much pleasure.

They were halfway between the Molalla River and Oregon City when she felt the vibration change in the floor. It was a faint difference but one she knew could mean trouble. She piped Ely to shut down the engine. The current would carry them the last few miles. The engine stopped, and then Thad raced up to the pilothouse the way he always did after an unexpected stop.

Thad burst in gasping for breath. "Ely said he'd•have the engine workin' in a few minutes, good enough to get us home."

"Thank goodness." She glanced at Thad. "We've made good time. Tell Ely we'll take it easy, and I'll talk to him later."

"Yes, ma'am."

Less than five minutes later, the engine started, and she continued downriver, the *Maggie* limping along with the southerly wind at her back and the strong current. Soon, Canemah and Oregon City came into sight. She blew the whistle and guided the boat into home port. They docked, she went down to the main deck, as usual, and set the gangplank. The last passenger had stepped onto the bank as Sam and Jeremiah joined her.

Cap nudged Jeremiah's hand with his nose before he trotted down the gangplank. Jeremiah patted Mr. Sam's arm. "Can I go with him?"

Sam glanced at the dog. "You better not. He'll be back."

Maggie turned to leave. "I have to see Ely."

Taking Jeremiah's hand to insure he wouldn't stray, Sam walked along with her. "What happened?" When he had heard the change in the engine, he had started for the pilothouse but changed his mind.

She paused at the stairwell leading down to the engine room. Ely didn't welcome outside advice, but she didn't have the patience to deal with the peculiarities of male pride at that moment. She shrugged. "That's what I'm finding out." Going downstairs was as close as she wanted to get to walking into a furnace. She found Ely with his shirtsleeves rolled up, bent over one of the valves. "What happened?"

"The dern thin' must a slipped when we took that bend."

She shrugged out of her jacket and hung it on a peg. "I'll check the connections."

"Maggie girl, I'll secure it. No need fer ya gettin' oily too." Ely grabbed a dirty cloth. "Ya kin git me a cup o' coffee, while I see jist what all needs work."

She nodded. "You'll come up for supper?"

He shook his head. "Better stay here till I know what we got."

"All right." As she reached for her jacket, one of the steam pipes caught her attention and she leaned over to take a closer look. "Grannie's biscuits," she mumbled. "This pipe's got a crack in it."

"Might be more, but we'll fix'm." He patted her arm. "We always do."

"Thanks." Yes, they always managed to fix the old engine, but one day his clever patches wouldn't be enough. She grabbed her jacket and went back up on deck. The chilly breeze felt good after the heat in the engine room.

While talking with Thad, Sam had kept the stairs leading below in sight. Maggie finally came back up and walked over to the rail. Facing the wind as it tugged at her hair and whipped her skirt, she kept her shoulders back and her chin held high, as if she were defying some unseen force. She was magnificent. Jeremiah was sitting with his arm around Cap not far from her. "Thanks for telling me, Thad," Sam said.

Thad glanced at Maggie. "She's a fine pilot, and she's been good to me."

Sam nodded and walked over to her. He stared at the river, searching for what held her attention, but he didn't notice anything out of the ordinary. "What did Ely say?"

"The engine shifted—again." Rivers rushed their banks, cutting new courses, she thought. That was their nature, ever changing. The last rays of sunlight vanished as if in a puff of smoke, and the dark quickly hid not only Canemah, a mile south, but also the riverbank and the fir trees.

He brushed against her arm as he leaned on the rail. "All riverboats suffer that problem." What he was really thinking was how wondrous dusk and dawn seemed aboard a steamboat. He had forgotten those times until now, though maybe this seemed more special because he was with Maggie.

She gazed over at him and took comfort from his nearness. "Can you tell me why someone hasn't designed a way to anchor that blamed thing in place?"

Her voice and the tilt of her head struck a familiar chord. He came close to wrapping his arm around her waist but caught himself before he had embarrassed both of them. "I'll take a look at the engine, if you want me to."

She reached out and rested her hand on his chest. Grinning slightly, she shook her head. "I can't ask that of you. You're a friend, paying a visit. I'll see if I can't rig up something." She let her hand slip down.

He caught and held her fingers before she could pull free. "I'm offering." He turned her hand over and stroked his thumb over her rough palm. "Won't you let me play, too?"

His touch was featherlight and, but for her pounding heart, nearly entrancing. She grinned and prayed he couldn't tell how it was affecting her. She was a widow woman, not a young girl, and she felt foolish. "If that's your idea of playing, you may join the fun." When had he become such a charming gentleman? she wondered, and who had he polished that charm with?

Sam was on his hands and knees, removing the sheered-off bolt from one of the engine supports. He doubted the part had been replaced since the boat was built. The biggest problem with steamboats was their length of service. The wear and tear usually shortened their usefulness to three to five years. He stood up and held the bolt out for Maggie to see. "We'll have to replace all the bolts. A pair of wedges at each of the legs should keep it in place."

Maggie had just loosened one of the steam pipes. She lifted it free and picked up the bolt from his outstretched hand. "We tried that once but all we had to use was wood."

"We'll use iron this time." He glanced at the cracked pipe. "You want to make a list of what we'll need to do? We should be able to have her running, but you'll have to stay in port tomorrow." Her fingers closed around the bolt until her knuckles turned white.

Losing a day's earnings wasn't so much, except that each coin was needed—but so was the engine, in good running condition. She chucked the piece of bolt across the room. "One day. I'll finish checking all the steam pipes." Ely was working on one of the valves. "Ely, think we can do it in one day?"

He gave an indifferent shrug as he kept working.

Tired and rather impatient with his stubbornness, she

frowned at his back, then met Sam's warm gaze. "We'll do it." She set the pipe aside and saw Jeremiah sitting on the stairs, his head resting against the dirty wall, and she realized that he was sound asleep. "He needs to go to bed, Sam."

Sam held up his hands. "You're not as dirty as I am. Would you?"

"He's not my . . . He's your—" *Responsibility* hovered on her lips, but it wasn't true. To their knowledge, she was the closest relative the little boy had. She woke Jeremiah up and walked him to his cabin.

Jeremiah sat on the edge of the cot while his aunt buttoned his nightshirt. "Is Mr. Sam coming to bed?"

She poked the last button through the hole. "Not now. But he'll be in a little later. He's helping with the engine." She pulled the covers back and motioned for him to climb in bed. "Jeremiah, do you remember ever seeing any other aunt or uncle?"

"Mama said the Lord took Aunt Effie to live with him." He lay down. "Did he take Mama and Papa, too?"

Maggie swallowed hard. She'd never had to face a question like that. "Yes, honey, he did." His lips quivered and his eyes filled with tears. She pulled him to her and held him close. The poor little tadpole.

He didn't want to move from the warmth of her arms. "How come he didn't take me? Was it 'cause I was bad and snuck the biscuit?"

"Oh, no. Don't think that. Don't ever think that." She rocked him, hoping for a flash of wisdom she didn't possess. "You still have to go to school and grow up. There are so many things you haven't done yet."

He sobbed and took a deep breath. "Will he take me then?"

"I hope not. Not until you're an old, old man." She sat him up and dried his tears with the edge of the sheet.

"Like Ely?" He lay back down.

She bit her lips to keep from laughing. "Mm-hm. He's lived a long time, and he's still going strong." *He's a treasure,* she thought, *I simply must find him a good family.*

"Aunt Maggie, how come you don't have any young'uns?"

"Well," she said, wondering how she was going to get out of this one. He was too young to understand but old enough to ask. "I don't know." She tucked the covers around his chin. "You go to sleep now. We'll be in the engine room for a little while."

"Night."

She strolled out to the bow and let the wind revive her. Jeremiah's simple questions had more than surprised her. They had been unnerving. And the worst part was that she knew she hadn't answered him properly, not the way his mother would have. She'd had no experience with little boys. She shivered and rubbed her arms. She had to get back to work, back to what she did best.

By the time she returned to the engine room, she was pale and quiet.

Sam was tightening the pipe joint. "Is he all right?"

"Fine." She moved to the other end of the engine and sat on her heels to inspect a joint and avoid Ely's keen eye—Sam's, too. "What have you found?"

Sam looked to Ely, who instantly became totally absorbed in the value he was fiddling with. "It needs two pipes and the wedges, plus whatever Ely's found."

Maggie stood up and stared at Ely. She loved him like a father, but she had had enough of his cantankerousness. "Ely?"

"The valve lever came loose and the cam rod worked itself off. It's fixed now." Ely grabbed a rag and wiped his hands. "I'll tighten the other lifters in the mornin'."

"Yes. We can finish this tomorrow." Ely left, and she glanced at Sam. She wished she was better at reading his thoughts. "I appreciate your help."

"My pleasure. How about some fresh air?" Noticing how weary she looked, he couldn't help wondering what had caused such fatigue in such a short time. Surely, he thought, Jeremiah hadn't given her trouble.

She put on her jacket, turned the lamp down, and followed Sam up on deck. He offered her his arm, and she accepted the friendly gesture.

She felt grateful that he and not a stranger had brought Jeremiah to her. It didn't have any bearing on her suitability as his guardian, but at least Sam hadn't simply dropped the boy off and departed. "What are we going to do with him?"

Sam glanced sideways at her as they strolled along the deck. "I don't think you would consult me about Ely, so you must mean Jeremiah. Did something happen when you put him to bed?"

"No—yes. His questions surprised me, and I'm certain I didn't tell him what he wanted to know." They were crossing the stern of the steamboat, and she stopped, staring at the big paddle wheel. The shaft that supported the wheel would have to be inspected also. Too bad she couldn't peer into Sam's thoughts as easily.

He wondered what the boy had asked that had upset her so much. "He's curious about you and your boat. I think that's a good sign. Don't you?"

"He didn't ask about the boat." She reached out and ran her hand along one of the paddles.

"What kind of questions?" She struck him as an off-the-cuff, straightforward type of person, who could handle about anything, and yet she was so uncomfortable.

She stared ahead. "He wanted to know if the Lord had taken his parents and asked if he hadn't taken him because he'd been bad." She shook her head. "Jeremiah shouldn't be worrying about dying or if taking a biscuit made him so bad the Lord would think he wasn't a good boy. That's nonsense."

"I agree." He lowered his arm and held her hand. "Were you able to put his mind at rest?"

"We'll have to watch him. I'm not sure." She met his gaze. He really cared about the boy, and she wanted to hug him for his understanding. "When he's sleepy seems to be a good time to talk to him. Maybe he'll be more at ease with you."

He nodded. "He moved firewood for Thad today and enjoyed himself. If he thought he was helping, maybe he would feel better." The interest shining in her eyes gave him the encouragement he needed, and they began walking again. He knew it wouldn't take her long to realize that she and Jeremiah needed each other.

Her hand felt warm in his. She was tempted to keep walking right down the gangplank into town, but they couldn't leave Jeremiah alone. "Since you've sold the hotel, what will you do now?" she asked.

He met her gaze and wondered why some man hadn't already slipped a ring on her finger. "Raise sheep."

"Sheep?" She grinned, then laughed softly. "Have you worked on a sheep ranch? I hear they're dumb as fence posts." When he gently squeezed her hand, it felt so good her heart skipped a beat.

"My partner, Chester Potts, has experience. We agreed to try it for two years—see how it goes." Her smile was beautiful, and he was glad he had made her laugh, though that wasn't his intention. "Starting a new enterprise is exciting." Business law had been interesting—until it had become routine.

"Where is this ranch?" She paused, gazing into his eyes. "Here . . . in Oregon?" *Wouldn't it be wonderful if he lived close enough to see once in a while?* she thought. "The Willamette Woolen Manufacturing Company is on Boon's Island in Mill Creek, just north of Salem. There are several sheep ranches in the valley."

Her eyes were bright, and she looked as if she actually wanted him to reply in the affirmative. He wouldn't enjoy disappointing her. "No. I met Chester in Sacramento. He needed backing. We struck a deal and found some acreage north of there." Her smile slipped away, but she shrugged and still held onto his hand. She was one hell of a woman. No pouting or tears, and he doubted she had ever whined.

"I wish you the best of luck." She pressed his hand. "With your talent for doing just about anything, you won't need luck." She eyed him playfully. "I never saw this side of you before." *If I had, would I have waited for him?* But there had been no reason for her to wait. Their romance had been alive only in her twelve-year-old heart and mind.

"You're a rarity—a sensible romantic."

When they came back around to the stairway leading to the upper deck, she stopped. "See you in the morning."

"Sleep well." He held her hand until she reached the second step, and he kissed her fingers before he let her go.

He held her gaze as her fingertips slipped from his. She smiled at him. "Night, Sam." She went to her cabin and dressed for bed, her spirits restored. When she was with Sam, she almost felt young and fanciful again.

Tomorrow they would not only complete the repairs, they must somehow include Jeremiah. She climbed into bed and closed her eyes. As sleep overcame her, she tried to recall her earliest years, what she did when she was five or six, what made her laugh, what made her happy.

Chapter 6

After breakfast, Maggie set off with Jeremiah to buy pipe for the engine. Ely made as many of the parts as he was able to but some things had to be purchased. She walked along the wagon track keeping pace with Jeremiah. There was a light, cool breeze, but the sun was bright and felt good.

Jeremiah watched a black bird swoop down ahead of them onto the road. "There's another one."

Maggie grinned. "How many crows have you seen so far?"

He looked at his fingers and held two down with his other hand. "This many."

"Three. That's a lot. Want to count how many we see until we get to Canemah?"

Nodding, he immediately started searching for more. He spotted a bird, but it wasn't a crow. "What's that?" he asked, pointing to the upper branch of one tree.

She shielded her eyes and stared at the branch until she saw it. "That's a blue jay."

He looked up at his aunt. "Why don't you count them?"

"Okay."

By the time they reached Canemah, they had walked backward, he had found a stick that resembled a snake, and he had seen his fifth crow. He was behaving like other little boys, which was a welcome sight. She took his hand as they entered Murphy's Warehouse. Murphy built steamboats and sold supplies. She led Jeremiah over to where old Murphy was working on the hull of a steamboat. "That's a beauty."

Murphy looked over his shoulder and smiled at her. "You

can have one just like this whenever you say the word." He climbed down from the ladder. "How you been? Haven't seen you lately."

"We're fine. Or will be if you have two lengths of pipe for me." She glanced at Jeremiah. "Murphy, this is my nephew, Jeremiah. Zeke's brother's boy."

Murphy held out his hand. "How do, Jeremiah."

Jeremiah looked at his aunt before he shook hands with Mr. Murphy. He was big and had a hole between his front teeth, but he smiled a lot.

"You helpin' your aunt run that boat of hers?"

"I don't know how."

Murphy chuckled. "You'll learn." As he went over to where his pipe stock was, he called, "What lengths do you need?"

She told him what she needed, and she paid him. "Thank you. I'll have to let you know about that new boat." It had been a running joke between them for at least three years. She turned to leave, but Jeremiah had followed Murphy.

"Mr. Murphy—" Jeremiah held out the note Mr. Sam had given him. "I wanna buy these."

Murphy read the note, then he looked from Maggie to Jeremiah. "You sure, son?"

"Yes, sir. And I got money to pay for'm." Jeremiah held out the coins Mr. Sam had given him.

Maggie stared at the coins. "Jeremiah, who gave you that money?"

"Mr. Sam." Jeremiah did just what Mr. Sam had told him to do; he watched Mr. Murphy.

"Well?" Murphy eyed her.

"Go ahead. He has the money." Botheration, why had Sam done that? The boy sure looked proud of himself, and she wasn't about to reprimand him. No, she'd have her say with Sam.

Murphy handed Jeremiah six bolts and took one coin in payment. "Thank you, Jeremiah."

Jeremiah grinned. "Yes, sir! I never bought nothing before." He poked the bolts into his trouser pocket and left with his aunt. When they started walking back to the boat, he looked up at her. "Can I count blue jays this time?"

Sam finished oiling the cam gear and stood back as he asked Ely, "Want me to check the reversing gear?"

Ely snorted and grumbled, "If it ain't broke, don't go pokin' round it."

As disagreeable as Ely was, he was completely devoted to Maggie. He was working on the valve gear. It converted rotary motion into intermittent reciprocating motion. Sam knew that part must be in top condition; it was essential.

Ely stood up and arched his back.

Sam hadn't seen Ely check the connection from the rocker shaft to the cam rods. He couldn't have forgotten, not with his experience, but neither could Sam ignore the gnawing doubt. He stepped over and reached out to the rocker shafts.

Ely moved with lightning speed and grabbed Sam's arm. "What'd ya think yer doin' there?"

"Look at this sleeve." Sam moved enough for Ely to see where he was pointing. "That rocker slipped."

As Ely stared at the shaft, he let go of Sam.

Sam adjusted the inner rocker shaft. "There. Right as rain."

"We'll see," Ely said grudgingly.

High compliment, Sam thought. "I'm going up top." He was thirsty and wanted to watch for Maggie and Jeremiah. After gulping two dippers of water, he went over to see how Thad was doing.

Thad grinned. "Ely drive you out?"

"We're done until Maggie returns. I see you've cleaned out the boiler."

Thad nodded. "Since the engine's down, I thought I'd better check the safety valve and clean the chimney. I'm ready to fill the firebox when Ely gives the word."

"Good." Sam stared at the road leading south.

"You ever work on a riverboat?"

"I did. Started when I wasn't more than a stripling boy,

hardly strong enough to keep up. By the time I left home, I'd worked most every job there is on a steamboat."

"Thought so."

As Sam stared at the road, Maggie and Jeremiah came into the clearing. It was obvious that she laughed, and then Jeremiah looked around and pointed at something overhead. It was a wonderful sight. Whatever she was doing with the boy was working, and better than Sam had hoped.

Maggie managed to keep Jeremiah near her side until they came within a few feet of the gangplank. Then he made a dash for the deck. "Slow down!" she called as she dropped the pipes and ran after him.

Jeremiah couldn't wait to show Mr. Sam the bolt things and called out, "I got 'em," as he raced up the gangplank. He reached into his pocket to pull one out.

She knew the moment he lost his balance. She made a grab for his arm, but her fingers barely brushed his sleeve as he fell into the river. She followed, jumping in after him.

Cap darted past Sam and jumped overboard, too. It all happened so quickly that by the time Sam reached the gangplank, Maggie had come to the surface of the water holding a startled Jeremiah above her head, and Cap was paddling at her side. Sam hurried down to the edge of the embankment and lifted the boy out of the water before he extended his hand to Maggie. When Sam thumped Jeremiah's back, the boy coughed and sputtered, getting rid of the river water. Sam went down on one knee. "Are you okay?"

Jeremiah rubbed his eyes and nodded. "What happened?" His mouth tasted bad and his throat felt funny. Cap licked his face and Jeremiah petted him.

Sam pulled the boy into a fierce embrace. "You fell into the river. Can you swim?"

"Unh-unh."

Maggie pushed her hair back from her eyes. Sam was holding Jeremiah with such affection. *Sam Adams, you're a liar,* she thought, *if you deny loving that boy.* She rested her arm across Sam's shoulders and ruffled Jeremiah's hair. "I think we should get into some dry clothes."

Sam lowered his arms. Jeremiah was pale, and his teeth

were chattering. "I'll give you a ride." Sam stood up with
Jeremiah in his arms and realized that the boy's hand was in
his pants pocket. "Is your hand stuck?"

"I was gonna show you the bolts." Jeremiah grinned and
pulled his fist free. "I got 'em for you. See." He held up one
of the bolts.

Sam chuckled. "You sure did."

Maggie picked up the pipes she had dropped and followed them up the gangplank. Cap waited on deck to see
which direction to go. She caught his attention and pointed
to the deck. "Cap, stay here. Sam, take him to my cabin. I'll
get his clothes."

Jeremiah ate a small bowl of hasty pudding and fell
asleep while Maggie told him a story about a frog and a
tadpole. She carried him down to the cabin he shared with
Sam and tucked him into his bed. When she stepped outside,
she found Cap sitting by the door and stopped to pet him.
He'd shaken most of the water off, but he was still wet.
"You can stay with Jeremiah and dry off."

After she let Cap into the cabin, she looked for the pipes
she had set by the door, but they were gone. She went down
to the engine room. "Sam, have you seen the pipes? I'm sure
I left them on deck."

He waved his hand at the engine. "There they are." He
glanced at the top of the stairs. "Where's Jeremiah?"

"Sleeping. After all the excitement, he was worn out.
How are things going here?"

Sam motioned to Ely.

Maggie nodded. Had Ely and Sam reached an understanding? It was almost too much to hope for. "Ely?"

Ely straightened up and glanced at her. "About ready to
try her out."

"Good, but I want to check the paddle-wheel connecting
rod first." She met Sam's gaze. "Would you help me?"

"Yes, ma'am."

She picked up her toolbox and went up on deck. As soon
as they reached the walkway leading to the stern of the boat,

she frowned at Sam. "Why did you tell Jeremiah to buy those bolts? Ely can make them."

He smoothly relieved her of the toolbox without missing a step. "The idea came to me while I was talking with Jeremiah last night. He was so excited about surprising you, and I thought Ely had enough to do. Did Jeremiah enjoy himself?"

"He did indeed. Proud as a rooster in a henhouse."

"Good. He certainly was happy when you returned."

She glanced at Sam. "How do we keep him busy without working him as if he were full-grown?"

"Keep his tasks simple. He likes to be around everyone, not shut up in the cabin." They stopped at the wheel. "Want me to take this side?"

She smiled and started inspecting the wheel support. Working with him felt so natural, as if they had always worked side by side. It took them less than fifteen minutes. "It looks fine."

It was in very good condition, he thought, better than the engine. "What next?"

"Thad can start the fire."

"He's ready."

When Thad had built up a head of steam, Ely started the engine, and Maggie clasped her hands behind her back. All the parts worked the way they were supposed to, and she sighed her relief. "We're in business."

Ely nodded at Sam and made himself busy.

Sam gazed at Maggie. "When are you planning to leave?"

"Not until morning. I'll go into town and see about getting the cargo loaded today." When they went up on deck, she heard Cap scratching at the cabin door. She grinned at Sam. "I think Jeremiah's awake."

The opportunity was too perfect to pass up. "Good. Now we can go with you."

They went ashore a short time later. Jeremiah held onto Maggie's hand, her arm was on Sam's, and Cap trailed behind. She noticed a few curious glances, but she greeted those she knew as if she usually went walking with a handsome gentleman and small boy. They made three stops, and she settled her arrangements in quick order.

In Peterson's store, Sam watched Jeremiah from a distance as the boy gazed longingly at a little carved and painted horse. It was on a wooden platform with wheels and had a small cloth figure of a boy riding it. Sam went over and pushed the horse back and forth. "Did you have a horse like this?"

Jeremiah nodded slowly. "Pa made it with his knife. It didn't have wheels. I made it walk."

Her business completed, Maggie found Sam and Jeremiah standing in front of a display of brightly painted wooden toys.

"Here." Sam handed the horse and rider to Jeremiah. "I think the man that made this would want you to have it."

"Oh!" Jeremiah held them with both hands. "It's the goodest toy I ever had! Thanks, Mr. Sam." The horse was brown with a *real*-hair tail; the boy had red suspenders and black boots.

"You're welcome." Sam didn't think he would ever forget the look of pure happiness on Jeremiah's face. Stepping over to the counter to pay for it, Sam passed Maggie making her way to Jeremiah. He shrugged. He didn't need to explain his purchase.

"That's a handsome horse." Maggie bent down to get a closer look. "Do you like horses?"

"Mm-hm. And see—" Jeremiah lifted the doll up. "The boy comes off."

"That's very clever."

Sam came back and motioned to the door. "Shall we go?"

"I believe we have everything." Jeremiah was still fascinated with his new toy, so she placed her hand on his shoulder to guide him outside.

When Cap came up to Jeremiah, he held the horse down to the dog. "See, Cap? The wheels go round."

Maggie gazed up at Sam. "That was nice of you. He's so happy." She felt good, too, and slipped her arm through his.

"It was my pleasure," he said, wondering what she secretly yearned for and never expected to have. If he hadn't had to meet his partner, he wouldn't have minded spending a few weeks helping her out on the steamboat. However, he was expected at the ranch by mid-November at the latest.

"It's nearly suppertime." Maggie grinned at Jeremiah, who was still showing the horse to Cap. "Are you hungry?"

Jeremiah rubbed Cap's neck. "Uh-huh."

"Then we'd better get back so I can start cooking."

Sam stopped and held her arm to his side. "Why don't we have supper at Barnhill's Home Restaurant? It's across the street."

Cap licked his lips, and Jeremiah giggled. "Can we, Aunt Maggie? Cap's hungry too."

Sam watched a man and his dog leave the restaurant. "Looks like Cap can eat with us. What do you say?"

It was so tempting—Laurel Barnhill was a friend and a wonderful cook—but it seemed like a waste of money to Maggie. "Sam," she said softly, "I'd better cook."

Sam arched one brow. "I thought cooking wasn't one of your favorite chores. Isn't their food good?"

"It's wonderful. I've known Laurel and Paul for years." It was embarrassing to admit she hadn't the money for an occasional meal out, but the truth was, she didn't. "Sam, people will stare. Please, let's go."

She thinks she'll have to pay for her meal, he suddenly realized. He leaned his head near hers. "I am inviting you to join me and Jeremiah for supper." He straightened up, and nodded to a passing woman, who was staring at them. He started across the street with Maggie in tow, without waiting for her reply.

He didn't appear to expect an answer. She really felt stupid. Any other woman probably wouldn't have thought about paying for her own meal. At times like this, though they were few, she wondered how different her life might be if she lived in town. Paul Barnhill's friendly greeting brought her musing to a halt.

"Maggie Foster. It's about time you paid us a call." Mr. Barnhill seated them at a window table. "Be right back." He pushed the door to the kitchen open and called, "Mrs.

Barnhill, you better take care of this party." He turned back to Maggie, grinned, and added, "Hurry up, woman."

Mrs. Barnhill came out from the kitchen, still wiping her hands on her apron, and glanced at her husband. "Mr. Barnhill, I was putting up an apple pie. What's got you riled up?"

"Did you clean that table?" He motioned to where Maggie was seated.

Mrs. Barnhill glared at Mr. Barnhill. "You know I don't leave tables dirty." She whirled around and marched over to the table in question.

Maggie burst out laughing. "Oh, Laurel, he's joshing you." Laurel's brown hair curled naturally. That and her contagious laughter and smile always brightened a room.

Laurel grinned. "I'll deal with him later. How've you been?" Then she looked at the man and boy. She grinned at Cap and petted his head. "And who are your dashing companions?"

Maggie introduced everyone and couldn't ignore Laurel's questioning gaze. "Sam and I grew up in Meyer's Ferry. How are Bobby and Colleen? Last time I saw them she was blaming him for scaring off all the boys."

Laurel chuckled. "They still tease each other, but she still manages to see the boys." She grinned at Jeremiah. "What is your favorite supper?"

Jeremiah shrugged. He wasn't sure what to say. No one had ever asked him that before.

"We have salmon, of course, roast of pork, beef steak, and fried chicken. What sounds good?"

Sam glanced at Jeremiah and Maggie. "Salmon for me, Mrs. Barnhill, and I believe Jeremiah's partial to chicken. Maggie?"

Everything sounded good to Maggie and not having to cook was a special treat. "Steak, I think, juicy red in the middle."

Laurel nodded. "Mr. Barnhill, these poor folks are parched. If you get them something to drink, I'll serve their supper." She winked at Cap. "I'll bring something for you, too."

"Never should have let her do the cooking. How was I to know she'd refuse to feed me if I rile her?" Mr. Barnhill chuckled good-naturedly. "What's your pleasure, folks?"

Sam reached over and tucked Jeremiah's napkin in the neck of the boy's shirt. "Milk and"—he looked at Maggie—"a light wine or maybe—"

"Excuse me, Sam," Maggie interrupted. She waited until the two men who had just come in had walked past their table. "They don't serve spirits." She looked at Paul. "Coffee will be fine for us, Paul." Paul left, and she leaned over closer to Sam. "The temperance movement is strong in this state. I'm sorry."

Sam nodded. He hadn't realized the movement had gained such a foothold in Oregon. "If the food is as good as the Barnhills are friendly, they must stay busy." They were dining early; the sun had just slipped past the western hills. Another family came in, then a man and woman. Sam didn't envy Mr. Barnhill having to hurry from table to table.

Paul Barnhill's laughter rang out, and he brought their drinks to the table. "Good thing you came in early. In a couple hours, there will be people waiting out front."

Soon Laurel brought their supper. She served Maggie, Jeremiah, and Sam, then set a bowl on the floor in front of Cap. "Call me if you want seconds."

Sam stared at the generous portions. "If we call you, it won't be for want of food, Mrs. Barnhill. This must be the whole salmon."

Laurel laughed. "I try to fill the plates, but you'll never catch me serving a twenty- or thirty-pound fish."

As Jeremiah chewed a bite of chicken, he watched the dog. "Aunt Maggie, what did she give Cap for supper?"

"Probably a little bit of everything." Maggie fully enjoyed her meal.

When Paul cleared the table for dessert, each of them declined. Sam paid for their meal, and they started to leave.

They were almost to the door when Laurel rushed from the kitchen to walk out with them. "I hope you come back real soon. What with my cooking and your boat, we hardly get to visit." She handed Maggie the apple pie she had wrapped up. "Take this back to the boat. There's enough for Ely and Thad, too." Cap licked Laurel's fingers, and she scratched him behind his ear.

"I shouldn't," Maggie said, grinning, "but I will. Thank you, Laurel."

Laurel hugged Maggie and whispered, "He's a handsome one. Don't be so blamed smart, lean on him a bit."

Paul Barnhill came to the door. "That steak's burning, Laurel."

Laurel threw up her hands, said, "Nice meeting you, Mr. Adams, Jeremiah. Hope I see you again," and dashed back inside.

They returned to the steamboat as the last crate was being carried aboard. Maggie handed the pie to Sam. "Would you mind taking this to the cabin for me? I really should check over the cargo."

Sam relieved her of the pie. "Sure." She didn't seem to have anything in her life that wasn't somehow connected to her boat, and that didn't seem right. She was a fine woman, but it was almost as if she were hiding. From what, he wondered. From life? But that didn't seem possible.

Chapter

7

Sam had helped Maggie verify the cargo, while Jeremiah played with his new toy with Cap. Later that evening, she insisted Ely and Thad join them in her cabin for a slice of Laurel's apple pie. By the time she went to bed, she was pleasantly tired. Although he had watched out for Jeremiah, Sam also appeared determined to assist her. She enjoyed his company, the smiles they shared, the way he'd rest his hand on her shoulder without seeming to notice, and the way his voice sounded huskier when he said her name. Too bad he's set on raising sheep, she thought as she fell asleep.

The next morning she dressed for the day in a flannel shirt, with trousers beneath her skirt. She ate a few bites of hasty pudding and left the pot to the side of the stove when she went down to start work. Only five passengers boarded. When she reached out to swing the gangplank aboard, Sam came over to help her.

She smiled at him. "Hello." She hadn't consciously thought about it, but when she saw him each morning she was pleased all over again to see him. Over the last few years, piloting her stern-wheeler had become all-encompassing in her life—until Sam arrived.

"Good morning." He was fascinated, watching her old hat flap wildly in the wind but staying put. It was amazing how well her work clothes hid most of her charms—all except for her beautiful eyes. "Have you had breakfast?"

"I left a pot of hasty pudding on the stove for you and Jeremiah." She rubbed her gloved hands together. "He isn't on deck, is he?"

Sam motioned to the boiler. "Jeremiah wanted to carry a few logs for Thad."

"If he gets tired of the cabin later, you can bring him up to the pilothouse. The company would be nice." She rested her hand on his arm. "I'd better get going. See you in a little while."

She hurried up to the pilothouse and blew the whistle before their departure. Piping orders to Ely, she reversed gears to back the stern-wheeler out of port, and then she switched to the forward gears to head south. The weather had turned cool and dark clouds threatened more rain.

Suddenly the rain started as if a great spigot had been opened overhead. It came down so hard she had to navigate more by instinct than by sight. She didn't see any signals asking her to stop and hoped she hadn't stranded anyone in the foul weather.

The current became fierce with the water rushing toward the Columbia River. The downpour continued for almost an hour before it calmed to a steady rain. By the time she made her first stop at Mission Landing, her shoulders were stiff, and she looked forward to moving about, even in the cold rain.

Cap was the first one down the gangplank. While four roustabouts unloaded several barrels and replaced them with a dozen crates, Maggie went over to warm up by the boiler and check on the supply of wood. "Thad, how're you holding up?"

"I'm fine, but we're sure goin' through those logs. I better go ashore for more while we're here." He opened the steam-escape pipe to lower the pressure while they were stopped. "I'll get my coat."

"Don't forget your galoshes and oilskin," she called after him. She turned her backside to the boiler and looked to see if Sam was on deck. She was beginning to thaw out when he come over to her, the hint of a smile at the corners of his mouth, and his eyes glowing softly. "You seem happy," she said. "What have you been up to?"

"Nothing in particular. Don't I usually look happy?" He had been told many times that he had a poker face, and he had in fact worked to perfect it: he had thought it was to his advantage. With her, he wasn't as certain.

She grinned. "Mm, sometimes. It's hard to tell." She glanced around. "Is Jeremiah in the cabin?"

"He's talking to Cap on the other side of the boiler." He motion to the backside of the firebox.

She stepped to his side, took his arm, and they walked over to where Jeremiah was talking to Cap. "Hi. Have you been playing with the horse?"

Jeremiah shook his head. "Mr. Sam showed me how to write my name." He petted Cap's ear. It was so soft. "I ain't good at it."

"You did very well for your first lesson. We'll work on it a little each day." Sam met Maggie's gaze. "How are you doing? The river's rough today."

"I always work a little harder in the winter. It isn't so bad." When he eyed her, she chuckled and rubbed her right forearm. A few more years behind the pilot's wheel, and she would have arms like a lumberjack.

"I'm ready for some hot coffee," he said. "I'll make a pot. Would you like a cup?"

"Sounds wonderful. Would you bring it up to me after we leave port?"

"Of course." He didn't speculate on which she wanted more, the coffee or his company—he might not like the answer. "I'll take some to Thad and Ely, too."

"They'll appreciate it. I used to take coffee to them, when Zeke was piloting the boat." She raised Jeremiah's jacket collar to cover his neck. "Do you want to stay with me? We can go up to the pilothouse in a few minutes."

"Okay." Jeremiah pushed the horse over to Cap's paw and petted it with the boy figure's little hand. "See, Cap, he likes you."

While Jeremiah talked to the dog and the doll, Maggie marveled at the change in him, and she felt a twinge of guilt. Although she had been straightforward with Sam about the fact that she couldn't raise the boy, it didn't seem fair that he should suffer. She had planned to spend the night at Independence, but if she made it down to Albany, she could call on Nellie Quint, who made it her business to know everyone within miles. She might know someone who would take Jeremiah.

The rain had stopped by the time Thad returned with two roustabouts who had helped him collect more wood. As soon as the men were gone, Maggie pulled in the gangplank and went back to Jeremiah. "Come with me. We have to leave now."

"Can Cap go with us?"

"Afraid not. He can't climb the ladder, and he's too heavy to carry." She smiled and held out her hand. "You can see him later."

He hugged Cap and kissed him near his black nose. "You be good." He picked up his toys and looked up at her.

"Let's put the doll in your pocket." She took his hand and hurried up to the ladder leading to the pilothouse. "You'll have to use both hands to climb. The ladder's still wet, so be careful." He was trying to put the toy in one of his pockets, but it was too big. He looked stymied, and she took pity on him. "I'll take the horse up for you. I'll be very careful. I promise."

He handed his horse to her and started up the ladder.

Maggie climbed step by step right behind him. If he slipped, she was ready to catch him. But he went right up and opened the door. When she reached the top, he held his hand out. She put the horse in his hand and smiled. Sam surely had given the boy more than just a toy horse to play with, he'd given his childhood back to him.

"Do you want to blow the whistle for me?"

"Uh-huh." Jeremiah grinned and raised his arms for her to pick him up. Then he gave the rope two tugs, just as she told him to do, and stared at the river. It looked cold and so far away.

She set him back on the floor and piped Ely. After she backed up and guided the stern-wheeler across the current to the west side of the Willamette, she glanced at Jeremiah. He was standing at the window with his hands cupped around his eyes and his nose pressed on the glass. "What do you see?"

"I can't see nothin'. It's sorta fuzzy."

She turned the wheel and avoided a fallen tree hanging over the bank. "You're standing too close. It's cold out, and your breath is warm. It fogs the glass. Step back a little."

"Oh." All he could see was big trees on this side. He went over to the other side of the little room. He could see the river and fields. He rested his chin on the ledge.

"Here comes another steamboat, the *Liberty*. We'll pass her in a couple minutes." She blew the whistle.

"Look! Gee, it's even bigger than your boat." Black smoke streamed out of the big pipe and hung in the air.

The *Liberty* came abreast, and Maggie waved to Captain Wymer. She counted at least fifteen men standing out on deck, and there were probably more inside. They were friendly rivals of hers, and she wondered how long she would be able to survive despite the two companies that owned nearly all of the boats on the river. Even if they bought her little stern-wheeler, which wasn't likely, they wouldn't allow her to pilot the boat.

Jeremiah stepped sideways along the windows until he came to the last one. A man waved. Jeremiah jumped up and down, waving back. "Are there any more boats coming?"

She grinned. "I don't see any right now."

He kept staring out the window. He saw one man walking on the path by the river, they passed another one on a brown horse. Then his aunt blew the whistle. "Do you see another boat?"

"A ferry, over there." She pointed to the east bank without taking her attention from the river ahead. "Wave to Mr. Ridley."

Jeremiah smiled and waved at the man. "He has a dog, too."

"That's Sassy. She goes everywhere with him."

Jeremiah watched for a few more minutes, but he was tired of standing there and sat down on the floor. He saw an old rag in one corner and pushed the horse over to it. He was taking the boy figure off the horse when he heard someone on the ladder. He scrambled to his feet and opened the door. "It's Mr. Sam!"

"Hi there." Sam stepped into the pilothouse and handed a steaming cup of coffee to Maggie. "Did you think I'd forgotten?"

The warmth from the cup seeped through her glove and felt so good. She cast him a quick glance. "No, but we've been busy, haven't we, Jeremiah?"

"Mm-hm."

Sam leaned close to her ear and said softly, "And I was hoping you missed me." He stepped over to Jeremiah. "Don't you want to watch for other boats?"

"We saw one, didn't we, Aunt Maggie?"

"Sure did. Why don't you tell Sam about it? He probably didn't see it." Jeremiah sure perked up around Sam, she thought, wondering if Sam realized it.

Jeremiah described what he had seen. "And he had a dog, too. Aunt Maggie said her name was Sassy."

Jeremiah's eyes were bright, and he was so enthusiastic, Sam couldn't resist the impulse to pick him up. "Sounds as if you've had fun."

Jeremiah put his arm around Mr. Sam's neck. "Yeah. But Aunt Maggie said she didn't see any more boats coming, and I wanted to play with my horse." Mr. Sam carried him over to one of the windows. "Not too close or we'll fog the glass. That's what Aunt Maggie said."

It seemed *Aunt Maggie* had made quite an impression on the boy, just what Sam had hoped for when he delayed bringing the coffee to her. Although her attention never left the river, he could tell by her expression that she was aware of them. "If you want to move around, Maggie, I'll take the wheel for you."

"Thanks, but Lincoln's just ahead and Salem's not much farther. We can stay in port and have dinner there. If it doesn't rain any more, we'll make Albany by this evening."

"I thought we were headed for Independence."

"We'll stop there. It's a few miles south of Salem, but we're making good time. I might be able to pick up a cargo in Albany." She steered around a mound of boards and branches that had washed up against the bank.

Jeremiah patted Mr. Sam's shoulder. "I'm thirsty."

"Want to go down to the cabin for a drink?"

Jeremiah nodded.

Maggie flashed him a quick smile. "There isn't much to do up here. Go on. I'll see you two later."

Sam draped his arm around her shoulders. "I'll put the gangplank out for you. Jeremiah can help me."

His breath skimmed her cheek, and a warm feeling rippled down her spine. "I'll see you on deck." She really had to concentrate on the river. Brush, tree limbs and all sorts of odds and ends had been carried along by the fast-moving current. As Sam left, she glanced at his back. He could easily become her current and sweep away her careful sensibilities—without even knowing it.

After dinner, Sam talked Maggie into taking a short walk around Salem with him and Jeremiah. They looked in shop windows and stopped for a few minutes for Jeremiah to watch a man laying bricks. Although Maggie enjoyed the outing, she was anxious to get back to the stern-wheeler, and Sam gave in to her wishes. He was making headway with her. A few more days, and he felt sure he could leave Jeremiah with her.

Earlier, Maggie had spoken with Ely and Thad about reaching Albany by evening. By the time they returned to the boat, a fresh supply of wood had been stacked on the main deck. She waved to Sam and Jeremiah on her way upstairs.

She hurried away, and Sam knew her mind was on her work, which certainly appeared to be her main enjoyment in her life. She was alone, and that didn't sit well with him, but he had no right to interfere in her personal affairs. He peered down at Jeremiah. "What do you want to do?"

Jeremiah looked at the firebox. "Can I help Thad?"

"All right." Sam fixed him with a firm stare. "Don't get in Thad's way or try to feed the fire. Understand?"

"Yes, sir." Jeremiah ran over to Thad. "I can help you!"

Thad looked at Sam before he answered. "Good. I could use some help. Just set the wood down here," he said, pointing to the side of the firebox.

Sam checked on Jeremiah from time to time and finally took a leisurely stroll around the deck. When he returned to the firebox, he found that Jeremiah had removed his coat, though the wind was still cold. He decided the boy had had enough. "Jeremiah, tell Thad you have to go now."

Jeremiah put down the big log. "Can't I stay? I'm helpin' Thad. Huh, Thad?"

Thad threw two more logs into the fire and stood up. "You've been workin' mighty hard. I think you should listen to Mr. Adams."

Jeremiah frowned. "Gee, I wish I was twelve."

Sam picked up Jeremiah's jacket and put it back on him. "Twelve. That's pretty old."

"Yeah. My pal, Will, was twelve and he got to do lots of stuff."

Sam cleared his throat to keep from laughing. He must look like a dotty old man in the boy's eyes, a thought he certainly didn't agree with. He was a long way from accomplishing all he had planned.

When they got back to the cabin, Sam built up the fire. "You must be thirsty after working so hard."

Jeremiah nodded, pulled his jacket off, and went into the kitchen. It was so hot. He drank water from the dipper, then put it back in the bucket.

Sam laid out a sheet of paper and pencil. There were still things to buy for the boy—chalk and a chalk board, mittens, and maybe a first reader for Maggie to help him study with. "Do you want to practice writing your name?"

"Un-huh. I'm sleepy."

"Do you want to lie down for a while?"

"Mm-hm." Jeremiah shivered and walked over to the sofa.

He looked as if the steam had gone right out of him. Sam was worried until he remembered the boy was only six years old. "You can rest on your aunt's bed. You'll be more comfortable." He scrutinized the boy. He looked a bit flushed. "I'm sure Maggie won't mind."

Jeremiah followed Mr. Sam into the bedroom and sat on the floor to take off his shoes. When Mr. Sam pulled back one of the covers, he climbed into bed. It was big and soft. "I forgot Cap."

"He's used to staying down on the main deck. We'll see him later."

"Okay. He'll want his supper."

Sam found a copy of the *Statesman* dated October 2, and he settled in the quilt-covered armchair. He read the first two paragraphs of an article by Asahel Bush, but Sam wasn't familiar with Oregon politics and couldn't appreciate the writer's vitriolic attitude. After perusing another article, he assumed name-calling was an accepted practice in the area.

He finally found a piece about Oregon's first state fair. Prizes totaling almost nineteen hundred dollars were being awarded in several classifications. A good sum, he thought. He'd ask Maggie if she had gone to the fair. He set the newspaper aside and went in to check on Jeremiah. The boy was a little restless and had kicked the cover off.

Sam pulled the comforter back up, and his hand skimmed the boy's jaw. It was hot. So was his forehead. He didn't know what to do, if anything, but he was sure Maggie would. He went up to the pilothouse, hoping she would put his mind at ease.

When Sam burst in looking more serious than usual, Maggie quickly noticed he was alone. "Where's Jeremiah?"

"He said he was sleepy. I hope you won't mind, I let him rest on your bed." They were making good time. As Sam oriented himself with her controls, he draped his arm across her shoulders. "I think he's got a fever, Maggie."

"You did build up the fire in the stove, didn't you? Make sure he was covered up?"

"Yes, Maggie. I didn't know what else to do."

His arm felt warm, though his touch was becoming less comforting. Instead, he aroused feelings she had thought were only for the young. When she gave him a quick glance, her nose brushed his cheek. If he hadn't been dead serious, she might have—She gripped the wheel. "What good would it do if *I* checked on him?"

"I'd feel better. I can take over here for you." He didn't

reach for the wheel. She had made it clear how she felt about handing over command, and the choice was hers. He reached out and put his hand next to hers but not quite touching the wheel. "I won't ground her. Promise."

She hadn't shared the wheel with anyone other than Zeke. Besides, she wasn't a mother. "What can I do that you can't? Just because I'm a woman most certainly does not mean I've been blessed with any special talent for doctoring."

"Maggie . . ."

"Oh—The only thing I can think of is sassafras tea. You can brew that."

He leaned close enough to her that he bumped her hat a little cockeyed. "Please, go see him. I may be wrong." He gently massaged her shoulder, wishing the circumstances were different.

She sighed and nodded. "Keep to the right of the channel. It's easy to see it along here. If you need me, yank that rope." She pulled the old chart off a small shelf and pointed out their location. "Independence is the next stop, but I'll be back before then." She pointed to marked pipes, one to Thad, one to Ely, and the signal rope Zeke had put in that connected to their cabin. "If—"

He interrupted her. "I'll be fine. Go."

She rushed out of the pilothouse before she could change her mind. She felt guilty. She shouldn't have balked when Sam asked for her help, but she didn't trust her instincts where Jeremiah was concerned, or where Sam was concerned, for that matter. As she entered her bedroom, she forced herself to slow down and step quietly so she wouldn't alarm the boy.

Jeremiah had thrown the cover back again. His face was flushed, and he was sleeping uneasily. Her hands were cool so she placed the inside of her wrist on his forehead. He did feel hot—hotter than he should be.

She went to the kitchen, hoping the sassafras tea would bring down his fever. But it might take a few hours to work. By the time the tea had cooled enough for Jeremiah to drink, his fever seemed worse, though she wasn't sure. If she had only paid closer attention to her mother's instructions all those years ago, she thought.

When she sat down by him, Jeremiah's eyes were open, but he looked so scared. "Hi, Jeremiah. Are you thirsty? I made some tea for you."

He stared at her.

His confusion was obvious, and she hoped her fear wasn't. She set the cup down on the little table by the bed and lifted him into a sitting position with the pillow behind him. "Did you have a bad dream?"

Jeremiah clamped his lips together. He was cold and hot. He felt funny, but he didn't want to cry like a baby.

She held the cup up to his mouth. "Try this."

He took a sip and swallowed hard. He made a face and shook. "It tastes bad. Can I have water?"

She nodded. "I'll be right back." After she poured a dipper of fresh water into another cup, she added a bit of sugar to the tea, hoping that if it tasted better he would drink it. He finished most of the water, then she traded cups. "I added some sugar. See if this isn't better."

Warily, he tasted the tea. It wasn't as bad. He took a sip, then another.

She watched him carefully. What had her mother done for her fevers? Kept her warm—and one time she remembered her holding cold cloths on her forehead. And . . . pennyroyal, that was it, pennyroyal tea. All she had was sassafras. She hoped it would work as well. "Do you want something to eat?"

He shook his head.

"Okay. Let's change your clothes so you can rest easier." She found Zeke's old red flannel shirt and soon had Jeremiah in the soft shirt, which hung down to his feet. She set the chamber pot out for him, but he climbed back into bed. "You rest now, honey." She tucked the covers around his shoulders.

He nodded. Her cool fingers slid down the side of his face. It felt so good. He closed his eyes and pretended his mama was with him.

Maggie stoked the fire in the kitchen stove. Broth might

be good for him, especially if he didn't want to eat. He could drink his nourishment. She set a pot of water on the fire and added vegetables and chunks of beef. Once she assured herself that Jeremiah was sleeping soundly, she hurried up to the pilothouse. Sam appeared to be enjoying himself and doing a fine job, but she couldn't resist the urge to see for herself. She rested her hands on his shoulder and peered around his other side. "Any problems?"

"No, ma'am. All's well here." He glanced at her. "How's Jeremiah doing?" Although she was being playful, she seemed a bit unsettled. Which bothered her more, he wondered, Jeremiah or seeing him piloting her boat?

"You were right. He's got a fever. He drank some of the tea." She raised her hand to reach for the wheel but stopped just short of grabbing it and lowered her hand to her side. Sam hadn't forgotten what he'd learned so long ago. "One of us will have to stay in the cabin with him."

He spotted a signal set out by someone wanting a ride upriver. "We can take turns." He blew the whistle and began easing the stern-wheeler over to the east bank.

"Yes, of course." She forced herself to stand by, say nothing and see how he handled the stop. So far it seemed he had remembered what she'd told him about the signals. That was reassuring. "I'll stay with him in the evening, and he can spend the night in my cabin."

"What?" He glared over at her. "You're not—"

She grabbed the wheel. "Wasn't that signal on the east bank?"

He reclaimed the wheel and guided the stern-wheeler over to the landing where a wagon waited. "We *will* talk about this later." He turned to leave.

She took a step toward the door and found her face pressed into his chest, his strong chest, with his hands gently holding her arms. She glanced up at him. "I'd better get down there and put out the gangplank."

He shook his head. "That's my job." He lowered his hands. "Unless I'm discharged." So many emotions flitted across her sweet face that for one long moment he believed she might take back command of her boat.

The offer was tempting. She wanted . . . She wanted Jeremiah to wake up feeling fine; she wanted to know what it would have felt like if Sam had embraced her—and kissed her. "Would you blame me for wanting to do what I do best?"

"No. I don't." He reached around her and pushed the door open. "Neither of us is used to putting a child ahead of our own interests." He tapped her chin and stepped around her. "I know. The last couple weeks have been an experience."

"Don't keep the passengers waiting." She realized that he felt as uncomfortable with the situation as she did, she realized, and knowing they shared the same uneasiness made it more tolerable.

He took the steps two at a time, then paused at the foot of the ladder and called up, "What fare should I collect?"

"Fifty cents to Independence, a dollar to Albany." She went down to the hurricane deck and watched him. He was a fine figure of a man, and handsome, too. He certainly had a way of making her feel special. She imagined there must be several women who would gladly become his wife and wondered why he had remained single.

Chapter

8

Sam set the gangplank and held out his hand to the man that boarded. "Welcome aboard. I'm Samuel Adams."

"How do. Giles is my name." He looked around the deck. "Did Mrs. Foster finally hire a pilot?"

"I'm just helping her out." Mr. Giles paid fare to Albany and went up to the main cabin. Sam swung the gangplank back aboard, then he stopped to speak with Thad.

Thad wiped his brow. "What's goin' on?"

"Jeremiah has a fever and Maggie is taking care of him. I'll be piloting the boat for a while." Sam looked at the woodpile. "Maggie's set on getting to Albany today. Do we need to cut more wood?"

"We better. Independence is on the west bank. Just south there's a good stand of trees."

"Thanks." Ely came up on deck. Sam explained to him where Maggie was and added, "She's none too easy about handing over the wheel, but she can't afford to have the boat in port until the boy recovers, either."

"I'll do my part." Ely stared at his hands. "Do her good to put her feet up fer once."

"I agree. I'll be leaving in a couple days. Until then I intend to help Maggie any way I can." With Ely's help, Sam knew there would be few, if any, problems.

He returned to the pilothouse and guided the stern-wheeler across the current. It was coming back; his awareness of the vibrations of the deck, his sense that all was running well, the feel of the wheel, and the lofty view of the river he had always loved. Since Jeremiah wasn't feeling well, and he wanted to spend a little more time with Maggie, he really should stay on another couple days. He'd still have more than enough time to get back down to the ranch.

Jeremiah slept most of the afternoon, and Maggie feared she had worn a path to her bedroom. While Thad and Sam gathered firewood, she had watched from the deck outside her cabin. Sam cut and carried wood as if he were a fireman or mate.

He had asked her how long she could continue working shorthanded and, for the first time, she began to wonder how much longer she could expect Ely to work as if he were forty years younger. Before Sam had come back into her life, she hadn't questioned her ability to maintain the old stern-wheeler. Ely had always been there but, deep down inside, she knew she couldn't depend on him forever.

Although she was with Jeremiah, encouraging him to drink more tea, she felt the boat's approach to Independence. She wanted to run up to the pilothouse and guide the *Maggie* into port. She didn't. Jeremiah wasn't any better, and she was afraid to leave him alone.

Jeremiah turned his face away from the cup and scooted down under the covers. "Can Cap stay here with me?"

"That's a good idea. I'll call him after he takes his walk."

He closed his eyes.

She quietly left him to rest and watched the men unload the cargo. She called to one of them and when he shouted back that since she had a new pilot she could take it easy, she laughed. He didn't know what the situation was, and she wasn't about to explain.

Sam was on his way back to the pilothouse when he met her on the walkway outside of her cabin. "He's still sleeping?"

"Pretty much. I told him I'd bring Cap up to stay with him." She glanced down to the main dock. "Guess I'd better get him." She took two steps and paused. "Albany is about twenty-four miles upriver on the east bank. You can't miss it." She frowned. "Never mind. I'll relieve you in a while."

"Maggie," he said, continuing on to the ladder, "I'll get us there. Don't forget Cap." She was anxious, and he understood. However, it occurred to him that she might have intentionally centered her life around the stern-wheeler to the exclusion of all else. If that were true, she needed the boy more than he'd realized. She was too young to cut herself off from life.

She went partway down the stairs and called Cap. A moment later he trotted over and stared up at her with his tongue lolling out of the side of his mouth. "Come on up, boy." Cap obeyed, but he looked at her as if wondering if she were all right. She dropped down and gave him a hug. "You're always there, aren't you, boy?" She kissed his muzzle and stood up. "Right now, Jeremiah needs you even more than I do."

Cap followed her into the bedroom when she went to check on Jeremiah. He was sound asleep with one arm hanging over the side of the bed. Cap walked over and licked his fingers. She grinned and pointed to the floor. "Lay down." Cap lay down with his chin on his front paws and stared up at Jeremiah.

Needlework and sewing had never ranked high among Maggie's talents, so she straightened up the parlor, made repeated trips outside to see what was happening, and finally gave up and started supper. After dipping a good part of the broth into a smaller pot to keep it warm for Jeremiah, she thickened the rest of the liquid for the stew. It was simmering long before Albany came into sight.

It was nearly dark when Sam finally blew the whistle signalling their arrival. Relief washed over her. She was anxious to speak with him. Being so far removed from the running of her steamboat made her nervous.

She checked in on Jeremiah twice, but Sam still hadn't come to the cabin. She couldn't stand the suspense any longer and gave in to her urge to see what was going on below. She looked around from the upper deck but all was quiet. The main cabin was empty, as she expected. Continuing on down the stairs, she finally heard Sam's voice. He was talking with Thad on the far side of the boiler.

She hadn't heard their conversation, but she couldn't help

wondering if what had kept him down there so long was something he wanted to keep from her. "What's wrong?"

Sam leaned over to Thad as if to share a confidence with him. "Think we should tell her about the gash in her hull?"

She smirked and eyed each of them. "You mean that canvas and tar patch didn't hold?"

Thad coughed. "Think I'll see what Ely's doing."

"You and Ely are having supper with us. It's ready to serve so tell him to get cleaned up."

Thad nodded.

"Thad," Maggie said, "if you two don't show up, you can look for work on another steamboat, and tell Ely I said that." After he made his escape, Maggie chuckled. Poor Thad. After two years on her boat he still didn't know what to make of her. "I guess it's up to you, Sam. Tell me what's going on."

"Not a thing." He gave her a speculative gaze, as if he were in court and she were on the witness stand. "Why so suspicious? I've never heard of a mutiny on a riverboat." She was as agitated as a wet hen but much more appealing.

"We've been docked for at least twenty minutes." She sighed as if the weight of the world were on her shoulders. "I expected you to come up and tell me how everything went."

"No mishaps to report, Captain. We have a good store of wood, the boiler didn't blow," he said, rubbing his chin, "we didn't go aground, hang up on a bar or send Cap over the side."

"You couldn't have. He's been in with Jeremiah." She gazed at him, wondering why she was *so* upset with him. She mumbled, "Blame my buttons," and then, "You aren't going to make this easy for me, are you?"

Sam slid his arm through hers and motioned to the stairs. "I couldn't resist." She softened and fell into step with him. "What's made you so jittery? Don't you trust me?"

"I know you wouldn't deliberately—" That wasn't what she meant. She didn't really understand herself. "It's just that I'm used to—"

He interrupted to complete her sentence. "Being in

command." He covered her hand with his. "If it helps any, I did enjoy being the pilot for a few hours." He paused outside of her cabin. "How is Jeremiah?"

"No better, no worse. I got him to drink some more tea and a little broth." She opened her cabin door and went in to see Jeremiah. On her way out, she left the door ajar. She found Sam in the kitchen sampling the stew. "How is it?"

"Not bad." He licked his lips. "Have any spices?"

"A few." Her gaze narrowed, hiding her surprise. She opened the cupboard where she kept her spices. "You cook?" And what else could he do, a small-minded part of her wondered, part the water? She must be tired. It wasn't like her to be so spiteful.

"Enough to keep me from starving."

"I put an onion in and salted it," she said, trying not to sound defensive. He added a little more salt, some peppercorns, and a pinch of what looked like mustard seed from a little box, stirred the stew, and tasted it. She stepped closer and peered around his shoulder.

He dipped the spoon into the pot, then held it out for her. "See what you think."

She held his gaze as she leaned forward to taste the sample. She dragged her lips along the bowl of the spoon and swallowed. His eyes seemed to smile. A bit self-consciously, she licked her lower lip. "You're hired. Can you bake bread, too?"

"About as well as you used to make tea cakes," he said, his gaze still riveted on her rosy lips, his mind imagining how they would feel pressed against his.

She set the table, while he added more seasoning and sampled the stew. "Save some for the rest of us. I'm hungry." She set the bowl of butter on the table. When she glanced over at him, he was watching her. The look in his eyes gave her a warm-all-over feeling as surely as if he were holding her in his arms.

"There's plenty." He hadn't realized how special she was before. He had called on and kept company with a fair number of ladies but none had that spark that Maggie possessed. He put the large spoon down and closed the cupboard door where the spices were stored. Leaving wouldn't be as easy as he had first thought. Seeing her had been such a surprise, and with each day their bond seemed to be growing stronger.

Ely and Thad arrived and took their usual seats. Maggie served them their plates and put another in the middle of the table with bread. "Start without me. I'm going to look in on Jeremiah."

A couple minutes later, she joined them at the table. Each of them stared at her with concern clear in their expressions. "He's still sleeping."

Sam folded a slice of bread. "Might be the best thing for him."

"I hope so." Maggie ate a few bites, glancing at Ely from time to time. He was a man of few words, but he usually said something. "How's the engine holding up, Ely?"

"Jist dandy." Ely took another bite without looking up. "Looks like those wedges're holdin' her tight."

"Good." Sam glanced from Ely to Thad. "We didn't have a problem getting upriver."

Maggie finished eating first and sat back. "I need to go into town, Sam, will you sit with Jeremiah while I'm gone?"

"Sure." He gazed at her, but she didn't look at him. "Must be important."

"Yes, it might be." Before he could ask more questions, she checked on Jeremiah. He was petting and talking to Cap. She didn't think she had ever been so happy to see someone awake. From the way the dog had positioned himself, she wondered if the animal knew Jeremiah was sick.

Jeremiah looked over at her. "Cap likes to sit with his chin on the bed."

"I see that." She smiled. Cap did seem content to sit next to the bed. "Ely and Thad and Sam are here. Would you like to go in and see them?" Jeremiah looked so little in her bed. Little and peaked. "I'll carry you in, if you want me to."

"Can Cap come too?" Jeremiah pushed the covers back and waited for her to pick him up. He wanted her to hold him and rock him the way his mama used to when his belly hurt.

"He'll follow us." Maggie lifted him to her chest. "Are you cold?"

"Not now." He rested his head on her shoulder and put his arms around her neck.

Her breath caught in her throat. She had never in her life felt such a flood of tenderness. Tears sprang to her eyes. He sighed and kind of nestled in, and she held him close. His little body was so hot against hers, but it was the warmth of his trust that surprised her most. She blinked to clear away the tears, then carried him into the kitchen.

Sam smiled when he saw Jeremiah. But his happiness was short-lived. The boy looked worse, and Maggie was supporting his full weight. "There you are. You almost missed having supper with us."

Maggie stepped over to the stove. She poured a ladleful of the lukewarm broth into a cup and sat down at the table. Repositioning Jeremiah on her lap took some doing, but when she cradled him within her arms, he relaxed again. She glanced at Ely. His stare was fixed on the boy, and he looked worried. If he was concerned, Jeremiah must be worse than she'd thought. She held the cup up to Jeremiah's lips, and he swallowed a few sips.

Sam cut the last piece of meat on his plate into five small morsels and offered one to Jeremiah. "You must be starving. Taste this. It's good."

Jeremiah stared at the piece of meat.

Ely braced his forearms on the edge of the table. "Try it, mate. Ya have to be big and strong to be a steamboat mate."

Maggie felt him sit up, then he leaned forward and took the meat. She smiled and nodded to Sam, hoping he understood and would offer Jeremiah another bite.

Ely grinned at Jeremiah. "Ah, lad, ya'll be a mate in no time. No time a'tall."

Mr. Sam held out the next bite, and Jeremiah opened his mouth. He chewed up the meat and reached for the cup. When Ely grinned at him, his big eyebrows wagged up and down, and Jeremiah smiled.

*   *   *

Fortunately, Nellie Quint lived only three blocks from where Maggie was docked. She made her way there by the light spilling from neighboring buildings and homes. Nellie greeted her warmly, and Maggie chatted with her for a few minutes.

Nellie leaned forward, as if sharing a secret. "Tell me, Maggie, I heard there's been gambling on some of the riverboats. Is that true?" She sat back, fanning her face with her handkerchief. "Terrible, terrible. I suppose they imbibe, also."

Maggie didn't want to become embroiled in a lengthy discussion about temperance and the sins of men. "Piloting the steamboat doesn't give me much time to visit with the passengers." She smiled. "There is something you might be able to help me with."

"Oh, my dear, I had completely forgotten, you're wearing that pretty green calico dress and all. Poor Zeke's been gone what . . . almost sixteen months, isn't it?"

"About," Maggie said, wondering why that had occurred to Nellie. "You're always so friendly and have been welcoming new settlers for years. I—"

Nodding, Nellie interrupted her. "It's my Christian duty, Maggie."

Maggie attempted a sociable smile. "Nellie, I was hoping you might know a *good* family, one who may want to adopt a wonderful little boy. He's only six, and he lost his family." She clasped her hands on her lap, while Nellie seemed to think about her request.

"Hm. There's the Dickersons. They have a farm up the Calapooya, and they're good church-going folks. He's got girls and they read the Scriptures like little angels. I could speak to him. Or there's a shoemaker up in Santiam looking for an apprentice." Nellie shook her head. "Most families have a passel of children," she said, leaning closer, "more than I think is decent—if you know what I mean."

Maggie knew exactly what she meant. What she hadn't known before was what a snobbish, unfeeling woman Nellie was. "The boy's a little young to work in the fields, and he's running a fever. In fact, I really should get back and see if he needs anything." She came to her feet, ready to run if necessary to escape. "Thank you, Nellie."

"Boil a red pepper in a half pint of water, strain and add a fourth pint of vinegar, heaping teaspoon of salt and a dash of powdered alum. Best tonic there is, works every time." Nellie walked her out to the front stoop. "If you change your mind, dear, I'll be happy to speak to the Dickersons for you."

Maggie forced a smile and said, "Thank you. I'll keep that in mind," hurrying down the walk. As she marched back to the boat, she resolved never to consult that woman again. She hadn't seen that side of Nellie before and hoped never to see it again.

Maggie turned down the lamp in the kitchen and carried two cups of coffee into the parlor. She handed one to Sam and settled in her little rocking chair. "Thanks for helping with supper. And for tempting Jeremiah into eating a few bites." She gave him a lopsided grin and added, "And for staying with him while I went into town."

"Ely was the one who tempted Jeremiah to eat. He perked right up when Ely talked about him being a mate. It was better than tonic for him." Sam thought her reaction to the boy had been just as revealing. Whether she knew it or not, she was mothering Jeremiah.

He watched her over the rim of his cup. "Ready to talk about what happened?" When she had returned to the boat, she looked ready to do battle. He found her magnificent with her bright flashing eyes, cheeks flushed, and her skirt fluttering out behind her as she charged aboard.

"Nellie . . . Quint."

"Hm, I don't understand. Can you give me any more clues?" She was still simmering, he realized.

"She's always seemed like a nice, friendly woman. She knows everyone within miles." Maggie took a sip of her cooling coffee. "I knew her as a passenger. I had no idea what a zealot she can be." Maggie glanced up. He still didn't understand. "I had hoped she would know of a nice family for Jeremiah, not one who'd think of him as a farmhand."

He realized that she was feeling desperate, and he hadn't intended for that to happen. "Maggie, it's all right. There are good, loving families, and we'll find one for him," he said, softly adding, "if it comes to that."

She swirled the coffee around in the cup wondering if his last comment meant that if all else failed, he would adopt Jeremiah. She looked in on the boy again; he was still sleeping. She sat back down. "Sam, was he sick before you got here?"

"No. I didn't notice anything until this afternoon, after he'd been moving wood for Thad." He took a swig of coffee. "I thought it might do the boy good to get away from me for a bit. And he was with Thad."

"Didn't you say he was six years old?" She stared at him, and he gave her a nod. "And you let him go down to the main deck alone? He could've fallen overboard. He didn't grow up on a river the way we did." She was dumbfounded!

"No. I walked down with him. I doubt he was raised in a nursery, either. He hadn't been out of my sight since the night of the fire, until we boarded your boat." Sam took a sip of coffee and studied her. "He wanted to find Cap, and he does like to help Thad. I think it makes him feel grown-up. He was happy, Maggie. Happier than I've seen him in weeks."

"He's not used to boats." With a tap of her toe, she set the rocker in motion. "This is why he can't live here with me. He's too young—by at least five years."

Sam shook his head. "We could keep him tied to your apron strings. . . ." He wanted to make her understand. "Our parents allowed us room to grow. Shouldn't we do the same for him?"

"Indeed, Sam." She slowed the rocker to an easy pace. "When he's feeling better, we must find him a suitable home, a real family with a mother and father, and brothers 'n' sisters."

He wasn't ready to agree with her just yet. They had gone head-to-head before but never was the issue so very important. Neither did he want a debate. "Are we going back downriver tomorrow?"

She nodded. "Would you rather stay here in a boarding-house or hotel? Being on the river might not be the best thing for Jeremiah right now."

"I don't agree. He trusts you, and you've seen the way he fancies Cap. It's warm and dry in here. He'll be fine." Sam stood up to stretch his legs and add more wood to the stove.

His jacket was hanging on the peg beside hers, as if it had always been there. She gazed at his profile. She wanted to comb her fingers through the wave his hair made above his ear, smell the clove scent of his hair tonic on her fingers and run her fingers along his strong jaw. *He's fitting into my life too easily,* she thought, *as if there's been a space waiting for him to fill.* Her life was full and satisfying, but the last few days had turned her routine world into a jumble—and her emotions into complete turmoil. "Want me to bring his cot up here?"

They heard Jeremiah whimper from the other room. "Please," he moaned. They both hurried into the bedroom, and Maggie turned the lamp up. Jeremiah stopped thrashing around and looked glassy-eyed. "What's wrong, sweet-heart?" She felt his forehead and pulled the discarded covers back up to his chest. The fever was worse; the tea wasn't working. Dear Lord, if she didn't get his fever down . . . She sat down on the side of the bed and looked over at Sam. "Would you pour a little warm broth in a cup?" She picked up the glass of water and let him sip from it.

Sam left and returned with the broth. "Try this."

Jeremiah swallowed some and shook his head, then Cap poked his nose over the side of the bed. "Hi, Cap." He slid back down in bed and closed his eyes.

Maggie motioned for Sam to follow her into the parlor. "We have to do something. He's burning up."

"How can he cool off with the covers holding the heat in? Why don't we set him in a tub of cool water?"

"That could kill him! Couldn't it?" She paced the width of the room shaking her head. She wasn't about to make him drink hot peppers, but they had to do something. "Well—

maybe barely warm water?" She stirred the fire in the kitchen stove, put pans of water on to heat and got the washtub out.

Sam helped fill the tub, then went to get Jeremiah. "This is a funny time for a bath, but I bet you'll feel better when we're done." He was so limp, Sam had trouble undressing him. When he finally managed, he hurried back to the kitchen with Jeremiah in his arms.

"It's ready. Ease him into the tub." The water felt nearly warm on the tender side of her arm. She slipped her hands under Jeremiah's arms to keep him from sinking in the water. "What now?"

"Keep him wet and hope that the bath and the air cool him off." Sam dipped his hand in the water and dribbled it over the boy's shoulders. "It isn't cold in here, but it must feel like it to him."

Maggie didn't know how long they stood by the tub keeping Jeremiah's face and shoulders wet. His teeth chattered uncontrollably, and he offered little resistance. She was numb with fear. Dear Lord, he had to survive this. She dampened his silky hair. His body was so white, so small. Pressing a kiss to his thin shoulders, she prayed his fever would go down. The last time she prayed had been for Zeke, after he was scalded helping Mr. Vernon repair his boiler. Her prayers hadn't saved him, but they had to be answered this time.

As she made her plea for Jeremiah's recovery, she included his need for a good home. She didn't want to care for him so much that she couldn't do what was best for him. It wouldn't be fair to him if he grew to love her. He had already lost his parents, and she feared causing him more pain.

She whispered in his ear, "You have to get well, sweetie. You just—" Tears blurred her vision and ran down her cheeks as she promised to find a wonderful family for him if only he would get well.

While she was crying and whispering to him with desperation, Sam decided he would dip the boy in the frigid river if that's what it would take to bring down his fever.

They wouldn't allow him to slip from their grasp without a fight. He raised one of Jeremiah's legs out of the water and fanned it, then raised the other leg. As Sam lifted Jeremiah's left arm, the boy struggled and murmured. Sam grinned at Maggie. "Did you hear that? It's working!"

Jeremiah began to pull back from them. He was so cold and they wouldn't leave him alone. "N—n—n—o—o—o."

Maggie pressed a kiss to his head. "Come on, Jeremiah. Keep fighting us." She beamed at Sam. "See if there's any tea left. He likes it with sugar."

Chapter

9

While Sam set up the cot in her room, Maggie rocked Jeremiah, and Cap slept nearby. The fever was lower, but the little boy was worn out. She thought about the women who had four, five, or six children and wondered how they managed. Jeremiah stirred, but he didn't wake up. She pressed her cheek to his forehead and sighed. As if he understood her concern, Cap sat up and stared at Jeremiah.

Sam watched her from the doorway and knew that image of her would always be with him. Part of him didn't want to disturb her quiet moment with Jeremiah, but she was exhausted and needed rest as much as the child in her arms. He went over and hunkered down by her side. "His bed's ready. You're falling asleep. I'll tuck him in for you."

She nodded and stood up with the help of Sam's steady arm. "He's still too warm."

"Give him time. If we have to, we'll bathe him again." He reached out to take the sleeping boy.

She kissed Jeremiah's forehead and lifted him from her chest. Cooler air replaced his warmth, and she felt the loss instantly. Sam shifted Jeremiah to his shoulder without waking him. She walked ahead of Sam to pull the covers back for him and discovered that he had not only made the bed but had gotten it ready for them to slip the child into. She felt a little like an eavesdropper with nothing to do but stand by as he cared for Jeremiah with such tenderness.

Sam draped the covers over Jeremiah's back and smoothed the boy's hair back from his eyes. "Sleep well." When he straightened up, he put his arm around Maggie and held her close to his side. "He's okay for now."

She nodded and walked back to the parlor in the shelter of his loose embrace. He felt wonderful. She hadn't realized how much she missed being held by a caring man. "I don't know what I would've done without your help. His own father couldn't have done more."

He stopped at her cabin door and put his other arm around her. He held her close and felt the pounding of her heart against his chest. "We did it together." He moved his hand slowly up her spine and encircled her soft neck with his fingers. He felt as if he were home.

When his fingers lightly caressed her neck, she quivered and clung to him. It must be fatigue, she decided. She felt as if a feather had fluttered down her bare back and around her belly. She rested her forehead on his chest a moment, then gazed at him. "You'd better get some sleep. It will be sunrise before we know it."

"Ah, if you had only said, 'we,' the invitation would be much sweeter." He pressed a gentle kiss to her hair—he didn't trust himself to allow his lips any lower—and stepped back. "To bed with you, you're almost asleep on your feet."

After he left, she wrapped her arms around herself, but it wasn't the same. *Maggie*, she thought, *you're too old for these girl's notions*. She dropped her arms to her sides and went in to check on Jeremiah. He slept peacefully, with his hand hanging over the side of the bed and resting on Cap's head.

Later that morning, Sam roused when he heard Ely and Thad talking as they crossed the deck. Washing his face with the icy water from the pitcher brought him full awake. He dressed and left his cabin to see how Maggie had fared with Jeremiah.

Sam tapped on her door and when there was no response, he quietly went inside. There wasn't a sound, until Cap stalked to the bedroom doorway with his ears back and hackles up. "It's okay, Cap. Just me." Cap relaxed and wagged his tail as he trotted to the door. After Sam let the dog out, he peered into the bedroom.

It looked as if Maggie had fallen in bed without remembering to take off her boots and had barely pulled the covers across her midriff. He shook his head and fought the urge to straighten the comforter over her. Jeremiah had kicked his blankets off, again, too. Sam built up the fire in the parlor and in the kitchen stove. After putting a large pot of coffee on the fire, he kept himself busy with making breakfast.

Maggie woke up with the taste of coffee in her mouth— remnants from her dream, she thought, until she wondered why she could also smell freshly brewed coffee. She sat up and stared at her boots. At four in the morning, dressing for bed had been beyond thought. All she had wanted to do was stretch out and close her eyes for a few minutes.

Jeremiah. She jumped out of bed and knelt by his cot. He was still too warm but no worse than when she'd fallen asleep. "Thank you," she whispered. It was then that she noticed the room wasn't cold. She heard someone in the kitchen and knew it was Sam. No one else would dare enter her cabin uninvited.

The sound of her boots was unmistakable, and Sam glanced at the doorway. "Good morning." He filled a cup with fresh coffee and handed it to her. "You look like you could use this."

She raised the cup to her mouth with both hands, took a sip and smiled. "It's good." His hair was slicked back and his deep blue eyes seemed even more striking than usual. Belatedly, she noticed the frying pan on the stove top. "What are you making? It smells wonderful."

"Smoked pork steaks, fried potatoes and eggs." He reached for the bowl he'd seen in the lower cupboard. "I was about to make flapjack batter. Hungry?" There were dark circles under her eyes, but a good night's rest would lighten those.

"Yes, but you, Ely and Thad can have the flapjacks. You're up early." She watched him from over the rim of her cup. "Jeremiah isn't any cooler. I'll go to the general store. Mr. Waller may have a fever remedy."

She finished her coffee, and he refilled her cup. "What about a doctor? Isn't there one in town?"

"I guess there must be, but I don't know." She blew on the steaming coffee and took a drink.

"Why don't you ask Mr. Waller while you're at the store? He should know. But first you'll eat. You don't want him to think you're the patient, do you?" He put a steak, a helping of potatoes and jumbled eggs on a plate and handed it to her.

She stared at the eggs and grinned. "You mixed them with bits of fried pork fat, the way your mother used to." She ate a bite. "Mm, as good as I remember." She wasn't sure how old she'd been when a lot of the children had spent the night one Halloween at Sam's house.

He shrugged. "I always liked talking to Ma while she was cooking, especially in winter. The kitchen was warm and it always smelled so good."

"I liked testing the blackberry jam to see if it was ready to set up." She smiled as she recalled standing on a chair and watching the fruit simmer in the big kettle. "Blackberries grow wild here, too," she said as Sam joined her at the table. She cut a piece of steak and ate it. "The Willamette Valley's a lot like back home."

That could be one reason he felt so comfortable here, he thought, but it was being with Maggie that made him feel at home, rather than the climate. There was a scratch at the cabin door. As he stood up, he said, "Cap," and he went to let the dog back inside.

Maggie watched for Cap. He came in and sat down in the doorway, just the way she'd taught him. He was such a good dog. She rarely gave him any food from her plate, but he'd been so loyal to Jeremiah she thought he deserved a treat. She set her plate by the sink and walked over to him. She held out a piece of meat for him, and he took it from her fingers with his short front teeth. As she bent to give him a kiss, Ely and Thad passed her on the way into the kitchen. "Good morning."

Ely peered around her into her room. "Sam told us about last night. How's the lad doing?"

"I'll let you know after I check him." Cap followed her

into the bedroom and licked Jeremiah's hand as Maggie reached out to feel his forehead.

Jeremiah felt Cap's wet tongue on his fingers and opened his eyes. "Cap . . ."

She dropped down to his level. "He spent the night by your bed." He was better! She struggled to sound normal so she couldn't alarm him. "How are you feeling?"

"My mouth feels funny."

She picked up the glass of water she had left on the little table and held it to his lips. "Sam made breakfast, and his jumbled eggs are good. Want to try to eat a few bites?"

Jeremiah swallowed and pushed the glass away. "What about Cap? I didn't feed him."

"You can after you have something yourself. Okay?"

He nodded and rubbed Cap between his ears.

She carried him into the kitchen. Ely and Thad were seated at the table, and she sat down with Jeremiah on her lap. "Sam, he'd like to try some of your eggs."

Sam grinned at him and dished up a small portion of eggs and a spoonful of potatoes. He set the plate down and handed him a fork. "I'll heat that broth and the tea. I think they helped."

Ely held out a fork full of eggs and potatoes and made a show of eating for Jeremiah.

Jeremiah opened his mouth, and Maggie gave him a small bite. Sam refilled her cup. She gazed up to thank him and saw her happiness reflected in his eyes. Sharing the pleasure with him made it all the more special. She mouthed, "Thank you," not wanting to draw Jeremiah's attention.

Thad cleared his throat. "Lucky you're better, Jeremiah. My ma used to make a poultice out of mashed onions. She'd smear it all over my chest, in my armpits and even on the bottoms of my feet." He made a face, then grinned at Jeremiah. "Boy, did I stink!"

Although she was nearly certain she knew the answer, Maggie couldn't resist asking, "Did it work?"

Thad shrugged. "I'm here, but I can't take raw onions."

Maggie hugged Jeremiah to her. Thad's experience made the cool bath more bearable. After Jeremiah had eaten several bites and half a cup of broth, he sipped on the tea. Then she carried him into the parlor. "It's warm here on the sofa, and Cap can sit with you."

Jeremiah twisted in her arms, looking for the dog. "I didn't feed him."

She set him down on the couch. "I'll fix his pan, then you can give it to him." She scraped what was left of their meal into the dog's pan and gave it to Jeremiah.

He set it on the floor for Cap and sat back on the sofa to watch him eat.

"I'll be right back." She hurried into the bedroom for the pitcher, added hot water to it, and closed the bedroom door behind her. Jeremiah was on the mend, and she had to start downriver. She stripped out of her wrinkled clothes, washed off and put on fresh clothes. When she returned to the parlor, Ely was talking to Jeremiah. She motioned for Sam to follow her outside.

Clean clothes didn't hide the weariness in her eyes. However, Sam knew what was on her mind. He followed her out and walked past the saloon with her. "Feel better?"

"Much." She glanced back at her cabin, then at him. "I didn't want him to hear us talking about him as if he weren't there. I've got to head back up north. He's doing better, but he still needs his rest. You'll have to stay with him."

He leveled his gaze on her. "Maggie, we are going to share that responsibility." She gritted her teeth, but he refused to give in to her. "You hardly got any sleep. Stay with him this morning and get some rest."

"I'm fine," she said, planting her hands on her hips. "I told you yesterday, I'll pilot and then stay with Jeremiah at night." She sauntered over to the jackstaff and turned her back to the rail. "Sam, it is my boat, and I'm responsible for it, the cargo, and the passengers."

He shook his head. She was so damned stubborn. "I'll get the boat to Wheatland for Mrs. Tillman, and you can take over there." He rested his forearms on the rail and watched the river. "I can be as bullheaded as you, Maggie. Look at that current." He waited until she looked at the water. "The sun will be at our backs. You know how easy it is to make a careless mistake when you're tired and steaming with the current with little to keep you alert."

She glared at him. He was right, and he was being so nice. She wasn't sure which irritated her more.

He tapped her chin. "I won't be replacing you, only relieving you for a few hours." When her gaze slowly met his, he added, "Think of it as a very late birthday present . . . or an early Christmas gift."

She couldn't resist his nonsensical reasoning, but she struggled not to give in to the grin she felt tugging at the corners of her mouth. "You forgot Halloween next week."

Although there was a steady breeze, the weather had turned mild. Sam made stop after stop at landings on his northbound course to Wheatland. Just past midday, he navigated a wide bend in the river, no more than a faded line on the old chart, and pulled into port at Salem nine minutes past one. They had made good time.

On his way down to the main deck he let Cap out of Maggie's cabin for a walk and he put out the gangplank. Fifteen passengers had arrived at their destination here and left the boat. As five others boarded for Oregon City, he made a command decision. When it looked as if all the passengers had come aboard, he asked Thad to lower the boiler pressure and watch the gangplank while he made a quick trip to the restaurant he'd noticed from the deck.

After introducing himself, Sam offered to pay double for five meals, plus the plates, if he could leave with the food within three minutes. His offer created quite a stir in the little dining room. It also had the desired effect. He returned to the steamboat with Cap at his side and five pot roast dinners complete with sour cream gravy and biscuits.

Thad and Ely chose to eat on deck. Sam carried the last three plates up to Maggie's cabin and eased the door open. To his surprise, she was asleep on her bed, and Jeremiah was asleep on his cot. He left their meals in the kitchen, motioned for Cap to go with him and took his plate down to the main deck to join Thad and Ely.

Thad wiped the back of his hand across his mouth. "This sure is good."

Ely sopped up some of the gravy with a chunk of biscuit. "Maggie and the boy sleepin'?"

"Mm-hm." Sam jabbed his fork into a piece of meat. "Think she'll throw it at me?"

"She may want to, but she don't like cookin'." Ely shook his head. "Mostly, she'll be steamed 'cause ya caught her snoozin'."

When Thad and Ely finished eating, Sam took his plate up to the pilothouse. He checked the chart, located Wheatland and noted an area to watch for; then he guided the stern-wheeler into the current. The river was still high on the bank, and he had no problem passing Darrow Chute. He blew the whistle as he approached Wheatland. When he came into port, Mrs. Tillman was waiting for them, and he went to greet her at the gangplank.

After she heard Sam hurry along the walkway, Maggie opened her cabin door and stood in the threshold watching the goings-on below. She had promised herself to stay out of his way, and she had. But it was unnerving, rather like riding in a driverless buggy, helpless as they careened down the road. She stepped out onto the walkway and peered over the rail.

Mrs. Tillman took Sam's hand and looked around the deck. "Where's Maggie? I've never known her to not be standing right in that spot, Mr.—" She frowned, as if vexed with herself.

"Adams, but Sam will do, Mrs. Tillman. I'm helping her out for a while." He collected the fare from three more passengers, while she remained at his side. He swung the gangplank back in place and held out his arm to her. "May I walk you to the saloon?"

"Thank you, Sam." She smiled, handed him her portmanteau and took his arm. "Now tell me, how did you talk Maggie into letting you help out?"

He gave her an exaggerated wink and grinned. "How could she defend herself against such charm?"

Mrs. Tillman chuckled. "I think she's met her match with you. Too bad you're so young."

Sam escorted her to the passenger saloon and met Maggie outside of her cabin. Her color was back and her warm brown eyes were glowing. "Did you find your dinners?"

"It was very good. But Jeremiah doesn't have much of an appetite. I'll save his for him." She leaned back against the rail and smiled at him. "Thank you, Sam." He looked wonderful—no, he looked positively dashing with his windblown hair, no collar, and the top button of his shirt undone, better than the Sam in her dreams. "Did you run into any problems this morning?"

He shook his head. "More stops than I expected. Oh," he said, reaching into the pocket. "Most of the passengers knew the fare." He handed the money to her. "I only had to guess with a couple."

"You did very well. Too bad you aren't interested in a job." She put her hand through the false pocket in her skirt and dropped the cash into her trouser pocket. "I'd better get going. Jeremiah's resting. There's broth and tea on the stove. Get him to drink as much as you can."

"Aye, Capt'n." He tipped her a snappy salute and listened to her laughter as she dashed up to the pilothouse, not that different from the way she used to run along the riverbank. He was glad she still had some of that little hoyden in her.

The homebound leg of the trip acted as a balm for Maggie's frayed nerves. It hadn't occurred to her before, but the pilothouse had become her haven, her refuge. She wasn't certain when it had started or why, but she was grateful there was one special place where she felt nearly dauntless.

After spending almost twenty-two hours in her cabin—terrified Jeremiah might die and feeling helpless with her lack of experience—she needed the security of the pilothouse to sort out her tangled feelings. Although he wasn't mending as quickly as she'd hoped, he was better than last night. But Sam was the one she couldn't figure out. He awakened her emotions as easily as he had stirred the pot of stew.

She must not forget that he was there on business. As she guided the stern-wheeler around Corey Bend, she thought about her friendships with other men. She hadn't had any problems there. If a man dared familiarity with her, she put him in his place without thinking about it. But not Sam's. She welcomed his frequent touches. Her problem with him was, she realized with a sinking heart, that he *hadn't* tried to take any liberties with her.

While musing, she almost passed Ray's Landing. Moving quickly, she blew the whistle, piped Ely and managed to bring the stern-wheeler to a stop. A family of seven boarded, and then she continued on downriver. Once again she was in her own element. She felt safer with her hands on the wheel and her mind on the running of the steamboat. Lord love a duck, she had come close to mixing an old fancy with reality.

She pulled into port at Oregon City. As usual, Cap was first down the gangplank, before Maggie saw the passengers off the boat. After speaking with Thad, she went down to the engine room. Ely had shut down the engine, and the room was quiet. "We had a good trip. Thanks, Ely." She hesitated. "Though I did almost miss Ray's Landing."

"Weren't nothin' we haven't done b'fore." Ely grabbed a rag and glanced at her as he wiped his hands. "Sam's a fair pilot. Leastways he didn't ground her."

She grinned. That was a high compliment for Ely. "Yes, he was good. He practically grew up on riverboats." *And he seems to have a knack for doing about anything he sets his mind to,* she thought.

"How's Jeremiah?"

"He hasn't shaken the fever yet." She idly checked a pipe joint.

"Give the boy time. He'll be right as rain b'fore long."

She nodded. "I'd better get supper on. Come up when you're done here." She went back on deck and waited for Cap before she returned to her cabin. Sam was sitting at the kitchen table writing. "Is Jeremiah sleeping?"

Sam set the pencil down. "Again. He wakes up, drinks some broth, a little tea, then goes back to sleep."

She stopped in the bedroom doorway and petted Cap as she glanced in at Jeremiah. "Is that normal?"

"I don't know." He watched her fingers sink into the dog's fur coat and envied the affection she so easily gave to the dog. "A doctor would. Who do you go to?"

"I haven't gone to any. And I haven't heard of one who has a wonder cure that works any better then those tonics at the mercantile." Women turned to midwives for birthing, husbands looked to their wives, and children to their mothers. Poor Jeremiah only had Sam and her. "I'll brew the tea stronger." She hung her jacket up in the parlor, washed her hands and set a kettle and two pots of water on to boil.

Sam narrowed his gaze. She was different, almost as if he had done something to upset her, but he'd been with Jeremiah all afternoon. "Have any trouble?"

"No. The engine's working better than ever." She smiled and motioned to the paper on the table in front of him. "If you're writing to your parents, please give them my regards."

"It's not a letter. Just some notes."

She nodded. "We're having rice and bacon for supper, but it won't be ready for a while. Why don't you get out of here? Take a walk. You must be tired of these rooms." *As weary of them as I am,* she thought. She set out half a dozen tomatoes on the table to scald in one of the pots.

He glanced at the notes he had made on the ranch and folded the page. "Yes, ma'am."

After he left, the tomato she was holding over the boiling water slipped from her fingers and splashed scalding water on her hand. Served her right for not paying attention. Oh, if only she could hire a cook. She dried her hand and went in to check on Jeremiah.

He was sleeping peacefully with Cap on the floor beside the bed. She loosened the bun on the back of her head, briskly rubbed her scalp and brushed her hair out. That felt better. She returned to the kitchen, put the rice on to cook and finished peeling the tomatoes, humming "Oregon Gals." Sam would be back soon, and she was looking forward to spending the evening with him.

Chapter
10

Jeremiah rolled over, and Cap's wet nose bumped his hand. "Hi, boy." He rubbed Cap's neck and sat up. He got out of bed and used the chamber pot. Cap walked over to the door and looked back at him. "Do you want me to come with you?" Cap wagged his tail, and he followed him into the kitchen. Aunt Maggie was stirring a pot. He walked over to her. "Can I have a drink of water?"

At the sound of his voice, Maggie almost dropped the spoon into the pot of tomatoes. She whirled around to him and smiled. "Of course." She filled a glass and handed it to him. He looked better and when she felt his forehead, he felt almost normal. "Are you hungry?"

He finished the water and nodded. "Some. Cap is, too, ain'tcha boy?"

Cap was sitting in the doorway, and she winked at him. "It won't be too long." She pulled one of the chairs out from the table. "Do you want to keep me company?"

"Okay." He climbed on the chair and kneeled on the seat. "Whatcha makin'?"

She picked up the pan of mashed tomatoes and added it to the cooked rice. "Rice and bacon." Next, she spooned in cooked bacon and stirred.

He peered into the big kettle. "Smells good."

She grinned at him. "Thank you." She continued stirring, then spooned a couple of bites into a bowl. She handed him a spoon and set the bowl on the table. "You can be my taster."

"Taster?"

She nodded, still grinning. "Tell me if it tastes good." He was so precious. She ruffled his hair. She used to pray for a little boy like him, but she hadn't been blessed.

"Okay." He scooped up some of the rice and put it in his mouth. "Mm, it's real good," he said with his mouth full, then swallowed.

"I'm glad you like it." She covered the kettle and put several slices of bacon into the big skillet. When she glanced at Jeremiah, he was scraping the spoon around the bottom of the bowl. *If Sam didn't return in the next few minutes,* she decided, *I'll go ahead and feed Jeremiah.* "Let's find some socks for you and another shirt. I don't want you getting cold." That sounds so normal, she thought, and so right.

She put an old pair of woolen socks on his feet and found a shirt to serve as his robe. As she rolled up one sleeve, it occurred to her that she was doing what any mother might do. *So this is what it feels like,* she thought. Maybe, for a short time she could really enjoy Jeremiah's company. He would be leaving before long and if she didn't make the most of this chance to love him as her own, she might always regret it.

She smiled and hugged him. His small hands pressed on her back, and she bit her lips to keep from weeping. No mother had ever felt more appreciated than she did at that moment. "I'm so glad you're feeling better." She lowered her arms and leaned back.

Jeremiah looked at her. She was getting more like his mama, and he liked it. "Can I go find Mr. Sam?"

"You can't go out until you're all well. But he'll come back soon, or you can have your supper now, if you want to? He'll understand."

Jeremiah frowned. She sure talked funny sometimes. "Unnerstan' what?"

"That you're too hungry to wait for him." She stood up and held out her hand to him.

"Please, Aunt Maggie, can't we look outside? Maybe he's down by the ramp." He held onto her hand as he looked up at her. "Please . . ."

"You're not dressed." He was so determined. She could hear her mother saying, *I said no. Now you git yourself back in there right now,* but she had the feeling that Jeremiah needed to see Sam. "We'll look from right outside the door." She wrapped him in her jacket and carried him out to the railing.

Jeremiah put one arm around her neck and leaned over the rail. "He's not there."

Maggie glanced toward town. "He may have walked up the street." *Where are you, Sam?* She had suggested he leave the cabin because he wasn't used to being cooped up. *Well,* she thought, *it's time to come back home.* Jeremiah's hand pulled on her neck as he suddenly leaned further over the rail. She leaped back against the bulkhead. "You could've fallen. It's a long way down to the main deck."

"I was holding on." He stared at the street. "Can't we go find him? Maybe he's lost. It's gettin' dark." Aunt Maggie didn't look upset, but Mr. Sam *never* left him, and that was scary.

She stared at the trees until she could keep a straight face. "I don't think so, sweetie." She stepped back into the cabin and closed the door. "I'm hungry." She sniffed. "Oh! Those bacon curls!" She put him down and dashed to the kitchen stove. They were curly—and black as cinders. Botheration, she'd only been gone a couple minutes. If Jeremiah had to depend on her for his meals he'd likely starve. She dumped the charred bits of bacon into Cap's pan and dished out two plates of the rice mix.

Jeremiah dropped her coat on the little chair and went over to Cap. He hugged him and gazed into the dog's big brown eyes.

"Come on, Jeremiah. We're going to eat now." She pulled out his chair. He was slow to join her. "You can feed Cap when we're done."

Jeremiah stood on the seat of the chair and tried to look into the big pot. "Is there more for Mr. Sam?"

"There's plenty." She grabbed the back of his chair to steady it. "Turn around now." He did as she asked, and she found herself feeling grateful he was an only child. She had no idea how she could handle more than one.

He ate real slow and chewed every bite real good, like his mama told him to, but Mr. Sam still wasn't back by the time he was full. Aunt Maggie fixed Cap's supper, and he fed him.

When Cap went to the door, she let him out and stood in the doorway searching along the dark bank for Sam. Where had he gone?

Jeremiah went outside. "It's so dark. Can Cap see?"

"Yes. He has good eyes."

He frowned and squinted, but it didn't help. "Don't I?"

She grinned. "Yes, of course you do." She stepped back into the parlor, taking him with her and closed the door.

"Then how come I can't see in the dark?"

How in the world, she wondered, was she supposed to know? "Well . . . that's a good question, but I don't know the answer."

"I'll ask Mr. Sam. He knows everythin'."

After reaching the northern end of Oregon City, Sam returned along the riverbank. When Maggie told him to leave, he had felt as though she had slapped his face. He had been more than willing to leave. It still didn't make any sense. Glancing around, though, he reminded himself that Oregon had gained statehood less than two years ago. She had been one of the pioneers, and her life couldn't have been easy. But he couldn't help wondering if she had become so accustomed to being alone that she was uncomfortable around people day in and out.

As he neared the *Maggie*, he stared at the little old stern-wheeler. The earlier settlers had certainly had to have grit, spirit and strength, traits Maggie possessed in spades. Nonetheless, he had also seen a softer side to her when she held Jeremiah in her arms and cried over him. Hell, he didn't know what to expect when he went up to the cabin and knocked on the door, although he did know what he was going to do.

Maggie opened the door. "About time. Come on in." He

had retreated to his former, proper self. "We didn't wait supper, we were too hungry." She glanced at Jeremiah. The poor little tadpole had fallen asleep. "He tried to stay awake till you came back. Ely and Thad ate, but they said they hadn't seen you. Have you eaten?"

He stepped inside, and she closed the door behind him. "No. I thought—" Did that mean she had changed her mind, wanted him to stay? he wondered. Jeremiah was stretched out on the sofa. Sam motioned to him. "Is he better?"

"Much, and he ate supper. I'll fix a plate for you," she said, hurrying to the cookstove.

Her disposition certainly had changed, and he noticed that she had let her hair down, too. He followed her into the kitchen. The change in her had to be because of Jeremiah's improved health; evidently her concern for him had been even greater than he had realized. He leaned against the doorjamb. She set a plate on the table at his place and gave him what felt like a heartwarming smile. "I'm not starving." He sat down at the table and pushed her chair out with his foot. "How about sharing this with me?"

She poured him a cup of coffee and sat down at the table with him. "I couldn't possibly, but I'll keep you company."

"Then I'm glad I missed supper." He tasted the rice concoction and nodded his approval.

Sipping her coffee she wondered why he'd say such a thing. "Why?"

He finished chewing the bite and swallowed. "Why what?"

"Why would you be glad you missed supper? What if I hadn't saved any for you?" After all didn't he know she'd made enough to feed fifteen people.

"I said that after you said you'd keep me company. What is the matter with you? First you tell me to *get out*, then you welcome me back as if you'd missed me. Now we're having the strangest conversation—all because I thought you were happy to see me." He wiped his mouth and stood up.

"Wait, Sam." She grabbed his hand. "You sound as if I were a fishwife kicking you out of the house. I thought you'd wanted to get out of here after being cooped up." She relaxed her hold and lowered her hand. "I was looking forward to seeing you, but I thought you wanted some fresh air."

"Oh, Maggie." He dropped back down onto the chair. "It sounded like you *told* me to go. It didn't make any sense, but I did decide it was time for me to leave."

"Leave? You can't go now!" She paused, staring at him. "Go where?"

He pushed the fork into the rice mixture. "To the ranch."

"Jeremiah's not that well." *Oh, please, give me another two, no, four days,* she thought, lacing her fingers together, *at least until Jeremiah's well enough to travel.*

Sam glanced at her. He didn't understand her, it was that simple. She might as well have been speaking Portuguese. "He's on the mend. He'll be fine, Maggie."

"Yes, if he gets enough rest." She loosened her fingers and picked up her cup. The boat rocked gently, a comforting motion, and she gazed at him. "You aren't leaving because we . . . because of our . . . what I said, are you?"

"A couple more days won't make any difference." From her crestfallen expression, he figured she had mistaken his meaning. "I'll stay a few more days."

She wanted to whoop for joy. Instead, she nodded and took a sip of coffee to calm her pounding heart. Thankfully, it was too soon for Jeremiah to travel. She didn't think Sam would have changed his mind if she'd said she wanted his company. For someone with such an uncomplicated life, hers had become a real tangle.

Giving up Jeremiah was for his own good, which she believed would make it easier for her to do. But when Sam left, she was sure she would never see him again. He wasn't ready to put down roots. His ranch was probably just another adventure for him—*unless he adopts Jeremiah,* she realized. "Is it still clear out?"

"Yes. The stars are bright." He gazed at her. "After Jeremiah goes to bed, want to walk around the deck?"

"Sounds nice." She glanced into the parlor. Cap put one

of his front paws on the sofa and started to creep up beside Jeremiah. "Cap, no." She pointed to the floor.

"Cap—" Jeremiah reached out for him and opened his eyes. "Hi, boy."

Maggie grinned. "Jeremiah, look who's here."

Jeremiah crawled to the other end of the sofa. "Mr. Sam!" He slid off of the sofa and ran into the kitchen. "I knew you'd come back."

When Sam held out his arms, Jeremiah took a running leap and landed on his chest. Sam held him tight. "Of course. I just took a walk." He looked at Maggie, but she was as surprised by the boy's reaction as he was. "Did you have a bad dream?"

Jeremiah shook his head. "I was scared. You never left me before." He hugged Mr. Sam real hard. He was back and everything was okay.

Sam relaxed his hold on the boy. "Want to help me finish my supper?"

Jeremiah nodded and opened his mouth.

Grinning, Maggie got up and poured a cup of broth for Jeremiah. He still needed nourishment to regain his strength, but he seemed to be getting better by the hour.

"Mr. Sam—"

"Just call me Sam. We're friends, aren't we?" Jeremiah's eyes were big and bright as he nodded enthusiastically. "Good."

"Sam, how come Cap can see in the dark an' I can't? Aunt Maggie said my eyes were good as his. How come I can't?"

Sam stared at Maggie, hoping she might speak up and help, but she only raised an eyebrow, shrugged and handed Jeremiah a cup. "Hm. A lot of animals see better at night . . . like owls and bats. It's probably because they need to, and we don't. We can use lamps and lanterns."

Sam looked at her as if to say, "Was that okay?" and she nodded. "Makes sense to me."

Glancing from Aunt Maggie to Sam, Jeremiah said, "Oh. Maybe it's 'cause his eyes are bigger." He stared at Sam's eyes, then his aunt's. "Will my eyes get bigger than yours? Like Cap's?"

"No—" Sam replied, attempting to keep his amusement from the serious little boy. "I don't think so."

Entering the passenger saloon ahead of Sam, Maggie lighted the first lamp they came to and then two more. "Have you been in here?"

Sam set the bucket for the ashes by the wood stove. "Jeremiah and I spent a couple of hours in here that first day." He glanced around at the sofas and chairs, which had been set in groups, as if in separate parlor settings. "It's homelike in here. Are the other riverboats as comfortable as this?"

Straightening the cushion, she glanced at the old furniture. "The newer steamboats are much nicer. This is showing its age."

"Everything does." He opened the woodstove door and started cleaning out the ashes.

She tidied the room, filled the lamps and washed the porcelain cuspidors. Most of the upholstery seams were frayed, and fabric that had once been crimson, ebony, green or cobalt blue was now dull, faded from the sun and wear. She set the cleaning pails and rags outside and began turning down the lamps.

He laid a fire and stood up. Light from the single lamp cast a soft glow and was reflected in the windows that lined the three walls. "Do you make night trips?"

"No. The Willamette's not the Mississippi and there's no need." She looked around one last time. "Ready?"

"Unless there's something else."

She turned the wick down and gazed out through the windows. Funny, she hadn't been here at night in months. She used to come to the saloon after Zeke fell asleep; she'd watch the town or Linn City across the river.

Sam stepped over to her side and gently clasped her arm. "This is nice. It's even better with the lights out."

He had come up behind her, and his trousers brushed against her skirt. "I think so, too," she said softly. Lights flickered in the distance, but her thoughts were on the way his fingers softly stroked her arm with a lazy, spellbinding course.

"Jeremiah was sleeping soundly when we left your cabin. Want to sit here a while and talk?" He lifted her hair with his other hand and let the strands slip between his fingers.

She led him to the sofa facing Linn City on the west bank and sat down. "At night, with the lights bright, this room's like a stage but when they're out, it's like a hidden window on the world."

He sat at one end with her by his side and rested his arm along the back of the sofa. "What's your schedule for tomorrow?"

"Unless someone needs to go farther south, Salem." She sank back and glanced at him. "There're usually a lot of stops on Saturday. *I'll spend half my time running up and down between the pilothouse and gangplank*, she thought.

He couldn't resist playing with her hair. It was so soft, and it seemed to put her at ease, he realized. "Do you want to pilot upriver or down?"

She smiled and closed her eyes. "Both." Her bones felt as weak as pudding. When he eased her head and shoulders over onto his chest, she didn't mind at all. Sharing the stillness with him was so nice.

He leaned his head down by hers. "If I stay, I help pilot. Why not take advantage of me while you can?" She murmured and it resembled a cat's purr. "I'm glad you agree." He rested his cheek near the top of her head.

"Did I?" She was dreaming; she must be. There was no other reasonable explanation for his tender ministration. His heart beat against her shoulder, and she felt his breath on her ear. "Or are you trying to coax me into agreeing with you?"

"Oh, you agreed, but if you would like to be persuaded, I will gladly oblige." He kissed the rim of her ear and slipped his arm down along hers and beneath her full breasts.

Her heart beat wildly, and she couldn't seem to fill her lungs with enough air or keep her thoughts together. If he continued with his persuasion, would she have the strength or the will to resist him? She didn't want him to stop. Not

yet. Maybe in a couple of minutes, when her pulse no longer
sounded like the paddles slapping the water as the big wheel
turned.

He discovered that a satiny spot at the back of her neck
was especially sensitive. He lost track of their conversation
when she pressed her lips to the back of his hand. Then she
traced the length of each of his fingers with the tip of hers,
and he wondered if she had any idea how seductive that
simple touch was to him.

She had never felt so wonderfully calm, yet aroused and
cherished—and so totally confused."Oh, Sam," she said,
resting her cheek on the back of his hand. "I can't think
straight like this."

He gently leaned his chin on her shoulder. "Me either. Do
we need to?"

She grinned and nodded. How could she tell him that she
had never cuddled with another man? Zeke had only once
kissed her hand and her cheek before they wed. He hadn't
been a tender romantic man, but he was kind and good to
her. Sam, however, challenged, teased and cajoled her, and
she felt more alive, like her old self—or at least what she
thought was her real self. "I'll take the boat as far as
Ridley's Ferry. You can pilot her to Salem and back to
Lincoln."

In the morning Maggie carried the coffee pot to the table.
"Sam, more coffee?"

"Please," he said, holding his cup up for her.

She found herself watching his mouth, the curve of his
lips as she remembered how they felt on the nape of her
neck. She started to pour the coffee and would have missed
the cup if he hadn't moved it. She wasn't one to take flights
of fancy, but she was becoming more distracted by him each
day.

He grinned. She actually blushed—and so prettily. Had
she had been thinking about last night? he wondered. The
idea that she had enjoyed their time alone as much as he had
was an inordinately pleasing one.

She quickly set the pot on the stove top to the side of the fire. "Jeremiah, do you want a little more milk?"

He shook his head. "I'm full. Can I give this to Cap?"

She picked up Jeremiah's plate, but he looked disappointed. Setting the plate back down, she said, "I'd better get downstairs. Would you scrape the food into his pan for me? And feed him?"

"Oh, yes." Jeremiah dropped down to the floor and set Cap's pan on his chair.

"And don't forget to leave him outside for his walk after he eats." Maggie smiled at Sam. "I'll see you later."

She went down to the main deck and began her day. She noticed odd looks from Ely and Thad from time to time, but otherwise her morning passed quickly and smoothly. She arrived at Ridley's Ferry a little before midday. By the time she came down to the main deck, Sam had put out the gangplank and was greeting the passengers. She nodded to one man she knew and glanced at Sam. "You're a little anxious to take over, aren't you?"

"Me?" He collected fares, and after the last couple boarded, he passed the money to her. "Jeremiah's in the saloon. See," he said as he raised one hand to her shoulder and pointed to the window where the boy stood. "He's watching us."

She waved to Jeremiah. "All right, I'm going."

He held out his arm to her. "It will be my pleasure to escort you upstairs, ma'am." Her smile was brighter than the sun and definitely more encouraging as he walked up the stairs with her. "We, the officers of the *Maggie*, offer the very best service, madam. We endeavor to satisfy our passengers at all times. Would you like me to straighten the course of the river today?"

She burst out laughing. "No. *Please* don't do that. The bends make the trip interesting."

"Yes, ma'am." He opened the door to the saloon. "Enjoy your passage, Mrs. Foster."

Chapter

11

It was Sunday, the one day of the week Maggie set aside to scrub and polish the sixteen windows in the passenger saloon. She finished rubbing out the streaks on the far side and moved to the windows facing the bow. It was sunny and calm out on deck, and she let Jeremiah play there with Cap for a while. Sam kept pace with her, cleaning the outside of the windows while she worked inside.

After she'd washed the front windows, she moved on to the ones facing the riverbank. She only had two more to do when she saw Caroline at the foot of the gangplank waving at her. Maggie glanced at Sam. He had discarded his jacket and rolled up his shirtsleeves; the top three buttons were open; and he was as handsome as ever. She dashed outside to where he was washing the window. "Caroline's come by for a visit. I'd like you to meet her. We can finish this later."

She went downstairs and met Caroline on deck. "What a nice surprise." Maggie glanced at Sam. "This is Sam . . . uel Adams. I think I told you about him the other day. Sam, Mrs. Caroline Dobbs."

Sam extended his hand. "My pleasure, Mrs. Dobbs." Her smile was warm and friendly, and he wondered just what Maggie had said about him.

Caroline kept smiling as she shook hands with Sam. "And mine, Mr. Adams." She brought a parcel from behind her skirt and handed it to Maggie.

"What's this?" The bundle was soft. Maggie eyed her friend. "You didn't."

As if she were surprised, Caroline glanced from Sam to Maggie and shrugged. "Didn't what?"

Pressing the package, Maggie spoke to Sam. "Caroline's a talented dressmaker, and she's been after me to let her make me a new dress." She looked down at what she was wearing, one of her oldest dresses, which was perfect for cleaning.

Sam smiled at Caroline. "Since she's your friend, I doubt she is trying to drum up business." He gazed at Maggie. "Aren't you curious? Open it up."

Caroline quickly touched Maggie's arm. "Maybe you should unwrap it in your cabin."

Maggie nodded, wondering what all was in the package. "You haven't met Jeremiah yet." She called him, and he came over with Cap. "Jeremiah, this is my friend, Mrs. Dobbs. And this is Jeremiah Foster, my nephew."

Caroline grinned at the boy and shook hands with him. "You're bigger than I expected, Jeremiah. Are you having fun on the boat?"

Jeremiah stared at the lady and nodded. "Do ya know Cap? We were playin' by the woodpile."

Caroline nodded. "Cap and I are old friends, aren't we, boy?" She petted the dog's neck.

"Sam," Maggie said, taking Caroline's hand, "if you'll excuse us, I'd like to see what she brought me."

He glanced from Jeremiah to Maggie. "We'll wait down here."

Maggie led the way upstairs. As soon as the cabin door closed behind them, she looked hard at Caroline. "What are you up to? I didn't ask you to make me a dress."

"Mrs. Cowin changed her mind," Caroline said, untying the ribbons holding her bonnet in place. "I made a few alterations and thought you might like it." She removed her gloves and glanced at Maggie. "Aren't you curious?"

Maggie grinned and yanked the string off. "You know I am." She pulled back the brown-paper wrapper and reached for the dress. "Caroline, you're a wonderful seamstress and a poor fibber." She held up the dress. "By the way, who is Mrs. Cowin?" It was beautiful and the prettiest pale yellow with delicate little brown spots. The neckline was plain, the way she liked, with dropped shoulder seams, full sleeves and three wide tucks above the hem of the wide skirt.

Caroline laughed. "At least you're looking at the dress. Try it on. I want to make sure it fits properly."

Maggie lifted the dress free of the paper and saw the petticoat. The fabric was fine and the stitching was beautiful. She held it up and stared at Caroline. "I wonder which lady in town decided she didn't want this lovely undergarment?"

Caroline grabbed the petticoat and went into the bedroom. "It was the end of the bolt."

Maggie followed her. "And I'm Governor Abernethy's daughter." She unbuttoned her old dress and stepped out of it. She put the petticoat over her head, lowered it to her waist and tied the strings.

Caroline helped Maggie into the dress. "I knew this spotted muslin would look good on you." Caroline swept Maggie's hands aside and fastened the eight buttons down the front of the bodice, then stepped back to gauge her work. "How does it feel?"

"Fine."

Letting her hand drift down one sleeve, Maggie smiled. "You knew I'd like it." She went over to the small mirror on the chest of drawers. The image that greeted her was startling, even more so when Caroline reached over and untied the piece of rawhide holding her hair back from her face.

"You're lovely, Maggie." Caroline checked the fit of the waist and the shoulders, and she looked to see if the button on either cuff needed to be moved over. "Walk into the parlor so I can make sure the hem is right."

Maggie went into the next room and slowly twirled around.

Caroline carried the mirror to the doorway and held it for Maggie to look at. "What do you think?"

"The dress is lovely, but my boots don't add a thing." Maggie quickly unfastened and stepped out of her boots. The difference was amazing, and she started laughing.

Caroline narrowed her gaze. "What's wrong?"

"Not . . . a thing," Maggie said, doing her best to act as if she were the lady she resembled. She motioned to the mirror. "That isn't me."

"Yes, it is. You have hidden your hair under that old felt hat and you've worn trousers beneath your skirts for so long, you've forgotten what being a woman feels and looks like. Try your shoes on."

When Maggie had gotten her shoes out, Caroline grabbed the brush and began brushing Maggie's hair down her back. Once the shoes were buttoned and Caroline quit fussing with her hair, Maggie turned around. "Thank you, Caroline." She stepped over to the peg where her trousers were and took seven dollars out of the pocket. She hugged Caroline, then pressed the money into her palm.

Caroline struggled to hand it back but stopped short of an all-out brawl. "It's a gift, Maggie."

"I'll accept your hard work, but that'll cover part of the yard goods. There must be six yards of cloth in the skirt alone. That won't pay for all of it, but I'll take you upriver anytime you want to go." Maggie handed her friend the mirror and stepped back. The shoes were a definite improvement. She set the mirror back in its place and started to undress.

Caroline clasped Maggie's hands. "Oh, don't take it off now. It's Sunday. At least show Mr. Adams." Caroline's gaze narrowed. "I should lower that neckline. I can have it ready by tomorrow night."

"Oh, no you don't," Maggie said, ducking away from her. "I like this neckline just fine."

Caroline laid the old dress across the foot of the bed. "I like your Mr. Adams, and you were right about Jeremiah. He's adorable."

Maggie spun around. "Are you thinking about changing your mind? He's still getting over a fever, but he's almost completely recovered."

Caroline vigorously shook her head. "I can't take on that responsibility but . . . you and Mr. Adams could. Why, the three of you *look* like a family already."

Maggie backed up and bumped into the doorjamb as she wrestled with the top button at the neck of her new dress.

Caroline stilled Maggie's hand. "What's wrong?"

"If this dress was made so I would—"

"You need it. You haven't had a new dress in years, and I didn't make a matching bonnet because I knew you wouldn't wear it." Caroline studied Maggie. "What is going on in your head? I've never seen you this flustered."

"Sam and I are friends. Nothing more. He'll be leaving in a couple days." Maggie stared at her hands and lowered them. "We don't always agree with one another, and I don't want him to think I'm out to trap him."

Caroline grinned. "If you're only friends, he'll probably compliment you on your new clothes and think nothing more about it," she said, brushing at Maggie's skirt.

Meeting Caroline's gaze, Maggie started laughing. "You're right. I'm acting like a silly young girl. Come with me." Before she could change her mind again, she left the cabin with Caroline. "Will you stay for dinner? I have no idea what we're having, but I wish you would eat with us."

"I would like to, but I already accepted Mr. Bennett's invitation to dinner."

Maggie paused on the last step above the deck and glanced at Caroline. "Has he proposed to you yet?"

"He talks about obligations and responsibility in marriage and his need to have a large enough bank account before he can consider such a step."

"Has he asked you what *you* need? You should encourage other men to call on you. Gilbert isn't the pick of the litter, and it's about time he discovered that." Maggie stepped onto the deck and walked over to Sam.

Sam's gaze went from the golden cast the sun gave to Maggie's hair down over the pretty yellow dress that showed off her nicely curved body to the tips of her shoes. "Pretty as a butterfly."

She glared at him. "What was I before? A woolly worm? You lummox! Caroline worked very hard to make this lovely dress—" She stopped. He was laughing!

"If I had said you were beautiful, you would've argued

with me." He took her hand and turned her around. She was beautiful, and he was certain she hadn't been told that often enough.

Jeremiah stared at Aunt Maggie. "You're pretty. You goin' somewhere?"

Maggie felt the blush heat her cheeks, but she was helpless to stop it. "Thank you, but we aren't going anywhere."

Sam noticed the amusement in Mrs. Dobbs's eyes—and a touch of sadness? She had understood his teasing before Maggie did and had kept it to herself. "Mrs. Dobbs, the dress is beautiful. Do you think she'll wear it? Or save it for special occasions?" Caroline's eyes lighted up with barely concealed merriment. On the other hand, Maggie looked bored, as though she wanted to appear weary of the subject.

"In all fairness, it really isn't suitable for work." Caroline gave Maggie a reassuring smile, then glanced toward the river and softly added, "If she had someplace to wear it, I'm sure she would."

Maggie couldn't believe her ears. Caroline was her closest friend. Why would she embarrass her like that? "You are both wrong. It's Sunday, reason enough to wear my new clothes." Maggie touched Caroline's arm. "Won't you reconsider dinner? You can even bring Mr. Bennett."

Caroline laughed. "Oh, no, Maggie. Thank you for offering. I do appreciate your thoughtfulness, but I've enjoyed enough levity for one day." She gazed at Sam. "It was a pleasure meeting you, Mr. Adams. Maggie, I really must be going."

"If you change your mind, you're welcome to join us." Maggie gave her a quick hug. "You know I love the dress. You're such a good friend." Caroline left, and Maggie glanced from Jeremiah to Sam. "I'll finish the last couple windows and start dinner."

"Jeremiah, take Cap to the upper deck." Sam linked arms with Maggie and started up the stairs. "Would you like to eat at the Barnhills' restaurant?"

"Mm-hm. There are many things I'd *like* to do." She

gazed at him. She really did appreciate his offer. "But it's a waste of money when I can fix dinner."

He raised one eyebrow. "That's no way to christen a new outfit." He tipped her chin up with his finger. "Find your favorite shawl. Jeremiah and I will get cleaned up, too."

"A dress isn't worth this much fuss." She started for her cabin, but he held her hand, preventing her escape.

"You are." He grinned and released her hand. "You've got five minutes to find where you stashed that shawl."

After a leisurely dinner and stroll around Oregon City, Jeremiah, Cap, Sam and Maggie arrived back at the stern-wheeler near sundown. She glanced across the road as she turned to the gangplank and noticed Mr. Peterson, from the general store, standing in the road looking their way. Everyone she knew seemed to have taken a Sunday walk. She called out a greeting to him and hurried up the ramp.

"Aunt Maggie, can I stay out here with Cap?"

Jeremiah stood with his arm draped around the dog's neck, and Maggie petted Cap. "No. It's getting cold." She motioned for Cap to go up the stairs, and she followed Jeremiah up.

"Where'd Sam go? He gonna come to your cabin, too?"

Maggie leaned over the stair railing and surveyed what she could see of the main deck. "I don't know, but he'll probably be up later."

"I'll look in our cabin."

As Jeremiah started down the steps, Maggie put her arm out and caught him. "Wrong way. Cap's already at the door waiting for you to open it."

Jeremiah backed up one step and stopped to look for Sam.

Maggie didn't move but watched as Jeremiah stopped on each step and searched for Sam. When he reached the deck, she caught up with him and walked him to her cabin. Cap was the first through the doorway, and she entered last. "Your horse is on the little table."

He picked up the horse and rider and sat down on the floor with them. If he was Cap, she'd let him go out. Or maybe if he was bigger. He held the boy doll up. "You're way smaller than me."

Maggie went into the kitchen and put a pot of coffee on the stove. One of the passengers had given her a jug of apple juice. She poured a small glass for Jeremiah and carried it to the parlor. But she didn't interrupt him.

He was pushing the horse over near the door and walking the doll in the same direction. "I wanna go out," he said in a squeaky voice. With a louder voice he said, "No! You're too little."

She listened to the back-and-forth conversation he was having with the doll. Had she sounded like that? She waited to see how he would end the make-believe game. Soon, he told the doll to go to bed. She stepped over to the sofa. "Would you like some apple juice?"

"Okay." He set the doll on top of the horse and pushed them over to her.

As she handed him the glass, there was a knock at the door. She called out, "Come in," expecting Sam—in fact hoping it would be him.

The door opened and Ely entered. "Jeremiah, just the mate I wanna'd to see." He handed the boy a small wooden boat.

Jeremiah scrambled to his feet and set the boat on the sofa. "Look, Aunt Maggie, it's your boat."

She smiled at Ely. "That's wonderful. I thought you gave up whittling."

Ely shrugged. "Thought he'd might like somethin' else to push round."

Jeremiah held the boat up in front of his aunt's face. "The wheel turns, just like yours!"

"A stern-wheel steamboat." She was nearly as intrigued with the boat as Jeremiah. The detail was wonderful. "There's the boiler and firebox, even tiny logs for the fire." She glanced at what she thought was a piece of wood. It had been hollowed out and coated with tar.

Ely rubbed his chin. "Ya can put some water in there so he can float the boat."

"You old softy." She wondered what he'd been like when

he was younger, but he rarely talked about himself. He could be a great grandfather; too bad he never had a family. "Have you seen Sam?"

Ely nodded. "He's finishin' the windows."

"Will you stay with Jeremiah a few minutes?"

"Go on."

She grabbed her shawl and went to the saloon. He had changed into his blue muslin shirt and sturdy brown trousers. "Why are you doing this? It could've waited until tomorrow." The light breeze had tousled his hair. She picked up his discarded jacket. She smelled his hair tonic on the collar and held it to her chest.

He grinned and rubbed out the last smear. "I knew you'd probably finish these in the morning." He picked up the pail of water and another one full of dirty rags. "I'm done." She was watching him with a slight smile, the way women do when they aren't about to tell you what's on their mind. "I'm glad you didn't change out of that dress. It really becomes you."

She glanced at the skirt, which was a little longer than the skirts she usually wore. "It's a Sunday-go-to-meetin' dress. I couldn't work in this."

"Of course not. But miners wash off the coal dust on their day off." He winked.

She brushed a bit of lint from his sleeve. "The coffee's ready. Leave those pails outside my door. Did you see what Ely brought Jeremiah?"

"I didn't pay any attention." He set the buckets down and went inside with her. Jeremiah and Ely were bent over a small trough filled with water. "That's a great steamboat. Is she fast?"

"Yes, and see," Jeremiah said, pushing the boat. "The paddle wheel turns 'round, just like a *real* one." He grinned at Sam. "You wanna run it?"

Sam pretended to ponder the idea. "Is Ely your engineer?"

"Uh-huh."

"Then I'll have to have his permission." It wasn't easy for Sam to keep a straight face. Jeremiah was so very serious, and Ely was obviously having as much fun as the boy. He had put a lot of time and work into the miniature of the *Maggie*, and it appeared to have been worth it.

Maggie watched the three of them from the kitchen. Three generations, unrelated, who could easily be mistaken for family. She filled three cups with coffee and sat down at the table with one, reluctant to disturb them. Jeremiah was getting the attention he needed; Ely finally had a little boy to whittle toys for, and Sam—He had been there seven short days, longer than he had planned, she was sure, but even three or five more days wouldn't give her enough time with him.

Jeremiah looked first at Ely, then Sam. "Come on. She's s'pose to make port 'fore they run outta wood."

Monday morning the *Maggie* steamed south with Maggie at the wheel. They were carrying cargo and several passengers, earning just enough to keep her in business. She had agreed to let Sam pilot the steamboat part of each day. By Wednesday, the new arrangement felt normal, and she was enjoying her time with Jeremiah. He was by her side while she greeted passengers at Fairfield Landing and collected the fares. She smiled at Ben Potter as he stepped aboard.

"Good weather for this time o' year."

"That it is, Mr. Potter. How far are you going today?"

"Champoeg. Will ya take these chickens for my passage? They're fat 'n' fresh killed."

"Yes, indeed. Just in time for me to cook them up for supper." He handed the birds to her, then the last man boarded. She turned to Jeremiah. "Do you think you can hold these birds for me? They're heavy."

"Sure I can." He held up both hands.

The chickens were tied by the legs with a length of twine, and she held the birds out so he could take the string in both hands. "You okay?"

"Mm-hm," he said, gritting his teeth. Those chickens were real big, and he couldn't hardly hold them up.

She quickly swung the gangplank aboard, waved to Sam

in the pilothouse and relieved Jeremiah of the chickens. "Thank you."

"Whatcha goin' to do with 'em?"

"Stew them for supper. Come on." She started walking to the stairs. "You can help me. Later we'll make dumplings."

"Do I have ta?" Jeremiah stopped at the bottom of the steps. "Cap stays down here. Can't I help Thad? Or Ely?"

"N—" But as she looked at him, the no died on her lips. "You don't like cooking?" He made a funny face and wouldn't meet her gaze. "I guess fixin' supper isn't as much fun as carryin' wood or bein' in the noisy engine room. I bet Sam would help me, except he's piloting the boat."

Jeremiah glanced up at her. "He would?"

"Sure. He's a good cook. " She went up one step, hoping her ploy would work. He would have to mind her, but she wanted to try a gentle hand before a firm one, this time.

"Well, okay."

He ran upstairs ahead of her, and she heaved a sigh of relief. Her mother had raised her with a firm hand, though sometimes it had been gloved to ease the sting of obedience. *This is so new to me*, she thought.

Jeremiah followed her into the kitchen and watched her chop the feet off of the chickens. He held up one foot. It was sorta red 'n' dirty. When he shook it, the toes bobbed up and down. "Can I have 'em?" he asked, reached for the other one.

As she plucked the birds, she stared at the foot. "That isn't a toy. Do you want to help me pull out the feathers?"

"Unh-unh." He picked up the other foot and walked them across the table and a chair.

When he hopped the feet across the front of one cupboard, she decided that boys did think differently than girls. She finished cleaning the birds, put them in her largest kettle with water, carrots, onions, peppercorns and a good measure of salt to cook.

"We'll make the dumplings in a little while."

Jeremiah crawled under the table with a chicken foot in each hand. "Okay."

At least he's busy, she thought. While the chicken boiled, she discovered that his imagination seemed to have no boundaries. With his help, the chicken feet rode the horse, danced on top of the woodstove and steamed downriver on his boat. He even showed her how to pull one of the white, stringy things in the end of the leg that made the toes curl. When the whistle blew signalling their arrival in Oregon City, she came close to grabbing his hand and running from the cabin. She didn't, though. "It's time to put the gangplank out."

He walked down to the main deck with her. "Can I go see Ely now?"

"All right, but don't get in his way. And *don't* go near the engine. Sit on the steps." He ran off, and she stood ready to set the gangplank in place when Sam pulled into port.

When the passengers had gone ashore, Jeremiah wanted to stay with Ely. Maggie returned to her cabin alone. She mixed the dumpling batter and dropped spoonfuls into the simmering broth. Thirty minutes later, she set the platter of stewed chicken ringed with dumplings on the table and grimaced. The balls of dough hadn't puffed up. No, they were the same size as when she scraped them off the spoon, and they were hard as pebbles. She called everyone in for supper and poured drinks.

Sam motioned for Jeremiah to remain standing until Ely and Thad had stepped around the boy's place at the table. "You've been busy, Maggie. Looks good."

She stared at the platter. "I'll be satisfied if it tastes all right." She passed out glasses of water and sat down.

When Maggie didn't move to serve Jeremiah, Sam put a chicken leg and a carrot on the boy's plate, and he was reaching for a couple of dumplings when Maggie laid her hand on his wrist.

She let go of him. "Don't. They're just for show."

"They aren't cooked?" He stabbed at one, but it rolled away.

"See." She couldn't help grinning. "I may have discovered the recipe for toy balls." Something else for Jeremiah to play with, she realized, then quickly decided they would be thrown out before he started batting them around with those chicken feet.

Ely winked at Maggie. "Ne'er did like eatin' fluffy thin's anyhow."

Chapter
12

After Jeremiah fell asleep on her bed, Maggie and Sam went to the saloon. She didn't light any of the lamps, preferring to sit in the dark and listen to a sudden shower pounding against the windowpanes. The lights across the river seemed to flicker. She gazed at Sam and covered his hand, which was resting on her leg.

Sam nudged her into a closer embrace and kissed her hair. "This is becoming my favorite time of day."

"Mm, mine, too." She curled her legs under her skirt and nestled against his chest, amazed anew by the strength she felt beneath her cheek. He might look lean, even wiry, but he was strong. She had learned to appreciate strength of body as well as character since coming west. Sam possessed both.

He bent his head near hers. "Whatever happened to those chicken feet?"

"What do you think?"

"Last time I saw one, it was in Cap's mouth as he ran away from Jeremiah."

She chuckled. "The carp had a late-night supper. I hope those dumplings didn't give them a bellyache." In the shelter of his embrace, she knew the saloon wouldn't be the same without him. If only the Willamette flowed down through California, she mused, snuggling his arm closer around her.

He combed his fingers through the length of her hair. "The other day Mrs. Dobbs mentioned you'd told her about me. What did you have to say?"

"That we grew up together, and that you're a rogue, an unredeemable rake," she said turning to him. "But I think I forgot to tell her about your big feet or how well you pitch a mean rock." *Or how gentle you are or how you make me feel beautiful.* She studied his eyes. "She's pretty, isn't she?"

"She's a handsome woman. I would say a good friend, too." He kissed the tip of her nose. "Why do I have the feeling you don't care for her Mr. Bennett?"

"She's so sweet and laughs so easily, except when she's with him." Maggie rested her head against his shoulder. "He's . . . oh, dull, arrogant."

He grinned, his curiosity growing. "Do you see them together at socials?"

She laughingly said, "I haven't gone to one in years, and I can't picture him kicking up his heels with her—or anyone. He's *too* dignified, if you know what I mean."

"I'm beginning to understand. Why don't you invite them to take a short trip with us upriver this Sunday? She may enjoy the diversion." *And you will, too*, he thought. He nuzzled her ear and the back of her neck.

Why does he ask me questions, then send my mind reeling like a whirlpool? she wondered. "That might be interesting, but Thad goes home on Sundays. You'd have to feed the fire. And I'd have to see if Ely would lend a hand." She gazed at the curve of his lower lip and the little dip on the upper one. They had grazed her cheek, her neck and even her ear. Where she wanted to feel them most of all was on her mouth.

He hadn't set out to seduce her, and he believed that she wasn't intentionally enticing him, but it was happening. Touching her felt as natural as breathing. Her skin was soft, her silky hair clung to his fingers as if of its own accord, and he loved the way she nestled in his arms, almost instinctively.

He drew his fingertips up the column of her neck to her upturned chin and covered her mouth with his. Her response was potent. She didn't submit to him—she returned his passion with a fervor that threatened his well-bred intentions. Her mouth was sweet and, even though she had turned around and pressed her breasts to his chest, he wanted still more of her.

Sliding her arms around his waist, she gave him greater access and gained more herself. It was as if she had just awakened after years of slumber. Every part of her quaked with a need only he could fulfill. There was a heat where their bodies touched. She grazed his cheek, drew her lips down his neck and fumbled with the buttons on the front of his shirt.

"Sweetheart," he murmured, gasping as he raised her hands to his mouth. He kissed her knuckles.

Sweetheart; the nicest word she had ever heard rang in her mind. This wasn't a girlish fancy—it was so *much* more.

"I never planned . . . or thought—I won't take you in a quick tumble, and that's where we're heading." He eased her down to his chest. "Maggie, I could give you a list of women who I'm sure would tell you not to waste yourself on me."

She laughed softly. "I'll wager I've known you longer than any of those ladies. I grew up a long time ago, Sam." His hand continued drawing lazy circles along her back, and she felt the heat building once more.

"I know. I wish I'd been there." He kissed the top of her head.

"There wasn't much to see, then." As his fingers traced her spine to its base, her hips rolled against his thighs. "Jeremiah's sleeping on my bed, but your cabin is empty."

"I've never been accused of gallantry, but I will do what is right for you." He hugged her and sighed. "You mean too much to me."

She was stunned. She had *never* been so bold with a man, but she had felt safe with him. "Did you make love to those women you mentioned?" Embarrassment and humiliation began to set in, and she felt ten times the fool.

"I won't answer that."

"No. I shouldn't have asked but—" She filled her lungs with air and let it out slowly to quiet her hammering pulse. "I almost wish you cared a little less for me."

"That's a fine thing to say."

She lowered her feet to the floor and sat up. She wouldn't beg him to make love to her. She needed him to desire her with the same passion she felt for him. "How about a cup of coffee?"

After a few short restless hours in bed Sunday morning, Maggie escaped her room long before daybreak. She started a pot of coffee, built up the fire in the parlor, then stepped out onto the deck. The icy wind went right through her woolen wrapper. She clasped her hands behind her back, tipped her head back and listened to the swaying trees and the rush of the river.

It was refreshing, and she needed to revive not only her body but her spirit. The last three days were taking their toll on her. She had tried her best not to let Sam know how abashed she had felt the other night. She hadn't been back to the saloon since then.

Mr. Bennett and Caroline would arrive by ten-thirty. Maggie stepped back inside. When she went into the bedroom for towels, Cap opened his eyes and closed them without moving from his spot at the foot of her bed. After putting water on to heat, she dragged out the tin bathtub and set it near the woodstove. Her last bath had been rushed. This morning it was early enough for her to have a leisurely soak and to wash her hair.

Sam carried the kettle of soup and one of the baskets of food up to Maggie's kitchen. So far, the rain had held off, and he hoped the wind would carry it over the mountains just east of them. He was curious to meet Mr. Bennett, but what he really wanted was to see Maggie smile again. He hadn't handled her advance the other evening well at all.

He hadn't had any problems in that area before—until Maggie. With her it had been different. God knew he had ached with desire for her, and declining her invitation had been as painful for him as it had been for her. However, his passion had seemed like a small thing compared to how she might feel about him—and herself—afterwards.

When he carried two other baskets up to her cabin, she was in the kitchen. "You're wearing my favorite yellow dress."

Her hand went up to the top button on her bodice, and she met his gaze. "Mine, too." She stared at the basket he set on the table. "You didn't have to go to all this trouble." *He really does care,* she realized.

He uncovered one of the baskets. "I'll be hungry after I play fireman. Ely will, too." He got the skillet out and set it on the stove top. "Mrs. Barnhill said we should keep the chicken warm."

"Does it still look like rain?" She felt more at ease, thanks to Sam's calm sensible manner. The only time she had seen him the least bit uneasy had been the other night. She glanced at him, unwilling to give up on him.

"Afraid so, but if it doesn't hold off until after our picnic, we can dine in the saloon." He finished emptying the second basket. "I'd better light the stoves in there."

As she stacked two of the baskets, she glanced at the third. "What all did you ask Laurel to fix for us?"

"Dinner. That's probably a pie."

"Didn't you look inside?"

"There wasn't time. I wanted to get back before they arrived. That chicken sure smells good."

She uncovered the last basket. "Apple dumplings," she said, smiling. "The fish won't get these."

He went to the saloon, and she set to work preparing for dinner. When she finished, she poured a cup of fresh coffee and took it down to Ely. He was sitting on a log talking to Jeremiah.

"Thought you might need this." She handed the cup to Ely. "It's still cold out here."

"Thanks." He held the steaming cup near his chin. "I'm a thinkin' it's gonna be a hard winter."

She watched Jeremiah a moment as he crawled around pushing his horse and rider, which never seemed to be out of his sight. "I think you'd better come up to the cabin with me."

"Can't I stay with Ely?" Jeremiah pushed the horse over to Cap. "I'll take Cap for a walk."

"No. He won't get lost. Come on." She fixed her gaze on him and held out her hand.

He hugged Cap. "I'm sorry."

Ely lowered his cup. "Yer callers're here."

She spun around and waved to Caroline. A steady mist had begun falling. "I guess we'll be eating in the saloon."

Ely stood up and ruffled Jeremiah's hair. "I better start the boiler fer Sam."

"No, wait. Mr. Bennett's coming aboard without Caroline." She watched him approach, his rounded top hat held in place with one hand and his fitted overcoat held down with the other. She motioned for him to join her under the upper deck. "Is something wrong? Caroline's not—"

Mr. Bennett interrupted her. "Mrs. Dobbs is quite fine, Mrs. Foster. Since it's raining, I thought it best to postpone the plans. I'm sure you understand."

"It rains a good part of the year, Mr. Bennett. I see no need to put off our visit." She made a fist with one hand in the folds of her skirt. "I assure you the saloon is dry." She glanced sideways at Ely. "We don't even have to leave port. You're already aboard, so I'll get Caroline. There's no need for you to get wet."

Before he could invent another excuse to cancel their visit, she dashed across the deck, down the gangplank and yanked the door of the carriage open. "Hi."

Caroline pulled her skirt aside so Maggie could climb inside. "What are you doing out here? You're getting soaked."

"I came for you." Maggie climbed in and sat across from her. "You haven't changed your mind, have you?"

"Well, Mr. Bennett—" She glanced at him. "He thought—"

"I know what he thinks. Sam had Laurel Barnhill cook us a wonderful meal. We can stay in port if you like and eat in the saloon. Sam arranged the meal and already has the woodstoves going." She grabbed the door handle.

Caroline stared out in Mr. Bennett's direction. "He really can be . . . difficult at times."

Maggie burst out laughing. "And you think I can't deal with him? You were invited to dinner and you're coming. Mr. Bennett can stay or leave." She unlatched the door and met Caroline's gaze. "Sam will be so disappointed if you don't join us. I'm afraid we piqued his curiosity last week."

Caroline grinned. "It would serve Mr. Bennett right. Besides, you've gone to a great deal of trouble." She handed the lap rope to Maggie. "Cover your head and shoulders."

With the coarse blanket ends under her chin, Maggie knew she could remain dry in any downpour. When Caroline had pulled the hood of her cape over her head, Maggie opened the door and they dashed on board. She pulled the blanket off, shook it out and handed it to Mr. Bennett, who glowered at her. Ely and Jeremiah were nowhere in sight. "Caroline was kind enough to offer me the use of your lap robe. You may need it when you leave."

She linked arms with Caroline. "Let's warm up in the saloon." As she started for the stairs, she cast a glance at Mr. Bennett. He was still glowering.

Sam heard them coming upstairs and opened the saloon door for them. Maggie and Caroline rushed in smiling. "I'm glad you came prepared, Mrs. Dobbs." He watched in amusement as Caroline's gentleman entered after them with refined haste.

Caroline pushed back the hood and grinned. "If you live here long enough, you learn to be prepared for rain. It's nice to see you again, Mr. Adams." She turned to Gilbert. "I would like you to meet Mr. Adams, Maggie's friend whom I told you about. Mr. Adams, Mr. Bennett."

Bennett appeared a bit rankled. Sam closed the door and held out his hand. "Sam. Glad to meet you."

Mr. Bennett shook hands with Sam. "Mrs. Foster seems set on this trip." He carefully removed one leather glove, unbuttoned his top coat, pushed aside the front panel and put his hand in his trouser pocket.

Sam gazed at Maggie and smiled. "We both are." He glanced at Bennett. The single-breasted jacket, straight-cut trousers and plaid waistcoat, plus his soft felt, rounded top hat were sure signs of success and wealth. However, his aloof bearing and expression said much more about the man. "I'll hang up your coat, if you'd like?" Sam had met his type before. He wasn't impressed.

Mr. Bennett glanced around the saloon. "Thank you, but I'm still rather chilled."

And it'll take more than a blazing fire to warm you up, Sam thought, as he joined the ladies. "Do you want me to play fireman now?"

Maggie came close to smiling at Sam. "We've been talking it over." She glanced at Caroline. "Would you mind if we stay in port and eat here?"

"Fine with me. We can do this again another time." His hand grazed Maggie's arm as he stepped over to the woodstove.

Caroline unfastened the ties at her neck and took off her bonnet. "This is nice." She slipped her cape off as she glanced around. "I don't think I've been up here before."

Maggie laid her cape over one chair near the stove to dry, set her bonnet on the arm and glanced at Caroline. "Your dress is wonderful. Where are you going after you leave here?" Her friend looked like one of those pretty fashion dolls. There were yards and yards of rose poplin in the skirt, set off by a dark mauve waist and sash. The full sleeves had white undersleeves trimmed to match her sash, and her cleavage was hidden beneath the beautiful wide lace collar crisscrossing the bodice.

"I could say you aren't dressed for work either, but it would sound peculiar coming from me." Caroline grinned.

"I have water on for tea or would you like coffee?"

"Tea would be fine." Caroline gazed at Gilbert. "Would you prefer coffee?"

Mr. Bennett nodded and walked past her to one of the windows facing Linn City.

Glaring at Gilbert's back, Maggie wondered how her friend could continue keeping company with the man. "I'll get our drinks."

"May I help you?" Caroline asked.

"Make yourself comfortable. I won't be long." Maggie hurried out of the saloon and stopped outside of her cabin. The air was refreshing. How was she going to spend the afternoon with Gilbert Bennett and remain civil? She stepped into her cabin.

Ely nodded at Jeremiah. "Told ya she'd be back."

Jeremiah looked up from the little steamboat. "Whatcha been doin'? Did that man go yet?"

"I wondered where you had gone. Sam and I have been talking with Mrs. Dobbs and Mr. Bennett. We invited them for dinner." She smiled at Ely. "You're eating with us, in case you thought you were getting out of it."

"Nah, don't think so." Ely watched Jeremiah. "Why don't the nipper 'n' me eat at the table in there?" he said, motioning to the kitchen.

At least he had agreed to eat with Jeremiah, Maggie thought. "All right. Jeremiah, you can go back with me when I take our drinks. I want you to meet Mr. Bennett and say hello to Mrs. Dobbs."

When Jeremiah looked to Ely, Ely nodded. "Yes, ma'am. But that man looks like he swallowed turpentine." Jeremiah shivered and pushed his boat in the water.

Maggie stared at him. "That is a terrible thing to say." It was true, but she couldn't allow him to think it was acceptable to speak his thoughts aloud. "You must remember not to speak your mind . . . at least until you're older."

Ely quickly changed the subject. "We're not goin' up-river?"

"With the rain, we decided to remain here. If there's something you'd rather do, Ely, you don't have to stay here."

Ely winked at Jeremiah. "Nah. I'll stay with my mate."

"I don't think you'll be sorry. Laurel Barnhill cooked our dinner—all of it." She patted his shoulder on her way into the kitchen.

She set out a tray. While the pot of tea steeped, she wondered if Caroline was talking with Sam. Was Gilbert still staring out the window? She filled a small bowl with sugar and set it on the tray. She picked up the tray and went to the parlor. "Jeremiah, would you please open the door for me?" She looked at Ely. "He'll be right back."

Jeremiah opened the cabin door for his aunt and followed her into the saloon.

Sam excused himself from Mrs. Dobbs and relieved Maggie of the heavy tray. He whispered, "I was beginning to wonder if you were coming back."

"Why, Sam—" She couldn't keep an innocent expression, and she smiled. "I wouldn't desert you . . . or Caroline," she softly confided.

"That's my Maggie." He grinned at Jeremiah. "Are you having tea with us?"

"Unh-unh." He crooked his finger at Sam to bend down. "Aunt Maggie said I had to say 'Hello' to that man."

"Come with us." Sam carried the tray to a table near where Caroline was seated.

Maggie almost floated over to the table near the wood-stove. "His Maggie" had such a nice ring to it. Maybe he'd changed his mind. She was glad she had his respect, but Lordy, didn't most men respect their wives? Their lovers? Well, maybe not, she realized.

Sam walked over to Mrs. Dobbs. "Jeremiah, you remember Mrs. Dobbs, don't you?"

He nodded and smiled at her. "Hello, Mrs. Dobbs."

Caroline grinned at Jeremiah. "Hello to you. I'm glad you're joining us."

Maggie stepped up behind Jeremiah and caught the end of Caroline's comment. "He's just here to say hello. Then he's going to keep Ely company."

Caroline glanced at Maggie. "Can't they eat with us?"

Resting her hands on Jeremiah's narrow shoulders, Maggie shook her head. "They were steaming the boat Ely made for him down his special river. Weren't you?"

"Yeah. It's just like Aunt Maggie's."

"My, that sounds like fun."

Caroline gazed at him with such longing, Maggie hoped that, very soon, some special man would come along and make Caroline's heart pound the way Sam made hers. She bent down and whispered to Jeremiah. "Say, 'it was nice seeing you again, Mrs. Dobbs.'"

Jeremiah's glance darted from Sam to the lady. "It-was-nice-seein'-you-again-Mrs.-Dobbs."

Caroline nodded. "I hope I'll see you again, Jeremiah."

He ran the words together as though they formed one long word, and Maggie knew she'd have to work with him. She led him to the window where Gilbert stood as if on guard. "Mr. Bennett, I'd like you to meet my nephew, Jeremiah. Jeremiah, this is Mr. Bennett."

Gilbert gave the boy a stiff nod.

Maggie whispered to Jeremiah what he should say.

"Pleased to meet you, sir."

"If you'll excuse us, Jeremiah has a boat to pilot." Maggie walked Jeremiah to the door. "Thank you. I'll see you in a little bit."

Jeremiah stepped out onto the deck and paused. "How come he don't like Mrs. Dobbs? She's nice."

As they say, she thought, *he sure can hit the nail on the head.* "He's just a bit formal."

"He's like old Mr. Lobb. He didn't like nobody either."

She watched him enter her cabin and sighed. For such a young boy, he certainly was clever. She went over to the tray. Caroline came over, and Maggie handed her a cup of tea.

Caroline picked up another cup, held it for Maggie and glanced at Gilbert. "I must apologize. I had hoped—"

"He'd be charming?" Maggie grinned.

Caroline chuckled. "You're terrible. He can be . . . engaging." She leaned closer to Maggie. "And I don't have to worry about him taking liberties."

Maggie raised one brow. "Isn't there anyone you would rather keep company with, one you wished would attempt a liberty or two?" She glanced over at Sam and was surprised he wasn't with Gilbert.

"No. My Todd was like that," Caroline said with a fanciful gleam in her eyes. "When I was with him, I feared my heart would jump right out of my skin." She shrugged, adding, "But I haven't met anyone like him since."

"Don't give up." Maggie glanced over at Sam and then at Gilbert. "We can't spend all day standing by the tray." Maggie poured two more cups of coffee. She took one to Sam. "It feels strange being up here during the day and not cleaning."

"Then we'll have to do it more often." He rested his hand on the small of her back and tilted her head in Bennett's direction. "Shall we?" Bennett hadn't moved from the window or said one word to either him or Mrs. Dobbs.

She walked up to Gilbert. "Mr. Bennett, your coffee. Won't you have a seat with us?" She motioned to where Caroline was seated.

Gilbert stared at her as if momentarily surprised that she had spoken to him. But he accepted the cup. "Yes, of course."

When he sauntered to the chair at Caroline's right and sat down, Maggie glanced at Sam wondering why Gilbert had chosen not to sit on the sofa with Caroline. There was no doubt about it: he was a cold fish.

Sam sat beside Maggie on another sofa, facing Mrs. Dobbs. His arm stretched along the back cushion, he seemed perfectly at ease. "Since I'm an outsider, Mr. Bennett, I'm not familiar with the area. Are you in business?"

Gilbert leveled his gaze at Sam. "Banks, Mr. Adams. I own the River's Banks, one branch here and one in Salem. What are your business interests, Mr. Adams?"

Sam let his hand slip down until his fingers came to rest on Maggie's far shoulder. "I recently sold my hotel and purchased a ranch. Thought I'd try raising sheep."

Gilbert nodded. "Hotel management isn't for everyone. You're wise to return to ranching, something you probably do quite well, I'd imagine."

"I hope you're right," Sam said, patting Maggie's shoulder, "though I doubt my law degree would be considered good preparation for sheep ranching."

Chapter

13

Maggie stared at the last half of her apple dumpling and set the spoon in the bowl. "Sam, you got too much food. Laurel cooked too much." With a crooked grin, she added, "And I ate enough for both of us."

He arched one brow and motioned to his empty bowl. "I couldn't eat this way every day either."

Mr. Bennett folded his napkin. "Very good."

Pushing her chair back, Maggie stood up. "Coffee, anyone? I think the tea's still warm, Caroline." She refilled Sam's cup and her own when Gilbert declined.

Caroline got to her feet and began stacking their bowls. "I'll pour my tea, Maggie. I need to move around."

"I'll get those. I don't want you spoiling your gown." Maggie put the coffee pot back on the tray.

Caroline brought her cup to the tray and poured herself the last of the tea. "Did Mr. Adams really arrange the meal?"

"That's Sam. He took pity on me." Maggie chuckled. "Or maybe he simply wanted a good meal. Actually, he's a good cook." *He would make a perfect husband or wife,* she thought and grinned. She glanced at Caroline. "What do you think of Sam?"

"Maggie, he's special. Your gaze follows him—it's almost embarrassing. And the way he looks at you." Caroline gave Maggie a sly smile. "I'm so very happy for you."

"I never realized what a romantic you are." Maggie shook her head. "He's special, but we are simply friends, no more." She glanced at him. "I don't understand why he isn't married."

"He hasn't found the right woman—or if he has, he hasn't told her. . . ." Caroline returned to her seat.

"Balderdash," Maggie mumbled. As she joined the others, a sudden gust of wind rocked the steamboat, and she patted Caroline's hand. "We're okay."

"Well," Gilbert said, pulling out his pocket watch. "It has been a delightful day, but it is getting late."

As if to cover his rudeness, Caroline quickly added, "Yes, thank you so much, Maggie, Mr. Adams. Dinner was wonderful." Gilbert assisted her to her feet and handed her cloak to her.

"I wish you didn't have to leave." Maggie opened the door. "You might want to cover up with that lap robe, Mr. Bennett. It's really coming down." She gave Caroline a quick hug. "I'm so glad you came."

Sam stood at Maggie's side and leaned closer to her. "We still owe you a trip, Mrs. Dobbs."

"I might take you up on that offer," she said as Gilbert took her arm. She saw the lap robe tucked under his other arm. "Aren't you going to cover up? She's right. It really is raining now."

"As you said, it rains frequently." Mr. Bennett patted her hand. "I won't melt."

Maggie choked and coughed, thinking that he couldn't have melted even in the fires of Hades.

Sam gently tapped her back. "All right, now?"

With her lips clamped together, she nodded.

"Thank you, again," Mr. Bennett said, starting out the door, "Mrs. Foster, Mr. Adams."

Sam took Maggie's hand and followed them to the deck. "Our pleasure." When Caroline and Gilbert rode away, Sam went back into the saloon with Maggie. "I wish I could offer you something stronger than coffee."

"Gilbert does have that effect on people." She gazed at him, wondering why he didn't know what she would have liked much more than a drink. "Zeke kept a jug in his trunk.

I think I can find it." She took one step toward the door and paused. "Or you could go to the Mudd Hole."

"You said the state was dry. Didn't you?"

"Not entirely. The saloons do a thriving business."

"I don't *need* a drink, though if Bennett had stayed much longer, I would have." He picked up the tray of dirty dishes. "It was an interesting visit, wasn't it?"

"Yes." She opened the door for him. "Yes, it was."

She realized that his feelings about her hadn't changed, but she wasn't sure what that meant. She didn't believe for one moment that he would hesitate to tell a woman he loved her. But could he fall in love in a couple of weeks?

Maggie piped Ely, while acting quickly to avoid what looked like part of an outhouse riding the current. It was still raining Tuesday, and the water current was swift. The poor old steamboat was getting a workout. Fortunately, a few people braved the chilly rain to travel. The trip south was difficult, but she'd make good time steaming back down-river.

She blew the whistle at their approach to Wheatland. She was actually looking forward to turning the wheel over to Sam for the next half of the voyage. After tying her old hat down with a scarf, she left the pilothouse to put the gangplank out.

Three passengers hurried aboard, and one merchant had his men load a dozen crates bound for Independence. Sam helped her swing the gangplank back in place, then ran for cover with her. When she gazed into his eyes, her arms didn't feel quite as stiff or her shoulders nearly so tired. "You're spoiling me. I actually looked forward to your taking over."

"I'm enjoying it, too." As they walked to the stairs, he casually put his arm around her shoulders.

"The river's running fast." *And so's my heart,* she thought. "Do you have your gloves?"

He pulled a heavy pair out of his jacket pocket. "You might want to take Jeremiah down to watch Thad or Ely. He's been in the cabin all morning, and he's a bit restless."

When they reached her cabin, she unlatched the door. "We'll have dinner while the cargo's being unloaded in Salem."

He nodded. "If the rain lets up, you can bring Jeremiah to the pilothouse for a while." With one last gaze, he raced up the ladder.

He signalled Ely to reverse gears, to back away from the riverbank, and then change to the forward gears. As Sam guided the stern-wheeler to the west side of the current, he couldn't miss the strain on the engine. Forward, reverse, stopping and starting, many times in rapid succession, were taking their toll on the old engine. How much longer would it last?

When he stopped in Salem, Maggie was waiting by the boiler for him. "Stay here," he said. "There's no need for you to get wet."

She watched as he ran out onto deck to set the gangplank in place, then she went in search of her nephew. She found him in the engine room talking with Ely. "Hi. Are you two hungry?"

Jeremiah nodded. "Can I eat with Ely?"

"Of course you can. We're eating together at the kitchen table." She held her hand out to him. "Why don't you come along with me?"

Ely nodded to the boy and looked at Maggie. "I'd jist as soon eat here."

Jeremiah tugged on his aunt's hand. "Can I, too? I won't feed Cap off my plate."

Ely winked at the boy. "It's okay with me."

She eyed Jeremiah. "You mind Ely. I'll bring your dinner down."

Jeremiah watched her leave, then he looked at Ely. "How can I mind you? You don't tell me nothin' to do."

Chuckling, Ely rubbed his chin. "That's a real per'dicament. Mebbe ya should help me wipe up this oil. Ya better git a rag from that barrel."

"Yes, sir!" Jeremiah ran over to the barrel and grabbed a rag. Boy, he was gonna work with Ely. "Am I a *real* mate now?"

"Aye, this makes ya a real mate." Ely saluted Jeremiah and helped him mop up the oil.

After supper, Jeremiah fed Cap and they waited for him to return from his walk. Thad and Ely left, and Sam dried the dishes that Maggie washed. She handed him the last spoon. Since Jeremiah and Sam had arrived, her life had changed in so many ways, she wasn't completely sure she had noticed just how much.

After Sam put away the last piece of flatware, he hung the drying towel over the back of his chair and stepped up behind her. "That's enough for you." He took the rag from her hand and tossed it into the dry sink.

She felt him behind her and leaned back against his solid body. She was continually amazed at how her body felt so different when he was near, as if he were some sort of revitalizing elixir. Only there was no way to bottle what he did to her, that heart-pounding reaction and the way she felt all bubbly inside. "For a while," she murmured.

He trailed his fingers along the back of her neck, and her head tipped forward. He placed a hand on each side of her shoulders and kissed her hair. "I'll check the fire."

The impulse to touch her, satisfy his desire to be near her and hold her in his arms grew stronger each day. As he added wood to the parlor stove, he knew he had to talk to her about returning to California—that night. Then tomorrow afternoon, he would have to leave. He wouldn't stay away too long, but he had obligations he simply couldn't put off.

She went into the parlor and sat down in the rocker. Her day wasn't over. Maintenance on a boat couldn't be ignored. As soon as she rested a moment, she'd go down and take care of a few chores.

When Cap returned, Sam gave Jeremiah two old towels to wipe the dog down and sat down in the easy chair opposite Maggie. Her eyes were closed as she gently rocked. *She's working too hard,* he thought, but he doubted anyone could slow her down. If only his situation were different, though, he would like to be the one to try.

Jeremiah wrapped one towel around Cap's head like a scarf and giggled. "You look like a gramma."

"Sh." Sam put his finger to his lips. "Your aunt's resting."

"She's not asleep," she said softly, as if she were sharing a secret, while peering through her lashes.

He winked at her and was rewarded with her lazy grin. "I guess you aren't. Jeremiah, why don't you show Maggie how well you write your name?"

"Okay."

Sam went to the small corner desk, wrote the boy's name in large letters across the top of the paper and handed it and the pencil to Jeremiah.

Pointing with his finger the way Sam had showed him, Jeremiah traced his name. He used the pencil the next time, but his lines were wiggly.

Maggie watched him struggle with the strangeness of controlling the pencil. He frowned, and his tongue poked visibly against his cheek. She recalled her own frustration with penmanship. Sam had the right idea, but Jeremiah needed to practice each letter separately before putting them together. "It's hard, isn't it?"

"Yeah."

She sat down on the floor next to him. "Let's try just writing the letter *J*." She filled the line with the *J*'s, then she showed him how to hold the pencil and covered his hand with hers. "I'll help you so you can see how it feels."

Sam sat back regarding how she held the boy's attention. She was just like a mother. He knew she would be this way, but he hadn't anticipated his reaction to her. Her hair was held back with a ribbon, but several strands had worked loose and were clinging to her cheek. She held him captive, and she wasn't even aware his attention was on her.

"That's very good. See if you can fill the rest of the page." She stood up, pushing the loose hair behind her ears, and met Sam's gaze. "Would you stay with him? There's something I need to do."

"Of course." She'd switched gears in the blink of an eye, he realized, and wondered what was so important.

"Thanks," she said, putting on her heavy coat. "I'll be back in a little while."

She didn't pull her work gloves out of her jacket pocket until she was walking along the deck to the stairs. After she gathered the tools she'd need, she went to the firebox. She wouldn't be able to inspect the inside until it had been cleaned. That was one of Thad's duties, but it was her job to make sure the pipes and seams were tight.

Sam yawned. Unless Maggie returned now, she would find him *and* Jeremiah asleep in her parlor. Sam started pacing. Each time he thought of her, his irritation increased. If nothing else, it was down right rude of her to leave him believing she'd return in a few minutes. Inconsiderate. Selfish.

No need to wake the boy, he decided. He scooped him up, the blanket wrapped securely around him, and left her cabin. The boy should be in bed, and he did not intend to sit or stand around waiting until she happened to come back.

There were lights on the main deck, which seemed peculiar. He assumed Thad was repairing something and didn't give it any more thought—until he passed the firebox and saw Maggie. More accurately, he saw her boots, skirt, and her derriere poking out of the front of the open firebox.

He opened his mouth, but he didn't want to wake Jeremiah. Sam quickly put the boy to bed and went back out to her. "Is that the 'something' you had to do?"

"What?" She backed out and came face to face with Sam, and he was glaring at her. "I couldn't hear very well. . . . Did something happen to Jeremiah?" She glanced around before she realized Sam wouldn't have brought him outside.

Her face was smudged and her hair in complete disarray, but he'd be damned before he would allow himself to be distracted by her charms now. "Do you have any idea how long you've been down here?"

"No, I don't." She pulled at the fingertips of one glove. "Where's Jeremiah?" She pulled off the glove and turned up the collar on her jacket. He was seething, and she was beginning to feel a little miffed herself.

"He's sleeping on his cot. Why the hell didn't you tell me what you were going to do? And just how long is 'a while' to you?" He wanted to throttle her.

"Sam, I didn't think I'd be so long, but I needed to check this tonight." She wiped her face with the hem of her skirt and gazed at him. "What are you so blamed mad about? Did you think I'd run off?" *Grannie's buttons! She never thought he'd be such a fuss-budget.*

"How the devil was I to know what you were up to?"

A horrible idea came to her, and she narrowed her gaze. "You didn't let Jeremiah think I'd left him, did you?"

"Of course not! After he worked his way to *m*, he couldn't keep his eyes open. He was so proud of his letters, and he wanted you to see them." He jammed his hands into his trouser pockets. "Do you make a habit of working at night like this?"

"When there's work to be done, and I have to." She shook her head. His anger made no sense. She collected her things, dropped the rags in one bucket and closed the boiler.

He couldn't recall the last time he'd been so frustrated. He reached for one of the two buckets, but she was faster. "We have to talk."

She brushed her arm across her forehead and gazed at him. "I'm so tired, I can hardly think." She put the lamps out and picked up the other bucket. "I'll see you in the morning. We can talk then. Night, Sam."

Jeremiah woke up and heard a grumbly noise. He pushed back the covers. He still had his clothes on. He put his shoes on and stepped over to Sam's bed. He was on his back with one arm stretched out, and he was making that funny noise. Suddenly, Sam's other arm flopped toward the edge of the bed. Jeremiah covered his mouth and jumped back. As he tiptoed out of the room, he grabbed his coat and put it on.

Thad was at the firebox, and Jeremiah stopped to talk to him. "Whatcha doin'?"

"I'm cleanin' out the smokestack." Thad looked around. "You out here alone?"

"Yeah. Sam didn't wake up yet." Jeremiah stepped closer. "Can I help you?"

"Not with this. This soot's real messy." Thad raised the long-handled brush to the open end of the smokestack. "I think you better go see about breakfast."

"Did you eat?"

"No. I will when I'm finished here. Would you tell Maggie that for me?"

"Sure." Jeremiah went up to his aunt's cabin and eased the door open. When Cap saw him, his tail wagged, and he came over to him. "Hi, boy."

Hearing Jeremiah's voice, Maggie went to the kitchen doorway. "Morning. Where's Sam?"

"Sleepin'." He rubbed Cap's neck. "Can't I stay?"

She grinned. "Well, of course you can. Do you want breakfast?" He looked so dear with his rumpled clothes and hair. She was sure going to miss him when he left with Sam.

"Uh-huh. Whatcha makin'?"

"I haven't started anything yet. What sounds good?"

He thought a minute. "Sam's taters and jumbled eggs. Oh, 'n' Thad wanted me to say he'll be up after he's done cleaning the smokestack."

"Good." She held out her hand. "You can help me." As they worked together, she wondered why Sam hadn't joined them. Last night he'd been as mad as a cornered badger, but she felt sure a good night's sleep would improve his humor. It had done wonders for her. By the time the eggs and potatoes were ready to serve, Jeremiah licked his lips. "That sure looks good."

She picked up a plate and grinned at him. "Now we'll see how it tastes." She put a large spoonful of eggs and another of browned potatoes on the plate. "Turn around and sit down."

"Aren'tcha gonna get Sam? He'll be hungry, too."

She mulled over the idea. It would give them a chance to talk privately. "Eat, and don't touch the pans on the stove."

"I won't," he said, as he chewed a mouthful of potatoes.

She paused in the doorway, eyed Cap and pointed to the

floor. He lay down and rested his chin on his front paws. "Good, boy."

She hurried down to Sam's cabin and tapped on his door. When he didn't answer, she quietly entered, although his snoring was loud enough to drown out most any noise. Her eyes adjusted to the darkened room, and her gaze halted on Sam. He was uncovered down to his hips . . . and he didn't even seem to be wearing drawers.

She swallowed hard. She had never seen so much of a man's body before, not even her husband's. Unwilling to ignore her fascination with Sam, she stepped to the side of the bed. The hair on his chest appeared to grow in dark swirls. Her heart thundered, and she felt breathless and spellbound.

His smile was easy and so handsome. She was tempted to lean down and kiss him awake, but she had never done such a thing. She couldn't . . . could she? She glanced at his hair, his eyelashes, and she listened to him breathe as she struggled with her desire.

The worst that would happen was that he'd get mad, and she wasn't really concerned about that. She leaned down, staring at his mouth and gently pressed her parted lips to his.

Sam wrapped his arms around her back and held her close. He deepened the kiss. Some dreams do come true. "It took you long enough."

Her mind reeled, from the heated kiss and his words. "I thought you were asleep. That I'd wake you slowly." Even she didn't believe the last part.

"You succeeded. Now what're you going to do?" He drew her down on top of him, and oh, she fit his form perfectly.

"I—" She felt his arousal, and she rocked to one side, then the other. "Oh." Her heart pounded and her belly felt like melted butter. She lowered her mouth and kissed his chin and along his jaw. Lying on top of him gave her a heady feeling, and she sank onto his chest, her hips still pressed to his.

He slid one hand down her spine and rolled over with her. She moaned, and her deep throaty sigh surged through him with the energy of the river plunging over the falls. His blood rushed through his body, and his arousal throbbed. Caught in the web of her unspoken plea, he skimmed her ankle with his fingertips and slowly drew her skirt up to her waist. His body pulsed, and he gasped for breath. In that brief moment, Ely's voice drifted into the cabin.

She groaned and held him close, her heart pounding. She struggled to clear her mind of the desire he ignited so completely. "Jeremiah . . . he—He's eating. And he knows I . . . came down to wake you. He'll ask them where we are." She pressed her lips to his shoulder.

"I'll get dressed." He started to move away from her, but her gaze held him after her hands grazed his sides. One more taste of her before they returned to reality, he thought. He traced the line of her lips with his tongue and delved deeper.

Trembling, too weak to move, she watched him dress. His body was beautiful, magnificent. She hadn't known men could be that stunning, and she would never forget how his wonderful body made her feel.

That afternoon while Sam took his turn piloting the steamboat, Maggie was on her knees scrubbing traces of moss off the stairs and walkways. The day passed quickly while the memory of his kisses lingered at the edge of her mind. When she pulled into port at Oregon City, Sam saw that the cargo was unloaded.

When everyone had gone, she smiled at him. He was like a shaft of sunlight shining through the clouds. "At last, and it's early. It won't be dark for another hour."

He laid his arm around her shoulders. "Why is that important?" Tonight he *must* talk with her, but he couldn't leave tomorrow. It was too abrupt and might seem as if he had taken advantage of her. It was Wednesday. Friday was soon enough in one sense, far too soon in another. That morning, it felt as if her body had awakened to his. Just remembering, he breathed harder, and his heartbeat increased.

"I need to work on the decks. I don't want anyone to slip or fall." She rested her head on his shoulder. "I need to finish this section tonight. Even the weather's cooperating. It's only misting."

"Let's get busy. I think I can remember how to scrub a deck."

Jeremiah heard his aunt and hurried over to her. "Can I help, too?" he asked, patting her arm.

While she considered Jeremiah's offer, she held his hand. "It's cool and wet out here, and you were sick. I think you'd better wait in the cabin. Cap's not staying outside either."

Sam waited for her to ask him to stay with the boy. He had never seen a woman more determined to do exactly what she wanted, without help from anyone. She soothed the boy's feelings, and he wondered if she planned to do the same with him. And yet this driven woman was the same one who had leisurely gazed at him and kissed him so passionately only a few hours earlier. She inspired desires and fascinated him more than any woman had ever managed to do.

"Sam, if you're set on scrubbing the deck, I would appreciate your help. I'm sure Ely'll lend you his oilskin." His surprised expression was worth what little discomfort she felt about his working as if he were a deckhand.

He resisted an almost reflexive impulse to thank her. "I'll be right back." He left for the engine room.

She walked Jeremiah upstairs and Cap followed. "You can wait in the saloon or my cabin. Where would you like to go?"

"The saloon."

She grinned. "I like that room, too. Let's get your horse."

"And the boat."

She watched him gather his toys, then settled him and Cap into the saloon. "We'll be right down on deck. If you need me, just call from here. I'll come right up. All right?"

"Mm-hm." He dropped his arm around Cap's neck. "We'll be okay, won't we, boy?"

"I know you will." She ruffled his hair and went down to the main deck. Wearing Ely's oilskin jacket, Sam had started without her. She grabbed the bucket, stiff brush and started scrubbing forward from the walkway toward him.

The work was monotonous and required only a strong arm; it gave him plenty of time to think. He couldn't understand how she had managed to keep the boat as well as she did with so little help. The other riverboats he had seen were newer than hers, and all appeared to be adequately crewed.

She met him on the well-worn path from the gangplank to the cargo area. His hat was soaked as were his trousers, but he seemed happy. Sitting back on her feet, she wiped the mist from her face and grinned. "Thank you, Sam. Let's dry off and have supper."

"All right." He set the buckets by the firebox and walked her to the stairs.

She took his hat off, shook it and handed it to him. "Don't forget to bring your clothes up to dry." A wave of his hair was plastered to his forehead, and his cheeks were pale, but his eyes were bright. Her pulse skipped a beat. She lowered her hand to the banister and smiled as she started up the stairs. It was strange how she felt caressed by his gaze. *I'm being foolish,* she thought.

As soon as she reached the saloon, Jeremiah opened the door and came out hugging his toys to his chest. She grinned and impulsively scooped him up in her arms.

He was glad she was so happy. "Can we go with you now?"

"As soon as I turn down the lamps." It was only a moment before she carried him to her cabin.

She added wood to the fire in the parlor stove, while Jeremiah played with his horse. After she set up the drying rack in front of the woodstove, she changed clothes and hung her pants and stockings at one end. She was in the kitchen when Sam came in, and she watched him talking with Jeremiah as he hung his clothes on the drying rack. Sam was less guarded with him than he was with her, and she prized those moments.

Jeremiah picked up the hollowed-out log Ely had made for his steamboat. "Can I fill this with water?"

Sam shook his head. "Maggie's making supper, and we'll eat before long. Maybe later. I'm going to see what smells so good." He walked into the kitchen and eyed her, from her soft hair down to her slippers. "You're almost as pretty in that dress as you were in pants."

She gave him a saucy grin. "You look rather dapper yourself." Then she lost her playful tone and added, "You should wear blue more often." She turned to the table where she had been slicing the ham and picked up the big knife. Her hand shook so badly, she quickly set it back down. "It won't be long. Did you see Ely or Thad?" *This is nonsensical.* There was no reason for her feeling so jittery around him. She'd been fine a few minutes before.

"They'll be up shortly." He moved to her side and picked up the knife. "Want me to slice more ham?"

"Please. Two more should be enough," she said, reaching for a baking pan, "or whatever you think." Determined not to embarrass herself further, she kept busy until she served supper and had to sit down with everyone at the table.

After they finished eating, Ely and Thad left them alone, even though she had tried to interest Ely in a game of checkers. She had felt Sam's gaze on her during their meal, and the way he watched her brought back that deliciously weak, trembly feeling she'd had that morning. She shoved her hair behind her ears, again, and smoothed her skirt.

"Aunt Maggie—" Jeremiah held up the pages of letters he had written the night before. "See? I did *all* these."

She looked at each of the pages. "My, you worked very hard. Do you want to try the *i* now?"

"Uh-huh." He got the pencil and gave it to her.

"Thank you." She sat down on the floor with him. She wrote the letter *i* and held his hand while she filled the line with the letter.

He grinned. "I like those." He showed Cap what he'd done. "See, these're *i*'s and I made 'em."

Maggie met Sam's gaze before she said, "Don't forget to dot each of them." She dotted three *i*'s to show Jeremiah what she meant, then sat in the rocking chair near him.

Sam couldn't seem to keep his attention from her fingers. They were strong enough to control the wheel of the steamboat or hold him captive, gentle enough to cradle

Jeremiah's hand as if it were fragile glass or soothe his brow. The boat gently rocked. "The wind must be up. Good thing you wanted to scrub the deck before it got dark."

"You learn not to put off chores here—never know what the weather'll be like." She glanced at Jeremiah's progress and back at Sam. "But I still do, sometimes."

After Jeremiah falls asleep, Sam thought, *I'll talk with her.* "How about a game of checkers?"

His suggestion surprised her, but she shrugged. "Why not?" She brought out the crate Zeke had painted with black and red squares. "We can sit on the sofa." She got the checkers from the desk and joined him on the sofa.

He set out the wooden disks. "Unusual colors," he observed. "Do you want blue or green?"

She chuckled. "Those were Zeke's favorite colors. I'll take blue."

"Green it is, then." He began setting up his pieces. "What'll we play for?"

She thought it over a moment. "How about the loser makes breakfast? I'd like to sleep in one morning besides Sunday."

He raised one brow. "You would? I thought you were an early riser?"

"Usually, but I also try to be a good sport." She set up her pieces.

"You're on." He glanced sideways at her, wondering if she realized she had given him a perfect excuse to lose the game. He doubted it. In any case, he intended to make her earn the game.

Five plays later, she sat back. "King me."

He did and matched her. "Your turn."

Jeremiah showed her his paper. "Looky, I made a lot of *i*'s."

"You sure did." She gave him an encouraging smile. "Are you ready to try an *a*?"

"Yeah." Jeremiah stared at their game. "Sam, are you winning?"

Sam moved one of his pieces. "Not sure yet."

"Oh." Jeremiah looked at his aunt. "Is that a *A*?"

"Yes." She wrote three for him and held his hand, guiding it while he filled the remainder of the line.

Jeremiah sat back down on the floor with the paper and pencil. "*A . . . A . . . A.*"

She looked at Sam, and he nodded at the game board. "Hm." He thought he was humoring her, she just knew it. She'd wanted to claim his kings and win. Now, she'd settle for the game. She found the opening she wanted and jumped a king of his.

"Out for blood?" He jumped and claimed one of her pieces. She pushed her thick hair back from the left side of her face and tucked it behind her ear. He flexed his fingers and realized she had noticed. "Warming up."

"Be my guest. It's your turn." She couldn't hide her amusement and laughed. He wanted to win as much as she did. The times she had played with Ely, she never thought his heart was really in the game, and Zeke hadn't challenged her either. Sam was enjoying the cat-and-mouse game—so was she.

He had captured four of her pieces and still had a little hope of tying the game, when she snatched his last king. "Wanna give me another chance?" He flashed her a lopsided grin. "Two out of three?"

She laughed. "Sounds fair." They played two more games, and Jeremiah worked on writing a page of *h*'s. Sam won the next match, and she the last one—by two pieces. "Jeremiah and I like the way you make those special potatoes."

"I concede," he said, stacking the pieces. "Breakfast it will be in the morning."

Jeremiah went over to Sam. "Will you tell us a story?"

After putting the game pieces away, she sat back down on the sofa near Sam. Thank goodness he'd asked Sam, she thought; she was too tired to think of anything interesting.

Jeremiah dropped his paper on the desk and went back to Sam. "Can I sit on your lap?"

Sam lifted him up and waited until the boy got comfortable. He put his other arm around Maggie's shoulders. "Jeremiah, do you know the story about the bear and the mountain lion?" That story should put the boy to sleep—anyway, he hoped so. After waiting all evening to speak with her, now he wasn't as sure as he had been about leaving.

Jeremiah stared at Sam. "Unh-unh."

Sam pulled Maggie closer as he started spinning the tale. "A long, long time ago there was a big mountain . . ."

She drew her legs under her bottom and snuggled up against Sam. He spoke in a deep, soothing voice. It wasn't long before her eyelids grew heavy.

He was just getting to the part about the bear and the mountain lion's disagreement, when he realized both Jeremiah and Maggie were sound asleep. He kissed the top of her head and whispered, "There's always tomorrow."

Chapter

14

Sam woke up just before dawn the next morning, though it couldn't be seen through all the clouds. He dressed quickly, quietly, without disturbing Jeremiah, and went to Maggie's cabin. Cap appeared in the bedroom doorway prepared to defend her, until he recognized Sam. He pulled her door almost closed and added wood to the parlor stove before he lighted a lamp in the kitchen and latched that door.

It only took him a few minutes to find where she stored the potatoes, bacon and a sharp knife. He peeled, cut, and dumped the potatoes in a large skillet before he seasoned them. He placed several slices of bacon in another pan. After he stirred the embers in the stove and added wood, he put a pot of coffee on the fire. He wanted to surprise her, not wake her up with the aroma of breakfast.

As soon as the coffee was ready, he poured two cups and set the skillets to the side of the fire to cook slowly. He tasted his coffee and removed his shoes. Once he had lighted a lamp in the parlor, he carried the second cup into Maggie's bedroom. The lights from the kitchen and parlor cast a soft glow in her room. She was sprawled on her side, and her loosely braided hair lay over her shoulder.

Cap perched as if ready to spring up onto the bed. Sam snapped his finger, the way Maggie did to gain the animal's attention, and pointed to the floor. Fortunately, the dog was obedient and lay down.

She murmured and stirred, and Sam held his breath. He was sure his heart was beating loud enough to wake her, but it didn't. One of her arms was under the pillow, the other lay

156

along the top of the covers. Even in the dim light, he could follow the line of her back down to the curve of her hip. She slid one knee closer to her chest, while the other leg remained straight. He reached out and carefully loosened her hair. When he combed his fingers through the silky length, a few strands caught on one of his fingers.

The room was so quiet, her breathing sounded like a whisper. Hoping the floorboards wouldn't give his presence away, he walked round the bed and eased down onto the mattress. The support ropes creaked, and he waited for her to wake up with a start. When she only mumbled, he stretched out on top of the covers behind her, wondering if he was out of his mind. But then he realized this is what it would be like to wake up next to her. He recalled how she had roused him; he wanted the pleasure of seeing her come full awake.

Slowly, he rolled onto his side and molded his body to the curve of her back. That special excitement, that energy streamed through his limbs, intensifying his desire to make love to her. His intentions weren't to seduce her, but cuddling with her felt as natural as breathing. He eased one arm around her waist. She murmured again and snuggled back against him.

He nudged her hair back and kissed her neck. He held her close and said, "Good morning."

Instantly, her eyes were open. She *wasn't* dreaming! "What . . . are you doing?" He was in bed with her and holding her in his arms. "Mm—" For one thing, his hand gently kneaded her waist, and it was all she could do not to turn over and face him. Moreover, his body was fitted to hers as firmly as a glove on a hand.

"Did you have pleasant dreams?" He blew on the back of her neck. She trembled, and he tightened his hold.

"I . . . I'm not sure where they ended, and you took over." She covered his hand with hers, fighting the urge to raise or lower it.

"Are you hungry?"

She pressed his hand to her belly. A soft moan escaped. "Ah, the game."

"Mm-hm. Your breakfast is cooking while we lie here keeping each other warm."

She dropped her hand to the mattress. "Shouldn't you make sure it won't burn?" *Oh, damn.* Was everything a game to him? "I can smell the bacon."

He wanted to see her lovely face. He moved enough so he could tip her onto her back. "You sure are pretty in the morning." He bent over and kissed her.

He looked so sincere, she couldn't believe he wasn't, or she didn't want to believe he would be so underhanded. She wrapped her arms around him, held him close and gave free rein to her desire. She inhaled deeply when his lips glanced across her cheek and down her neck.

He pressed his lip to the hollow of her neck, then leaned back. Her face was rosy, and there was a glint in her eyes. "I brought you a cup of coffee. But it's probably cool by now."

She glanced at the table by her bed and smiled.

"If a cup of coffee made you smile, maybe I shouldn't have started the potatoes so soon."

"I'm glad you did." She gazed at him and then down at the bed. "Nana once told me about the old custom of bundling. Is that what we're doing?"

He chuckled. "The way I heard it, the couple spent the night in bed together—not always alone." He playfully nipped at her chin. "That's something to keep in mind, though."

A movement near the door caught her attention. Cap had his nose in the air. She sniffed, too. "Sam, I really think you should check on the bacon."

"I don't suppose you'll wait right here?"

She grinned and combed her fingers through his hair. "Jeremiah'll be awake before long."

Later that afternoon, Maggie was humming when Ely came up to her. "It was a good day, wasn't it?"

Ely stared at her and shrugged. "Appears it was fer ya."

She put her arm around his shoulders. "Out with it. What's put you in such a state?"

"Me?" He arched one bushy brow. "Nothin' botherin' me. I ain't the one grinnin' like a blockhead."

"Oh, Ely," she said, hugging him. "I'm happy. Is it that unusual?"

"Nah, guess it's 'bout time." He looked her in the eye. "Jist watch out fer eddies, gal. Ya said yerself, Sam'll be leavin'."

"I haven't forgotten. But he'll raise Jeremiah, and I'll go see them from time to time." She kissed his whiskered cheek. "It'll be enough. When I'm an old woman, the children can tell tales about the crazy ole lady steamboat pilot."

"That's a heck of a life ta look forward to." He shook his head. "Maggie girl, me 'n' this ol' boat won't last ferever. I'd hate t'see ya pass up someone who makes ya this happy."

"I'm not. He's not ready to marry, and I know I'm not either. But I value his friendship—and yours, you old curmudgeon, so don't get all steamed."

He grinned at her. "Ya always was a sassy li'l snippet."

She winked at him and lowered her arm from his shoulder. "If I wasn't, I wouldn't own this steamboat and be the pilot. Now, I'm going to town for supplies. What do you need?"

"Not a thin'."

"Please yourself. I'm feeling so good, I might agree to whatever you wanted."

"Yeah, that's what concerns me."

He ambled over to where Thad was talking with Sam near the boiler, and she shook her head. He meant well, he really did. And she agreed with what he'd said about the boat not lasting forever. The problem was that she couldn't imagine being this happy doing anything else. She walked over to Sam.

He eyed her. "I see you finished scrubbing the deck. Why didn't you wait?"

"It didn't take all that long. Besides, I need to get supplies. Want to come along?"

"Sounds good. I'll get Jeremiah."

She watched him leave, but she felt Ely watching her and turned to him. "I—" She shrugged. There really wasn't anything to say. "Thad, what do you need?"

"Can't think of a thing, but it's early. If you don't mind, I'd like to eat at home tonight."

"Please tell your parents hello for me." She looked at Ely. "Care to take a walk with us?"

"Nah. I'm athinkin' mebbe I'll stop by Miz Hanson's."

She didn't smile, but she felt her lips twitch. He had known Mrs. Hanson for years, and she had been widow for half that long. Maggie cleared her throat. "Enjoy your meal." She wished those two would get together. He was getting too old for this work. She really had to give some serious thought to how she would replace him.

Jeremiah ran up to her. "Sam said we're goin' to the store. Cap's comin' with us, isn't he?"

She grinned at him. "He sure is. I want to change jackets. Will you wait right here for me?"

"Uh-huh." Jeremiah hugged Cap.

She dashed up to the cabin, traded her old hat for a bonnet and put on her long heavy coat before she returned to the main deck.

Sam fastened the last button on Jeremiah's coat. "There. Know what? You need a hat." The boy's eyes looked ready to pop out, and he nodded.

"Gee! Not a stocking cap—a *real hat*?"

"Let's see what the store has, but I promise it won't be a stocking cap." Sam looked at Maggie as she came up to them and gave her a slow, appreciative smile. "You're mighty fetchin', ma'am, and it's a fine afternoon for a stroll to the mercantile." Her cheeks turned a becoming shade of pink, and she moved her head just enough for the brim to shield her face from him. He linked arms with her. "Shall we go?"

"Mm-hm." She held out her hand. "Jeremiah?"

He took her hand and stared up at her. She looked real different, more like a ma. "Sam said I could get a *real hat*."

"You don't have one?" She glanced at Sam and back to

Jeremiah. "Then you certainly need one." She looked at Sam. "You're not wearing one either."

He shrugged and winked at Jeremiah. "Guess we'll have to buy two hats."

They crossed the deck and walked down the gangplank. She was glad when Sam thought to carry Jeremiah over the mucky ground. A few minutes later, she remembered why she rarely wore this bonnet. It was like wearing blinders, and she was soon tiring of swiveling her head from side to side.

Sam noticed her fussing with the bonnet. "What's wrong?"

"This thing needs windows in the brim so I can see you." She made a face. "I wasn't cut out to be a lady."

"You're wrong, Maggie. Very wrong." He hugged her arm to his side and gave her a reassuring gaze.

After they passed the livery, the first boardwalk they came to in front of the harness shop had so much grime tracked on it, it wasn't much better than the street; fortunately; the second one in front of the barbershop was better. She led the way into Kirkland's and went straight to the display of men's hats. "What's your pleasure?"

After glancing around, Sam held up a cloth hat with a hard peak. He popped it on his head and struck a rakish pose. "What do you think?"

"Ah . . . well—" She burst out laughing.

Jeremiah giggled and handed Sam a big tall hat.

Sam changed hats. "Any better?"

Jeremiah shook his head. "Nah."

Setting the hat back on the shelf, Sam reached for a bowler and glanced at Maggie. She shook her head, and he picked up the one he liked. It was a wide-brimmed, wool felt hat, more serviceable than the others.

She nodded. "Try it on." *Oh, Grannie, he's a treasure*. He set the hat at a slight angle and pulled it down over the top of his forehead. She heard soft whispers and glanced over her shoulder. Three women were watching him, and from their not-so-modest smiles, they also thought he was handsome.

"Maggie?" He tapped her shoulder. "Like this one?"

"Very much." She motioned to the young women standing by a display of lace. "I think they do, too."

He tipped his hat to the young ladies and picked up Jeremiah. "Now we need to find some smaller hats for you."

Jeremiah pointed to one like Sam's. "That one."

Sam handed it to Jeremiah. "See how it fits."

Jeremiah put it on and stared up at the brim.

The hat came down near his eyebrows. Biting down on the side of her tongue to keep from grinning, Maggie took the hat off him. "It's just a tad too big."

"Here," Sam said, holding his hand out. "Let me see something." She handed it to him, and he felt the sweatband. "You really like this?"

"Oh, yeah! It's not too tight, and I'll grow into it."

"You will." Sam put Jeremiah down and went over to speak to the clerk. After the pleasantries, he asked, "Would you have this hat in a boy's size?"

When Maggie joined Sam, the man glanced up, stared at her and smiled. "Mrs. Foster. Nice to see you again."

"Hello, Mr. Kirkland. Will you be able to help us?"

Mr. Kirkland thought a moment and checked the hat.

Jeremiah patted Sam's arm. "I'll eat a big supper, an' I'll go to bed right after. Ma said I growed at night. Maybe it'll fit better tomorrow."

Mr. Kirkland grinned at him. "Son, there's no way this'll fit that soon. But maybe I can fix it to give you some more time." He looked at Sam. "If you can give me a little while, I think I can help."

"That will be fine. We'll be back." Sam paid for both hats and thanked Kirkland. He looked into Jeremiah's anxious face. "It's yours. You can wear it back to the boat later."

Jeremiah hugged Sam's leg. "Thanks, oh, thanks."

"You're welcome. Now let's see what Maggie needs to get."

Sam carried him down to their cabin and tucked him into bed. True to his word, Jeremiah had fallen asleep not long after supper, though Sam was sure it was a coincidence. He walked out on deck and saw Maggie standing near the bow

without her coat. It had stopped raining, and she stood there
with the wind blowing her hair and billowing her skirt out
behind her.

He stepped up behind her and slid his arms around under
her breasts. "He didn't wake up. But I did set his hat at the
foot of his cot."

"He wasn't happy about taking it off for supper, so I
wasn't too surprised when he feel asleep with it on." She
tipped her head back on his shoulders and smiled at him.
"You made him so happy."

"I wish you would've picked out a new bonnet. Wouldn't
that yellow one with the lace and little flowers go with your
new dress? The brim swept back to your ears, so you could
glance sideways at me."

"You're impossible." The river was choppy, and she
loved the rocking motion, especially when she was on deck
or in bed. And it felt even better with his arms around her.

When she shivered, he held her tighter. "It's getting cold
out here, and I need to talk with you. Want to sit in the
saloon? I'll light a fire."

"And I'll make some cocoa." She turned around within
the circle of his arms and gazed at him. A chill that wasn't
caused by the night air slid down her spine, and she laid her
cheek on his chest.

"Sounds good." He kept his arm around her as they
walked up to the saloon.

She left his warm embrace. "I won't be long."

Sam lighted one lamp near the door and built up a fire in
the woodstove at the other end of the room. Telling Maggie
about his departure would be difficult, but actually leaving
will be worse. Timing. *Sometimes, luck, good fortune,
whatever you want to call it*, he thought, *all comes down to
timing*. And his was damned poor.

Maggie carried a tray into the saloon. Sam was pacing
between two windows and didn't hear her enter until she
crossed the room.

He cleared the six-day-old newspapers from the small
table for her. "Looks good."

She poured cocoa into one cup and handed it to him. "It's

not too sweet, but here's the sugar bowl," she said, pushing it over to him. "You can add more sugar if you like." She filled her own cup.

He tasted his cocoa. "Just the way I like it." He motioned to the sofa and sat down with her. He took another sip and set the cup down on the table in front of them. "It's hard to believe . . . but I've been here almost three weeks."

This isn't any easier for him than it is for me, she thought, holding her cup with both hands. "Doesn't seem like it, or does it?" She took a sip. She believed that problems were best met head on. "When will you be leaving?"

He stared at her, wondering how she managed to do what he least expected. "I should leave Saturday." Her lightly trembling hands gave the lie to her calm attitude. "Chester's due the first part of December with the sheep. I should be able to come back up in February." He rested his arm on the back of the sofa and laid his hand on her shoulder.

Trying to hide her disappointment she gulped, and attempted a smile. "I'll look forward to your visit." She wanted to set her cup down, but she needed something to hold on to—and she didn't think it was a good idea to reach for him. "I'll take you down to Corvallis."

He gently kneaded her shoulder. "Thank you . . . leaving you won't be easy. Will you be all right?"

"Business isn't bad." She lowered the cup to her knee. "In fact, I'm thinking about hiring a man to work with Ely."

He eyed her. "Really?" He had no idea chicken, jam and pork were so profitable. That wasn't fair, he thought. She had been working hard, and he didn't know what she had earned from hauling cargo. But he doubted it was enough to pay another man's wages. "What does Ely think of that?"

She glanced at her cup and raised it to her lips. "I haven't told him yet." She sipped the warm cocoa. "Jeremiah's changed so much. I bet he claims one of the sheep for a pet."

"They aren't pets, but he can see that for himself if you bring him down for a visit." He skimmed his knuckles down her cheek. "I hope you can. You may like it there."

She frowned and set the cup on the table. "That doesn't

make sense, Sam. He'll be living with you. I want to see you and him—"

"Maggie—" He waited until she looked at him. "Why do you think he'll be *living* with me?"

She rolled her eyes. It wasn't like him to be dense as a fence post. "Because he can't stay here. You've been here long enough to see that." She swiveled on the seat to face him. "Don't try your fancy lawyer tricks with me. You know as well as I do that I'm no mother. You'd have to be blind not to see that." She glared at him. "He can't stay here."

He couldn't, would never actually do what he was about to threaten, but he had to make her understand how much she cared about the boy. "Would you rather have him in an orphanage? There must be one up here. Or I could see if that family, the one the preacher in San Francisco knows, still wants him." There wasn't an easy way to do it. He could only hope she would forgive him later.

"You wouldn't! He adores you." *He's bluffing*, she thought, *I know he is.* "And don't think I haven't noticed how you dote on him." *Anyway, I hope he's just trying to dupe me.* His expression was blank. *He must be a great poker player.* However, she was determined—for his sake, and for Jeremiah's.

He cocked his head, still holding her gaze. He must be missing something. If he viewed her as if she were a stranger . . . "Are you afraid to raise him?"

Chapter

15

"It scares the bejeebers out of me," she said after a stunned silence. "*You* can do anything you want and earn money. I can't sew a straight seam, my pie crust would make better pie tins and no one would want me for a housekeeper. But I am a good pilot. If this steamboat blows, sinks or collides with another riverboat, I'd be lucky to feed myself." She leaned back against the armrest. They had to thrash this out and put an end to it.

"Thought you were making enough money to hire another man. I'll wager he'll cost you nearly as much as Ely earns."

She brushed aside his comment as if swatting at a fly. "You haven't said why he can't live with you. You're as frightened as I am, and you want to walk away. If we were strangers, and say I was a lady of the evening, would you leave him with me?" His poker face slipped away, his mouth fell open and his eyes grew huge. She understood his frustration, shared it. The fire popped, and she flinched, but she refused to look away.

He bound to his feet, glaring at her. "Good God, woman, I thought I knew you!"

"I believed you did, too."

If she had slapped his face, he couldn't have felt worse. "How could you think so little of me?" He stalked over to the window. *Damn*. His insides felt as if he'd ridden a log over the rapids.

"I—" *Don't* died on her lips, and she shook her head.

He interrupted her and continued as if she hadn't spoken. "And *no*—I wouldn't leave him just anywhere."

"I never said that." She scrambled to stand up. "But it seems as if you think it's all right to leave him here just because you know me."

"Maggie, you're his aunt, the only relative either of us knows about." He stared into her eyes. "We're both in the same position. I have to work the ranch. There's no one who could watch him, at least not now. There isn't even a house yet. That's why I have to get back."

She stepped over to the window and rested the side of her head against the glass. "I'm his aunt, according to the law." She watched Sam. "It's not fair. Not fair to any of us. If I gave up my boat, it won't help him or me."

"No." He reached out and took her hand. "But would you agree to keep him until next spring if I helped with his expenses? I'll leave you money." Her hand was cold, and she looked so aloof. He slipped his arm around her.

Oh, Grannie, I want to hold on to him, even just for a moment, and believe everything will work out. But she couldn't agree with him. "No. He'd be better off watching you build the ranch house. I won't drag him around the way I did my doll when I was his age. You've seen me work. I can't do it." She wanted to rail at someone. Instead she sighed. "I can't do everything, and I won't ask Ely and Thad to watch him. They are overworked as it is."

"Jeremiah would get used to spending most of his time in the pilothouse, and he'd be with you." He rubbed her back with feathery strokes and she leaned into him, her breasts pressed into his chest. His response was immediate and gripping. If only a solution would come about as easily.

She stirred, slowly, recognizing the ripples of desire pulsing below her belly. She felt as if she were being torn apart—as if her mind and her body were two separate parts, each seeking its own satisfaction.

He kissed her hair. "We'll work it out." He tipped her chin up and kissed the tip of her nose. "If it will help, I'll stay on another couple of weeks."

She lowered her lashes and savored his offer. It was

almost too much to hope for. "How can you? What about the ranch house? Your partner?" *Would that be long enough for her*? she wondered.

"I'll send him a message telling him to hire a couple of men to start the work. As long as I'm there to meet Chester, it'll have to be all right." Feeling her shudder he tightened his embrace. "Want to sit down by the fire?"

"Mm-hm." It was settled—for the time being. She curled up at his side, encouraged by their agreement. "Tell me again what's so interesting about sheep."

He leaned back against the end of the sofa and stretched out his legs. "It sounded like a good investment. There's a market for the wool and the meat, and we should be able to sell the hides, too." He stroked her arm. "Haven't you wanted to try something new?"

She glanced up at him. "Once or twice."

"What would be more exciting than piloting a riverboat?"

"Riding for the Pony Express," she said with a crooked grin, "but the riders are men, and I'm too old to pose as one."

He studied her a moment. Yes, that choice suited her. "You'd never be mistaken for a man." She snuggled against him and laid her hand on his chest. He took a deep breath. He should say or do something to distract both of them. He didn't want to; each time her body rubbed against his, his heart pumped faster and his blood rushed through his limbs. He wanted her, and he didn't know how much longer he could stand the exquisite torture before giving in to his need. "I'd better make sure Jeremiah's still asleep."

Her hand slid down his chest and caught on the buttons on his pants. "You're coming back, aren't you?" As she gazed into his eyes, the buttons pressed against her hand.

Her voice flowed over him like warm sorghum, but when she touched him so intimately, a jolt shot right through him. He inhaled deeply and waited for his strength to return. "I shouldn't be long."

She had barely sat up, when he almost sprang to his feet. It suddenly felt warm in the saloon. She fanned her face and loosened the top two buttons on her dress.

On his way out he turned and stared across the room at her slender neck and then lower, and he felt the same heat. He quickly stepped outside. The air was cold, bracing, and he hoped it would help change the course of his thoughts. He checked on the boy. When he returned to the saloon, she was lying on the sofa and the smile on her face couldn't have been more beautiful or more inviting.

She pushed herself up with her elbow. "Was he sleeping?" He came back to her. Until that moment, she hadn't allowed herself to consider otherwise. The disappointment and pain of a second rejection would have been too great. When he gazed at her, she felt as if he'd brushed against the length of her body.

He nodded. "Soundly." He sat at her side and draped his arm around her shoulders before he realized it. He hadn't known a woman like her, or one he looked forward to seeing each morning, one he couldn't resist touching and the only one he wanted in his bed each night.

"I'm glad," she murmured, scooching up onto his lap. She wrapped her arms around his neck and kissed his jaw. His heart thumped against her breast, and she nestled closer. With each move, her hunger for him grew stronger. As a girl, she'd dreamed of a chaste kiss—the woman wanted and needed so much more from him.

He closed his arms around her and rested his forehead on hers. He couldn't believe he was holding this woman he wanted so desperately, knowing he couldn't do what every part of him craved. Her bottom squirmed on his lap. He groaned and clutched her tighter.

She wasn't imagining his desire for her. It was real, and it was as urgent as hers. Her pulse quickened, and with concentrated effort, she slowly began unfastening the buttons on his shirt. His clove-scented hair tonic was intoxicating, and the hair on his chest was soft. She sank her fingers into the swirls of dark hair and grazed his skin. His muscles flexed beneath her palm. Her heart pounded with anticipation.

He held her hand still with his. "Maggie, I'm not made of stone."

She grinned. "I know." She slid her hand from his and parted his shirt. "You're flesh and blood—" She pressed a kiss to the middle of his chest. "And you feel so good."

He gasped and let his head fall back on the sofa. "You-know-I . . . have-to-leave . . . in two weeks." He inhaled deeply, but it didn't help. "When I return, then we can see if you still feel the same or if you've changed your mind."

"I don't want to wait, Sam. I need you *now*." She raised her skirt and straddled his thighs. His eyes were wide with surprise, his lips parted. She nibbled the corner of his mouth and around to his ear. "You know I was never long on patience, but I've waited fifteen years for this moment."

"Oh God." He framed her face with his hands and covered her mouth with his. She tasted sweet, and he wanted to bury himself in her. "You were headstrong all those years ago. Seems you still are." His muscles were taut with anxiety. She was Maggie. He'd grown up with her. He respected and cherished her friendship, but he couldn't ignore his attraction to her. It had grown stronger with each passing day. He wondered why the man was expected to decide what was right for the woman and discount her feelings—or was he making excuses to himself?

"Mm-hm." Rocking back on his lap, she tugged his shirt from his pants and slowly finished unbuttoning it. "We're grown-up now."

Each time she shifted her weight, his body responded. He opened the front of her dress, eased the bodice over her white shoulders and pushed the sleeves down past her hands. As he peeled her garments away, he exposed her beautiful breasts and creamy smooth skin. She was lovely— his image of perfection.

She had never experienced such dizzying excitement and braced her hands on his shoulders. She stared at him in wonder as his lips caressed her, and his tongue teased her nipples. She moaned and settled on his lap, increasing the tension coiling below her belly. She needed him, wanted to feel him inside her. When he looked at her, they were both breathing hard. She held his gaze as she unfastened the buttons on his pants.

He groaned, trembling with desire. She seemed to glow in the soft light. He raised her hands to his lips, then he drew one of her fingers into his mouth and slowly released it to sample each one in turn. Her pupils widened and her hair spilled down over her shoulders. She swayed, and he shifted her to the cushion in a rolling motion that brought him to his knees on the deck with her seated in front of him.

When he loosened the waist of her dress and petticoats, she raised her bottom, and he pulled her clothes down over her knees. He quickly removed them and tossed his shirt aside. His trousers landed on the mound of discarded clothes. His gaze blazed a path down her exposed body as he lightly trailed his fingertips over her curves and hollows.

At times she forgot to breathe, at other times she inhaled sharply. It was as if he were wrapping her in a magical cloak of overpowering sensations that continued to build beyond imagining. When his hands lingered on her knees, she opened to him with a whimper and held out her arms to him. She wanted to hold him close, feel his skin against hers, his weight bearing down on her.

He moved into her embrace and lay down on top of her. Her warmth and passion were remarkable. He nibbled her lips and explored her mouth with all the fervor he had held back until now. She wrapped her legs around his, and he rubbed the length of his body against hers. He wasn't prepared for the surge of energy that exploded in him. He wanted to taste her, learn her most sensitive spots that even she had yet to discover, but their need was too great. She seemed to be as driven as he was to join their bodies completely.

His strength inflamed and fed hers. She had never felt the freedom to touch, taste and feel at will, and it was thrilling. She ran her hands up and down his back, delighting in his trembling response. Her need grew so great, she pressed her hands on his bottom, urging him to fill her. He slid his hand under her hips and in one gliding move, he thrust into her, and she cried out her pleasure. Tears filled her eyes. She pinned his legs with hers to make that first breathtaking moment last, as waves of ecstasy whirled through her.

He felt her tears on his cheek, and fearing he had hurt her, he gazed at her. She smiled and rocked her hips. Pressing his mouth to hers, he withdrew to enter her anew. She met each thrust with a hunger he felt as well. All too soon, she cried out as her tremor shook them both. Her inner hold gripped him as firmly as if with her hand, and his release claimed him.

Lingering desire still pulsed through her veins. She reeled as she wrapped her arms around his back and pressed a kiss to his shoulder. She didn't want it to end. She had never known such complete and glorious pleasure. Her plain face and figure didn't seem to matter to him, and she loved him all the more for it. Her breathing slowed, and she sighed with heartfelt happiness.

He kissed the smooth skin between her breasts. "Do you feel as good as I do?"

"Better." She playfully grabbed his bottom with both hands, and she grinned. "I've never felt so wonderful. I could fly above the clouds."

"Not without me." He nuzzled her neck and wound strands of her hair around his finger. "How about swimming upstream with the salmon?"

She parted her lips, inviting his kiss, and he obliged with such passionate tenderness, she could have cried. "I think we already have."

Chapter
16

Maggie stood outside of her cabin with a cup of fresh coffee. Rays of light filtered through the treetops as she watched the sunrise through a break in the clouds. Her pulse quickened at the thought of seeing Sam when Jeremiah woke up and the two came up for breakfast. They had said good-night at her door, and she remembered reaching for him at least three different times during the night. She sipped her coffee. They had two more weeks together.

By the time her coffee had cooled, she was ready to start her day and went inside. She tossed her robe aside, put on a work dress, tied her hair back with a ribbon and started their meal. Bacon and fried potatoes were cooking, and she was stirring the batter for griddlecakes when she heard the cabin door open. She set the bowl on the table and went to the kitchen doorway.

Jeremiah had his new hat on. He stopped to greet Cap and set it on the dog's head.

Sam pushed the door closed and smiled at Maggie. "You look good this morning." She always did, but this morning she had a special gleam in her eyes.

She laughed. "You do, too."

"I'll give you a hand." Sam walked into the kitchen with her and drew her out of the boy's sight.

"Sam—" She peered around the corner of the door to see if Jeremiah had noticed, but he hadn't. She grinned at Sam and slid her hands up his arms. "Good morning."

He poised her chin with his first finger and covered her mouth with his. When she leaned into him, he wrapped his arms around her and held her close. "I could spend the day here."

Two weeks ago, she'd never kissed anyone with her mouth open; her husband had always kept his lips clamped together. Now, it was perfectly natural. The urge to grind her hips on Sam's also felt normal, but very unseemly with her nephew in the next room. "If I don't turn the bacon, it'll end up in Cap's pan."

He held her a moment longer before releasing her. "Leave it to me." He turned the bacon and potatoes, while she started the griddlecakes.

Jeremiah left Cap and came into the kitchen. "Can I help?" He pushed his chair in between Sam and his aunt and stood on the seat.

"You certainly can." She put her arm around him. "You can tell me when the tops of the cakes are bubbling."

He stared at the white cakes on the griddle. "I will."

"Don't forget—the stove's real hot. Don't touch it." She glanced at Cap. He was watching every move Jeremiah made.

He grabbed the back of the chair while he stared at the pan. "They're not doin' nothin'."

"Nothing," she said, correcting him. "There is a *g* on the end." Since he would be staying with her for a few months, she might as well start acting as if she were his mother. "But 'they aren't doing anything' sounds better."

"Okay." He sighed, glaring at the cakes. "They aren't doing anything. They aren't . . ."

She cleared the table and set it for breakfast. Ely and Thad arrived. She poured four cups of coffee and set them out on the table.

"There they are! Aunt Maggie," Jeremiah called, "they're bubblin' *all over*. Sam, look—" He pointed to the cakes.

Sam peered at the pan and chuckled. "Those are good bubbles."

Maggie stepped over to Jeremiah's side. "They sure are. Time to turn them over." She grinned at him and flipped the cakes.

He bent down to get a better look, but he couldn't see anything. "How can I see the bubbles?"

"There won't be any now. You can watch the next batch." She held the plates for Sam while he dished the generous portions of potatoes on them and placed the bacon on top. "That looks pretty. You're spoiling us."

He grinned at her. "Then you're too easily pleased."

She eyed him. "Only in the kitchen." She served Thad and set Ely's plate down. She knew Ely had been studying her. "The cakes will be done in a minute."

Ely shrugged. "I'm in no hurry."

She glanced at Sam and back to Ely. "We'll go down to Corvallis today, or at least Albany."

Ely nodded but didn't say a word.

She stacked the cakes on one plate and started four more. "Jeremiah, you don't have to watch these, if you want to start eating."

"But I do. I wanna see a bubble pop."

"I don't." She patted his shoulder and served the griddle-cakes to Ely and Thad.

Sam filled their cups with coffee and sat down at the table. His attention repeatedly veered to Maggie. She stirred a wealth of emotions, and he found himself deciding to hire a few extras hands to help him complete the work on the ranch sooner than planned.

Ely ate a bite of his griddlecake and grinned. "Ya did a fine job, Jeremiah."

Jeremiah grinned at him and turned back to the stove. "Can I make one for Cap, Aunt Maggie?"

Maggie wanted to pilot the steamboat all the way to Albany and that suited Sam just fine. It gave him the morning to write to Lewis, the ranch hand he'd hired before leaving. Sam explained his delay and gave him instructions. To the best of his knowledge, the man was reliable, but he felt better giving him detailed guidance, leaving nothing to chance.

They were making good time, and he kept track of the boat's progress upriver. When the whistle blew on their approach to Albany, he tucked the letter in his coat pocket. "Jeremiah, get your coat. We might go into town."

"Can I wear my hat? It won't blow away, will it?"

Sam glanced outside. "The wind's died down. I think it'll be safe." He made a mental note to look for a chin strap for the boy's hat. He put on his coat and hat, made sure Jeremiah's buttons were fastened correctly and left the cabin with him.

Maggie walked over to Sam after the last passenger stepped off the gangplank. "We'll leave for Corvallis in ten minutes."

"You don't have to go that far for me. I'll post the letter here."

"All right. The general store is just down that first street."

"I told Jeremiah he could go with me. Won't you come too?"

"I'll get dinner ready. You two have fun."

"Jeremiah—" Sam playfully eyed her. "Last chance."

"Go on." On her way up to her cabin she stopped to tell Thad and Ely they would be heading north after dinner. It didn't take her long to make the beef log and put it in to bake with potatoes and carrots filling out the pan.

Later, Ely and Thad joined her, and she gave them each a cup of coffee. "How did it go this morning? Notice any problems?"

Thad shook his head. "Everythin's fine on deck. Didn't you have enough steam?"

"Plenty. I just don't want any surprises." She studied Ely. He looked tired. It was no longer something to consider, she must hire a striker, an assistant for him: "I'm sorry it was so hard for you this morning. It seemed like I was piping you every two minutes."

Ely shrugged. "I don't jump round like a striplin' boy. Been finaglin' that old engine long 'nough to know what I'm doin'."

"You better." She grinned. If she were too serious, he'd not only feel insulted, he'd get cantankerous. She was about to refill Thad's coffee when she heard Sam's voice.

Jeremiah opened the cabin door and let Cap go in first.

Ely and Thad were there. "Hi. Look what Sam got me." He pulled off his hat and held it out. "See—it's a chin strap, so the wind won't blow it off."

Ely winked at him. "That was smart thinkin'."

Maggie grinned. "That looks real fine." She held out her hand to Jeremiah. "Dinner's almost ready. Come wash your hands in the kitchen." While he washed up, she eased the biscuit balls into the hot grease. "You can call everyone in for dinner after you dry your hands. Oh, and hang up your jacket."

"Do I have to put my hat away, too?"

"Mm-hm. Sam doesn't wear his hat inside. You can put yours on my desk, or one of the tables."

He turned the hat over. "Okay." Gee, she wanted him to remember a lot of things.

Sam waited to speak with Maggie until after Ely and Thad had left. Jeremiah was playing with the dog and the toy horse. Sam caught her attention and motioned outside.

She went out with him. "Seems like you and Jeremiah enjoyed your outing. That chin strap should keep his hat in place so he can enjoy it."

He put his arm around her waist and kissed her forehead. "Did Jeremiah tell you what else I bought?"

"No." She looked at him. "What?"

"A first reader, more paper, another pencil, some clothes." He tapped the tip of her nose with his finger. "I left the packages on his cot."

"It'll take time to replace what he lost." *And what he needs most,* she thought, *neither of us has the power to return to him.*

"It's a start." He brushed his cheek against her hair. He had to stop touching her at every turn. The first step was to keep talking, it might help. "Jeremiah's certainly taken to Ely."

"I think it's good for both of them." She turned her back to the rail and faced him. "Ely was worn out after this morning. It seemed like I piped him every few minutes." She leaned back on the rail. "I have a big favor to ask."

"Anything."

"Instead of piloting the boat, would you help Ely in the afternoons? He's too proud to admit he needs it, but I saw it in his eyes before you got back."

He nodded. "Have you said anything to him about this?"

She shook her head. "I wanted to speak with you first."

"Leave it to me. Want me to start today?"

"If you don't mind. Jeremiah can go with me."

After Maggie had pulled the stern-wheeler out into the current, Sam brought fresh coffee down to the engine room. Three lanterns lit the room. The noise would take some getting used to, but he'd done it before. He hung his jacket on a peg and took a sip of coffee. Not wanting to startle Ely, Sam waited at the foot of the stairs for the older man to notice him.

Ely finished oiling the reversing gear. He straightened up with his hand on his lower back, groaning as he did. He heaved a sigh as he looked at the cam rod gear. Maggie piped him to slow the engine. He changed gears and saw Sam. "When did ya start deliverin' coffee?"

Sam handed one of the cups to Ely and leveled his gaze at him. "Call it a peace offering. I'm going to help out down here." Sam raised his cup and took a swig.

Ely sputtered, and the hot coffee sloshed over the brim of the cup, which he slammed down on the nearby bench. "The devil ya are. This's *my* engine room. I had me an agreement with old Zeke." He shook his head. "Maggie'd never go back on his deal." He glared into Sam's eyes. "She'd never do that to me. Not her." Ely turned his back on Sam and picked up the oilcan. "Git out."

"You're right. She wouldn't." Stepping over toward the rocker shafts, Sam nodded his agreement. However, her concern for Ely's safety was an overriding fear and that took precedence over whatever agreement Zeke had made in the past.

Ely glanced sideways and sputtered, "Are ya deaf, man? I said git out!"

"Not yet—I'm just plain stubborn." Sam stared at Ely.

"Probably almost as stubborn as you are." He picked up a rag. "I got tired of piloting," he fabricated, then enlarged upon it. "And Maggie wanted to take the boat downriver herself."

"Then pester Thad. The boy's not so set in his ways."

As Maggie's voice came through the pipe for full steam ahead, Sam stood his ground. "Say what you will, I'm not leaving. You can waste your strength blustering at me or you can say, 'what the hell,' and figure if I'm dumb enough to work down here, who cares."

Eventually, Sam outmaneuvered Ely. They took turns answering the piped signals, with Sam taking his cues from Ely. Ely was good, and Sam had no intention of causing him any further indignation. But he knew his own stubborn determination would match the older man's. He remained in the engine room until the end of the day when the stern-wheeler stopped at Oregon City.

After they had completed the routine end-of-the-day tasks in the engine room, Sam grabbed his jacket from the peg and picked up the coffee cups. "See you at supper." Ely didn't answer, and Sam didn't wait for one.

Their evening mealtime was unusually quiet. Sam spoke with Maggie and Jeremiah about their day, and he included Thad. Ely ate and left without saying one word. Sam glanced from Maggie to Thad. "Mind if I give you a hand in the morning?"

Thad grinned. "Of course not. Well—" He looked at Maggie. "Long as she doesn't mind."

She nodded. "Fine with me."

Thad wiped his mouth and drank the last of his coffee. "See you in the morning."

Jeremiah got Cap's pans and scraped the few leftovers into it. He showed it to Aunt Maggie. "That's not enough. What else can I feed Cap?"

"There isn't enough of the beef log left to make us another meal. He can have that." She broke it up and added it to the pan along with the vegetables. "That should fill him up."

Jeremiah nodded. "Thanks."

He ran off to feed the dog, and she cleaned up the kitchen with Sam's help. When they finished, she refilled their cups and led the way into the parlor. "I'm not surprised you asked that. Ely was so quiet. What reason did you give for helping him?" She handed him one cup and sat down by him.

He grinned. "I said I was tired of piloting, and you wanted to take the wheel on the return trip." He grinned at her. "I didn't think you would mind a slight exaggeration."

"Of course not. But how did he take it?"

"Blustered and roared, then he was silent." He raised the cup to his mouth. "I thought he might warm up with you."

"I'll have to speak with him." *And hope he listens,* she thought. "What about tomorrow and the next day?"

"I'll take each day as it comes. I didn't take over, though I did move a little faster than he could a couple times. But he responded to his share of the calls."

Jeremiah came back into the cabin. "Cap's taking a long walk. I better go find him."

Sam fixed the boy with a stare. "The dog knows his way around much better than you do. He'll be back."

Jeremiah put Cap's pan away and went to the parlor stove. His hands were so cold. He held them out to the heat and frowned. "Sam, how come Cap doesn't need shoes?"

Sam glanced at Maggie. "Dog's feet don't feel the cold as easily as ours do."

Jeremiah looked at him. "Are you sure? Mine are cold, an' I have stockings and shoes on."

Maggie lowered her cup. "Dogs like to wander around, and Cap's not a pup. He'll be back. He likes to sleep at the foot of my bed. It's better than outside in the winter weather."

Sam nodded. "After you warm up, Jeremiah, you can practice writing your name."

"Would you show me how to write Cap's name? And yours and Aunt Maggie's?"

"All right." Sam gave Maggie a hopeful look. "I'll bring the reader up tomorrow. We can see how he takes to that."

Jeremiah went to the desk and got out the paper and

pencil. He gave them to Sam and squeezed in between him and his aunt. "Do Cap first."

Maggie grinned at Sam over Jeremiah's head. He was so good for the boy. "While you two work on that, I'll see how Ely's doing."

"He's not sick, is he, Aunt Maggie?"

"No, honey. He's fine. I just want to talk with him." She looked at Sam. "I won't be long—promise."

"Sure." He would have liked to be a beetle in the woodpile and eavesdrop on that conversation. "We'll be right here." He nodded at Jeremiah.

She stepped into her room and got a leather pouch from the back of the bottom drawer in the chest. After tucking the pouch in her pocket, she went down to the main deck. Ely's cabin was on the far side of Sam's. She rarely went there, but she wanted to soothe his wounded pride. A dim light shone on the deck under his door. As she knocked, she hoped he would at least talk to her. There wasn't a sound inside, but she waited. The wind was light but the air was cool.

A few minutes later, she rubbed her upper arms. "Ely, it's cold out here." She glanced down the stairwell to the engine room, but it was dark.

The door opened partway. Ely peered out, looked around and pushed the door all the way open. "Somethin' wrong?"

"Might be. May I come in?"

He stepped back and turned the light up.

As she glanced around, she realized his cabin hadn't changed much since she'd last seen it. The yellowed drawing of the side-wheeler *Caledonia* was still opposite the window. The little mirror and a chart of the Missouri River hadn't been moved either. There were only two places to sit: the bed and an old comb-back rocking chair with a frayed pillow on the seat. She sat down on the side of the bed. "Aren't you talking to me?"

He closed the door and added two pieces of wood to the stove. "What do ya have in mind?"

"Sam." She turned to face Ely.

He sat in the rocker. "If ya want to run the o' girl with him, jist say so. She's yers."

"I'm not so sure." She raised one brow. "I meant to ask you about that. You and Zeke were partners, weren't you?" He looked at her with Sam's reserve, and she wanted to shake him.

"Why'd ya think that?" Ely rocked the chair slowly.

"Zeke rarely made a decision without talking to you, and your pay hardly compares with any other engineer on the river." She smoothed a wrinkle in the bedcover. "I've let it slide, hoping to increase our profit, but it hasn't worked like I'd hoped. I don't know how or when I will be able to repay you."

"Ain't nothin' to repay. Zeke done that long time back." He laid his head back on the headrest. "He knew this old tub made ya happy an he hoped it'd make ya some money."

"It has. I can't imagine not steaming up and down the river on her. But I worry about you. If Zeke were alive, he'd hire a striker to help you out."

He stopped rocking and sat forward, his stare fixed on her. "He'd not do that to me."

She didn't think Zeke would mind her fibbing for his friend's sake. "Over two years ago we talked about it. He was worried about you working so hard." *He's getting upset,* she thought, and she changed tactics. "Besides, every other engineer has at least one assistant." She hoped appealing to his sense of status would soften him.

"Balderdash. If ya don't want me round, I'll leave. Jist tell me to git."

"Don't want you?! You stubborn old buzzard," she said, praying Zeke's endearment would settle him down, "how would I make it without you?"

He shrugged and started rocking. "Ya'd manage. Ya have a knack for it."

She grinned. "You always knew how to get around me, but this time I won't budge." She pulled the pouch from her pocket and tossed it to him. "I set aside your share. I think you should have it. It's no fortune, but it is more than a couple months' pay."

"My pay's 'nough." He threw the pouch and it landed on the bed by her hand.

She glanced at the bag and shrugged. "You better find a place to stash it. I'm tired of the responsibility. Now, back to Sam," she said, leaning forward. "He'll be helping you until he leaves, in a couple weeks. If you have any trouble with him, tell me."

He looked at the far wall. "Yer still in yer prime, Maggie girl. Ain't right fer ya to be alone. Sam's not a bad sort. I hope ya don't send him away on my account."

She grinned at him. "He owns a ranch in California and will be raising sheep. I'll see him and Jeremiah from time to time, but you know how often I take trips to visit someone."

"Nev'r. Yer as set in yer ways as an old mare."

"Thanks." She went over to him and kissed his rough cheek. "See you in the morning."

Chapter

17

The next several days passed all too quickly for Maggie. The rain continued and the temperature dropped, but at least Sam and Ely were working well together, and Ely didn't look as tired. The only problem was that she and Sam were both so tired each night, they parted when Jeremiah couldn't keep his eyes open any longer.

As she steamed against the swift current, she dodged occasional logs, tree branches and even a fence post with two rails still attached. It was noontime when she reached Independence. She held out her hand to Jeremiah. "Come on, honey. We have to put the gangplank out, and you can visit with Sam."

"Okay." He got to his feet and looked out the window. "We gonna be here long?"

She glanced at him. "I'm not sure. Maybe a half an hour. Why?"

He moved to the door. "The only time I get to see Cap or Sam or Ely or Thad's when you stop."

She went down the ladder first and watched him. "It isn't much fun, is it?"

"Mm, it's okay sometimes."

She waited while he made a trip to the water closet, then walked down to the main deck with him. "Jeremiah, you can go see Sam. I'll be busy for a while." He ran off. She swung the gangplank into place and Cap trotted to the bank. She noticed a woman waving at her and saw her friend, Kathleen Barron. "Come aboard." Five passengers got off, and Kathleen made her way up on deck. Wisps of her unruly carrot-red hair slipped free of her bonnet, and Maggie grinned.

"It's been too long, Maggie Foster. I came for the cargo myself for it's the only way I'd have a chance to see you."

Taking her arm, Maggie hurried under the upper deck. "Kathleen Rafferty Barron, it's good to see you, too. This trip I promised myself I would see you." She glanced at the wagon. "Where's little Eagon?"

"He's not so little." Kathleen lowered her voice and added, "Come next spring, he won't be the baby of the family. That's one reason I left him at home with Hattie."

"Oh, Kathleen, I'm so happy for you." Maggie laughed. "I should've known by the peaches in your cheeks. You are pleased about it, aren't you?"

"Yes, but this'd better be the last one. I'm getting too old to be a brood mare."

Maggie grinned and shook her head. "Not you, but I think I can understand how you feel." After a few weeks with Jeremiah, she didn't envy her friend her five children. Even two sounded like a handful to her. "How's Mr. Barron?"

"He hasn't changed. I sometimes wonder how many boardinghouses it will take to satisfy him." She smiled and shrugged.

"I'm glad you're happy." Maggie looked around, hoping Sam had come up on deck for some fresh air, but she didn't see him. "While your cargo's being unloaded, I'd like you to meet someone."

Kathleen's gaze narrowed. "I do see a sparkle in your eyes I've never seen before." She grinned. "Where is he?"

"He?" Maggie struggled to keep a straight face. Were her feelings for Sam so plain for everyone to see? "Sam's been helping Ely." She glanced around again. "While you tell the roustabouts where to load your goods, I'll go get both of my visitors."

Kathleen raised one auburn brow and nodded.

Maggie grinned and left for the engine room. "Jeremiah," she said, holding out her hand. "Sam, I want you to meet a friend of mine. We won't be leaving for a little bit."

"Of course." Sam rinsed off his hands, dried them on a

clean rag and shrugged into his coat. "Shall we?" He grabbed Jeremiah's jacket and followed Maggie and the child on deck. "Jeremiah, you'd better put this on."

Maggie led them over to Kathleen and introduced them. Kathleen was petite, shapely, and pretty to boot. Maggie watched Sam. Kathleen was so engaging and spirited, most men were instantly charmed by her, and Maggie was curious to see if he would be.

"Mrs. Barron, it's my pleasure." Her coffee eyes held a glint of amusement, and he wondered what he'd said that she found entertaining.

"Mine, also, Mr. Adams." Kathleen gazed at him a moment, then smiled at Jeremiah. "Hello, Jeremiah. Looks like you've made a friend."

"Uh-huh." Jeremiah shook hands with her. "He's Cap, Aunt Maggie's dog." She was pretty. "Do you have a boy?"

"We have two boys and three girls. Annie's the oldest. She's thirteen," Kathleen said, smiling at him. "But they're all in school, except for Eagon, and he's only two."

Maggie put her hand on Jeremiah's shoulder and spoke to Kathleen. "She couldn't be that old. Has it been *that* long?"

Kathleen nodded. "She's taller than me." She laughed and added, "That isn't too surprising, is it?"

A roustabout came up to them and waited for Kathleen to notice him. "Ma'am, your wagon's loaded."

"Thank you. I'll be right there." Kathleen looked at Maggie. "Will you stop by for a *real* visit one of these days?" Kathleen glanced at Sam. "Both of you?"

Maggie glanced at Sam, who she guessed wouldn't object to the idea. "I really will try."

Sam put his arm around Maggie's waist. "I hope we'll see you and your husband soon."

Kathleen smiled. "I'm looking forward to it." She took Maggie's hand. "See you soon."

Maggie walked her to her wagon. "Kiss the children for me and take care of yourself."

"I will." Kathleen glanced back at Sam. "I like Mr. Adams, and I'm that glad he makes you happy." She gave Maggie a quick hug and climbed to the wagon seat.

Maggie waved and returned to the steamboat. Jeremiah was playing with Cap, but Sam was waiting for her. "Want a cup of coffee?"

"Sounds good." He walked up the stairs with her. "Mrs. Barron is certainly a cheerful woman. It wouldn't be difficult to plan a stopover here, wouldn't it?"

"No," she said, surprised he was looking forward to meeting Mr. Barron. Did Sam really plan on staying that long? "You'd probably get along very well with her husband, too. He's a wonderful businessman, well respected throughout the valley." She entered her cabin, went straight to the kitchen and set the coffee pot over the fire.

"Maggie, you didn't introduce me to her to test me, did you?" he asked, a step behind her.

She shook her head. "I wanted her to meet you." She glanced over her shoulder at him. "Honestly? I was curious to see if you reacted the way most men do around her. She's a lovely woman."

He turned her around. "You've nothing to worry about." He held her close. "She is attractive. So is Mrs. Dobbs. I like your friends." He leaned back and tipped her chin up for a lingering kiss. "But neither of them are as beautiful as you." He kissed her once more. "Want me to change my mind?"

"Unh-unh." She held him tight. "You're a nice man, Sam." His heart thundered beneath her cheek, and her pulse leapt in response. She wanted him, and she didn't need to feel beautiful to know he cared for her.

He slid his hand down her back and pressed her against him as he covered her mouth with his. She opened to him, and he wanted to bury himself in her, show her how much he cared for her. He gently sucked on her lower lip and kissed her temple. "How soon do we have to leave?"

"Any minute." She wondered what it would be like to make love to him in the daylight, and she smiled. "I'd better find Jeremiah." She nuzzled his chest. "Think we'll be able to stay awake long enough to make love tonight?"

"Count on it." He swatted her bottom. "Don't run us aground."

She gave his backside a nudge and stepped back. She

filled two cups with coffee and handed him one. "See you later." She gave him a quick kiss and walked to the door.

"Jeremiah can visit with me and Ely. The change will be good for both of you."

"Thank you." She paused on the walkway. "And would you pull in the gangplank for me?"

"Aye, Capt'n."

Her grin threatened to split her face, and her steps to the pilothouse were light. She blew the whistle and piped Ely to reverse the engine. Waving to Kathleen, Maggie backed the stern-wheeler away from the bank and continued on upriver. The rain came pouring down just south of Buena Vista and persisted until they reached Albany. The roustabouts earned her gratitude and sympathy as they toted the barrels and crates in the heavy rain across the muddy ground.

She stayed in port until she and her crew had eaten dinner and started back home. A mile or so beyond Doak's Ferry, Maggie spotted dark smoke rising above the stand of trees along the riverbank. Her reaction was second nature; she blew the distress signal, piped Ely to stop the engines and pulled the stern-wheeler over to the riverbank near where she had spotted the smoke. The instant her feet touched the deck, she ran. Ely, Thad and Sam were waiting for her on the main deck.

"I want to see what's burning. Jeremiah, stay with Ely and keep Cap here with you. Sam, will—" Before she could ask, he was in motion.

He swung the gangplank into place and followed her down. "Do you know who lives here?"

"I'm not sure." She paused at a patch of dried berry vines, hiked her skirt up exposing her trousers and ran through the brambles.

She's one of a kind, he thought, but there wasn't time to dwell on that. Beyond the trees was a cabin nearly burned to the ground, and a family of three was trying to extinguish the fire in the barn. Sam ran over to the man. "Did you get the livestock out?"

"Yeah." The man grabbed the bucket of water his wife

passed to him and hurled the contents on the flames.
"Weren't so lucky with the house."

Sam took the next bucket passed to him by the daughter
and worked alongside the man. Soon, six men who had been
traveling on the steamboat joined them with more pails and
kegs to haul water.

The air was thick with smoke from the smoldering cabin
and the barn as Maggie helped the woman and young girl
fill the buckets with water from their stream. It felt like
hours before the last flames were doused and the smoke
turned light gray. The girl ran to her mother and held onto
her.

Maggie pulled a hanky from her pocket, wet it and wiped
their faces with the cool cloth. "What can I do for you?"

Clutching the girl to her bosom, the woman stared at the
barn, while tears streamed down her face. At one point she
opened her mouth but no sound came out.

Maggie set off to see what she could do. Not far from the
cabin she found a mound of things that must've been
rescued in haste. A few timbers had survived but most were
still smoldering. Holding her skirt up around her thighs, she
picked her way through the rubble searching for anything
that might have survived. A ladle, a pan, a tea cup—even a
button would have been a welcome sight.

Two thirds of the barn had been saved. While Sam helped
pull the charred debris a safe distance away, the rain started
coming down. He went over to the landowner. "Were you
able to save any of your tools? I think we can board up that
one opening so your family will be dry."

Instead of answering Sam the man held out his hand.
"Harold Overmeyer."

"Sam Adams.""

Mr. Overmeyer stared at the barn. "It's a start. I'd
appreciate a hand patching that wall on the storeroom. That
was Martha's idea, bless her."

Sam foraged around and found enough pieces of wood to
cover the opening. He set to work with one of the passengers from the stern-wheeler. Others helped him move what
was left of the family's possessions into the storeroom, then

he watched as Maggie led Mrs. Overmeyer across the yard.

Maggie entered what remained of the barn with the woman and girl. "Here, sit down on this bench." She found a blanket and wrapped it around the woman and her daughter. Among the ashes, she had discovered a small book of poems. The edges were singed, but the pages had survived. She pulled the volume from her pocket and placed it in the woman's hands. "Maybe this will help."

The woman sobbed and looked up at Maggie. "Bless you."

Maggie and Sam followed the passengers on their return to the steamboat. The rain smelled clean and sweet. It cleared the smoke from the air and hopefully from their clothes. As they rushed through the stand of alders, she glanced at him and felt very grateful for his support and quick thinking. His face was smudged. The rain only made the sooty coating worse, but his beautiful eyes were as clear and as caring as a caress. "You didn't get burned, did you?"

"Fortunately no one did." He looked back at the lone structure and shook his head. "At least the Overmeyers have a dry place to stay until he can rebuild." He took her arm when they came to a fallen tree.

"Overmeyer," she repeated softly, stepping over the tree trunk. "She was so distraught, I didn't even ask her name. She barely said one word, and her daughter wasn't any better."

They boarded the steamboat, and the six men who had helped fight the fire hurried up to the saloon. Sam stopped to speak with Thad, and Maggie looked for Jeremiah in the engine room . It was empty, as were Ely's and Sam's cabins. When she realized Cap was sitting as if on guard at the foot of the stairway, she dashed up to her cabin.

Ely was sitting in the big chair holding Jeremiah in his arms. The boy was pale and trembling. She dropped to her knees at the side chair and softly asked, "What happened?" She felt his brow and was relieved to find it a little cool.

Ely glanced at Jeremiah. "Smell of smoke was purty strong, and he got all skeered, poor li'l mite."

She skimmed the back of her fingers down his cheek.

"Jeremiah, will you sit with me a while?" He flinched, buried his face in Ely's chest and screamed. She smelled her hands and her sleeve. "Ely, I'd better change clothes. Be right back."

She stepped into her bedroom and closed the door. Everything had happened so quickly that her concern and her thoughts had been on anyone who might have been in danger from the fire. It hadn't occurred to her that the smoke would be such a painful reminder for Jeremiah or would frighten him so.

She tossed her coat, dress and trousers in a heap by her boots. They'd have to be washed immediately and the boots polished to rid them of the lingering smoky odor. She scrubbed her face, hands and arms. As she buttoned the fresh dress, she caught a glimpse of herself in the mirror.

Her hair was a mess. She brushed it out, whiffed the ends and tied it back with a ribbon. Suddenly remembering her special honeysuckle toilet water, she dashed some on her neck and wrists.

She started a fresh pot of coffee and returned to the parlor. "Ely, I'll take him. Would you please tell Sam I need to talk with him?"

Ely nodded and loosened the boy's hold on him.

She placed a hand under each of Jeremiah's arms and lifted him off Ely's lap. "Come on, honey, we'll rock for a bit." Nothing had prepared her for his struggling against her as if she were going to beat him. She clamped her teeth together and pulled him to her before he mistakenly struck Ely.

He pushed and kicked, but she wouldn't let him go. "No, no, no . . . I want my mama. I want —"

"Jeremiah, everything's okay." She sat in her rocker and held him in her arms, hoping the gentle motion would calm him. After Ely left, Jeremiah settled on her lap and silently wept. A few minutes later, she heard Sam's footsteps on the deck.

He entered her cabin quietly. After what Ely had told him, the memory of the hotel fire returned twofold. "How's he doing?" She shook her head and shrugged one shoulder.

Sam went down on one knee and laid his hand on the boy's back. "Jeremiah, we're safe. Everyone is. No one was hurt."

Jeremiah peered at him. His face was all black and he was stinky like the men—"No, go 'way." He squirmed to get Sam's hand off his back. "Where's Mama? I want my mama 'n' papa—"

Sam cringed at the agony in the boy's voice. "Jeremiah, this fire wasn't like the one in San Francisco. We talked about what happened there. Do you remember? Your—" He gazed at Maggie. She wasn't any more prepared for this than he was. "Son, your mama and papa are in heaven."

Jeremiah shook his head against his aunt's chest. "No, no she isn't. She wouldn't leave me. She wouldn't!" He peeked at Sam. "Maybe she's lost . . . 'n' she can't find me."

Sam rubbed the boy's back. "She isn't lost. She's safe and happy because she knows you are too." The boy squirmed and held on to Maggie. Sam lowered his hand.

Maggie mouthed, Thank you, before she spoke aloud. "Would you pilot the boat for me?"

He nodded. "And I'll speak to Ely and Thad." When he looked up, he noticed water spewing out of the coffee pot spout. "I'll move the pot to the side."

"I made a full pot—enough for us and the men in the saloon. Would you mind—"

He kissed her cheek. "Rest easy. We'll be fine."

"You'll have to stop at Matheny's, Fairfield and the Mission landing."

He set her cup of coffee on the table by her chair. "Yes, ma'am." As he poured the rest of the coffee, his attention repeatedly veered to Maggie. She handled emergencies well, but he wondered if she was burying her feelings. She was almost too strong, too good to be true. She appeared to be as content rocking Jeremiah as she was at the wheel of her steamboat. The fact that she looked prettier each time he saw her only added to his frustration with his inevitable departure.

After Sam had spoken to everyone, he piloted the steamboat to their next stop, Matheny's Landing. It was late in the day, and there were no waiting passengers. Half an hour later he stopped at Fairfield. The trip to Mission Landing took nearly an hour. After the last two passengers disembarked, he stopped by Maggie's cabin.

He eased the door open, and she gave him a warm smile. "Is he asleep?" In her relaxed state, she looked as cuddly and soft as a kitten. But she was no kitten; she was a mountain lion—and he liked big cats.

"Resting, I think. " With her arm around Jeremiah supporting him, she sat forward and arched her back.

Jeremiah mumbled, glancing around, then sat up. "Where's Cap? Thad said—"

"He's down on deck," Sam interrupted, hoping to allay the boy's fear before it could take hold. He stepped out on deck, called the dog and watched Jeremiah's smile when Cap trotted straight over to him.

Jeremiah slid off his aunt's lap and knelt down to hug Cap. He was wet, but Jeremiah snuggled with him.

Maggie got a couple of towels and handed one to him. "I'll help you dry him off before you get wet, too."

"The last two passengers left the boat," Sam said. "No others boarded and all the cargo's been unloaded. It's difficult to believe, but we're finally alone." When she stood up, he stepped over to her side and put his arm around her shoulders. "How're you doing?"

She gazed into his eyes. "Better. You?" She slipped her arm around his waist, rested her head on his chest and let the steady beat of his heart wash through her.

"Me too." He embraced her and closed his eyes. He had never felt more at home than when he did now holding her.

When he got done drying Cap, Jeremiah stood up and carried the towels over to his aunt. "Whatcha want me to do with these?"

She rubbed her hand on Sam's back as she turned to Jeremiah. "I'll take them." She studied his face and combed his hair away from his face. "Are you feeling better?"

He nodded. "The smoke was scary." He bit his lips. He wanted his mama so bad.

Tears filled his eyes. She picked him up in a fierce hug.

"Oh, sweetie, it's okay to cry and to miss your mama and papa." She stared over his head at Sam. How were they, two people headed in different directions, going to care for this child? she wondered.

Sam encircled Maggie and Jeremiah in his arms. He couldn't shield the boy from every danger or fear but the desire to do so was nearly overwhelming. He kissed Maggie's forehead. "It's getting late."

She looked out the window. "It's almost dark. We can spend the night just downriver on the narrow side of the small island ahead."

After Sam left, Maggie hung the towels over the back of her kitchen chair and smiled at Jeremiah. "You know, I can't remember the last time I got to sit in the saloon while we went upriver. Want to go in there with me?" It was true, and she hoped it might cheer him up a bit.

He looked at Cap. "Can he go with us?"

"Mm-hm. Him too." She carried Jeremiah and Cap followed. Someone had lighted four of the lamps, but it was cool in the saloon. She put the boy down. "Would you help me add wood to the stoves?"

"Yeah." No one ever let him do that before. He got two pieces of wood from the pile and took them to her.

She opened the door on the front of the stove. "Does the smell of the woodsmoke scare you?"

"Unh-unh." He looked into the stove and held out one of the pieces of wood. "But I don't wanna get burned."

"I'll put them in for you." As she poked the wood into the fire, she talked to him. "Fire isn't always bad. It cooks our food and keeps us warm."

"But big fires are bad."

She closed the iron door and put her arm around him. "Sometimes accidents happen. Today a family lost their cabin, but they weren't hurt."

He chewed on his tongue a minute. "You sure?"

"Very. If you smell smoke, or if you see any, I want you to tell me or Sam. Okay?"

"I will."

She hugged him, then pressed a kiss to his forehead,

much the way Sam had done to her. "Let's look out the window."

After Jeremiah fell asleep on the sofa, Maggie and Sam went for a stroll along the upper deck. Clouds passed over the moon from time to time, lighting the bare limbs of the alder trees. She stopped outside the cabin and faced him. "Isn't the quiet wonderful?"

"So's the privacy." Without reaching for her, he bent his head down and covered her mouth with his. She parted her lips and flattened her body against his. As he deepened the kiss, he held their hands in the folds of her cloak. The effect was maddening, exciting. He nibbled her lips and rained kisses down her neck.

She stiffened her arms, giving her leverage as she arched her back. Her cloak rubbed against his jacket, making a raspy sound. Her pulse surged, and she trembled. She wanted to open his coat, feel his chest, hold him closer. When she tried to slip her hands from his loose grip, he laced his fingers with hers, and she could have sworn she felt him smile. She had never been so delightfully frustrated. She stood on tiptoe, longing for him, and she groaned. "Sam . . ."

He nuzzled her neck and trapped one of her legs between his. "Yes?"

"Please . . ."

"Right here on deck?" He had just about reached his limit too, but that was a good part of the pleasure.

"Ugh— I've heard there's a fine line between someone with their wits and madness. I don't want to find out."

He chuckled. "Neither do I." He released her hands and framed her sweet face. "Let's go inside." His heart pumped furiously. He loved the way she melted into him.

Thunder boomed in the distance, and she rested her cheek on his chest. Her pulse raced, and she panted as the dizzying need grew even stronger. Tussling with her riotous emotions, she finally stepped back and opened the cabin door. Jeremiah was still asleep.

Holding her hand, Sam led the way into her bedroom. "Now, it's our turn."

Her cloak dropped to the floor along with his coat. They kicked their shoes off, and she rid him of his shirt. She wanted to skim her fingers through the wavy hair on his chest, press her hips to his and feel the muscles on his back move beneath her fingers. Her hands moved with an urgency she wouldn't deny. She stepped out of her dress. His pants landed nearby.

He loosened the ribbon holding her petticoats in place and then he began untying the bows on her chemise, one by one, until he had uncovered her full breasts. She swayed and nearly tumbled him onto her bed, but he kept his balance with his hands planted on her waist. He lifted her off the floor and kissed his way down to the tender skin between her breasts. He looked into her smoldering eyes. "One of these days I'll have to teach you the pleasure of patience."

"Not now, " she said. "You've stretched mine to the limit this evening." She wrapped her legs around his waist. He gasped.

"No, not now." He lowered her to the bed and feasted on her beautiful body. Her arms had strength hidden underneath the smooth skin, as did her shapely legs. He kissed her belly and grazed her breasts with the back of his hands. She thrashed and tugged at his shoulders.

Slowly, ever so slowly, his mouth made a fiery trail up to hers. Desire coursed through her, demanding release. At last, his hips pressed her to the mattress, and that wondrous swell of sensation flooded through her. Wrapping her arms around his neck, she rolled her hips and sank down until he filled her.

He felt as if she had drawn him into her, but he set their pace, burying himself in her, withdrawing slowly and lingered at her threshold before he repeated the sinuous bliss. Over and over again, he filled her until he could no longer delay the instinctive fulfillment of their passion.

She clung to him, amazed anew by her hunger for him, some part of her mind wondering if they could remain joined like this forever.

Chapter

18

Maggie didn't want to wake up and leave the shelter of Sam's warmth, but her eyes drifted open against her wishes. The sun came up later each morning in winter, and it wasn't her habit to laze about in bed. She rolled over to her back and reached out to embrace him, only to discover she was alone in her bed. Wide-awake then, she remembered he had left during the night.

She hugged his pillow to her chest and smiled. Oh, just thinking about him brought back the delicious feelings. It began in her belly and spread outward in waves. She moaned softly and heard the arousing sound as if it had not been her own. *We're caught in a swift current,* she thought, and prayed they weren't going in different directions.

Eventually the practical, sound part of her mind began thinking about her day. She wanted to collect a few supplies for the Overmeyers, and she needed to see about cargo going upriver. Reluctantly, she left her bed and pulled the covers up. After she let Cap outside, she completed her morning ablutions.

She started a pot of coffee and a pan of oatmeal. Soon Jeremiah came in with Sam right behind him, smiling and more handsome than a man had a right to be. "Good morning." Her pulse quickened, and she blurted out, "Breakfast'll be ready in a minute."

"Good," Sam said, stepping to her side. A lovely woman's smile could inspire lecherous thoughts in any man. However, Maggie's beauty aroused desires and longings that went beyond physical pleasure, and he was beginning to

197

think it would take him a lifetime to explore each. "I seemed to have worked up a healthy appetite." He tipped her chin up and kissed her.

"Me too." Jeremiah glanced up. Sam was kissing Aunt Maggie. Jeremiah hugged Cap and whispered, "She must like him a whole lot. She looks happier than mama when papa said her supper was specially good."

She grinned at Sam. "Then I'd better put on some bacon or ham, too." Knowing Jeremiah couldn't see Sam, she reached out and caressed his backside before she turned to finish cooking their meal.

Before long, she had put breakfast on the table, and both Ely and Thad had arrived. They talked about the steamboat maintenance and possible cargo, and she told them she would be in town for a couple of hours. "We can leave after the Rival arrives below the falls."

Cap cried. Jeremiah went over and petted him. "I'll get your food right now." He set Cap's pan on the seat of his chair and scraped food from the dishes into it.

Maggie washed each dish as he finished with it. He took Cap outside to feed him, and she glanced at Sam as she dried her hands. "Want to go along with me?"

He nodded. "I'll rent a buggy and come back for you."

She draped the hand towel over the back of her chair. "You don't need to go to the expense."

"It isn't much, and it's raining off and on." He went into the parlor and grabbed his coat. "I won't be long."

She was a step behind him and put her hand on his arm. "We'll go together. No need to be making an extra trip."

Practical as always, he thought, and smiled. "Get your cloak."

She bundled up against the elements and put one of her scarves around Jeremiah's neck. They left the steamboat and hurried across the muddy ground with her in the lead. She dashed into the Moss livery, and the strong odor of manure made her blink. She pushed her hood back and tipped Jeremiah's hat so the rain ran off behind him. The owner came through a side door. "Sam, that's Mr. Moss."

Sam met the man near the horse stalls. "Mr. Moss, we

need a buggy with curtains and a large boot." A little while later they rode out of the livery in a roomy old coach. Sam handled the reins and looked at Maggie. "Where do you want to stop first?"

"Just down the street at the steamboat office." He pulled up out front and she ran inside. After she settled her business, she told everyone in the office about the Overmeyers' fire and explained their loss. In times of trouble, people gave one another a hand, and she felt certain that as word spread, the Overmeyers would receive enough goods to get them through the winter.

She returned to the coach, and they continued with their rounds. They stopped at Ainsworth and Dierdorff's, Dannenbaum and Ackerman's, Kirkland's Mercantile, Charman, Warner and Company and, last of all, the Excelsior Market. Then they returned to the steamboat and unloaded the goods and supplies she had collected for the Overmeyers. Everyone had been generous. There were cast-off clothes, even a winter coat and cloaks, a pair of shoes for each of them, kitchenware, two bolts of yard goods, and a variety of food, including the necessities.

Sam set a keg of nails down in the cargo area and wiped his brow. "I'm amazed at the variety," he said, watching Maggie stack the yard goods on top of a crate. "It's as if you had planned all this."

She sat down on a barrel and brushed the hair from her face. "I did suggest different items to each person I spoke to, and I'm sure others will help put up another cabin."

"I'll return the buggy and be right back." He gave her a short, sweet kiss and ran to the wagon. His coat was wet and little protection against the cold rain. Everyone else appeared to take the almost daily rain in stride, but he wasn't sure if he could adjust so easily.

Maggie made the customary stops on her route south, with an additional one at the Overmeyer farm. She set the gangplank in place and asked Jeremiah to stay with Ely until they were done. She wrapped many of the dry goods in a tarp, which she slung over her shoulder.

Sam hoisted a barrel of flour to his shoulder, and they set off for the barn through the brambles. It didn't take them long to reach the clearing. The west end of the barn still looked to be sound; the other half was charred beams and framework. He went over to what had been the storeroom door and knocked.

The door opened and Maggie smiled at the girl. "Hello. Remember us? We were here the afternoon of the fire."

"Oh, yes. Mama—" The girl pushed the door open all the way.

Maggie stepped inside. "Mrs. Overmeyer, I hope you won't mind, but we collected a few things for you." She set the canvas bundle on the dirt floor. "Everyone I spoke with wanted to help you. There's more on my steamboat—we'll bring it over. Sam has a barrel of flour that Mr. Dierdorff sent."

Mr. Overmeyer came around the side of the building with an armful of logs. "Adams, isn't it? Sam Adams? Didn't expect to see you again." He dropped the logs and dusted his hands on his trousers.

"You've a good memory, Harold. Where do you want me to set this flour?"

"In there." Harold picked up two short logs and entered the room. "You folks shouldn't've gone to all this trouble." He set the logs on the dirt in one corner.

Sam followed him in and set the barrel down on the logs. "It was Maggie, Mrs. Foster, who collected everything." He glanced at her and at Mrs. Overmeyer. "Hello, ma'am."

Mrs. Overmeyer looked from the dry goods to the barrel. "Thank you both so very much."

"There's more," Sam said, meeting Maggie's gaze.

"Get your shawl, mother—you, too, sis." Harold glanced at Sam. "No need your making another trip here."

Returning to the steamboat with the Overmeyers, Sam was certain they were in for a surprise. Even he had been amazed by the number of things Maggie had collected.

When Mrs. Overmeyer saw the stack of goods, she pressed her hand over her heart and reached for her husband's arm. "Mr. Overmeyer, this must be a mistake."

Maggie shook her head. "No. This will help see you through the winter." She handed her the list of the people who had given them something and what they had sent.

Tears filled Mrs. Overmeyer's eyes, and she hugged her daughter.

Her husband patted her back. "Now, now. We have to get busy so these good people can be on their way." Harold picked up one of the crates. "We'll stack these on the bank so you can get going."

While they stacked most of the goods on the ground, Sam carried the sacks of food stuff that should be kept dry back to their room. He returned and moved the last keg ashore. "Are you sure you don't want help moving all this to your barn?"

Harold shook his head. "You folks have done too much by far. We'll be just fine." He looked to Maggie and held his hand out. "I don't know how we'll repay you, Mrs. Foster. If you *ever* need our help, we're here."

Maggie shook his hand. "These goods came from many folks in Oregon City. Your wife has their names. I just delivered everything for them." She glanced at Sam and back to Mr. Overmeyer. "I do need to get my passengers upriver. You take care." She took Sam's hand and dashed up the gangplank.

The following days they steamed up and down the Willamette River. Maggie knew if she worried about when Sam would have to leave for California, she wouldn't enjoy the time they did have together. She carried enough cargo to keep busy and spent the evenings with Sam and Jeremiah. Each time she watched Jeremiah write one of their names, she was as proud as any mother.

She woke up Sunday morning to sun spilling into her room. After she let Cap outside, she stirred the fires, added wood and started the coffee. She was fastening the last button on her dress when Jeremiah opened the cabin door.

"Aunt Maggie, didja see the sunshine?!" Jeremiah hugged Cap. "Maybe we can go outside today."

Maggie came out of her room. "I sure did. You can't miss it."

Sam kissed her cheek and went into the kitchen. There were two cups on the table, and he poured the coffee. He felt as happy about the sun as Jeremiah did, and he started breakfast, since Maggie didn't.

Jeremiah looked up at her. "What're we gonna do?"

"I don't know." She went into the kitchen and peered around Sam to the skillet on the stove. "What would you like to do today? It's too nice to stay indoors."

He turned the slices of smoked ham over and glanced at her. "Didn't you say you have a cabin not too far from here?"

"About fifteen minutes south of town." She rested her cheek on his arm. "It's probably occupied with critters, but we can go down there if you'd like."

He broke an egg in a second skillet. "Shall I rent a buggy? Or do you ride horseback?"

"I haven't ridden in years, but we'll take the boat. It's on the west bank." She helped him finish cooking and called Ely up for breakfast. As she finished eating, she realized they sounded like children being let out to play.

Jeremiah set Cap's pan on his chair and started scraping the dishes.

Ely handed the boy his plate. "Mebbe we kin do some fishin'."

"Oh, can we, Aunt Maggie? Sam said you used to fish. That true?"

She laughed. "Mm-hm. I used to go fishing with him."

"Didja stick a worm on the hook?"

She grinned at Sam. "Sure did. And I dug them up, too." She scraped what was left in the pans into the dog's pan. "That should fill him up."

Sam stood up. "Ely, I'll take over for Thad—fill the firebox and watch the boiler."

Ely glanced at him. "S'pose ye've been a fireman, too."

Sam shrugged. "I did spend my summers on riverboats."

"Figures." Ely made his way around the table to the kitchen door. "I'll be in the engine room."

Maggie glanced at Sam. "We can leave as soon as we've built up a head of steam."

Jeremiah ran past Ely as he darted into the kitchen. "Cap's done eating. I told him to hurry 'n' poop real fast."

Ely laughed out loud.

Fighting the urge to laugh, Maggie clamped her jaw shut and put the dog's pan in the corner. She didn't want to hurt Jeremiah's feelings, and Sam wasn't much help. He was chuckling.

As Jeremiah looked at everybody, he frowned. "What's so funny?"

Sam hunkered down by Jeremiah and put his hand on the boy's shoulder. "It was funny because it is hard to make a person do that in a hurry, and Cap probably didn't know what you said." Sam ruffled the boy's hair. "Don't worry. We won't leave without him. You can help me on the way to Maggie's cabin."

"Oh, gee! Thanks, Sam." Jeremiah grinned and ran out to the walkway to look for Cap.

A short while later, Maggie turned the stern-wheeler up river and across the current. In less than thirty minutes, she blew her whistle—for Jeremiah's sake—and eased her steamboat up to the old landing. She met Sam, Jeremiah and Ely on the main deck and stared at her cabin. "This is it."

It was in better shape than she'd expected, which wasn't saying much. The land was as pretty as always, but then it needed no tending—if you didn't care about the wild blackberry vines that grew uncontrollably.

Jeremiah looked around and asked Ely, "Aren't we going to get off the boat?"

Ely nodded as he watched Maggie. "In a minute, mate."

Sam stepped up to her side and put his arm around her shoulders. "This is a beautiful spot. The cabin appears solid. From what you said, I expected a dilapidated shack."

She chuckled. "It was well built. But the dampness is hard on buildings that aren't maintained." She helped him set the gangplank. As usual, Cap was the first one down. She smiled at Ely and Jeremiah. "Come on. What are you waiting for?"

Jeremiah ran past his aunt and down the gangplank after Cap. The grass was almost as high as his knees, and Cap looked short, like he had little legs.

"Jeremiah," Maggie called, "there're probably a lot of mole holes hidden in the grass." She glanced up at Sam. "They are permanent tenants."

Sam stepped onto the riverbank and surveyed the area. The land was fairly level, with alder and willow trees. There was a small narrow island, about the length of Maggie's steamboat, away from the bank. If her husband had tilled the ground, all traces had been covered by the dense foliage and thick grass. Sam took her hand and headed for the log cabin.

"The shutters are still in place." She tried the door, but it barely gave.

"Let me try." He put his shoulder against the plank door and applied his strength. The third time he shoved, the door gave way, and he pushed it wide open. Dust floated above the rough wooden floor in the shaft of light. He stepped inside and motioned her forward.

As she entered, she covered her mouth and nose. The floor felt sturdy. She went over to the window nearest the door and laid her hand on the glass. It had been a dear extravagance, but Zeke had insisted she have two windows to start with, and he had put in a third in their second year. All three windows opened inward on hinges, like little doors. She unlatched the window, opened it and did the same to the solid wood shutters. The fresh air smelled wonderful. "It's in better shape than I expected." She glanced at the doorway and saw Ely watching her. "A lot of soap and water, and this place wouldn't be too bad."

Jeremiah and Cap ran inside, and the dust clouded the air. "Whew, it sure is dirty in here," Jeremiah said.

Ely shook his head. "Weren't so bad till ya stirred it up." He walked around behind the stone fireplace and came back holding three old fishing poles. "They were still there!"

"Looky!" Jeremiah ran over and stared at the poles. They were bigger than Ely. "Can we use 'em?"

"That's what they're for." Ely eyed Maggie. "Right?"

"Certainly. I'll find a shovel. There must be one around here somewhere." She grinned at Sam.

He motioned to the cupboard below the dry sink. "Mind if I look for an old tin or something to keep the worms in?"

"No. I moved our . . . my things aboard the steamboat years ago."

Jeremiah and Ely went outside, while she stared at the one-room cabin. The old bedstead was at one end, the dry sink and cupboards at the other, with the fireplace in between, opposite the door. It really wasn't a bad place. Without looking, she felt Sam's nearness as surely as if he were holding her hand. *How would it be living here with him?* she wondered.

He found two chipped bowls in the back corner of the cupboard. When he turned around, she was staring at him with the most delightfully soft, suggestive smile. He glanced at the open door and back at her. "They might wonder . . ."

Slowly, he came into focus. "About what? Oh, you did find something. I'd better see about that spade." She went to the storage shed, found a shovel and met Sam in front.

As they walked toward the river, he gave her an appraising look. "Want to make a wager?"

"On the worms or the fish?"

"Why not both?"

A grin hovered at the corners of his lovely mouth. She wasn't sure what he was up to, but he was in such a playful mood, she had to go along with him—if only to satisfy her curiosity, she convinced herself. "We'll need prizes. Hm—I haven't anything to offer. You've already had—a trip to Corvallis? Breakfast in bed?"

He nodded. "Breakfast in bed for the one who digs up the longest worm. That's suitable. Now for the fish." He gazed into her eyes. If he did happen to lose, he could just manage it. However, if he won, it could prove to be an opportunity for both of them. "One week. If you catch the biggest fish, I won't leave as I planned, at the end of the week. I'll stay for Thanksgiving." The heat shimmering in her eyes had a predictable effect on him. When she parted her lips, he was tempted to lead her into the woods and make love to her.

She forced herself to take a deep breath. It sounded too good. "And if you win?"

"You'll go back to the ranch and stay with me for a week," he said, supporting her elbow as they stepped over a log. She trembled, and he tightened his grip.

His wager had turned serious, at least in her mind. It was a devil of a temptation, and she didn't think she had the willpower to treat it lightly. But she must try. "You aren't serious. I can't leave and certainly not for that long." She thought a moment. "The river's high. If you win, I'll take you down to Springfield or as far south as we can go."

Staring into her eyes, he shook his head. "One week. Ely and Thad shouldn't mind a rest, and I'll pay their wages." He was making it difficult for her, but damn it all, he wanted her to see his ranch. He also needed to know if she could be happy living there. The Sacramento River was less than a mile away, but she wouldn't be able to see it, and he didn't know how important that might be to her.

"Why?" When they were children, their bets had been paid with cookies or tea cakes. She was no gambler, especially not with so much at stake. Had he become too important to her? More important than her obligations? Her steamboat? Herself?

"Why? Because I want you to see my ranch. And I have the feeling this is the only way I'll get you to visit." He watched her struggling. He understood her pride, her stubbornness. He hoped it wouldn't douse the sparkle in her eyes, wouldn't dent her spirit. "Anyway, you probably know the best places to fish." He grazed her arm and clasped her hand. "Come on, before Jeremiah starts digging with his hands."

As she walked with him, her mind raced. It seemed so ridiculous to think so much about the consequences of a fishing match. She used to win most of the treats. And if she won, he wouldn't leave at the end of the week. Cap ran around them with Jeremiah close behind. "All right. You're on—and we'll eat my winning fish for supper." She grinned, hoping to bolster her own confidence as well as reassure him that she wasn't overly concerned about the outcome.

Jeremiah tugged Sam's sleeve. "Come on. Ely an' me are waiting." He ran over to his aunt's side and reached for the shovel. "I'll take it to Ely."

She moved it out of his reach. "No, Jeremiah. You — Sam will help you." As she watched Sam, she prayed luck would be with her because she didn't know of any special places to drop her line. He started running and pulled her along.

He stopped several feet from the bank. "I smell worms."

She burst out laughing and handed him the shovel. "Good luck." It slipped out, but she realized that if he won this, the second contest might not be as difficult for him to lose.

He set the cracked bowls down and dug out three large mounds of earth. Cap watched him for a moment, then started his own hole with great enthusiasm. Sam smiled at Jeremiah. "I think he's digging your worms, Jeremiah." He handed the shovel back to Maggie. "Good luck to you, too."

Jeremiah got down on his knees by Cap and stuck his hand in the dirt. "How do I find 'em?"

She grinned. "Feel the dirt. They're in there." She picked up one of the bowls and walked several feet away. She dug a good-sized hole and sifted through it, tossing each worm she found into the bowl. When she finished, she went over to Sam and held up her best worm.

He held up his. "Jeremiah, you be the judge. Which one is the longest?"

Jeremiah went over and studied at each of them. "Yours, Sam."

She smiled and dropped hers into the bowl. "Congratulations. You'll have breakfast in bed any morning you choose." She scooped up some dirt and spread it over the worms to keep them content.

"Gee, can I help, Aunt Maggie? I can take him his coffee."

She covered her smile. "We'll see."

Ely rolled his eyes and shook his head. "I hope the fishes are waitin' for ya."

Maggie smiled at Sam. "Guess we'd better get started."

Ely handed one of the fishing poles to Sam, another to Maggie, and the last one to Jeremiah. "Since they're havin' a contest, I'll show ya where the best place is to fish."

"Okay." Jeremiah walked at Ely's side. "Do you know where the biggest fishes hide?"

"Mebbe."

Maggie hesitated, curious to see which direction Sam would go, but he seemed to be wondering the same about her. She glanced to the right. "I'll take the south point over there," she said, motioning to a minuscule point of land.

He raised his fishing pole in a salute, and she smiled. "Good luck." She would win in either case, although he didn't believe she realized it yet. He walked along the riverbank until he came to a likely spot and baited the old hook.

She recalled a comment about the best place to fish her husband had made years earlier and wound her way through the thick brambles and brushes to a pool she had almost forgotten. She poked a fat worm on the hook and dropped it into the water. If she leaned forward, she could see Jeremiah. He sat straddling a piece of driftwood with Ely right behind him. She had never seen Ely so content, and Jeremiah fairly shone in the glow of the elder man's attention.

Something pulled at the pole, and Jeremiah jerked it back. "Ely, help me. Something's trying to get my pole."

Chuckling, Ely put his arms around the boy and steadied the pole. "Ya got a fish, lad. An' that humdinger's givin' ya a fit."

"I got one!" Jeremiah let go of the pole and cupped his hands around his mouth. "S-a-m, I got one! A-u-n-t Maggie, I got one! Ely said it's a humdinger!" He waved to Sam.

"Ya gotta help me, mate." Ely grinned. After Jeremiah grabbed onto the pole, Ely gave a firm pull.

The fish popped out of the water and landed nearby on the grass. "Gee, *looky!*"

Sam tossed his pole on the grass and ran over to him. "That's about the biggest fish I've ever seen." He picked up Jeremiah and whirled him around.

Maggie came over and ruffled Jeremiah's hair. "I hope Sam's catch isn't that big." She kissed his cheek.

"What am I going to do with him?" Jeremiah stared at the fish. It flopped around. "Is he hurt? Can't we take the hook outta his mouth?" Sam put him down and went over to the fish.

Ely pinned the fish down and removed the hook. "It's out. He's a fine trout, boy, a steely. Ya did real good."

Jeremiah reached out to pet it, but it flapped around again, and he jumped back. Cap started barking at it.

Ely hunkered down by the boy. "I bet Maggie'll fry 'im up for ya tonight."

"Cap!" Maggie pointed to the ground, and the dog lay down.

Jeremiah stared at her. "No! You can't *cook* him. Put him back!"

"Easy, mate, that's the way of it." Ely put his hand on the boy's shoulder.

Jeremiah pulled away. "No. Sam, put him back. You gotta. *Please*."

"All right, Jeremiah." Sam tossed the trout back in the river. "See him?" Sam wrapped his arm around the boy and pointed down into the water. "He's okay."

Jeremiah went over to Ely. "I don't wanna fish."

Ely patted the boy's back. "Ya don't have to, mate. We'll take a walk with Cap."

Maggie walked with Sam toward where he had been fishing. "Do you think he's all right?"

He kissed her forehead. "It's all part of growing up. I guess I'd forgotten what it was like to be six years old."

She stopped and faced him. "Think we should call off the contest?"

He shook his head and patted her bottom. "No, ma'am. I can already taste my fish."

She gave him a fun-loving frown. "You're mistaken. That's mine you're tasting." She ducked away from him and ran back to her pole.

Later Jeremiah and Ely brought Maggie and Sam a light dinner from the boat. The sun passed overhead and their shadows grew longer. When her back was tired and her limbs were stiff, Maggie lifted her line out of the water and laid the pole down. She had caught three fish but kept only the largest. She stretched and went over to see how Sam had done.

He glanced up. "I've had enough fishing for one day, too." He looked at his catch. "A carp and two bass." He held up the larger bass. "This's a good size where I come from. Where's yours? I saw you pull in more than one."

"I threw two back and kept the salmon." She met his gaze. She had never seen him look so disappointed. She couldn't muster even a hint of a smile to lighten his mood, and she felt no elation in besting him.

"I've heard stories about the salmon here. I'd like to see one." He slung his arm around her shoulders. "Why so serious?"

She gave him a weak imitation of a smile. "Tired, I guess." They reached her spot, and she motioned to the salmon. "It's a chinook."

"Whew, that's a good size. Beats mine six ways to Sunday." He stared at the salmon. It had to be over two feet long. He picked it up and judged its weight to be close to twenty pounds.

"It's a small one, but they're larger than bass."

He laid it down. Being careful not to touch her with his hands, he put his arms around her. "Congratulations." He bent his head and kissed her slowly, coaxing a response from her. "That's better. Winners should be happy." His consolation was that he would have another eleven or twelve days with her. Not what he'd hoped for, but he would find another way to get her to at least visit the ranch.

She held him close and rested her cheek on his chest. She felt terrible. There was no pleasure in winning the wager. She remembered how she used to dance around, how she had delighted in devouring every morsel of her prize. Now, however, she wondered what she had lost. Instinctively, and belatedly, she knew it was much more than she had believed was at stake.

"How do you like your salmon cooked?" she asked.

Chapter

19

Later that afternoon Sam built a fire in the firebox and made a quick trip up to the pilothouse. He still wasn't overjoyed with Maggie's winning the wager, but she didn't seem especially happy with her victory either—not as he had expected. He stepped into her domain. "You should come back here more often."

She shrugged. "I see it every day, or almost." She watched him gazing out the window. "Something wrong? I thought we were leaving."

"I just wanted to come up for a minute." He stared at the distant hills. "Is that snow?"

She moved to his side and looked at the Cascade Mountains. "It's beautiful, isn't it? A little more than usual for this time of year." She smiled at him. "If you had to cross those mountains to get home, you'd have to stay the winter and wait for the thaw."

He frowned. He hadn't considered the weather posing a problem. The mountains at the Oregon-California border were high. If they too were covered with snow when he reached Jacksonville, he would have to continue south by way of Eureka, California and travel down the coast, which would make the return trip many days longer. Regardless, he was committed to staying another eleven days, and he would.

Although he enclosed her in a gentle embrace, their kiss quickly became heated. He found her so warm, exciting, bold, vibrant—and she held his heart in her hands. He hugged her a moment longer. "I'd better add fuel to the fire."

She nodded. "Oh, when do you want breakfast in bed?"

"Surprise me."

As she looked at him, she pictured him in bed, sleepy eyed, reaching for her, and she smiled. "All right."

Maggie really enjoyed working with Sam. Over the next three days, she again wondered if she had allowed the steamboat to become too important to her. Before he had come back into her life, it hadn't mattered. It probably still didn't, she realized with a strong dose of practicality.

He'd said he wanted to be surprised with his breakfast. Thursday morning she woke up early and prepared his meal. She had decided it should be special, so after she poured the flapjack mix in the skillet, she added bits of spiced beef and smoked ham to other cakes. If nothing else, they'd be filling. She stirred the pot of hasty pudding. She had saved two boiled potatoes from supper the night before. She cut them up, browned them in the second skillet and added three beaten eggs.

At daybreak, she set two full plates of food on a tray with a cup of coffee and stared at the food. It was lumpy and didn't look very appetizing, but at least she had remembered to salt and pepper the food. Maybe she shouldn't have attempted to improve the recipe. Hoping it would taste better than it looked, she carried the meal down to his cabin.

Cap appeared at the door and entered ahead of her. She balanced the tray on her hip and parted the curtains. Cap stretched out on the deck by Jeremiah's cot. She stepped up to the side of Sam's bed. Sprawled on his back, he was bare as far as she could tell.

She set the tray on the floor. Hoping he wouldn't call out and wake Jeremiah, she leaned down and pressed a kiss to Sam's mouth. As if he had been waiting for her, his arms pulled her down on him as his tongue slid between her lips. She felt weak and excited. She wanted to lie beside or on top of him, but she didn't dare.

He whispered in her ear. "You taste even better than the food smells."

After a quick glance at the cot, she traced her hand down his chest to where the sheet stopped at his hips. His breathing grew harsh. She grinned and kissed his chin. "Good morning." The next moment, the covers rustled on the cot. She quickly pulled the sheet up to Sam's chest and stood up, certain Jeremiah had been watching them. When she glanced over, he seemed to be asleep, and she sighed.

Sam chuckled and raised her hand to his lips. She looked so delightfully ruffled. "Why not wake him and get it over with?"

"You're right." They'd had a few moments to themselves, more than she had expected. "Jeremiah . . . want to have breakfast with Sam?"

"Huh?" Jeremiah rubbed his eyes and stared at his aunt, then Sam. "Now? But I gotta get his coffee."

She sat on the end of Sam's bed. "I'm sorry, honey. It was so early—But it's on the tray. If you want to eat with him, I'll bring you a plate."

"Okay." Jeremiah saw Cap and grinned. "Hi, boy. Didja come to wake me up?"

Sam grinned as Maggie set the tray across his upper legs, then stared at the amount of food she had served him. "This looks wonderful, but there's enough for all of us." He grinned at Jeremiah and patted the mattress. "You can crawl in bed with me."

Jeremiah hopped out of bed and hugged Cap. "Can he sit on the foot of the bed?"

"No," Maggie said, shaking her head. "He can stay right there on the floor."

Jeremiah rubbed his cheek on the dog's head. "Sorry." He climbed onto Sam's bed and crawled up under the covers. "What're the brown things in the flapjacks?"

Maggie tried not to smile. "They are pieces of ham or spiced beef."

Sam swallowed the bite of flapjack, handed the spoon to the boy and gave him a slight nod. "It's polite to taste a small bite of the food first. The flapjacks are good. Try some." Next, he tried the eggs and winked at Maggie. "Delicious." He took her hand and drew her down to sit on the bed by him. "I've never had eggs and potatoes cooked this way. An old family recipe?"

She laughed. "Hardly. More like a hopeless attempt to make something a little different." She shrugged. "You know I'm not much of a cook. It wasn't a fair bet."

He gave her a cockeyed grin. "I'm not complaining. It's delicious. Here," he said, feeding her a bite of eggs. "I bet you haven't even sampled any of this."

Each day Sam marveled at the rain. It seemed incredible and, with the exception of last Sunday, there didn't seem to be an end to it. The ground was soggy in places, and outright boggy in others, and he wondered how the farmers managed to raise anything in the mud. The inclement weather continued all week. When Sunday came round again, none of them minded staying aboard.

Jeremiah took Cap's pan back into the kitchen. "Can I run my stern-wheeler down that little stream by the gangplank?"

"No, Jeremiah." Maggie handed Sam the last plate and dried her hands. "You'd get soaked."

"But it's there in the dirt an' my steamboat could really work. Please—"

Sam fixed him with a stern look. "Maggie said no. That's the end of it." He put the dry plate in the cupboard. "Jeremiah, why don't you give Ely and me a hand with the engine?"

"Really?" Jeremiah looked from his aunt to Sam.

She nodded. "Sam wouldn't have said it if he didn't mean it."

"Oh, gee." Jeremiah dashed to the walkway outside to look for Cap.

"Thank you for backing me up. I never would've dared ask papa anything after mama had said no." She grinned. "One of them would have skinned me alive."

He put a hand on each side of her shoulders. "He's a little boy, and he'll need a firm hand from time to time." He pulled her to him and held her close. "Try to give him time with Thad and Ely—especially Ely. He's the closest the boy will come to having a grandfather, and he'll be firm if he has to be."

She slid her arms around his waist. "They're going to miss one another." In a few days Jeremiah would have to say good-bye to Ely, and she knew it would be painful for all of them.

"Mm-hm. At least they'll have time together now." He kissed her temple. "And we do, too. But right now, I'd better get down to the engine room before Ely's convinced I'm a lazy, no-account drifter." He still refused to believe Maggie hadn't come to love the boy. And he felt sure that by the time he returned in the spring, they would be discussing more than where the boy would live.

As she nodded, her cheek brushed his chest. "He's soft as a kitten."

He chuckled. No wonder they got along so well, he thought. He tipped her chin up and kissed her. "Why don't you take some time for yourself today and call on Caroline?"

"I've got the decks to do and then the saloon." She watched him leave with Jeremiah, and she set to work.

There was a certain amount of comfort in following the same routine, day in and day out, for years. She could do the work while her mind roamed free to dream about Sam's ranch. Before the *Maggie*, she had been content living on the land. What she tried to work out in her mind was, had she been happy because the Willamette bordered the land? Or would she have been as satisfied without the river at her door?

Oh, Grannie, why did he have to come back only to leave again? I was happy with my work. Now I'm not so sure. One thing she was sure of was that she *needed* no man to put food on her table or to manage her life. Oh, but she wanted him in her life—but she would allow no man, not even Sam, to break her heart because of her *own* muddled fancies. When Zeke died, she had lost her best friend. It hurt like the devil, and she didn't want to test her ability to survive another loss again so soon.

*   *   *

Maggie stared at the ceiling and counted to fifteen. She had told Jeremiah he couldn't fill the trough for his toy boat. So what was he doing? Taking cup after cup of water into the parlor, as if she would believe he had drunk three cups of water! He returned to the water bucket the fourth time. "No more, Jeremiah! I told you you couldn't fill that trough, and I meant it!" She grabbed the cup out of his hand.

Jeremiah pinched his lips together and backed out of the room. He went over to Cap and sat down. He wished Ely hadn't gone to bed so early.

Sam studied Maggie. It wasn't like her to scold the boy and let him walk away on the verge of tears. But lately she had been impatient and irritable—definitely not herself. It started the day after they went fishing, but the last two days had been the worst, and his patience with her was about tapped out. "Feel better?" His tone was sarcastic, his restraint stretched to the limit.

Biscuits and muffins, she was tired. All she wanted to do was take a turn around the deck and go to bed—alone was a given. For some reason, she and Sam had been at odds lately. "What?" She glanced at him over her shoulder.

Her absentminded response pushed him over the edge. "Never mind." He stood up, shoved the chair under the table, and took Jeremiah with him down to their cabin.

He tried to smooth over Jeremiah's hurt feelings and tucked him into bed. After he had fallen asleep, Sam grabbed his jacket and went out on deck. The day after tomorrow would be Thanksgiving, and he would leave Friday. Evidently, he had overstayed his welcome. He didn't feel that way, though. He . . . cared for her—so deeply. *Oh, hell, why mince words?* he thought. *Why not say it?* He loved her. He wasn't sure when it had happened. But it had. He loved her and by God he wasn't going to let her irritating attitude put him off. He knew she cared for him. The question was, how much? He would find out before he left.

Maggie returned to Oregon City earlier than usual on Wednesday. It was still light—and still rainy, too—by the time the last of the cargo had been unloaded. Tomorrow was Thanksgiving, and Sam would leave the day after. She wanted to have one nice dinner before he left. If only she knew of a way to slow the days, make it last for . . . But how could she expect him to want to stay after the last few days? She snapped at Jeremiah, and she had ignored Sam. Mealtimes were more like a punishment, and she had looked forward to doing the dishes alone.

Wanting to ease his departure, at least for herself, she had kept her mind busy with work or chores or the weather, on anything but how very much she cared for him. When he came back, then maybe she could trust her feelings, her instincts. Now, she didn't believe she could allow herself that luxury. It was too easy to confuse what she wanted to see in him with reality. When he smiled at her, was it with love, as it felt to her? Or was it simply a gesture between two friends?

Ely's voice startled her, and she wondered how long she'd been standing there. She walked over to the boiler. "Everything shut down?"

Ely nodded.

She looked around for Sam but saw no sign of him. "Where's Jeremiah?"

Ely motioned over his shoulder. "Saw him go in his cabin with Sam."

Thad put his jacket on. "Maggie, is it all right if I leave for home now? I'd like to surprise Ma."

"Sure. Have a good Thanksgiving, and tell your mother hello for me." She and Ely were silent until Thad left. "Do you have any special plans for tomorrow?"

"Nah. Old Roker must be snowed in from what I saw."

Her gaze swept the deck, including the door to Sam's cabin. "I'm going to the general store. When I bought the supplies, I forgot about tomorrow." Cap trotted up the gangplank, straight to Sam's cabin, and slapped his paw on the door. "Need me to pick up anything for you?"

"If they got any spare smiles, get one fer yerself. Ya been a mite short on 'em lately."

She felt the heat rise in her cheeks. "I'll see what I can

do." She kissed his whiskery cheek and hurried to get the milk pail before she dashed out into the rain.

When she reached Kirkland's General Store, she shook off her hat and went inside. The warmth blended the aroma of tobacco with the pungent smell of vinegar, and the kettle of spiced cider on the wood stove added a touch of holiday to the atmosphere. The elderly Kinney brothers were in their usual spot near the stove, playing checkers while three others looked on. She stepped over to the counter and greeted Mrs. Kirkland. "I know it's late, but do you have a turkey or a couple of chickens or maybe a haunch of venison left?"

"Oh, Maggie, why'd you wait so long? Let me see."

While Mrs. Kirkland went in the back room, Maggie browsed. She skimmed her fingers over a bolt of fancy poplin, looked at one of the solferino shawls she'd seen advertised in the *Oregon Argus* and saw a pair of men's boots she wouldn't mind having. Then she saw Mrs. Kirkland come back out grinning and held up a fine turkey. "You're an angel."

"And you're lucky. It was behind the venison." Mrs. Kirkland smiled. "What else do you need?"

"Oysters, a pail of milk, cider, a couple penny weights of cloves, a couple cinnamon sticks . . ." Maggie purchased everything she thought she might need for their meal, except for the pie. That, she wasn't going to attempt. "Mrs. Kirkland, would you hold this for me? I have one more stop to make, and I'll be right back."

"Sure, Maggie."

She dashed down to the Barnhill Restaurant and right through the back door to the kitchen. It smelled wonderful, and her stomach rumbled.

Laurel stared at her a moment and set the mixing bowl down. "Is something wrong?"

Maggie gave a short laugh. "I need one of your delicious pumpkin pies . . . or anything you can spare. Can you help me?"

Laurel smirked. "If you have an hour, I can show you

how to make one, but I bet you don't. Yes, you can have a pumpkin pie."

Maggie impulsively hugged her. "Thank you, Laurel. You've saved the day—and not the first time. Ely, Sam and Jeremiah will be so grateful."

She returned to the steamboat loaded down with the makings for their holiday dinner. After she set everything on the kitchen table, she stared at the mound of food. All she had to do was cook it.

Slowly, she cleared the table, moving the packages to every other flat surface in the room, and put the oysters and turkey in the cold cupboard. When she finished, she stirred the fire in the stove and put a pot of coffee on. Her stomach rumbled again, and she realized she'd completely forgotten supper.

An hour later she went down to the main deck. After telling Ely supper was ready, she knocked on Sam's door. She heard Cap on the other side of the door before it opened. Jeremiah gave her a curious look, then he glanced over his shoulder at Sam.

"Jeremiah, let her in." She was disheveled, there was color in her cheeks, and she met his gaze with a tenderness he hadn't seen recently. Lord, she looked good.

"I'm sorry supper's so late, but it's on the table now. Are you still hungry?" She could see Sam's mouth soften. She wasn't sure if he was happy to see her, but at least he hadn't told her to leave. She dropped down, balancing on the balls of her feet and petted Cap. He licked her cheek, and she hugged him. Cap was so understanding. She didn't want Sam leaving on a sour note and hoped he felt the same.

He glanced at Jeremiah. "We sure are." Sam handed the boy's jacket to him and grabbed his own. "Let's see what she made for us."

The wind had picked up and was driving the rain in sideways. They ran up the stairs and followed Ely up into her cabin. "Give me your jackets and start eating before it's as cold as that rain." She draped the coats over the furniture near the woodstove and added logs to the fire.

After serving Ely and Jeremiah, Sam placed a fried potato cake on Maggie's plate and another on his own. He was ladling soup into their bowls when she joined them at the table. "Smells good," he said.

She noticed her plate and smiled. "Thank you." She set a loaf of bread down by Ely and handed him a knife before she sat down. He didn't look as tired, now that Sam was helping him out. This Sunday, she must see about hiring a striker. She tasted the soup and realized she was doing it again, avoiding Sam. She gritted her teeth, wondering why it was so difficult to be herself now.

As he stared at her, he couldn't help thinking something must be wrong. "Don't you like the soup?"

"What . . . oh, no. It's all right." She broke a piece of the potato cake off and looked at Jeremiah. "Have you had fun helping Sam and Ely in the engine room?"

"Yeah. Ely lets me help him oil the rod, when the engine's off." Jeremiah grinned at Ely.

Too bad he's not ten years older, she thought. "Sounds like you're a good helper." She looked at Sam and smiled at the errant wave of hair over his ear. Instead of thinking about missing him, she set her mind to recalling the month he'd spent with her. When he caught her watching him, she quickly looked away.

Jeremiah nodded. "An' sometimes, I carry the little logs over to Thad, too."

He was taking to the steamboat, maybe too much. She hoped he would like the ranch as well. She glanced at Sam. "How're those wedges holding up?"

Sam nodded. "The engine's running well. It should last you another year or so." She seemed to be relaxing a bit. If he hadn't known her so well, he might have guessed she'd been nervous. No, not Maggie. Nothing much made her uncomfortable, unless something was out of her control.

Ely looked at Sam. "She's good as new, hasn't budged."

After supper, Ely excused himself, and Jeremiah worked on a drawing in the parlor, while Maggie dried the dishes that Sam washed. By the end of the meal, she felt more like herself. She handed a plate back to him. "You missed a spot."

He gazed at her. "I never said I was a good dishwasher." Her throaty laughter was better than a shot of whiskey, as sensuous as a caress. If his hands hadn't been in the warm water . . . Oh, what the hell. Before she picked up the next dish, he slipped his arm around her shoulders and kissed her. It had been too long since he'd felt her lovely body mold itself to his, the way it was doing now.

It was as if the last few days hadn't happened. She melted into him and deepened the kiss. She hadn't realized it before, but this was what she wanted—this was where she longed to be. She rested her cheek on his chest, closed her eyes and listened to the pounding of his heart. His fingers traced her spine down below her waist, and he pressed her hips to his.

Holding her so close had been a mistake. Now wasn't the time to make love to her, not when he would be gone in forty-eight hours. He gave her bottom a playful swat. "I'd better finish the dishes before the capt'n of this boat discharges me."

She grinned. "I'll put in a good word for you." Jeremiah was still busy drawing and playing with Cap when they finished cleaning up the kitchen. "I got a turkey for dinner tomorrow. If I don't get the feathers plucked tonight, we won't eat till midnight tomorrow."

"If we do it together it won't take us long." Sam got the old bucket for the feathers.

The evening passed too quickly for her. They laughed and teased one another while they plucked the bird clean. She returned the turkey to the cold cupboard. "There's some coffee left. Want to share it?"

He put his arm around her. "It's getting late. I'd better get Jeremiah to bed." He gave her one chaste kiss and left with the boy. If he made love to her, he wasn't at all certain he would be able to leave, and he must. He had already put it off far too long.

She closed the cabin door and leaned against it. A tear ran down her cheek. The evening had gone so well. She'd been sure he had forgiven her. Had she fooled herself? she wondered. He *had* kissed her with the same passion she had felt. She wrapped her arms around her waist, waiting for Cap to return and scratch on the door.

Chapter

20

The next morning Maggie let Cap out and went into the kitchen. She stirred the fire in the stove and added several pieces of oak and a couple of small lengths from a branch of an apple tree. Whenever she found limbs from fruit trees, she always set them aside for baking, though she didn't always remember to use them. She started the woodstove in the parlor and put on a pot of coffee. *I should get dressed,* she thought as she waited for the coffee to boil. But she decided Sam wouldn't be up for a while.

She set to work preparing the turkey. An hour later, she put her hand in the oven and began counting. She made it to twenty before she had to pull her hand back out and shut the oven door. The temperature was just right, and she put the turkey in to cook.

Cap hadn't come back, and she didn't see him on the bank. Knowing how close he was to Jeremiah, she was certain he was waiting at Sam's door. Pleased with her start on dinner, she refilled her cup and sat down at the table. Slowly, it dawned on her—breakfast. Setting a skillet on the stove top, she wondered if she could serve the pumpkin pie for supper.

She was standing at the stove when Ely came into the kitchen. "Hi. You must be hungry to be up here so early."

"Maggie, girl," he said, laughing. "Where ya been? It's half past nine."

She glanced down at her wrapper. "I didn't realize I'd been up that long."

"Ya're not workin' t'day. Ya don't have to fancy yerself up for no one."

"Well, I can't serve Thanksgiving dinner dressed in this, either."

Ely stepped over to her side and took the fork from her hand. "I'll finish the bacon."

"Thanks." She dashed into her room and closed the door. With only a moment's hesitation, she laid out her new dress, petticoats, and good kid slippers. As she fastened the ties on her prettiest camisole, she heard Jeremiah and Sam arrive. She quickly slipped into the rest of her clothes, brushed her hair out and joined everyone in the kitchen.

Sam paused with the cup at his mouth and gazed at Maggie. She was lovely. "Good morning." His fingers closed around the cup, but he'd rather have buried them in her long shimmering hair. He gulped the hot coffee and nearly choked on it.

Jeremiah crawled out from under the table, pushing his horse. "Hi, Aunt Maggie."

"Hi, yourself. Did you bring Cap up with you?"

"Yeah. He's in there by the stove." Jeremiah pushed the horse out of the kitchen.

She smiled at him and then at Sam. "Would you believe I almost forgot breakfast?" She felt her cheeks heat up and began searching for the apron her mother had made as a wedding gift for her.

He chuckled. "I'll help you with dinner. Did you get some oysters?"

"Mm-hm." She found the apron. The embroidered yellow-and-orange rosebuds across the top of the bodice and along the hem were still as pretty as when it was new. She tied the sash, and he handed her cup to her. "Thanks, on both accounts."

"You're welcome, and I'll make the oyster sauce."

She grinned. "Good. Mine might not be too creamy. Last time it was hopelessly lumpy."

After they ate breakfast, Jeremiah left with Ely. Sam helped Maggie clean up the dishes so they could dirty them again in a few hours. He peeked into the oven and grinned.

"Smells delicious. There's nothing like the aroma of turkey roasting. Come here." He took her hand, led her over and opened the oven enough for her to see the turkey. She bent to look inside, and he put his arm around her waist. When she straightened up, he drew her into an embrace. "You feel so good, Maggie."

"Mm . . . you do, too." She hadn't been embraced for so many years before he came back into her life, she had forgotten the warmth, the flood of pure happiness she now felt in his arms. She rubbed her cheek on his shirt. She loved him so much, it frightened her to even think the words, as if it might bring bad luck. She locked her arms around him. "I wish this day wouldn't end."

"Oh, Maggie, I'll come back to you as soon as I can. No later than April—I promise." He kissed the top of her head and gently rocked her. The sound of Jeremiah running to the cabin door signalled the end of their privacy. He kissed her forehead and released her.

"I don't understand how Kathleen's managed to have so much time alone with her husband to have so many children," she said. She grinned when he burst out laughing. She set the kettle on the stove top, poured the apple cider into it and added a bit of sugar and some cloves. She broke the cinnamon sticks up and set them on the table to remind her to put one in each cup.

"Sam—" Jeremiah dropped his coat on the floor and ran into the kitchen. "See what Ely's making for me?!" He held out the wood. "It's gonna be Cap. See his nose?"

Sam held up the piece of wood Ely had whittled. "It's good. That does look like Cap's nose." When he handed the dog back to Jeremiah, he whispered, "Don't forget to thank Ely."

"Oh, I won't, Sam."

They talked about past holidays; Maggie and Sam teased one another; and they avoided the subject of his departure as the morning became afternoon. When the skin had turned brown and crispy and the juices ran clear, Sam lifted the turkey out of the oven and set it in the middle of the table for her. The meal was coming together better than she'd hoped. The pan of biscuits was put in the oven to bake. A bowl of boiled carrots and another with potatoes were also put on the table. Jeremiah set the flatware out, and Sam showed her how he made the oyster sauce.

When they were seated at the table Sam glanced at her, she nodded, and then motioned for Jeremiah to bow his head. Sam said grace, his low-pitched voice rich and somber. She silently asked for guidance.

"Amen." Sam glanced around the table. "Let's eat. Maggie, would you pass the plates?"

She held each one while he carved and served the turkey.

When she picked up Jeremiah's plate, he sat up on his knees to see the turkey better. "Can I have a leg?"

"Sure can." Sam pulled the leg outward and stuck the tip of the knife in the joint to separate it. "You must be starving." He set it on the boy's plate.

"No, but I'm hungry an' I like legs." Jeremiah stared at the leg and grinned at Cap. He'd give it to him after dinner.

The first chance he had, Sam tasted a bit of the turkey and winked at Maggie. "You did a good job. It's delicious."

Ely nodded. "That ya did, girl."

Jeremiah nodded as juice dripped down his chin.

She sighed, cut a bite for herself and tasted it. The meat was moist and savory. "It must be the apple branch. I'll have to remember that." She dipped another bite in the oyster sauce and smiled. "Mm. This is good."

Jeremiah poked his fork in a gray thing in the sauce. "What's that? It's slippery."

"A piece of an oyster." Sam gave him an encouraging nod. "Try it."

Jeremiah frowned. "But *what* is it?"

Maggie reached over, speared the bite with his fork and handed it to him, while she told him where oysters lived. She got one of the shells from the bucket and gave it to him to look at.

Sam marveled at the way she interested the boy in her explanation while they ate. He asked Ely what he thought of lowering the charges for cargo to increase their load. Before he knew it, he had cleaned his plate and felt too full for comfort. "Who wants to take a walk?" He smiled at Maggie. "I'll help do the dishes when we get back?"

She stood up. "Sounds good to me. Let's get our coats."

Ely shook his head. "M'legs're jist fine. See ya later."

Maggie studied him, wondering if he felt all right. "You're welcome to go with us."

"Call me when ya serve up that pie."

She grinned. "I won't forget."

While they were busy talking, Jeremiah stuck the turkey leg in his pocket, and got his jacket. He flopped it over his shoulder, and went out on deck. "It's not raining." He went inside to his aunt. "Aunt Maggie, it's too hot for coats."

She went outside to see for herself and smiled at him. "You're right. It isn't cold. The deck is drying out."

As they walked down the stairs, across the deck and gangplank to the bank, Cap trotted at Jeremiah's side. He grinned. "In a minute, boy."

Maggie linked arms with Sam as they walked south alongside the muddy road to Canemah. "Have you noticed the way Cap has stayed at Jeremiah's side since before we left the cabin?" Maggie glanced at Sam. "When I take walks with him, he usually runs ahead and back again, as if he wants me to run with him."

"He does seem to be acting a little strange, but they're enjoying themselves." Sam hugged her arm and smiled. A light breeze rustled the treetops and carried the strong smell of pine and woodsmoke.

She liked this stretch of road through the trees. There was something about the breeze whispering through the trees and the sound of the fast-flowing river that reminded her of church, or what a church should be. The change in the weather almost seemed like a sign. Somehow, they would work out their differences.

Jeremiah stopped by a bush and looked back at Sam and his aunt. They weren't paying him any mind, so he pulled the turkey leg out of his pocket and held it up high. "Cap, sit up." Cap sat up, staring at the bone in Jeremiah's hand. "Good, boy." He gave the bone to him and squatted down to watch him chew it up.

Sam looked ahead and saw Jeremiah with the dog. "See," he said, motioning to the boy. "That's why the dog followed him so closely. Want to bet it's what is left of the turkey leg?"

"The little stinker. He thinks he's fooled us."

He stopped and turned her face to him. "Why not let him have this one?" He kissed the tip of her nose and grinned. "Don't you remember how much fun it was to put one over on your parents?"

I remember so many things, she thought, and nodded. "It won't take Cap long to finish the bone." *Oh, Sam, there must be a way for us to weave our dreams together—with forbearance but hopefully not taking too much time.*

Against her wishes, the day seemed to pass with lightning speed. All too soon, the kitchen had been cleaned up and they had enjoyed generous slices of Laurel's wonderful pumpkin pie. Ely turned in for the night, and Jeremiah fell asleep on the parlor floor with Cap.

Sam tugged Maggie back from the kitchen doorway and wrapped his arms around her. "You must be tired, though you certainly don't look it."

She gazed into his eyes, feeling anything but weary. "I'm not." *Besides, I'll have time enough—more than I want—to rest up after you and Jeremiah leave,* she thought, but couldn't bring herself to say it aloud. She put her arms around his neck and pressed her mouth to his. She couldn't tell him what she was feeling, but she could show him. Parting her lips, she deepened the kiss.

When her tongue caressed his and she flattened her hips over his arousal, Sam was hopelessly caught in her web of desire. His manhood throbbed, and he knew he had to put a stop to this heavenly madness before she hated him for using her and walking away. He held her tight, stilling her movements. "You know I have to leave tomorrow."

She nestled in his arms. "I can't think of a better way to say good-bye." *Or a better way to say I love you,* she thought, working her feet out of her shoes.

"Oh, woman, you're making it damn difficult to do what's right."

She smiled against his chest. "I'm trying to make it impossible for you to be so confounded proper."

He swung her around. "I adore you, Maggie." He tipped her chin up and framed her lovely face with his hands. "You're almost too good to be believed."

"Try." She put her hands on his waist, slipped her fingers under the band of his pants and listened to his gaspy breathing.

He scooped her up in his arms and carried her into the bedroom. "Ma used to tell me you were one determined young lady." He grinned. "She didn't know how very right she was."

His kiss was gentle. His lips grazed hers, teasing, taunting her with featherlight strokes. Her pulse quickened to one murmur of longing for him. She loosened the top buttons on his shirt, while his lips continued to send a tide of desire through her with seemingly little effort.

He had never exercised so much control as it took to slow his need for her, to allow him time to express his love for her in ways that words could not. She tried to reach the buttons on his trousers, and he smiled. "I'd better close the door." He eased the door closed, carried her to the bed, laid her down and covered the length of her with his body. Her breathing was as harsh, as uneven, as his own.

Again, she reached between their bodies to unfasten his trousers, but he laced his fingers with hers and held their arms out toward the edges of the bed. She rolled her hips from side to side, nearly frantic with her craving for him.

He shifted to one side and slid his knee up the inner side of her thigh. She momentarily stilled, and he smiled. "Remember telling me you weren't long on patience?"

"Mm-mm." Another moan escaped and she clamped her legs together on his. "Do we have to talk *now*?"

"Mm-hm. This is the only time—for what I have in mind." He kissed her throat where her pulse throbbed, then with one hand, he unbuttoned her dress.

She decided he must be trying to drive her mad. In frustration, she grabbed a button to help him, but he drew her first two fingers into his mouth and sucked on them, sending white-hot tremors down her spine. "Why won't you let me help?" His knee pressed against her. "Ohh, please . . ." She felt as if she were afire but weak and lightheaded.

He raised himself up on his knees and brought her to a sitting position. "Think of us taking a longer, more leisurely, more scenic route to our destination." He pushed her dress back over her shoulders, slipped the chemise away and quickly removed his own shirt.

Unrestrained, she combed her fingers through the wavy hair on his chest and rubbed her palms over his hard nipples. "I do like what I see . . . and feel." His muscles tightened beneath her hands. She bent her head and pressed her lips to his chest. His arms closed around her. As she explored his firm body, she understood that he had given her the confidence and freedom to venture anywhere at her will.

When she grew anxious for what was just beyond her grasp, he gently pushed her back. His heart pounded as he slowly eased her skirts down, and he skimmed his knuckles over the curve of her hips, down along her smooth legs to her trim ankles, then tossed her clothes aside. As he caressed and tasted her silky skin, his arousal strained for release.

She moaned and twisted and tugged at him, impatient to feel his weight on her. She hadn't known a body could feel so many different sensations, each wondrous, thrilling, and exasperatingly delicious. She moistened her dry lips and sank her fingers into his hair. "If you don't take off those pants, I'll rip them off."

His tongue completed the circle on one passion-hardened nipple, and he grinned at her. "Sounds interesting."

Oh, his deep, velvety voice was nearly her undoing. "This sweet torture . . . is driving me . . . ohh . . . senseless."

He kissed her belly and nearly tore off the bothersome boots and trousers. He covered her naked, quivering body with his as he plundered her sweet mouth. She rocked her hips, and he groaned, his need for her becoming almost painful. He raised his head and held her gaze as he drove into her trembling body.

She swallowed the cry rising in her throat. He filled a space he had created within her. She twined her legs around his and moved with the rhythm he set. She wanted this never to end—she wanted to soar the rapids with him. He withdrew and entered her anew, over and over, until she grabbed his bottom and sank down on him.

Not yet, he thought, but she drew him along with her, and he gave in to his release. They were in a place apart from the rest of the world, in an atmosphere of pure sensual delight and fulfillment, where the feel of her, the heat, the taste of her was all he needed.

The next morning, Maggie listened to the birds chatter in a pine tree just down the bank. As if someone had decided they'd had enough cold weather, the day was promising to be springlike. A perfect day to . . . enjoy the trip south. Cap returned from his walk and went back inside with her.

The morning was like most of the mornings for the last six weeks. Jeremiah played with the dog before and after eating. Ely, Sam and Maggie talked about the day ahead, as if it were no different from any other—except for Sam and Maggie's lingering, almost hungry glances. By nine forty-five, the cargo was stored aboard, and Maggie stood by the gangplank until the last passenger boarded.

Sam spoke to two men he had seen before, then made his way to her side. "Everyone appears to like the warmer weather."

She nodded. "It happens sometimes, and it's always appreciated." It was more humid than normal, and his hair was wavier than ever. *Oh grannie, he's handsome, and he makes me feel so good.* She wished she'd had a daguerreotype made of him, but it was too late for that now. Her memory would have to serve.

He helped her replace the gangplank and walked to the stairs with his arm around her shoulders. He was glad he would be working with Ely. At least it would keep his hands busy, although his thoughts would have a constant struggle. He tipped her hat back, kissed her forehead, then lowered the hat brim. "See you at the next stop."

She grinned. "I know." She looked around. "Have you seen Jeremiah?"

He motioned to the firebox. "He was talking with Thad."

She kissed his hand, which was still resting on her shoulder. "We'd better get going." *It's any other day,* she told herself, *until we reach Corvallis.* She took Jeremiah up to the pilothouse with her and held him up to pull the line for the whistle. She backed the stern-wheeler away from the riverbank and started upriver. The tree branches were bare. The current was churning and the water looked muddy, not a good sign. The first stop was at Mission Landing.

Jeremiah pulled the cord and waved at the people down by the river. "Can I blow the whistle again?"

"Sure can. I'll find a crate for you to stand on so you can see a little better." She wanted him to enjoy his last trip with her and have good memories. Normally, she didn't have the tolerance to entertain anyone in the pilothouse, but this was a special day.

"Gee, I wanna tell Sam and Ely." With the chin strap tight to hold his hat on, he went down the ladder and ran to the stairs.

"Jeremiah, walk!" She ran after him. Though it was still warm, it was raining again. The moment the gangplank was set, the roustabouts raced aboard and carried the cargo ashore.

While Jeremiah told Ely all about his adventure in the pilothouse, Sam joined Maggie on deck. "Jeremiah can't stop talking. I'd say you've made quite an impression on him."

"I was hoping to make the day a little special. He's blown the whistle before, but he wasn't as interested then." As they crossed the deck, she held his hand and felt happy for no particular reason. "I have to find a crate he can stand on."

"I saw one in the storage room." He located the crate and walked back to the stairs with her. "The current's still strong. How're you doing?"

She glanced at the river. The movement of the currents had always fascinated her. "It's a winter river. With the rain, there's more rubble in the water." She stared at him, momentarily captured by his warm gaze. She took a deep breath and let it out slowly. "Thanks for helping Ely today. I'll see about hiring a striker soon."

"Good." As he leaned over to give her a chaste kiss, Jeremiah ran into him, and Sam came close to knocking her down to the deck. He straightened up, steadying her at the same time. "Jeremiah, you've got to watch where you're going, son."

"Yes, Sam, but I didn't want her to forget me." Jeremiah looked from Sam to his aunt.

She lightly tapped his hat and smiled. "That won't happen. Come on, we'd better get going."

As they steamed up the river, Maggie occasionally checked the old watch in her pocket. The last she'd heard, the stage departed for points south of Corvallis around midafternoon, and she meant to have him there in plenty of time.

She served a cold dinner during their short stop in Salem, then continued south. After she pulled out of Albany, she smiled at Jeremiah. "Would you like to steer the boat?"

"Oh . . . gee!"

In his excitement, he made the crate wobble, and he toppled off. Without looking away from the current, she caught him with her arm. "Careful, honey." She positioned the crate with her foot while her focus remained fixed on the river.

He climbed back onto the crate in front of her, and her arms were around him. "What do I do now?" Gee, they were so high up he could see a long way off.

"Put your hands here. I'll help you." He gripped the wheel, and his little knuckles turned white. "Don't hold it so tight. Your hands'll cramp up."

He couldn't believe it. He was steering the big stern-wheeler up the river! He saw a man riding a horse. "Can I blow the whistle to him?"

She smiled. "Okay, this time." She held him up with one arm while he pulled the rope, then set him down again on the crate. "Now you have to watch the current. It's rough here with the twisting turns."

He did as she told him. It seemed he had hardly been at

the wheel very long when he saw a town on each side of the river. "Do we gotta stop at one of them?"

"Yes, Corvallis is on the right bank," she said, pointing out the town. "That's Orleans on the other side of the river." After he blew the whistle, she let him hold onto the wheel as she guided the steamboat to the bank. She followed him down to the main deck wishing he wasn't in such a hurry. He didn't seem to know the importance of this stop. She caught up with him and Sam.

Sam looked at her, and it was as if a mule had kicked him in the gut. Her tongue darted across her lower lip. Dread was so clear in her eyes and her rigid stance, the knot tightened in his stomach. "I'd better go check on the stage schedule. I won't be long."

Jeremiah pulled at Sam's sleeve. "Sam, can I go with you?"

"If Maggie doesn't mind." He rested his hands on Jeremiah's shoulders to keep from reaching for her, which would have made it even more difficult for both of them.

She forced herself to smile at Jeremiah and prayed her voice wouldn't betray her. "Of course you can. The stage stops right down that street at the mercantile."

Jeremiah grinned. "Bye, Aunt Maggie. Come on, Sam."

"We really won't be long." He hardly recognized his own voice and cleared his throat.

"You'd better go before he pulls your arm off." She wanted to turn her back, but she couldn't tear her gaze from him. *Oh, will this afternoon ever end?*

Chapter

21

Sam stared at the man behind the counter at the mercantile. "You are certain there isn't a stagecoach or mail wagon going south? How about a drummer? I'll ride with anyone. I must get to California."

The man shook his head. "Not even a mud wagon. Sorry, mister. The roads is either washed out or the mud's hip-deep." The man glanced at Jeremiah. "The next one's due here late Monday and will leave just after first light Tuesday morning—if they can get through. Want a buy your ticket now?"

Sam nodded. "Sacramento. One way." Although the delay caused problems, it was unavoidable—and it gave him three more days with Maggie. He should be distressed over being held up. He wasn't. He was delighted.

"Two?"

"One." Sam glanced at Jeremiah. He was staring out the window. Sam paid the fare. As he pocketed the ticket, he passed a shelf that held, among others, a pretty bonnet with a brim that narrowed about where her cheeks would be. Brown with a wide green ribbon and a little bunch of roses on one side—he thought it would be perfect with her new dress. "Jeremiah—" The boy came over and Sam kept him at his side. He gained the attention of the clerk, and she came over to him. "Would you mind holding that brown bonnet up?" He pointed it out, saying, "The one with the green—"

"Ah, yes, the brown leghorn." The clerk held up the hat. "This is a pretty one, and it's faced with gold crepe."

"Yes, that's the one." He leaned down to Jeremiah. "Think Maggie would like it?"

Jeremiah shrugged. "She likes her old hat."

Quickly smiling, the clerk turned the hat. "The cabbage roses are so nice. Is the lady here to try it on?"

"No. It's a gift." He'd never purchased a lady's bonnet before, but he could see Maggie in it. It also fit her requirement that the brim not block her side view. "I'll take it."

After the lady walked away, Jeremiah patted Sam's arm. "She'd look funny steering the boat with that hat on."

"Maybe, but it will look nice with her yellow dress." The clerk handed Sam the hatbox. He paid her and went outside with Jeremiah. The rain was steady, and the road was close to becoming part of the river. Sam scooped up Jeremiah. "Hold on and wrap your legs around my waist so you don't slip."

Jeremiah put his arms and his legs around Sam. As Sam ran down the street and onto the boat, Jeremiah held on tight, bumping up and down. It was sorta like playing horsy with papa. When Sam stopped in front of his aunt, she looked real funny, maybe a little scared.

She fought the tears threatening to spill down her cheeks. He was so very happy. She hadn't expected that, and it hurt. "Did you finish packing?"

Sam set Jeremiah on the deck. "I did, but I'll have to do it again Monday." Her hands were behind her back. He reached around behind her, took her hand and looped the hatbox cord over her fingers.

Feeling completely befuddled, she stared at the box. "What's this? What's it for?"

"A little surprise." He grinned. "I have another one, too." She stood there as if he had handed her a basket of snakes. "The stage already left. Won't be one through here till Monday evening. The roads are—"

"What?" She frowned. She'd missed something. He didn't seem to make sense. "What are you saying?"

His hands gently circled her upper arms, and he waited for her to look at him. Slowly, she lifted her chin. "The roads are washed out or too muddy to pass," he said. "You're stuck with me until dawn Tuesday, that is, if you don't mind spending Monday night here." The light flashed back into her beautiful eyes, and he nodded.

She threw her arms around him and squeezed. She had always liked the rain, but she had never been so very grateful for it. "We'll spend Monday night right here. Promise."

The hatbox whacked the back of his legs, and he chuckled. "Guess that means you won't mind having me around for three more days." He lifted her off the deck and kissed her. He didn't give a damn who watched or what they thought.

She felt light as a feather, as if a great weight had been cut loose from her shoulders. "Then I'd better get this old stern-wheeler moving. Mrs. Tillman will be waiting for us."

"Yes, ma'am." He gave her a quick kiss.

Jeremiah watched them. Grown-ups surely act funny sometimes. "Aunt Maggie, aren'tcha going to see what Sam gotcha?"

She grinned from him to Sam. "I certainly am." She tipped the lid back and lifted the hat out of the box. "It's beautiful. What's it for?" It really was pretty, but she would've thought he knew how she felt about bonnets.

He replaced her old hat with the new bonnet. "It'll be pretty with your yellow dress." She looked so adorable. He touched the side brim. "And it doesn't have a blind side, either."

She glanced sideways and grinned. "Thank you, Sam. It's lovely." She held the wide ribbons and kissed him. "I'll wear it Sunday with my dress." She carefully placed the bonnet back in the box, closed it and hugged it to her chest. "I'll always treasure this."

He plopped her old hat back on her head. "I'd be satisfied if you enjoyed wearing it."

"Oh, I will." She grasped the cord and held out her other hand to Jeremiah. "Want to help me?"

Jeremiah glanced from her to Sam. "Can I stay in the

engine room with Sam and Ely? I wanna tell him about the wagon stuck in the mud."

Sam nodded, and she smiled. "That'll be fine. If you change your mind later, you can come up with me."

She gazed at Sam and held the hatbox up, saying, "Thank you." Then she dashed up the stairs. She left her new bonnet in the cabin on the way up to the pilothouse and soon guided the stern-wheeler out into the current. The river was running fast, and she retraced their course in less than half the time the southbound trip had taken, even including many stops along the way. When Wheatland was in sight, she blew the whistle and piped Ely.

As the stern-wheeler came to a stop, she spotted Mrs. Tillman standing on a nearby porch and waved to her. The engine stopped. Maggie hurried down to the deck and swung the gangplank over to the bank.

Mrs. Tillman bustled aboard and took cover under the upper deck. "Gracious, Maggie, when is this going to end? We'll all need rowboats if it doesn't stop soon."

"It can't last forever, and I don't need any more competition." Maggie smiled. "I hope you had a nice Thanksgiving with Lavinia."

Mrs. Tillman nodded and gave Maggie a smug grin. "And *she's* spending Christmas at *my* house." Mrs. Tillman glanced down at the package in her hand as if she had forgotten about it. "Oh, here, dear. Lavinia thought you might like a loaf of pumpkin bread." She handed it to Maggie.

"How nice. Thank you. That was so sweet of her." Maggie glanced around but there were no other passengers. "If you wait till I swing the gangplank back aboard, I'll walk with you up to the saloon."

"Of course, dear." Mrs. Tillman held the bread for Maggie, handing it back to her when they started up the stairs. "Mr. Adams hasn't left, has he?"

"No. He's helping Ely."

Mrs. Tillman nodded. "Ah, he would." She stopped at the saloon door. "He likes you, and he likes working this old steamboat of yours." She patted Maggie's hand. "Give him a bit of encouragement but don't give the berries away until the bush is his."

Maggie clamped her teeth down on her tongue to keep a straight face. "That's good advice. Thank you."

She turned on her heel and hurried up to the pilothouse before she laughed out loud. Mrs. Tillman was a dear, and she'd be horrified if she had any idea how many "berries" Maggie had given away. She laughed so hard, she doubled over and tears ran down her face. The dear woman didn't understand that she wasn't husband hunting. She and Sam were very close friends. They didn't need to recite any vows.

The last leg of the return trip passed quickly. The current was so strong, she began slowing down the engine on the gentle curve before she came within sight of Canemah. It didn't help much, and as the little settlement loomed ahead, she feared they might go over the falls if she couldn't bring the steamboat to a stop. Her palms were slick with sweat, and she suddenly felt sticky all over.

She rang the emergency signal and piped for Ely to reverse engines, while she fought to ease the steamboat as close to the bank as she could without running aground. The deck vibrated, the engine whined, and she gritted her teeth, praying for the strength to control the boat.

The boat's speed lessened a bit—but not enough to make the necessary turn at Canemah to swing into Oregon City and avoid the falls. She was breathing hard. She had to think. There must be a way of stopping the steamboat. There were so many lives in danger. She filled her lungs and exhaled slowly, forcing herself to concentrate. Suddenly, she saw the small, brush covered outcropping ahead. Reacting instinctively, more rapidly than she could think, she sounded the general alarm and wrenched the wheel, turning the stern-wheeler into the small piece of land, praying the ground was soggy enough for her to glide ashore without ripping the hull open.

She braced herself for the impact. The current shoved the steamboat over the low riverbank. The boat shot into the brush. The hull scraped through brambles, shrubs and vines with loud screeching and groaning noises. The boat came to a sudden halt just short of the alder trees. Her heart pounded furiously, and she felt lightheaded, but at least they hadn't plowed into the trees. She ran down to the saloon to check on Mrs. Tillman and the two male passengers.

The older woman was on her hands and knees on the deck. Maggie ran over and helped her to the couch. "Did you hit your head?"

"No, girl." Mrs. Tillman rubbed her forehead. "I'll be fine. What happened?"

"The current's too strong," Maggie said, helping the woman back to her seat. She assured herself the other passengers were not injured and raced down to the main deck. Part of the cargo had sailed over the forward deck into the bushes. She hurried to open the safety valves on the boiler, releasing the steam. She found Thad near the bow muscling his way out from among the crates. "You all right?"

He gave her a slow nod. "If not for the alarm, we'd be over there in the trees, wouldn't we, boy?" he said, moving aside to let Cap out from behind a crate.

"Cap!" The dog ran over to her, and she patted his rump. "Thanks for watching out for him, Thad." She grinned at Cap. "I know a little boy who'll be as happy to see you as I am."

"He's a smart one. I just stayed with him."

"Sit down and rest, Thad. I have to see how the others are. I'll be right back." She climbed over crates and around barrels, and she shoved several logs from the stairwell leading to the engine room. Somehow, Cap had wound his way to the stairs and darted down ahead of her. Jeremiah's strong voice relieved one part of her concern.

She ran down the steps to Sam sitting at the bottom with Jeremiah in his arms. She embraced both of them while she frantically searched for Ely. "Ely!?" He had to be all right. If anything happened to him—

Sam wrapped his arm around her back and kissed her cheek. "Maggie, thank God you're safe." Her warning had saved them, but he had feared for her safety. The pilothouse wasn't always the safest place to be in a collision.

"I'm right here, girl," Ely said, climbing out from under the stairs. "The boy had a fright, but we're fine." He slapped the rag in his hand on the reversing gear. "The old girl did her best, and those wedges held her in place as safe as a babe in its mama's arms."

Maggie let out a long sigh. She began trembling and tightened her hold on them. "Jeremiah, how're you doing?"

Cap licked Jeremiah's face. He rolled around in Sam's arms and looked at his aunt. "Sam said we went aground. Did we?" He was so scared. The lantern had bounced around and there was a really loud groaning noise like the boat hurt. But Sam held him tight. And he felt safe. Now Cap and Aunt Maggie were there, too.

She nodded. "We sure did." She glanced from Sam to Ely. "The river's too fast. It wasn't this morning. I can't recall a current this strong." Later, when Jeremiah was asleep, she would be able to speak more plainly. She stared into Sam's eyes. If he'd made the stage, he and the boy in his arms would have been saved this frightful ordeal. Was it selfish to be glad he had missed the stage? If so, she was guilty.

Sam sat the boy up on his lap and studied Maggie. "Where are we?"

"At the south end of Canemah." She glanced at both men. "Would you take a look outside? I'm not sure I can get us back to port, but we can try if you want to. I'll send a wagon for the crates on shore." She moved back and sat on the stairs. "It's up to you."

Sam smiled at Jeremiah. "Let's get some fresh air." Amazed, he realized that though she was shaken she was still in control.

Ely started up the stairs. "Come on, boy. Let's see if it's still rainin'." He held his hand out to Jeremiah.

She moved aside, then followed them up on deck with Sam. He helped her make a quick inspection of the boiler, firebox and steam pipes. "It looks okay." She glanced at him. "But we'll have to start the engine to see."

"I'll check the hull. No use worrying about the engine if

she won't float." He gave her a quick kiss and turned to leave.

"Wait—" She didn't release his arm. "No need getting your boots and things mucked up in the river. Change into some old clothes I keep on hand for just such a predicament."

He quickly exchanged clothes and waded into the river. The water was so murky, he couldn't see under the water and had to run his hands over the hull to check the damage. Working forward from the stern-wheel, he finally made his way to the slippery riverbank, studying the exposed hull. He climbed aboard, and Maggie covered him with a blanket. "How set are you on getting her back to the city?" He dried his face and hands. The weather was so muggy, at least he wasn't cold.

"The river could stay high for weeks, and there's no telling how long I'd have to wait for the current to slow down." She walked with him back to his cabin. "Is the hull damaged? It looked okay when I leaned over the bow."

He reached out to put his arm around her, but his sleeve was dripping wet. "I didn't find any cracks or holes."

"Good." She smiled at him. "Thanks for mucking around for me. You've probably worked harder these last few weeks than in the last few years." She took his hand in hers. "There must be a way to get this old boat home."

"Weight, we need extra weight to help fight the strength of the current. I once saw an old riverboat captain tie tree trunks to the sides to drag along the riverbed." He met her gaze. "Want to try it? Might work."

She faced him and placed her hands flat on his chest. He'd given her hope. She gave him a quick kiss. "We'll have to get a wagon to take the passengers into town. Maybe there's something heavy at the ironworks, barrels of scrap, anything."

"We can ask the blacksmith, too. An anvil or block would do the job, but we'd never get either here over the roads."

While Jeremiah and Cap watched from the saloon, Sam, Maggie, Ely and Thad put the cargo back in the hold. Two men in a wagon arrived to lend a hand. The passengers were taken to Oregon City, and Sam and Maggie went along. After renting a sturdy wagon, they visited the ironworks and the blacksmith at the south end of town and returned to the stern-wheeler shortly before dark.

Ely had fixed supper and saved two plates for them. Maggie and Sam ate while explaining their plans to Ely and Thad. Late that evening they finished securing the barrels of scrap iron and larger iron chunks to the sides of the boat with stout ropes. Sam leaned against a stack of crates in a small crevice and watched Maggie rolling her shoulders and stretching her back. "She'll be ready to move at first light."

She raised one brow. "Why not now? With any luck, it won't take us half an hour."

Sam stroked her back. "You want to try it tonight?"

"We'll set every lantern we have out on deck. With the lights from town that will be enough. I want to get back while those weights are in place. There should be enough drag to get us back." His touch helped ease her aching back. "I just want to get home." She called to Thad and told him to build a head of steam.

"Let's go then," Sam said. He took her hand and gently pulled her in front of him, her feet between his. "A kiss for luck." He hauled her against him and covered her mouth with his. If any of those tonics or elixirs in the general store could revitalize a body the way she did, it would be worth a gold mine, he thought, deepening the kiss.

She wrapped her arms around his neck. As he rekindled that ever present flame of desire, her thoughts scattered, and she molded herself to him. For a moment, the only thing she was aware of in the shelter of his embrace was their pounding heartbeats. She sighed. "This feels too good. I could spend the night here."

He splayed his fingers above her waist and set her away from him. "You're right. And I'd much rather sleep in bed with you than out here on deck."

With those sweet words ringing in her ear, his smile quickened her already fluttering pulse. She felt the blush creeping up from her throat. If only he could spend the whole night in her bed, but it wasn't possible. She pressed her lips to his and returned to the pilothouse.

When she felt the familiar vibration in the deck, she took a deep breath, piped Ely to reverse gears and gripped the wheel with both hands. The paddle wheel churned the water, and the dried brush scraped against the hull as the stern-wheeler eased backward off the bank and into the water. Another command, and the steamboat moved forward with the current. The weights dragged along the riverbed as she guided the boat to the wharf.

After the *Maggie* had been secured, she made a pot of hot cocoa. They all sat at the kitchen table and enjoyed the warm drink. Glancing at Ely, Thad and Sam, she raised her cup. "Here's to all of you for working so hard. I appreciate your help." After her toast, she warmed her hands on the cup. "Thad, you can go home now if you like, or in the morning. I need to survey the damage. We can't leave before Monday, if then."

Thad dragged his coat sleeve over his mouth. "I'll stay till tomorrow. It won't be easy getting those weighted barrels up." He gulped the rest of his drink and stood up. "I'll see you in the morning."

"Wait fer me," Ely said, shoving his chair back. "It's been a long day."

Jeremiah had fallen asleep on the sofa, and Sam lingered over the last of his cocoa. He was bone weary but reluctant to leave Maggie. She was overtired, too. He slid his hand across the table and held hers. "This day seems like it was as long as three. Why don't you go to bed before you end up sleeping in your chair?" He stood up and, holding her gaze, drew her up in front of him. "Sleep well, Maggie. There's no need to rise early." He gave her a gentle kiss, wondering how many similar situations she had survived before this one.

Maggie woke Saturday morning with only the sheet covering her, the comforter having been shoved to the far side of the bed. Her room was light and it was already warmer than it should be. When she rolled over her stiff muscles and sore limbs rebelled. Cap licked her nose with his big wet tongue, and she opened her eyes. "I know. I should make some sort of lever for you to work the door with, as if I sleep late every day."

She forced herself out of bed, let the dog outside and stirred the fire in the kitchen stove so she could start a pot of coffee. Although she would have preferred a quick dip in a cool stream, she bathed, dressed and made breakfast. Jeremiah and Sam came up, both looking a bit tired; soon after, Ely and Thad arrived.

As soon as they had eaten, they set to work. The warm Chinook wind didn't discourage the rain.

By midafternoon the weighted barrels had been pulled out of the water and returned to the ironworks. Maggie sent Thad home, then went with Sam and Ely to inspect for damage.

She wiped her brow and glanced at the other riverboats moored nearby. "Guess I'm not the only one unwilling to fight the current."

Sam studied the west bank below Linn City. "I may be wrong, but the river seems to be at the top of the bank." He looked east, curious to see if the mountains were still covered with snow, but the high bank across the road blocked his view.

"No, I don't think so. The basin at the bottom of the falls is rising, too, and there's more rubble in the water." She watched him a moment, wondering if he'd thought about the stagecoach. Unless the rain stopped very soon, he'd have to board the stage in Oregon City early Monday morning rather than Corvallis the following day. "I'd better check the pipe connections at the boiler. Thad's a good young man, but he hasn't the experience yet."

"He'll be fine, but I don't think he loves the river life the same way you and Ely do." *Or the way I did,* he thought. The last few weeks with Maggie had been wonderful, but he now realized he didn't want to spend the rest of his days working on a steamboat. Neither did he want Maggie laboring as hard as a roustabout and growing old before her time.

Chapter

22

Since Saturday had been spent working, Sam wanted Maggie to enjoy herself Sunday. After breakfast, he excused himself and left the steamboat. The roadway resembled a stream, which stiffened his resolve to take Maggie away from town for a few hours. He made his way to the livery.

He found Mr. Moss grooming one of the horses. "Good morning. That's a handsome horse."

"Yes, it is." Mr. Moss looked up. "Adams, isn't it?"

Sam nodded. "Do you have a buggy with a fixed top?"

"Yep, ah do. When do you want it?"

"Today. Thought it would be nice to see some of the country around here." Sam patted the horse's neck.

Mr. Moss shook his head. "You can have the rig, but I've had two others returned. Most of the roads are under water. You can take your chances, but I'd hate to have you stranded in this weather." He started brushing the horse again. "Up to you."

"Thank you, but I think I'll wait until I return in a couple of months. Should be dry by then. " Sam started for the wide, double doors.

"Might be, might not." Mr. Moss laughed. "Never can tell round here."

Sam paused outside of the livery. Was it too much to ask for a respite from the infernal rain? He wanted their last day together to be special, and a ride through the country had sounded so good. He returned to the steamboat none too pleased.

Maggie looked up when the door burst open. Sam yanked

246

off his muddy boots, then came in and shed his coat with short, jerky movements. She couldn't imagine what had him so upset.

"Sam, see what I wrote?" Jeremiah sat up and looked at him. He didn't think Sam wanted to see his paper.

"Jeremiah, maybe you should show him later." Maggie eyed Sam. When he left, he'd been happy, very happy, so she felt certain he wasn't angry about anything she or Jeremiah had done. "There's cold coffee. Want a cup?"

He closed the door and leaned back against it, feeling a little foolish. "Sounds good." He glanced at her and saw she'd changed clothes. Then he saw her new bonnet on her desk, and he felt even worse. On his way to the kitchen, he bent down by Jeremiah. "That's very good. Your handwriting keeps getting better." He smiled, hoping that would put the boy at ease, and petted Cap.

Maggie lifted the coffee pot out of the bucket of cold water she was using to cool it, and when he came into the kitchen, she handed a cup to him. "What happened?"

He took a sip of the cool coffee. "I thought a ride would be nice." He stared at her. "You look so pretty. I wanted to spend the day away from the boat—see some of the country with you." He glanced out the window. "How do you bear the rain?"

She smiled. "You get used to it." She sat down at the table, which was safer than standing in his embrace and wanting more. "That would've been nice." Just knowing he'd planned a special day was enough for her.

He gave her one nod and sat down in his chair facing her. When he told her what Mr. Moss had said, she was amused, and he didn't blame her. "What are your plans?"

She grinned. "Nothing. Ely went in town to see some of his cronies. I'd be happy staying here." *With you,* she thought. She finished her coffee and got up to refill her cup. "I have a couple apples. Want to dunk for them? Or, we could try making taffy and have a pull."

He chuckled. "Sounds like fun. Have you ever made taffy?"

She glanced around. "Once or twice." She called Jeremiah in and told him what they were going to do.

They spent the afternoon making taffy. The second batch was successful, and she and Sam took turns pulling it with Jeremiah. Supper became a contest, with each of them making a different dish. Later they made shadow puppets with their hands, and Sam traced Jeremiah's silhouette on a sheet of paper.

When one of them ran out of ideas to entertain Jeremiah, the other would think of something. It was almost as if she were afraid to be alone with Sam, and he with her. She thought about how easy it would be to tell him she'd go to the ranch with him—the weather was a perfect excuse, if she needed one—but she couldn't bring herself to that. There was too much left unsaid. Eventually, Jeremiah had trouble keeping his eyes open, and she realized she didn't want to make love with Sam. It would make his leaving all the worse. She had been prepared to let him go Friday— now she wasn't so sure.

Jeremiah had dozed off against Sam on the couch. Sam glanced at Maggie sitting on the other side of the boy. She looked as sleepy as the child. He was, too. Neither of them had let up since noontime. The thought of three extra days had spun dreams, but the reality hadn't been the same. He couldn't help wondering if she was as uneasy about his leaving as he was. "I'd better put Jeremiah to bed."

She took a deep breath. "I have avoided thinking about it, but you'll have to board the stage here early in the morning. The river's no better, and I don't think we can make it to Corvallis with this current." Her tongue darted between her dry lips, and she met his gaze. "I hate long good-byes. I'm no good at them, Sam. I'm sorry."

He grazed her soft cheek with his knuckles. "I'm not either." He slid his hand down and rested it at the back of her neck. "The important thing to remember is that I'll be back for you—and of course Jeremiah."

She gaped at him. "What? He's going with you."

"He can't, you have to see that."

"No. I don't. You've seen how I live. How can you

possibly expect him to stay here?" Her irritation with him, at that moment, was as great as her love for him. "Besides, I thought you bought your tickets."

"One," he said, looking into her eyes. "Just one."

She couldn't believe she had misunderstood him. "He needs more than I have to give. You have a ranch with plenty of room for him, and you must know how he dotes on you."

"I've told you there is nothing there—no house, no cabin, no outbuildings. That's the reason I have to return now." He ran his fingers through his hair. "Do you really believe he would be better off spending the winter in a rough camp, than here with you?"

"I do." She gazed at Jeremiah a moment. "There're too many ways he could be hurt here. If anything happened to him, I wouldn't be able to forgive myself. He's been through so much, he deserves a safe home."

"And love." Sam couldn't recall feeling this frustrated when he had argued cases in court. "And he needs a mother. You're his aunt—I'm not even related to him."

She narrowed her gaze at him. "He already has your love, and what about a father? Children need those too." She shook her head. "He's not staying here. I can't do my job and look after him at the same time."

Her expression made it very clear—her mind was set. No matter what her feelings were for him or the boy, or what he said, she was refusing to keep the child. He realized it wouldn't be in Jeremiah's best interest to wear her down in order to change her mind. He couldn't believe his judgement had been so wrong, but he knew when to yield.

"Please . . . understand. He's so dear . . . if he were only a little older . . ."

Sam rested his hand on her shoulder. "I won't argue." He gave her shoulder a light squeeze. "I'll return—this spring, when I can get away from the ranch and the roads are clear."

She leaned her cheek on his hand. "I'm looking forward to that, but you'll write, won't you? I want to hear all about how Jeremiah's doing and the ranch, and how you like being a sheep rancher." She watched Jeremiah. He had become so very dear to her. She smoothed back his hair. Oh, grannie, she was going to miss him.

He sat forward and scooped Jeremiah into his arms. "I've never been much of a writer. You better answer."

"Promise." *I'll start tomorrow night,* she thought. She walked down to their cabin with him, carrying their coats and hats. When Sam laid Jeremiah on his cot, she kissed the boy good night for the last time.

Sam pulled the sheet and one blanket up to the boy's shoulders and hung their coats and hats on the pegs. Jeremiah was still sound asleep, so Sam stepped outside the door with Maggie. The sound of the rain would have been soothing if it hadn't become so tedious. Maggie seemed to enjoy it. The only hint that her composure wasn't so complete was the way she was keeping her hands clasped behind her.

Every time she smelled the scent of cloves, she would think of him. His errant wave had slipped down to his forehead. As she lowered her hands to the folds of her skirt, she flexed her fingers and gazed at him. "I'll have breakfast ready early. Sleep well, Sam." For one brief moment as she stared into his eyes, she wavered and almost leaned forward to kiss him. She ached to hold him close, to feel the warmth of his embrace. He looked as miserable as she felt, and she couldn't chance letting her guard down. Instead, she clasped his hand. "See you in the morning."

"Night, Maggie." He had never known a woman with such resolve. It was one of the qualities he most admired and loved about her. She firmly believed she was doing what was best. He didn't agree with her but that didn't detract one whit from his feelings for her.

After a fretful night spent tossing about in her bed, Maggie gave up trying to sleep and was up and about, stirring the fire in the kitchen stove at a couple of minutes past five. For some reason—maybe because she was alone in the kitchen hoping for some bit of wisdom to see her through the next few hours—she thought about her mother, Elizabeth. She had been the kind of woman who showed her love in a thousand ways and who took a measure of pride in sending visitors off with a lavish meal. "I wish I could be more like you, mama. If only for this morning."

Maggie rummaged through the drawer where she kept the napkins and various odds and ends. Crumpled at the back was the paper she'd been seeking. Her mother's recipe for apple rolls. As she measured, mixed and kneaded the dough, she hoped the saying, "Food made with love tastes better," was true. While the rolls baked, she started bacon and pan fried potatoes.

Sam and Jeremiah came in as she was taking the rolls out of the oven. She set the pan on the table and smiled. "Good morning." Jeremiah still looked sleepy, but not Sam. His wave was slicked back, and his eyes were clear—and they were trained on her. She picked up a plate, dished generous servings onto it for him and set it on the table at his place.

"Smells wonderful," he said, watching her fix another plate. There was a soft, almost nervousness about her he found very dear. He wanted to wrap her in his arms, hold her close and assure her he would return. He knew he couldn't leave without embracing her, but this wasn't the time yet. "You've been busy." Her hair gently swung over her shoulders while she rushed to serve Jeremiah.

As soon as his aunt set his plate down, Jeremiah picked up the roll and took a bite. "This's *real* good."

"I'm glad. My mother used to make apple rolls." She joined them at the table with her own plate, though she wasn't hungry.

Sam understood why she had gone to the trouble of preparing a special meal and appreciated it all the more. "You aren't going to try steaming upriver today, are you?"

She looked at him over the rim of her cup. "I've been working this river for years. We'll be fine." *That's the least of my worries,* she thought.

He nodded. "It has to stop raining sometime—soon, I hope." Everything tasted delicious, but he noticed that she hardly touched a bite. He finished eating and grinned at Jeremiah. "Are you about full, son?"

"Uh-huh. This is Cap's." Jeremiah got the dog's pan and scraped his food into it.

Maggie smiled. "You did just fine." After he walked outside with Cap, she glanced at Sam. "Does he know you're both leaving this morning?"

"I told him earlier." Sam gripped the cup and gulped the last of the coffee, then checked his pocket watch.

"Did he understand?"

"He hasn't said anything, but he seems okay." He shoved his chair back from the table and stood up. "We'd better get going. I can't miss this stagecoach. I was expected at the ranch last week. Chester said he'd be there by the first week in December and this is already the second day of the month."

"I'll walk with you." She almost knocked her chair over in her rush to join him. "It isn't far. The stage stops in front of Peterson's General Store." Watching him put his coat on, she felt as if someone had pulled a rug out from under her.

Jeremiah brought the pan back inside. "Cap's taking his walk." His aunt and Sam didn't look happy. Jeremiah set Cap's pan in the kitchen and put his coat on.

It was time to go. As she set her hat on her head, she felt a bit calmer. No more dreading this moment. Knowing it would be over very soon, she felt a sort of peace settle over her. When they were gone she would have a good cry, which she desperately needed, and then she'd get back to work.

Jeremiah went outside to wait for Cap, and Sam turned to Maggie. "I'd rather say our good-byes here." She looked up at him, but her eyes were hidden by her old hat. He tossed it toward the sofa and placed a hand on each of her shoulders. "I'm going to miss you more than you want to believe." Her chin was set at a determined angle; her rosy lips were slightly parted; her cheeks were pale, her eyes overbright; and her pride kept her spine rigid.

She stared at him fearing he might disappear if she blinked. His expression was unreadable, his grasp gentle, and his deep, husky voice sent a ripple of longing through her. She attempted a smile. "That goes for me, too."

He slid his arms around her and wrapped her in a tight

embrace. "I'll be back. I promise, Maggie." He loosened his hold, raised her chin and kissed her, showing her how very much he loved her the best way he knew, slowly and thoroughly.

As he stormed her senses, she felt lightheaded and clung to him. Her heart seemed to pound in her ears, and she pressed her hips to his. When he finally ended the kiss, both of them were breathless. "We'd better leave," she said, "before I don't give a fig if you miss that stage."

She retrieved her hat, plopped it back on her head and walked out of the cabin while she still had the courage. Leaning against the bulkhead, Jeremiah looked nearly as lost and lonely as she felt. "Don't forget your hat, honey."

He nodded and went in after it. He didn't want to leave, and he didn't think Sam did either. No one was happy. Jeremiah put his hat on and went over to the desk. His writing papers were on top, but he didn't want to take them. He ran outside. "Cap's going with us, isn't he?"

She nodded. "He'll walk to the stage with us." The rain was still coming down, and she didn't bother to even glance at the river. She led the way down to the main deck. "Have you said good-bye to Ely?"

Sam shook his head and motioned to Jeremiah.

"I'll get him." She went over to Ely's door and knocked. When he opened it, she straightened her shoulders. "They're leaving."

Ely harrumphed and followed her over to Sam and the boy. "Ya sure picked a soggy day to travel." He stared past them to the road. "Don't rightly see how a stagecoach's gonna make it through that, less'n it sprouts oars."

She spun around and stared toward town. The river had overflowed its banks during the night. The tree stump near the side of the livery, which had been there as long as she could remember, was covered with water. She ran to the far side of the deck and stared across the Willamette. The same had happened at Linn City, possibly worse, and the Island Mills looked to be in danger of being flooded out. "Sam," she called, recrossing the deck. "I don't think—"

"I know." He looked back at the livery. "I'm going to see

what's happening in town. I *will* be back, " he said, staring straight into her eyes.

"Go on. See if we can help." Sam had just rounded the corner of the livery when Thad came aboard. The young man was drenched. At least the wind was warm, though wet. "How's your mother doing?" she asked.

Thad shook his head. "The field and yard look like a lake, and the cellar's full of water." He stared out at the river. "Never seen it so muddy or rough."

"You go back home and help your mother. I won't be going upriver today. From the look of things, it'll be at least two, maybe three days. Check back Wednesday afternoon."

After checking the boat again, Sam ran down the gangplank and paused at the foot. The water came almost to his knees. "Where's Mrs. Dobb's house? Down here? Or up above?" He motioned to the cliff.

"Up above." She frowned. "Do you think it's that bad?"

"Probably not. We can check on her later if you want to." As he waded through the muddy water, he brushed past a tree stump and stumbled over a root. He paused at the livery. It was wall-to-wall water but at least the horses had been moved out. As he continued up the street, he wouldn't have known where the boardwalk started had it not been for the corner post. After glancing into a few stores, he stood in the middle of the road and looked north. As far as he could see, the road had turned into a stream—and there was no sign the rain would stop any time soon.

Although he was certain he knew the answer, he went to Peterson's General Store. Mr. Peterson, his wife and daughter were busy moving goods off of the floor. Sam gave them a hand with a barrel of pickles. "Don't suppose the stage will be able to get through this morning?"

Peterson shook his head. "Got that right."

"Can you send a telegraph to Sacramento, California?"

"Corvallis. That's as far south as the line goes."

Sam thanked him and made his way back to the sternwheeler. Maggie was waiting for him near the boiler. "From what I saw, you're better off than the stores on Main Street."

She helped him take off his sodden coat. "It's really that

bad?" She'd heard talk about a terrible flood back in '44, but there were few settlers and hardly any towns back then. In any case, her old stern-wheeler certainly seemed to be more of a haven than she had realized.

"If this infernal rain continues . . ." Water ran down his arms and back as if he had been standing under an open spigot. "Needless to say the stage isn't running, and the telegraph line only goes to Corvallis." *As if that's the end of the world,* he thought with no small amount of sarcasm. "I'm going to get out of these clothes."

"Come on up to the cabin." She started wringing out his coat. "Don't forget to bring your wet clothes." She stared across the river and watched the *Enterprise* start up the Willamette. Below the falls the *Onward* looked ready to steam south, too. She wished them luck. The river flow was so fierce she doubted it could be crossed safely.

Maggie returned to her cabin with Sam near sundown. "What if the water keeps rising? Much of this area is low."

He closed the door behind him. "With the volume of water pouring over the falls, it's hard to believe the city's still flooding."

She glanced over her shoulder at him. "Do you have any more dry clothes?"

"I think so." He pulled the door back open. "Be right back."

She had wrung out her skirt on deck, but it was still dripping wet. She smiled at Jeremiah and Ely. "How're you two doing?"

Ely looked up from the checkerboard. "Keepin' dry. More'n ya did."

She crossed the room to her bedroom door. "Who's winning?"

Ely frowned at her. "Hard t'tell, girl."

Jeremiah hugged Cap and whispered, "I hope it never stops raining, and we can stay here with you."

Maggie quickly stripped off her wet clothes and dumped them in her washbasin. Her nightgown lay across the end of the bed. She glanced at it, longing to slip into it and lie down for a rest. Instead, she put on her old, comfortable work dress and moved the drying rack closer to the woodstove in the parlor.

After taking down Sam's dry clothes, she hung hers across the strips of wood and went in to start supper. It was so warm she decided not to heat up the kitchen stove; the pot of coffee could be set on the parlor stove. She spread slices of smoked ham on a plate, cut the last third of a loaf of bread and opened a jar of spiced peaches she'd been saving.

Sam came in and hung his clothes by Maggie's. Jeremiah was talking to the dog as he pushed the boat around with the horse teetering between the upper and lower decks. "How're you doing?"

Jeremiah glanced up at Sam. "Okay. Where'd ya go all day?"

Sam hunkered down on the other side of the dog. "We were helping some people move their things out of the water."

"Aunt Maggie won't let me fill the trough for my boat. Why was their stuff in the water?"

Sam rubbed the dog's neck. "It's rained so much, the river went over the bank into town and into the stores."

Jeremiah looked at him. "They need a boat like Aunt Maggie's. We stay on top of the water, huh?"

"That we do." *So far, anyway,* Sam thought.

Maggie called them for supper. The kitchen was warm, and none of them was very spirited. Jeremiah ate, but she suspected he was saving a good portion for Cap. Ely didn't waste any of his meal, but he rarely did. When he had cleaned his plate, she passed the platter of meat down to him for seconds. "Did you have a chance to speak to any crewmen from other steamboats?"

"Harry stopped by fer a spell. Said fields are flooded out south of here. The mill's standin' in water, too. Them's that gotta cross the river can't. It's a sorry sight."

Sam took a swig of water. "Mr. Moss's thinking about renting rowboats instead of buggies."

"If I can ever get the old girl upriver, maybe I should try

working on the Tualatin River." She glanced from Ely to Sam. "The flatlands flood in winter, but never this bad. It might be easier on the old boat."

Sam stabbed his fork in the last bite of meat on his plate. "Would there be enough cargo to keep you going?"

She shrugged. "I'll have to ask around."

Everyone seemed to slow down like an unwound clock. Ely said good night. Jeremiah scraped off the dishes and handed them to her. She washed them and Sam dried. When they finished, they stepped out to the walkway. "Want to go in the saloon? Jeremiah can watch for Cap from there."

Sam held the door open and followed Jeremiah and Maggie inside. The room had stood empty for three days. It was cooler than the cabin but stuffy. And with the boy with them it was also safe.

"Aren'tcha going to light a lamp?" Jeremiah stumbled over a table leg before he climbed onto a sofa by the window.

Sam smiled at Maggie. "You can see out better without one. It's not really dark in here." *And if you don't want to be seen,* he thought, *it's perfect the way it is.*

Jeremiah pressed his face against the window and watched the pane get all foggy. He moved down the sofa and did it again. "Sam, do you know how to play checkers?"

"I think I can remember. Do you want to learn?"

"Ely showed me an' said I need to practice. What'd he mean?"

Sam grinned. "Just that you should keeping playing the game. We can play when Cap gets back."

"Okay." Jeremiah kept staring out the window. "Can dogs swim?"

Maggie grinned at Sam. "Yes, they're good swimmers."

Cap came back a few minutes later, and they all went back to the cabin.

While Sam and Jeremiah played checkers, Maggie relaxed on the sofa gazing at Sam, and listening to him explain his moves. His voice had a lulling effect on her. Their day had been so hectic, this was the first chance she'd had to realize that Jeremiah and Sam wouldn't be leaving right away.

She stretched her arm across the back of the sofa, smiled and rested her head. The next thing she knew, Sam was saying good night, and she was kissing him. It felt so good. In her drowsy state, she didn't think; she just savored the scent of his hair tonic and the feel of his lips.

Chapter 23

Early Tuesday morning the stern-wheeler shook violently. Cap barked and ran to the door. Maggie jumped out of bed and dashed to the window. The river hadn't just spilled over the bank—it was surging into town. She grabbed her robe and ran outside with Cap. He dashed ahead. It was already light out, later than she'd thought.

She watched from the deck to make sure he didn't fall off the gangplank or have trouble in the water. When he reached a low outcrop at the bottom of the cliff, she hurried to Sam's cabin and lightly tapped on the window. As if he'd been waiting for her, Sam looked out the window.

He quickly pulled on his pants and shrugged into his coat before he eased the door open. "I was wondering if I should check on you. What happened? A gust of wind hit us?"

She pointed toward town. It was still hard to believe. Even though the riverbank wasn't low here, it hadn't contained the river.

The steamboat rocked again, and he grabbed her hand. "We'd better get another line or two secured to the wharf." He carried one rope and ran down the gangplank. The current was strong, and he didn't trust the old wharf. He tied the rope to a stout tree. He waved to Maggie and shouted, "Throw me the other one."

She threw the line to him and dashed back along the rolling deck to Sam's cabin. She was almost at the door when it flew open and Jeremiah ran out. She caught him up in her arms and braced her feet to absorb part of the motion of the deck. "Did you just wake up?"

Jeremiah wrapped his arms around her neck and held on. "Where's Sam? I fell outta bed an' I couldn't find him."

"He'll be right back. He's okay." He trembled against her, and she rubbed his back to calm him. "The river's pretty rough, isn't it?"

"Uh-huh." He looked around and finally saw Sam coming up the gangplank. "Where's Cap? I wanna see Cap."

She glanced where she had last seen the dog. "I'll call Cap." She passed Jeremiah to Sam and went over by the gangplank. She hadn't needed to use her signal for Cap in months and hoped he hadn't forgotten it. She put her first and fourth fingers between her lips and let out three piercing whistles. Cap barked and swam to the foot of the gangplank.

"Cap!" Jeremiah yelled. "He's coming! He's okay!" He wriggled in Sam's arms. "Put me down. Put me down—I got to get Cap."

Sam lowered the boy to the deck but kept a firm hold on his hand. "He'll come over to you." He hunkered down by the boy. "Jeremiah, look at me." He waited, and the boy finally obeyed. "You *must* stay with me or Maggie or Ely at *all* times. Do you understand?"

Jeremiah nodded. "Can I stay with Cap, too?"

Sam hugged him. "Yes. You two'll stay together with one of us."

Ely came out of his cabin and made his way across the pitching deck to where they stood. "Maggie girl, mebbe ya better see if ya can stay ashore with a friend. This ain't good." He gave Jeremiah a halfhearted smile. "How ya doin', mate?"

Jeremiah grinned. "We're fine. Cap's a good swimmer." He looked at his aunt. "And Aunt Maggie's a real loud whistler."

With her gaze on Sam, she spoke to Ely. "If I leave, this stern-wheeler doesn't stand a chance. Sam, do you want to get a room at the hotel till you can catch the stage?"

Sam shook his head. How could she ask him that? "No, but I agree with Ely. It isn't safe to stay here."

She nodded. "I'll ask Caroline about—" She motioned to Jeremiah.

"I'll go with you." Sam tugged at Jeremiah's hand. "Let's get dressed."

An hour later they were standing at Caroline's front door. When she invited them in, Maggie hesitated because of the mud they would track into her house. "Do you have a few rags? It's awful out."

Caroline took Maggie's arm and dragged her into the entry. "At least wait here out of the rain."

After they had wiped some of the mud off, Maggie stepped to the parlor door. "Have you been in town this morning?"

Caroline shook her head. "What's happened?" She looked from Maggie to Sam. "You didn't have a wreck, did you?"

"No, no. The river's over its bank and flooding the city. I've never seen it like this. Would you keep Jeremiah for a day or two?"

Caroline smiled at the boy. "Of course, but you both must stay here, too."

"Thank you, I can't. I'll lose the *Maggie* if I leave her to that river." Maggie dropped down to Jeremiah and explained why he had to stay with Caroline. "We'll see you soon, but I—" She glanced up at Sam. "We have to make sure the steamboat doesn't float away." Jeremiah's lips quivered, and she hugged him. The poor little tadpole had been through so much. How could he understand all this when she was having trouble with it herself?

Setting the boy's bundle of things on the floor, Sam bent over and put his hand on the boy's narrow shoulder. "I want you to be brave, as brave as Maggie. We'll be back, and Mrs. Dobbs will take good care of you." He stood up and smiled at Caroline. "Thank you. I'll return as soon as I can."

Caroline took Jeremiah's hand, gave him a gentle squeeze and smiled. "We'll be fine." She bent over and said, "I think you'll like Tucker, my cat. He's a boy, too."

He looked around the parlor, then outside. "Cap—Cap's gonna stay here, too, isn't he?"

Maggie shook her head. "I'm sorry, sweetie. He's been with me since he was a tiny pup, and I don't think he'll stay here. Besides, he can't come inside. He'd get Mrs. Dobb's house all dirty and wet, but Tucker's a good cat. He'll keep you company."

After a hasty good-bye, Sam took Maggie's hand and led her out of the house. He started running at the end of Caroline's walkway and didn't stop until they neared the foot of the hill and the water-swollen street. He pulled Maggie into his embrace and held her tight. "It was best to leave him with Mrs. Dobbs. He'll be fine."

She cried against his soaking-wet chest. "Yes, but he looked so unhappy, and he must wonder if he'll ever be safe."

He gently rubbed his hand over her back. "I know. I know. But he'll be safe with her."

She kissed his jaw. "Thank you, Sam. But I'd feel better if you stayed with him. My steamboat isn't your worry."

"*You* are, Maggie. And don't forget that—no matter what happens."

They returned to the steamboat. Like a nightmare come to life, parts of fences, roofs and even planks from a boat dock washed downriver on the raging tide. Foundations of buildings and homes crumbled and were carried away by the river. Ely, Maggie and Sam helped people move their belongings, rescued a couple of stranded cats who had taken refuge in a cedar tree, and helped a family move their wagon loaded with treasured belongings above the rising water.

Across the river, Linn City appeared to be suffering even more than Oregon City. By midafternoon, the underpinnings of the island warehouses gave way under the mounting pressure of the debris-strewn river. Huge timbers and cribwork erupted from the building and were swept over the falls and downriver. The roar of the cascading water was terrifying.

The evening was no less frightening. Weakened by the torrent of water eroding the ground and foundations, buildings began breaking apart and washing away. Men and women clung to their children as best they could, grabbing hold of anything within reach to keep from being swept away. Some took refuge on floating logs, others on their rooftops or in sturdy trees. Torches and lantern lights seemed to bob in the darkness as cries for help could be heard and people searched for family and friends in the turbulent water.

Concerned for Mrs. Tillman's safety, Maggie was separated from Sam when she made her way to the older woman's home. The front door was open, and the water ebbed and flowed from the house. Shouting for her as she waded through each room, she finally discovered Mrs. Tillman perched on top of a wardrobe in a bedroom. "Are you hurt?"

"Oh, goodness, Maggie! I'm so glad you came!"

Maggie pulled a chair over through the knee-deep water, climbed on it and held out her hands. "How did you manage to get up there?"

"Frankly, my dear, I have no idea. When the water reached my knees, I became quite desperate."

Maggie helped her down to the flooded floor. "Where's your valise? We'll pack a few things and get you to higher ground." Fortunately, the older woman wasn't as frail as she appeared and she was able to keep pace with Maggie up to Mrs. Petty's boardinghouse. Maggie hugged her. "You'll be fine, but don't try to rescue any of your belongings until the water goes down."

Mrs. Tillman held onto Maggie's hand. "You're not going back down there tonight! You can't, child."

Maggie laughed and kissed her softly lined cheek. "I'll be fine. Besides, I have to find Sam. He's out there helping others, too." She hurried back down to Main Street, wondering if Sam had found a skiff, the easiest way to navigate the street. Every once in a while she caught sight of her stern-wheeler as she continued to do what she could.

Sometime during the night, she heard cries coming from an old oak tree and followed the sound. By the time she found the tree, Sam was climbing up to help a boy down. When he passed the child to her, she recognized the nine-year-old boy. "Timmy, hold on to me." She carried him over to Second Street and up above the flooded Center Street. "What are you doing here alone?"

"Pa told me to stay here. Have ya seen him, Miss Maggie?"

"No, I haven't, but you go to Mrs. Hanson's. Billy Ward's spending the night there, too."

She watched until he disappeared into Mrs. Hanson's house, then she went back down and joined Sam near the wharf where he was staring at her steamboat. She slumped against his side. "I'm almost numb. How're you doing?"

He held her close to his side and rested his chin on top of her head. "Bone weary. But every time I think of crawling into bed with you, I hear more frightened cries. If there's a hell, this must be close to it."

She yawned and shivered. "I haven't the strength to do any more tonight. Let's turn in."

"I won't argue. Where can we find a dry bed?"

She tipped her head back and looked up at him. They had been out in the rain so long, neither of them seemed to notice it washing over them. "The steamboat. At least it's still afloat."

So far, the lines were holding the old girl, and he sent up a prayer they would remain secure. "Sounds wonderful."

With a last burst of energy, she waded through the waist-deep murky water to the boat. After peeking into Ely's cabin to reassure herself that he was safe, she took Sam's hand and went up to her cabin. Cap was waiting outside her door. He jumped up, put his paws on her shoulders and his head below her chin. She hugged him. "I missed you, too, boy."

Sam opened the door, and they went inside. A few minutes later he was peeling drenched, muddy clothes from her shivering body. He toweled her dry with brisk, warming strokes and tucked her under the covers.

She gave up and lay still. "What about you?"

He dropped his shirt in the bucket on top of her chemise. "It won't take me a minute to climb in beside you."

As her gaze followed the course of his pants down his muscled thighs, she smiled. "Hurry. You have a wonderful body, but I'm falling asleep."

After one last brisk rub with the towel, he tossed it aside

and slid into bed behind her. She snuggled back, molding herself to him, and he kissed her shoulder. "We finally get to spend the night together, and we're too exhausted to do more than sleep." His eyes closed, and he mumbled, "This's truly an injustice."

Later that morning Sam woke up as his palm stroked Maggie's belly. They had slept with their bodies as close together as two pages in a book. He slowly opened his eyes. A hank of her hair was draped over her shoulder, and he realized more was under his cheek. He spread his fingers across her belly and pressed his hips to her nicely rounded backside as he kissed her shoulder. The steamboat rocked. She moaned and nestled back against him, and he smiled. "Morning." He slid his open hand down to the top of her thighs and back up to her breast. "You're a snuggler. I'm glad."

She giggled and squirmed her bottom. "You do know how to wake me up." She stretched her legs out and tried to ignore the boat's pitching and the roar of the falls as she trapped his knee between her thighs.

When she cringed, he knew they couldn't avoid the inevitable much longer. "I don't know what time it is, but the room's light. It must be late."

She rolled over, pressed him back on the mattress with the length of her body and kissed him hungrily. She wanted to forget the rest of the world, while at the same time she knew they couldn't. She started to rock her hips and paused. They didn't have time to make love. She braced her hands at his sides and raised herself up. Her nipples brushed his chest, and she trembled.

Knowing they both ached with the same need, he couldn't leave. He watched her eyes grow large with understanding as he put his hands on her hips. He pressed her down and filled her in one swift motion. He had never felt so complete as he did when their bodies were joined. Her open enjoyment of their lovemaking aroused him beyond control.

She'd needed him more than she had thought and gave into the swell of sensations spinning through her. She loved the feel of his skin rubbing hers, the perfect way they fit together as if two parts of a whole, and most of all, she had never felt more womanly than when she was making love with him. Impatient to satisfy her hunger, she arched her back and welcomed the last rush of pure pleasure as it surged between them.

The bed jolted violently. At first he assumed it was from their energetic lovemaking, but he quickly realized it was the boat. They landed on the floor within moments of each other. He grabbed his pants.

She struggled into her robe on her way to check for damage. The moment she stepped out onto the deck, the overwhelming roar of the river filled her mind, and she covered her ears till she could adjust to the terror it represented. Then she glanced ashore and was shocked anew by the mayhem. Three walls of the livery were gone, and she didn't see a horse or wagon anywhere. Other buildings were missing doors, walls or windows. The stern-wheeler shuddered violently again. She grabbed the rail and braced her legs. As she stared ahead, she noticed that two nearby houses had shifted off their foundations, and another was gone altogether.

When the deck settled to a jerky rocking motion, she made her way around to the deck in front of the saloon and surveyed the area. She stared across the Willamette to Linn City. The devastation was more than she could grasp. The foundry, Island Mills, iron works and machine shop were crumbling, and a large portion of the buildings had already washed away. Homes and storefronts that she had seen every day and paid little attention to were no longer there.

As if it were a dying buffalo, the old stern-wheeler creaked and groaned under the immense power of the water pounding her side, shoving timbers and debris into her. Another deeper rumble was the distinct sound of her planks being wrenched apart. Maggie leaned over the rail and screamed for Ely, then took the stairs two at a time down to the main deck. Before she reached his cabin door, he came out lugging two canvas bags. She gave him a hug. "Thank goodness you're all right." *And you're not bent on saving the steamboat single-handed,* she thought, although she was also surprised he wasn't going to try.

Ely carried the bags over near the gangplank and set them down. "Is Sam gettin' yer trunk?" Cap ran over and licked his hand. Ely ruffled the dog's fur and winked at him.

She shook her head. "Not yet." She couldn't tell him they had just awakened. "Where will you stay?"

He pointed beyond the cliff. "There's a shack a ways back. I'll be there if ya need me." He eyed her a moment longer. "Ya okay, girl? Is Sam gonna take ya and the lad back with him?"

"Not me! Why would you think that? Everything I have is right here." *Well, almost,* she thought. "And it's not going over the falls if I can help it."

As he stepped over to the rail and stood in the rain, Sam fastened his coat and noticed the bags. He hurried down to see what was going on. "Are you leaving, Ely?"

"If'n yer half as smart, ya'll git, too." Ely stared at Maggie. "These old timbers won't hold much longer. It's too late fer wishes 'n' prayers."

Sam put his arm around Maggie. "I heard the death rattle, too. It won't take us long to pack up some of her things." He gave her an encouraging gaze. He hadn't wanted to bring it up so abruptly but since it was out in the open, he wasn't about to deny the fact that the stern-wheeler had taken such a pounding that he didn't believe the boat was safe.

When she hugged Ely again, she asked, "Is that shack big enough for all of us?" She knew Jeremiah must be frightened and wondering if they had forgotten him.

He patted her back. "Surely is." He gave her cheek a quick peck and picked up his canvas bags.

That was the third time he had kissed her cheek in all the years she'd known him—the second time had been after Zeke was put to rest. Tears streamed down her cheeks. "We'll get Jeremiah and be there."

As they watched Ely trudge through the water, Sam stood behind her with his arms crisscrossing her breast, holding her safe as the deck continued to pitch. "He's right. We haven't much time to pack up your things."

She clamped her teeth down on her lips to keep from crying out and nodded. As she struggled to collect her fragmented thoughts, she couldn't tell Sam she wasn't ready to give up on the old boat just yet. Once her plan was set in her mind, she sighed and raised his hand to her lips. "We'd better get busy." Cap bumped her leg trying to sit as close to her as possible. She reached down and scratched the top of his head.

She had been tense, but now she was quiet within his arms. He sighed, relieved she was taking it so well. She hurried back to the cabin and went through the motions of packing, but he could tell her heart wasn't in it. She packed her clothes in a large old valise. "Is that trunk full?"

"Pretty much, but it's too heavy to lug to Ely's shack." She pulled out Zeke's old canvas bag and stuffed it with the rest of her things and the few precious mementos she couldn't bear to part with. Sam pushed a cup of coffee into her hands, and she gratefully gulped down half of it.

He found a heavy duck bag in the rag bin and filled it with as much food as it would hold; then he tossed Cap's pan on top and pulled the drawstring to close it. He set it by the cabin door and put her two bags there, also. "Ready to go? We can stop by Mrs. Dobbs's and get Jeremiah after we leave these things at the shack."

She nodded and stared around at the cabin that had been her home for what seemed like most of her life. It wasn't pretty, or even especially nice, but it was cozy, and it was hers. She took a deep breath, put her coat on, plopped her hat back on her head and picked up a valise with each hand. "Ready." She smiled at Cap. "Come on, boy."

Sam followed her down to the main deck carrying the bag of food and retrieved his portmanteau from his cabin. When he went to meet her, she had already made the dangerous trip down the swaying gangplank on her own. He gauged the shifting planks and made a dash for it. She was standing in water halfway up to her waist and staring at the stern-wheeler. The dog had enough sense to wait further up the hill just beyond the water. "We'll come back later and check on her."

She nodded and, with Cap at her side, waded to Second Street, following the track Ely had taken. They walked in silence, as if mourning the fate of her steamboat, though that fate wasn't yet sealed in her mind. When Ely saw them coming across the soggy ground to the shack, he was clearly startled, and she had to laugh. It had been worth lugging her belongings up there just to see the surprise in his craggy face. Cap ran ahead, greeted Ely and trotted inside.

Sam entered the shanty right behind her and set his bags down by hers. There was one room with a crude fireplace, but it had a split-log floor, and it was dry. "This's nice. Is it yours, Ely?"

"Nah. An old tracker an' me built it b'fore anyone owned the land."

Maggie eyed him. "I've never known about this place."

Ely shrugged. "No need fer ya t'know till now."

"You're a cagy man, Ely Cole."

"I'm not the only one," he muttered with his back to her.

Sam heard him and grinned. The old man knew her well. He turned his back to the fire and glanced at her. "Want to get Jeremiah before we settle in here?"

She moved the canvas bag and frowned, pretending she had misplaced something. "Why don't you get him? I can't find my hatbox." She glanced at him and shrugged. "I'll go back and get it. I can meet you at Caroline's if you like." She had to return to the steamboat, and she needed to go alone.

"We can go together." That idea didn't appear to set well with her, but he didn't intend to leave her any choice. Now that he'd had a chance to think it over, he realized she had agreed to abandon the steamboat much too easily.

"Oh, there's no need for you to do that. You're already drying out." She hugged Cap and told him to stay with Ely. She wasn't about to take a chance with Ely. "I'll be right back." Before he could speak, she darted out the door and nearly ran down to the river. All the way down the last block, she stared at the little stern-wheeler being battered about in the swollen river.

She ran up the heaving gangplank. Halfway up, she fell to her knees and had to crawl the rest of the way for fear of being thrown into the water. She landed on the deck facedown, with her heart racing. She kissed the deck and laid her cheek down for one moment. "I haven't given up on you—not yet."

She heard someone shout her name from the shore and got to her knees. "Mr. Peterson, how're you doing?"

He waved his arms in the air. "Storefront's still there, better than most. Have you heard about the Overmeyers? Their farm's under five feet of water."

"Oh no, not after—" *Those poor people,* she thought.

"The warehouse full of grain down at Wheatland got soaked and blew up. Seven thousand bushels, I heard." Peterson shook his head. "Livestock, outbuildings, people . . . so much lost in a couple days." He brushed at the rain streaking down his face. "Do you need any help?"

"I'm fine. Just checking over the boat."

"Take care, Maggie."

"You, too." She went up to the pilothouse and looked at the falls. The basin was still rising and the falls was only half as high as it had been. She noticed a movement out of the corner of her eye and turned in time to see three logs bound together and heading straight at her. She mumbled, "Oh, grannie—" and the piling was driven into the side of her hull.

The steamboat lurched, and she grabbed the wheel to steady herself. Suddenly, the river surged, spewing remnants of buildings, a wagon bed, even the carcass of a cow, straight at her boat. The lines screeched under the strain and gave way, one by one. Instinctively, she blew the whistle. The water swelled, and she wrapped her arms around the wheel. Suddenly the stern-wheeler rose up and plunged over what had once been the riverbank. She was completely helpless as the bow of the steamboat careened into the south wall of the old warehouse.

She reeled from the impact and slumped over the wheel. After she caught her breath, she pried her stiff fingers from the wheel. Her legs gave out, and she slid to the tilted deck. She lay there listening as the death rattle of the *Maggie* jolted her body. Her tears ran along the deck. The stern-wheeler had become her life, it represented all she had made of her life; it was her past, and her dream for the future.

And it was gone.

Chapter

24

Sam had given her a head start and hadn't boarded the boat until he saw her in the pilothouse staring toward the falls. Then something rammed the starboard side of the hull, and almost immediately the ropes whined and snapped. He staggered up the stairs and ran as best he could along the walkway to the ladder. Halfway up, he felt the boat shoot forward, and he braced for the collision. He was thrown from side to side, but he managed to hold fast.

The steamboat finally came to a jarring stop, and he became aware of shouts aimed at him. Loosening his grip, he waved them away before he climbed the last three rungs, yanked the door open and dove into the pilothouse. She was curled up on the deck. "Maggie!" He scrambled to her side and leaned over her. "Oh, sweetheart, I thought—" He pulled her into his arms and rocked her. "You're all right. Thank God, you're all right."

She was numb. His words didn't make any sense. Didn't he understand? She pushed away from him, still sobbing. "How can you say that?! I was a steamboat owner, and I was a pilot. I earned my own keep. Now I've nothing—no steamboat, nothing to pilot. As if all those years didn't count. All that work went for nothing." She wrapped her arms around herself as the tears washed down her face. "Gone . . . all gone."

"Sweetheart," he said, smoothing the wet hair back from her face. "You've lost replaceable things, but we're safe. I can't imagine what I'd do if I lost you or Jeremiah. And you're a hell of a lot more than a riverboat pilot or boat owner. So much more." He tipped her chin up with his curved index finger. "You are a hell of a woman, and I love you very much, Maggie Carter Foster." He wrapped his arms around her and held on, determined to see her through this disaster and convince her that her future was with him.

Slowly, the warmth of his body eased the tightness in her limbs, and his voice helped soothe her anguish. She lowered her arms. Her mind worked sluggishly. She didn't know how much time had passed before she heard him saying, ". . . love you." She stared at him. "What did you say?"

"That you're—"

"No— That's not it." Her heart pounded in her throat as she waited for him to say it once more.

Keeping his expression as bland as possible, he met her stare. "I love you? Is that what you wanted to hear?"

"That's what I thought I heard." She wound her arms around him and held him for fear he too might be snatched from her. "Oh, Sam—" His words had reached that cold, empty place inside, and she trembled. "Just hold me. I need you to hold me."

He pulled her onto his lap, content to have her in his arms, until the slanted deck shifted again. He loosed her grip enough to cover her mouth with his, hoping to convince her how very much he loved her. After he ravaged her sweet mouth, he gazed into her sparkling eyes. "Don't you think we should get that hatbox and get back on shore?"

She nodded. "I thought we were already ashore." Rolling to her knees, she gave him a weak smile and grabbed the wheel to pull herself up.

He got to his feet and braced his back against the doorjamb before he reached out and took her hand. "If this deck gives out, we'll land in your bedroom in short order."

She nodded and stepped onto the ladder. Without looking around, she went down to her cabin. She worked the latch, but the door was stuck. As Sam helped her, she suddenly wondered how he had found her so quickly. "What brought you back here?"

They shoved the door open, and he smiled at her. "I followed you." He put his hands on her shoulders. "Where was the hatbox?" He wanted to keep her focused on their purpose for being there, not the chaos. Areas of the deck were weak and in danger of giving way—they didn't have time to waste.

"The bedroom, and I'm glad you followed me, though I would've been mad had I known. I'd planned to ride this out alone." She stepped around her rocking chair, pushed the little table aside and paused in the bedroom doorway. The furniture had been anchored to the deck and was still in place for the most part. The mirror had fallen, and then she saw her broken water pitcher and basin on the floor. "No, oh no. The red primroses were so pretty." She clamped her mouth shut.

He stepped around her and searched until he spotted the hatbox under the mirror in a pool of water near the pitcher. He pulled it free and handed the wet string to her. "We have to leave, Maggie. It isn't safe here."

She stared at the mashed box and burst into tears. "Not this too, not my beautiful new hat."

When she started to sink to the deck, he caught her around the waist and pulled her to his chest. "It's just a hat. You can pick out a new one." He started walking her back to the door.

"I don't want another one!" She stopped in the parlor and tore the top off of the ruined hatbox. "I want this one." She held the hat up and shook it. "It'll clean up."

"Easier than you will if this deck gives way." He kissed her forehead and pulled her along with him.

Caroline stared at Maggie and Sam. "But you're all right? You weren't injured?"

Maggie grinned at Sam. "I'm better than ever." She glanced at Jeremiah. After his first flurry of questions, he sat down on the floor and wriggled a string for Tucker. "I hope he wasn't—"

Caroline waved off the inquiry. "He's been a wonderful help with Mrs. Williams, taking water to her and showing Tucker to her."

"Mrs. Williams? I had no idea you had house guests,

Caroline." Maggie felt terribly guilty for having imposed on her dear friend. "I would never have—"

"Maggie," Caroline said, interrupting her. "Mr. Moss and Mr. Peterson rescued her from the river and brought her here yesterday evening, while the others searched for Mr. Williams."

Maggie glanced toward the hall leading to the bedroom and spoke softly. "Have you heard any more about her husband?"

Caroline shook her head. "She prayed all last night, but there's been no word." Her gaze darted to the hallway leading to the bedrooms. "She told me they were crossing the river to get to Dr. Lindly's. I'm afraid she'll have the baby before he's found."

"Oh, dear. Surely no one could cross that current. Is it near her time?" Maggie glanced at Sam. She was so grateful for his consideration and discretion.

Caroline nodded. "She'll be fine—I must believe that."

A woman's groan drifted down the hall, and Maggie glanced in that direction. "Jeremiah," she said, holding out her hand. "We have to go. Don't you want to thank Mrs. Dobbs for her hospitality?"

He nodded and walked over to Mrs. Dobbs. "Thank you for letting me play with Tucker. He likes the top of his head rubbed with one finger."

She laughed and hugged him. "You can come visit him any time Maggie says it's okay."

Sam smiled at Caroline. "If you need any help, we'll be at the shack on the knoll just south of here."

"Thank you, Mr. Adams. I hope I'll see you again, soon."

Jeremiah gave Tucker one more kiss and laughed when the cat scrunched up his face. "You keep Mrs. Williams company, okay?" Tucker blinked, and he nodded. "Aunt Maggie, Tucker's almost as smart as Cap."

"I know he is. Come on, Cap'll be happy to see you." Maggie hugged Caroline. "Thank you so much. I'll call on you soon." She hurried outside.

Jeremiah walked down the road with his aunt on one side and Sam on the other. "How come you didn't bring Cap?"

Maggie darted a quick glance at Sam before she answered. "He's keeping Ely company."

Her old hat kept most of the rain off her face, but it ran down the back of her coat. As they sloshed across the soggy field to the shack, she wondered if it would ever stop raining.

That evening, Ely, Jeremiah and Cap, Sam and Maggie sat in the small cabin with only the fire in the fireplace for light. Ely and Sam had made a trip to the steamboat for bedding and returned with one more object that was very dear to Maggie—the stern-wheeler's placard. She sat down on the rough stone hearth and stared at the placard leaning against the wall. She wondered where she would end up living.

Jeremiah put the boy doll on Cap's back. Everyone was so quiet. "Aunt Maggie, can't we *ever* go back on your steamboat?"

"We'll see it again, but you can't go aboard." She glanced at Sam. "Besides, there may not be much left in a day or so."

Jeremiah crawled over to Ely to see what he was whittling. "My dog. You finishing him?"

"Sure am." Ely rounded off a sharp ridge with the edge of his knife and ran his little finger over it. Seemingly satisfied, he handed it to Jeremiah. "There ya are, mate. Yer very own dog."

Jeremiah held it with both hands. "Oh, gee, Ely, it looks just like Cap. It's the best dog in the whole world—'sides Cap." He threw his arms around Ely. "Thank you."

Ely gave Jeremiah a bear hug. When the boy showed the carved dog to Cap, Ely looked up and saw Maggie watching him. He cleared his throat and swiped at his nose.

As she glanced around, she wondered what she and Ely would do after Sam left with Jeremiah. She had the money she had managed to save, but it wasn't a drop in the bucket for what she'd need for another steamboat. When Jeremiah stretched out on the floor and used Cap's side for a pillow, she carried him to the bed she'd made for the three of them and kissed him good night. Now, she suddenly realized, she could keep him with her. A thrill ran through her, until she remembered she had no way to support him. "Oh, sweetheart," she barely whispered, "I love you," and kissed him.

Ely stared at the fire and waited until she sat down by Sam. "Have ya thought about what yer goin' to do now, girl?"

"No. I can't get another steamboat, though there might be enough salvage from the *Maggie* to make a ferry of sorts." She crossed her legs the way Jeremiah did on occasion and rested her elbows on her knees. "How about you, Ely? You going to see about working on the *Onward* or the *Enterprise*?"

"Nah. I'm too old 'n' stubborn to break in another steam engine." He looked over at Jeremiah. "Maggie girl, it's time I took old Roker up on his offer. He's got a place in the Cascades. After today, it sounds real nice."

Sam didn't seem surprised by Ely's announcement, but she certainly was. He'd been a good friend, sometimes a father to her. "Why? We'll find something. You love the river. What will you do in the mountains?"

He glanced at her and shook his head. "I wasn't always a riverman, girl. An' you weren't raised on a riverboat, either. You have to get on with your life—or pine away fer what never was like poor old Mrs. Merritt." He shook his head. "She's still livin' back in '37." He eyed Maggie as if she were a wayward child. "A good boat captain knows when to change course."

Oh, grannie, I'm going to cry again, she thought, *I'm turning into a spigot.* "We'll go back to the boat in the morning. You don't have to decide tonight."

"Already did, Maggie, girl. I'll tell the lad in the morning b'fore I go." Ely set his cup on the floor and stretched out on his pallet.

Sam moved to her side and embraced her. The rain pelted the old cabin and rattled the door. She trembled in his arms, and he wondered if she would now consider moving to California with him and Jeremiah. "You two are a lot alike. You do what you believe is best—no matter how painful it may be."

"It's as if . . . he's always been with me," she murmured, holding onto him. "Everything's changing so fast, and I can't stop it." She brushed her cheek on his shirt and wished she could sit there forever in his embrace so he wouldn't leave, too. In the space of a week, she would have lost everything that was dear to her.

"We've had a hell of a day. Why don't we get some rest?" He kissed her temple. "Who knows, it may not rain tomorrow." *And we might even find a more than agreeable solution to both of our predicaments.*

She almost smiled.

After a rib-sticking breakfast of stirabout, Maggie refilled their cups and started washing the pot and three tin bowls. Jeremiah was talking with Sam and Ely. Their voices were the sweetest music she could imagine. She finished with the few dishes and refilled their cups again. Sam had been right. The rain had finally stopped.

Ely looked at Jeremiah. "Why don't we take Cap fer a walk?"

"Okay." Jeremiah got his coat and went outside with him. "Where we gonna walk?"

"Jist up here a ways." Cap trotted ahead, and Ely shoved his hands in his coat pockets. "Mate, I'm leavin' in a bit, goin' to stay with a friend of mine. I jist wanted ya to know that I think yer the finest mate I ever had."

"What?!" Jeremiah threw himself at Ely's legs and held on. "You can't leave me, Ely. You can't!"

Ely grimaced and patted the lad's back. "Ya got Maggie and Sam. An don't fergit Cap." He sat down on a tree stump.

Jeremiah climbed on his lap and put his arms around him. "I don't want you to go, Ely."

"It's time, mate. I been thinkin' on this fer a while." Ely rubbed the boy's back with awkward strokes. "Come on, now, everythin's goin' t'be fine."

"Who's your friend? Where's he live?" Jeremiah rubbed his coat sleeve across his nose and knuckled his wet eyes.

"Roker. Lives up the Clackamas River in the high

mountains." Ely smiled at the boy. "I'll git to feed deer, see long-eared rabbits and mebbe a moose or two."

"Gee. Can I go with you? Where is the river? I never seen a moose." Jeremiah sniffed to stop his runny nose. "I'll be real good, and I can help you. Please, Ely . . ."

"No, mate. Yer place's with Sam 'n' Maggie." Jeremiah's chin quivered, and Ely frowned. "Now, now, mate. Don't ya go bawlin'. They need ya." He glanced at the sky. "The Clackamas River's jist there," he said, pointing to the north side of town. "I gotta leave b'fore it gits any later."

Jeremiah almost ran to keep up with Ely. "Why don'tcha want me? I thought we were friends."

Ely didn't miss a step, but he didn't look at the boy, either. "We're more'n friends. We're mates, always will be." When they reached the cabin, he went inside, put his backpack on and picked up his canvas bag.

Maggie stared at him. "Now?"

He nodded.

She ran across the room and wrapped her arms around him. "I don't know how to say good-bye to you. I'm going to miss you so very much." She was helpless to prevent the first sob that escaped, then bit her tongue to regain control and stepped back a pace. "How can I get in touch with you?"

"Suppose I'll get to Varny's outpost every few weeks." He gave her a stern look. "Ya'll know what t'do when the time comes. Ya always did, girl." He held out his hand to Sam. "Good luck to ya. I'm thinkin' ya'll need it, son."

Sam shook Ely's hand. "It's been a real pleasure, Ely. Take care." Sam gave him a curt nod. If Maggie's eyes hadn't filled with tears, she would surely have seen the pain in the old man's eyes.

Jeremiah buried his face in Cap's neck and held him tight. He didn't want to see Ely leave, but he did.

Ely ruffled Jeremiah's hair and winked at Cap. "Don't fergit to feed him."

"I won't!" Jeremiah stood up and glared at him. "I won't ever feed him again!"

Maggie put her arms around him. "You can't mean that. Please, wish Ely well and a safe journey."

Jeremiah looked up at Ely. "Yeah, what she said, but I still don't want you to go."

Ely harrumphed and hurried outside.

Jeremiah ran out and followed, watching where Ely went until Aunt Maggie and Sam caught up with him.

Sam picked the boy up and held him in his arms. "Why don't we go down and see what Main Street looks like today?" He gazed at Maggie and read the resignation in her eyes. "We should be happy. The sun's trying to come out." He linked arms with her and started back along the grassy track.

Sam carried Jeremiah in his arms, then gave him a piggyback ride as they wandered around town. Maggie wished people well with her usual strength and sunny disposition. She was doing it for the boy, but Sam hoped it would eventually bolster her own spirits, too.

She stared down the street at the remains of George Abernethy's old brick store, the first brick building in Oregon City. Linn City was gone—it was as if it had never been there. They'd been told that Champoeg and Orleans had washed downriver, too, as well as the lower parts of Independence and Wheatland. There were so many towns carried away by the raging Willamette River, it didn't seem real—it was too much to truly understand.

She glanced at Sam. "At least we don't need a skiff to get down the street today. Before we turn back, I want to see how the Barnhills are doing."

He grinned at her trousers. "At least you're dressed for this walk."

"Sam," Jeremiah said, looking around from Sam's shoulders. "There's a steamboat! Looky."

Maggie scanned the upper river. "That's the *St. Clair*, with Captain Taylor at her wheel. She works on the Yamhill." Maggie waded through the mucky mess up to Laurel and Paul's restaurant. The front of the building had been torn off, and mud covered everything like cocoa icing.

Maggie picked her way past broken furniture, splintered pieces of wood and what looked like refuse from the livery on her way into the kitchen. Laurel was scooping mud out of the oven. "Hi, want some help?"

Laurel whirled around and grinned. "Well, I'll be. I saw your steamboat—everyone has. Mr. Peterson said you were okay." She smiled at Sam and Jeremiah. "Where've you been?"

"A shack up past the high-water mark." Maggie glanced around. "How are Paul and the children?"

"We're fine and grimy." Laurel pulled a towel from a peg and wiped her hands. "Have you ever seen anything like this? I swear, if Noah had been here, he would've needed his ark."

Maggie chuckled. "Are you going to rebuild?"

Paul came in the back door with two buckets. "Hi, Maggie." He nodded to Sam. "We certainly are going to reopen." He gave Laurel's backside a pat.

She swatted his hand. "I told him after we clear out this mess and put a new front on the place, *I'll* seat the customers, and he can cook." She gave him a satisfied smile.

Maggie grinned. "Sounds fair to me."

Sam laughed. "I hope you're a good cook."

"Oh, he is." Maggie stepped closer to the stove. "Have you seen Abernethy's?"

Laurel nodded. "Went during the night." She shook her head. "Never thought that building could fall ap—"

"Paul! Mrs. Barnhill!" Mr. Peterson shouted, as he ran into what was left of the dining room. "Oh, Maggie. You have to come out here and see this!" He stabbed his finger in the air toward the river. "The *St. Clair*!"

"Oh, no," Maggie said, running outside. "She's not going down, is she?"

Sam followed right behind with the Barnhills. He stepped to her side. "Take Jeremiah. I'll see what I can do." He turned and bent over to make it easier for her.

Peterson tapped Sam's arm. "They don't need help. Watch! The *St. Clair*'s going over the falls!"

"By God, it is!" Paul pulled Laurel forward. "That fool's going to do it!"

"I can see it, Sam!" Jeremiah tried to raise himself up to get a better look, but Sam pulled him back.

Maggie forgot to breathe as the *St. Clair* neared the falls. People were watching from both sides of the river, but she couldn't take her attention from the little steamboat as the bow tipped down and ran the falls. For a long moment, there wasn't a sound from the crowd of onlookers. Then the *St. Clair* landed in the basin below the falls and Captain Taylor blew the whistle three times. Everyone cheered loud enough to drown out the roar of the river.

Sam hugged her to his side. "Feel better?" She resembled a young girl at her first fair. Each time he thought about how very much he loved her, he was shaken anew. It really did amaze him.

She gasped and grinned at him. "People will be talking about this for years." Taylor had really done it. She admired his courage. A few others had tried it, but they hadn't succeeded. Of course Taylor did have the high basin, which helped.

The sun had slipped down past the western hills, and it was growing dark. Sam nudged her. "We'd better get back to that shack while we can still see. I don't think there'll be a moon tonight."

With a nod, Maggie turned to Laurel. "We'd better go. I'll see you soon."

"Come back for supper in a week. We probably won't be open, but we can eat."

Maggie and Sam reached the shack in the last traces of daylight. She fixed them a cold dinner, and they both kept Jeremiah occupied until she put him to bed on Ely's pallet. Cap lay on the floor by his side. She sat on the hearth with Sam's arms around her. "I'm tired, how about you?"

"Mm-hm. Keeping him too busy to think about Ely was hard work." He nuzzled her neck. "But there's something I'd like to ask of you."

She snuggled against him. "I'm listening."

"I've had a lot of time to think this over, and I know it's

right—at least for me." He'd been told he had a gift with speech. If at no other time in his life, he hoped it would be true now, when he needed it most. "I want to adopt Jeremiah—but only if you approve."

She sat up and turned around to face him. She had never seen him so serious. "Honestly? You want to raise him as your own?" She had hoped, prayed for this weeks ago, and she knew there couldn't be a better father for her nephew anywhere.

"After all we've been through with him, I can't hand him over to anyone else. And I couldn't love him any more if he were my natural son." He combed his fingers through her hair. "I do have a problem, though. There isn't anyone who can watch him while I'm working the ranch. I can hardly expect him to ride double with me for the next six years. At the ranch, he'll be as cut off from other children as he would've been on the steamboat." It was a calculated risk. His—no, their—future depended on her devotion, her deep-seated loyalty and her stubborn pride. He intended to raise the boy, but he wanted to do it with her.

That was all? she thought. For a moment, she'd feared there might be a real problem. "You shouldn't have trouble hiring a housekeeper, maybe a widow with a child of her own." She grazed his jaw with one finger. He wouldn't have any trouble finding a woman. She lowered her hand.

He shook his head. "That may sound easy to you, but I wouldn't know what to ask. I certainly wasn't any good at trying to find him a new family."

"Your heart wasn't in it. I don't believe mine was either—not really." She glanced over at Jeremiah. She loved the little guy and wanted the best for him. Knowing he would be happy made her feel better. The burning log flared, and she smiled at Sam.

He wanted to touch her, hold her, but he resisted the urge. He respected her too much to try seducing her into submission. "This may sound unseemly, and be an imposition, but would you consider going back with us to help me interview housekeepers?" He gave her a cockeyed grin to soften the proposal and added, "You said you'd visit if you had the chance. I can't think of a better time, can you?"

She blinked and narrowed her gaze. His offer sounded too desirable. "You're a smooth talker, Sam. You don't need my help."

"In court, no—otherwise, yes." He leaned forward and put his hands on his thighs, ready to stand up. "You don't have to decide tonight. There probably won't be a stage through here for another couple of days." He stood up and held out his hand to her. "Ready for bed? I can't keep my eyes open."

Chapter
25

Jeremiah buried his face in the pillow and covered his ears, but he could still hear Sam and his Aunt Maggie talking about him. Sam said he'd take him to his ranch, and she seemed real happy about that. Jeremiah didn't understand all of the words, but he knew his aunt liked her steamboat better than him.

He curled up in a ball and scrunched up his face, but the tears came anyway. She didn't want him. And Sam was just being nice. Ely likes me, he thought, he only wanted me to stay here 'cause he figured they wanted him. Jeremiah heard them go to bed, then it was quiet, 'cept for the fire and Cap's snorty noise. He reached out to the dog and sank his fingers in the deep fur as he went to sleep.

He woke up later. The cabin was dark. He sat up and looked over at the big bed. Sam and his aunt were sleeping. Cap woke up and licked his face. "If I go find Ely," Jeremiah whispered, "will you come with me?" Cap licked him again. "Good, boy."

Being as quiet as he could, he pulled the pillowcase off the pillow. He put a pair of trousers in it, his horse, and the boat and the dog Ely whittled for him. He put on his shoes and coat and accidently kicked Cap's pan. He crouched down and waited for one of them to call out. He waited a long time, but they didn't wake up. He added the pan to the pillowcase, picked it up and put on his hat.

Jeremiah tiptoed to the door, eased it open and stepped outside with the dog. After he closed the door, he patted his leg for Cap and ran toward the river that Ely showed him.

He hadn't gone very far when he had to slow down and walk. "This stuff's heavy, Cap." The dog looked at him, and he smiled. "We'll find Ely. I know where he went."

He started down the hill and remembered that Ely had gone toward the mountains 'cause his friend lived up there. Jeremiah did the same with the dog at his side. He walked a long long time and finally the sky got light. Cap drank from a creek, and Jeremiah got down like the dog and drank some water, too. He sure was getting tired. Ely had to be just up ahead. He had to be.

His legs began to hurt, and he was getting hungry. Cap ran into the field and came back. "I gotta sit down, boy. We'll meet Ely later." There were some bushes by the side of the road. He curled up on the river side in the shade and put the pillowcase under his head. "Stay here, boy. We'll find something to eat after we rest."

Maggie woke when the sun warmed her face. *Finally,* she thought. *We need many dry sunny days to dig out from under all the muck.* She stretched and slid out of bed without rousing Sam and shook out her wrinkled skirt. In the close confines of the single-room shack, it had seemed best to sleep in her dress. The last few days had worn down all of them. She stirred the fire and put a pot of coffee over the fire before she made a trip outside. When she returned, she noticed Jeremiah's messy bed. *He must be a restless sleeper,* she thought, and went out to wait for the coffee to boil.

When she stepped back inside, Sam was sitting up in bed grinning at her. "Looks like a nice day."

"Beautiful." She filled two cups and handed one to him.

He took a sip and glanced at Jeremiah's bed. "What happened there?"

"Most likely he had a nightmare. He's been quiet since I got up." It was strange that he hadn't roused, especially with them talking near his bed. With a glance at Sam, she peeked under Jeremiah's comforter, then tossed it off the bed. "He's not here! Neither's Cap—" She ran outside and shielding her eyes, searched as far as she could see in each direction.

Sam joined her, only instead of looking up and around, he

studied the wet ground. There were footprints all over, but two sets, one a child's and one a dog's, led away at a different angle. "Looks like he went after Ely." He showed the tracks to her.

"He couldn't be far. Let's go." She had taken only three steps before he caught her wrist and stopped her.

"Maggie, we don't know how long he's been gone. Pack up a meal, and we'd better see what he took—besides the dog."

They soon discovered what Jeremiah had chosen to take with him, and it wasn't long before they were following the tracks. When they neared the Clackamas River, they walked east. Maggie stopped in the shade of an oak tree and mopped her brow. "How could he have come so far? Are you sure we're going the right way?"

"Jeremiah's tracks aren't as clear, but Cap's are." Sam rolled his shirtsleeves up while he stared ahead. "He must've left during the night."

"I had no idea he was so unhappy. He seemed fine when he fell asleep." She glanced over at the swollen river as they continued on the rough path. *What if he*— She shivered, refusing to complete the horrifying thought.

Sam gave her hand a reassuring squeeze. "He has a lot of explaining to do." His father would've tanned him until he couldn't sit down or walk, but he wasn't sure that would solve the problem.

She looked over her shoulder. "How far have we walked? Could we have missed him? It's midday. He *couldn't've* come all this way by himself."

Sam pointed to the soft ground. "Looks like Cap did, and he wasn't alone, thank God. I'd say those two vagabonds have gone at least five miles." He stared at the mountains in the distance and shook his head. No matter how clever the boy was, he'd never locate Ely.

A short time later, she heard a steamboat in the distance and ran to the edge of the river. When it came into sight, she waved it down. The *River Queen* stopped and the fireman waved to her. She called out, "Have you seen a little boy with a brown dog?"

The man shouted, "Sorry. Not a one today, ma'am."

"Thanks." She glanced at Sam and they walked on in silence. She was tired, but she couldn't believe they had missed the boy. Suddenly, Cap ran out from some bushes ahead and came straight to her, barking the whole way. She hugged him, then asked, "Where's Jeremiah? Show us."

Sam grabbed her hand and ran after the dog. They found Jeremiah, hiding under a large bush. Sam lifted the boy out and stood him in front of himself and Maggie. "Well, boy, what do you have to say?"

Jeremiah stared at his shoes until Cap sat down next to him. "We're going to find Ely." Sam was mad, real mad. Jeremiah put his hand on Cap's neck.

His stomach growled, and Maggie smiled to herself. "Sam, if he doesn't like us any more, he might as well try to find Ely." She stared at the distant Cascade Mountains. "He might be a grown man before he finds him, though." She shrugged. "I don't know about you two, but I'm hungry." Knowing she had his attention, she sat down in the shade and pulled out the slices of smoked him and stale bread. "We'll eat and head back to the cabin."

Sam followed her lead. "Sounds good to me. I'll take a slice of ham." He sat down across from her. "And a piece of bread." Cap came over to him, and Sam gave the dog a bite of bread.

Jeremiah licked his lips. "Can't I have some?"

Maggie glanced over her shoulder, chewing her mouthful of meat, intentionally tempting him. She gulped down the dry bread. "Did you eat all your food?"

Jeremiah shook his head. "I don't have any, but I got Cap's pan. You want it back?"

Maggie had to struggle not to smile at that. "Yes, thank you. I'll need it when I feed him supper tonight."

After he pulled it out of the pillowcase, Jeremiah inched closer to them. "You mean he's gotta go back with you?"

"Sure. He's my dog." She started to take another bite, then hesitated. "If you find Ely, maybe he'll get you a dog." If he'd only sit down with them, she wouldn't have to be so hard on him, but he had to realize that running away wasn't the answer. She forced herself to eat one more bite of meat. It had to be his choice, and he had to make the first move.

Jeremiah shoved the pan closer to her. "Ely wants me."

Sam looked him in the eye and steeled himself to say what he must. "Did he tell you he wanted you to live with him?"

Jeremiah stuck his chin out and shook his head. "But he said you did . . . *an' you don't.*"

Maggie glanced at Sam and forced herself to sound calmer than she felt. "Why would you think such a thing?" She'd had no idea that Jeremiah had been so unhappy, and she felt guilty.

"Just do." Jeremiah kicked a rock and a splatter of mud landed between them.

The boy had overheard them talking, Sam just knew it. "I don't agree. In fact, I don't believe you really understood what you heard us talking about." He gave Maggie a slight nod. "I said, I *do want you*, that I couldn't love you more if you really were my own son." Tears sprang to the boy's eyes. Sam cleared his throat. "Does that sound like I don't want you?"

Jeremiah was really scared now, and he didn't know what to do. Sam was still mad, but he said he wanted him.

Maggie looked at him. "And I said I can't keep you with me. I work all day and I don't have a home—not because I don't want you or love you. I do, Jeremiah." It was so much for him to understand at such a young age.

He looked away from her. He wanted to believe her, he *really* did. She was nice and fun lotsa times, and she was like his ma sometimes, too. He chewed on his lip, wishing she'd tell him what to do, like a real ma would.

Sam knew how difficult that was for her and decided to try a different approach. "Have you ever seen sheep?"

"Unh-unh." Jeremiah shuffled his feet. He sure wanted to sit down, but he petted Cap instead.

"They're smaller than cows and have wooly coats." Sam ate a bite of meat before he continued. "They aren't too smart. We'll have a dog to herd them—keep them to-gether."

Jeremiah stared at him. "Is Cap going to do that?"

"Mm, I'm not sure about that." He wanted to see the look on Maggie's face, but he wanted to give her time to think that over while he concentrated on Jeremiah.

"He's *real* smart." Jeremiah inched closer to them. "I betcha he could do it."

"Maybe he could." Sam moved aside to make room for him. "The ranch is pretty big, and it isn't too far from the Sacramento River." He gazed at Maggie and wondered if she realized he was attempting to fascinate her also. "There's a lot of pastureland and some trees, a couple of creeks, and there'll be a house—if I get back to help raise it."

"I could help you." Jeremiah dropped down to his knees. "Pa said I was strong." He glanced at his aunt and licked his lips.

He's beginning to realize his mistake, Maggie thought, handing him a couple of slices of meat. "Don't eat too fast, honey, or you'll get a bellyache." Oh, that boy was stubborn, but then, so was Sam in his own way.

Jeremiah nodded and took the meat. "Are you going to the ranch, too?"

She felt paralyzed for the briefest moment. *Oh, grannie, I won't lie to him, but I can't be as outspoken as I'd like, either.* She glanced at him, wishing he weren't so serious. "Now, what would I do on a ranch?"

Sam continued nibbling on the meat, intrigued to see how she was going to answer when she finally addressed the question. In winning over Jeremiah, he'd won an ally, which was a pleasant surprise.

Sitting down between them, Jeremiah looked at each of them. "Lots o' stuff. You cook real good, and Cap'd like chasing sheep."

She nearly laughed at his compliment on her cooking, but if she did, he wouldn't understand. She shifted positions, uncomfortable on the damp log and with the direction the conversation was going. "I've never lived on a ranch, and I don't know anything about sheep." Even she thought that was a weak, roundabout answer, but the truth would put

Sam in an awkward spot and embarrass her. She loved him so very much, but it was absolutely necessary that he wanted her company because he loved her, not just to help with Jeremiah. Sam had said he loved her, but she knew he meant it only in a friendly way to reassure her after the accident.

She looked funny. Jeremiah glanced at Sam. He looked happy. "Don'tcha like Sam?"

Feeling trapped and more exposed than if she were naked, she stared at a beetle trying to cross a little puddle. She did her best to force an offhanded smile. "Of course I like Sam." Her gaze drifted to him, but she quickly glanced away. "We've been friends for years. Why would you think I didn't?" She was stretching the truth a mite, but she didn't believe Sam would argue the point. She gave Jeremiah the last pieces of meat and bread. "Shouldn't we start back?"

Sam nodded. "Yes, we should." She was uncomfortable, and he wanted to continue the conversation in private. During the long walk back to the shack, Jeremiah asked a multitude of questions, and Sam told him as much as he could.

Maggie said little but listened to every bit of Sam's description of the ranch. It sounded wonderful. She was grateful he hadn't pressed her further. They arrived back at the cabin just after dark, and she kept busy fixing supper. After the long day's walk, it would be an early night. She glanced at the bed she had shared with Sam. How on earth could she share it with him after today?

Occupying Jeremiah helped keep Sam busy until supper but not too busy to appreciate the curve of Maggie's mouth, the way her hair shone in the firelight, her frequent glances. After they ate, he made up stories about the cities he had seen. When the boy finally fell asleep, he put him to bed and joined Maggie on the hearth. "It's been quite a day, hasn't it?"

She nodded. "I'm glad it's over. He's excited about going to the ranch now. I don't think he'll run away again." *But I wish I could,* she thought, still uncertain about so much, especially how to handle the sleeping arrangements without making a fuss. His clove hair tonic seemed stronger, or was she imagining it? She brushed at her sleeve.

He stretched his legs out in front of him and leaned back, which afforded him a better view of her. "Have you given any more thought to why you don't want to go to my ranch?"

"You just can't give up and leave well enough alone, can you?" She wadded her shirt in both hands. "You don't need my help hiring a housekeeper."

He raised one hand and ran it lightly down her back. "I wanted you to see what I was offering you."

His touch felt too good, and she squirmed, her heart racing like a steam engine. "What're you talking about?"

He grinned. "It seems I'm not the 'smooth talker' you thought I was." Placing both hands on her waist, he lifted her onto his lap and circled her with his arms.

"Oh— What're you doing?" *Oh, please don't do this, Sam, please.* She should run out of there, she thought, but she really didn't want to leave the warmth of his embrace.

Crossing his hands over her waist, he turned her around and pressed a gentle kiss on her lips. Unplanned, the words spilled out, "Will you marry me, Maggie?" He shocked even himself. However, that was exactly what he wanted, even though he hadn't thought of it before. She held her back straight, but the quiver beneath his hands betrayed her.

"*Marry* you?" She didn't dare move, her bottom was on his thighs—he was holding her in an impossible position. Backed into the corner, she had to ask what she feared most. "Why, Sam? Do you really love me?" As she met his beautiful gaze, her mind spun, almost making a whirling sound.

"Yes, I do, I already told you the other day, after the accident." He kissed her chin, so close to his lips. "I love you more than I knew a person could love another. We made love, Maggie, I didn't know it at the time, but I wouldn't have touched you if I hadn't loved you." Her cheeks turned a pretty shade of pink, and her eyes fairly glowed.

He'd said what she had hoped to hear but suddenly, and against her wishes, she remembered a niggling doubt she'd had about him. She couldn't sit still another moment and almost bounded to her feet. "How long—" She glanced at Jeremiah's bed and motioned for Sam to follow her outside. After he closed the door behind them, she started again. "How long will the ranch hold your interest before you move on?"

"I'm not sure." He stepped up behind her and resisted taking her in his arms. She paced several feet in front of him, almost like a caged animal, he thought. Did the idea of marriage frighten her? Or was it him? "Is the ranch that important to you?"

She turned on her heel and looked into his eyes. "You can't seem to settle in any one place, Sam." She brushed at a moth. "I never thought of you as a wanderer."

"Neither did I." He stepped up to her and raised her chin so he could clearly see her eyes. "It isn't the ranch, is it? You're afraid I'll leave you. Isn't that closer to the truth?" Her lips quivered, and her sigh brushed his cheek.

"I—" His gaze was like a snare, and she didn't know if she could, or wanted to, break free of it. "Yes—"

He stepped closer, narrowing the space between them, bringing their bodies together but keeping his hands at his sides. "Don't confuse the damned ranch with my love for you. We will *always* be together—wherever that may be. More than that, I can't promise." Would that be enough for her? He had nothing more to offer—it had to be enough.

She smiled and leaned into him. "I'll marry you, Sam Adams." She touched her mouth to his to seal her pledge and give in to her need for him. His kiss removed the last shadow of doubt. She playfully eyed him. "Have you hired a cook for the ranch?"

"No." He grinned.

"You'd better. You've shed a few pounds since you came here. You'll be skinny as a post if you don't."

"Anything you say, Mrs. Adams." She melted against him, and he kissed her with all the passion and love he had for her, tenderly, then hungrily. She had a way of arousing him that was pure magic. He held her still to keep himself from taking her out there below the stars, on the wet ground. "Life with you will never be dull."

"Oh, I hope not." She kissed his forehead, his nose and his chin. With a quick backward glance at the cabin, she whispered, "I'm going to make sure he's asleep tonight."

Dear Reader:

The story you've just read, *Maggie's Pride*, is based on the December 1861 flood in Willamette Valley, Oregon. It was the first disaster of that magnitude ever experienced by the settlers. A month of rain, which the swollen rivers could not contain, when coupled with the added snowmelt in the Cascade Mountains, washed away homes, mills, warehouses, entire towns in some cases, and caused a number of deaths. The river crested at fifty-seven feet above the mean low water mark, which made it possible for the steamship *St. Clair* to successfully navigate the falls and arrive safely in the basin below.

My next book, *Humble Pie*, will be one of three launch books for Jove's new Our Town series in July 1996. I wrote *Humble Pie* under the pseudonym, DEBORAH LAWRENCE. The setting is Moose Gulch in the gold country of western Montana in 1873.

Kate Miller, the heroine of *Humble Pie*, has spent nearly half her life trying to escape her outlaw father's reputation. Working and living in Moose Gulch, Kate believes she has moved beyond her past. Parker Smith, the hero of *Humble Pie*, intends to even the score with the outlaw who murdered his father. When Parker discovers Kate's connection to the killer, he believes he has found the object of his revenge and that his lengthy search is nearing the end. Of course, we know better, don't we?

I hope you'll enjoy *Humble Pie*.

Best wishes,

Deborah Wood

Also writing as DEBORAH LAWRENCE

ROMANCE FROM THE HEART OF AMERICA
Homespun Romance

Homespun novels are touching, captivating romances from the heartland of America that combine the laughter and tears of family life with the tender warmth of true love.

__SUMMER LIGHTNING 0-515-11657-2/$4.99
    by Lydia Browne
__LOVING HONOR 0-515-11684-X/$4.99
    by Christina Cordaire
__TEA TIME 0-515-11721-8/$4.99
    by Dorothy Howell
__LILAC CIRCLE 0-515-11769-2/$5.50
    by Karen Lockwood
__HEAVEN MADE 0-515-11748-X/$5.50
    by Teresa Warfield
__HONEYSUCKLE SONG 0-515-11786-2/$5.50
    by Lydia Browne
__WINTER LONGING 0-515-11811-7/$5.50
    by Christina Cordaire
__MAGGIE'S PRIDE 0-515-11830-3/$5.50
    by Deborah Wood
__FOR PETE'S SAKE 0-515-11863-X/$5.99
    by Debra Cowan (April 1996)